The shining splen[...] on the cover of this book [...] of the story inside. Look for the Zebra Lovegram [...]ver you buy a historical romance. It's a trademark that guarantees the very best in quality and reading entertainment.

LOVING DECEIT

Nearly distraught with fear, Jonpaul swam to the spot among the reeds where he saw Nichole's hair floating in the water. He hauled her out of the pool, shaking her, flooded with relief when he discovered she was very much alive.

"Damn you, girl! I thought you were dead! Dead!" he raged. He carried her to the cave behind the waterfall, despite her flailing and punching him. As Jonpaul set her down he meant to tie her up so she wouldn't escape him again . . . but the instant he set eyes on her naked loveliness, his intent changed.

"Dear Lord," he whispered as he stared with the heated passion of his desire plain in his eyes. "Like Eve before the Fall you are, or Venus in a star-filled night . . ."

Jonpaul's calloused hands gently roamed her curves, excitement numbed her thinking. Still, Nichole's fingers crept toward the dagger hidden in her furs even as he expertly roused her senses to a feverish pitch she'd never before experienced . . .

FOREVER AND A LIFETIME

JENNIFER HORSMAN

ZEBRA BOOKS
KENSINGTON PUBLISHING CORP.

ZEBRA BOOKS

are published by

Kensington Publishing Corp.
475 Park Avenue South
New York, NY 10016

First printing: February, 1990

Printed in the United States of America

Chapter One

An autumn sun set on the court of Charles the Bold, lord of the realm of the Lucerne Valley, where the court presently convened in the castle of the Lower Lake. The castle was a product of the early twelfth century, and only one concept governed the grand fortress: defense.

Everything in and outside of the stone fortress had been designed for the sole purpose of beating back an attack. Like a mammoth stand of stone trees, four towers rose against a green hillside. These great monstrosities enclosed a space of more than two archers and threw lengthening shadows over the township of perhaps a hundred houses and a square-cut church that serviced the castle. The only entrance to the castle was a fortified gate positioned between guard towers and further protected by the portcullis. Another twenty-foot stone wall separated the inner and outer bailey so that the stables, barn and kitchen, the servants and guard barracks were housed a goodly distance from the keep—which now served only to give all but the most industrious servants a thirty-minute excuse for being late. The four tall stories and basement of the stone-and-wood keep—the solar rooms and chambers, the chapel, hall, and storage rooms—could only be maneuvered by climbing up or down the most treacherous spiral staircases, a winding menace that turned sharply upward to the right so that the knight coming up was hampered by the center post but the defender coming down was not.

Large with her third child, Lady Fiona, descending from her rooms in the solar to the main hall, was keenly aware of this. With one hand flat against the stone wall and her other hand gripping Sarah's, one of her serving women, she eased her cumbersome weight from one unseen step to another. "Anyway," she was telling Sarah, "there I was in the middle of a great large circle with God knows how many hands pushed against my belly to feel these sommersaults, when I looked up and saw Anne Marie. Such sadness! I half thought she would burst into tears, I did, and it made me think, why, Nichole is right—"

Lady Fiona stopped of a sudden as a clamor of noise and voices were heard shouting after someone from the great hall below. She braced against the cold stone wall as the sound of quick, soft footsteps rose closer and closer. A girl raced up the staircase beneath them. The narrow space burst into sudden colors: a plain bright yellow gown, pale skin, raven dark hair, all formed her—Nichole!

Startled blue eyes shot up and, breathless, Nichole pressed against the center post across from them. She closed her eyes against the torrent pounding in her head, trying to catch her breath as a litany of prayers rushed to overcome her disbelief at last. He meant it . . . He meant it . . .

"Milady." Sarah dropped a slight, unseen curtsey, holding tight to Fiona as they stared at the girl. Something terrible had happened, a wild kind of terror and rage marked the lovely, flushed face, and unnaturally deep quick breaths pushed her breasts against the low bodice of a plain yellow gown. The girl's legendary thick, dark hair was plaited thrice, each plait wrapped in a tight circle around her head to form a halo of black silk that seemed to catch and hold the torch's light. Only Nichole could change a plain unadorned dress and the simplest hairstyle into something remarkable and lovely.

A dual heritage drew the young lady's beauty, and a great and rare beauty it was. Everything about the lady Nichole Lucretia radiated the health and vitality of living in this land where nature's splendor was displayed on a scale so majestic as to be unequaled the world over. Like most Swiss, she was tall, slender, and admirably proportioned, blessed, too, with her countrywoman's famed complexion. Yet the long dark hair, the arrogance of her poise, and the formidable intelligence—she was too smart for a girl, everyone thought so—these things let no one forget that not only was her father the late Lord Charles of Lucerne but that her dear mother had been an Italian princess of the famous Medici family.

The girl's regular if delicate features belied her uncommon strength and character, misleading all those who did not know her better. Set in a heart-shaped face, two thin brows arched dramatically over lovely eyes. A bright rosy blush spread across her high cheekbones; and a small, straight nose added a beguiling element of whimsy to the picture, while the full, sensual lines that drew her mouth mischievously concealed the well-known sting of her tongue. A wild, rebellious nature—"like a wood creature she is"—mixed with the great wealth of her compassion, understanding, and kindness, often with disastrous results. She was an initiate to the old religion, too, and she freely dispensed that treasured knowledge—too freely, Nanna always complained. Yet even if she weren't so able and quick to help, she'd still be the jewel of the Lucerne court, loved by one and all. The magic of her charm captured the hearts and laughter of the men and the love of the women.

The women watching her were no exception, and with alarm Fiona reached to take her hand. The girl gripped it tightly. "Nichole, my love, what has happened?" The yellow dress reminded her suddenly . . . the color of mourning for the initiates. Dear, no! Nanna, has she . . . *mon Dieu,* has she—"

"Nay." Nichole managed to shake her head, and in a gasping, pain-filled voice, "Nay, by God's grace she is still with me—though I know not how. Yet, Fiona, 'tis bad—"

"What? What has happened?"

"Nichole! Nichole!"

Nichole's women and the ladies of her brother's court had overcome the shock of Nichole's defiance to race up the stairs in pursuit of the girl. Four ladies suddenly appeared below them and more behind, and there was a sudden chaos of cries and exclamations and scolding; Charles's curses rising over them. "God's teeth, don't let me get my hands on you, girl, for I will beat you sound for this . . . What goes on here?" Charles asked indifferently as he met the alarmed feminine faces, the ladies quickly parting for him. "Has my entire court adjourned to my staircase?" Then with a wave of his hand, "Be gone with you now. None can save my sister this time."

No one moved at first. "Go! Be gone!", then the women lifted skirts and fled the tight space of the narrow staircase, no doubt to hover just out of sight below, listening to what he would say to the rebellious girl who went too far this time. Fiona and Sarah were last to pass, Fiona searching Charles's face for a clue as to what had happened but learning nothing past the obvious—he was furious.

A formidable presence, Charles never hid his emotions. A scowl on his face sent fierce warriors scurrying like rats in a fire, while the wave of his hand dispensed whole crowds of hundreds. Eleven years her senior, Charles was more like her father to her, and with the exception of Nanna, Nichole could not love anyone more. He was and always would be a great hero in her mind, better than the next best ten men, and there was no greater prize than winning his laughter, his love, his admiration, a prize more treasured than all the others put together; until now.

Like their father, too, Charles was a handsome man, devastatingly so—a popular consensus. Ladies found the air of extreme danger and power emanating from him as attractive as the pronounced angular features were handsome: the flat rectangle of his forehead, the sharp arch of brows and long, narrow nose and wide mouth, the point of his goatee, and even the oddity of his mustache, how on one side he let the length grow uncut until it reached across his face and curled over his ear—for luck in battle, he said. Nichole knew him far better, though, and with her, only with her, he dropped his airs and pretenses, not often but long enough to keep him in the special place in her heart.

With the exception of the old woman upstairs dying, she loved her brother more than any other. Even before their parents died—their father first, followed tragically by their mother two months after that, who died with the birth of a stillborn child—even before then, Charles's love had replaced her father's. Charles loved her when their father did not. Since the day she learned to walk, she followed him about, clinging to each small toss of his affection as if it were a treasure from God, and it was, it was. Until now. Until he did this thing to her.

Charles stopped a step beneath her and leveled his gaze at her, the unnatural pale-blue color burning like the fires of a snow burial with the intensity of his anger. For all of it, though, if anger could be measured on a scale, Nichole's would be greater.

"How dare you unleash that tongue of yours against me in front of my court, young lady!" He pointed a finger of his legendary gloved hand, the hand that had been covered since the day of his birth, its disfigurement so distressing their mother. "Before I publicly take a hand to your backside, what do you have to say for yourself?"

"How could you, Charles?" She ignored his vacuous threats to go to the issue that ignited the night like a thunderclap, the surprise announcement of her betrothal. "How could you do this to me? You've never even asked—"

"Asked? Curse it, girl, you are as spoiled as winter fruit! Nichole Lucretia, you have known since swaddling clothes you would not choose your husband, for no highborn lady has the choice. 'Tis mine to make for you and for the better of Lucerne. And I can tell you this, no pope ever put as much deliberation and consideration into a treatise as I put to the question of your husband. Gustave de luc Froissart is the best man, I say! You should fall to your knees with gratitude, thanking me and God for the match. The duke is richer than even I, not too old and—"

"And a weasel! Less than a weasel! He is low, vain, and cruel! He is unjust." The last word was pronounced as an indictment, the damning fault. "The only time I met him, I had to intercede, as he ordered a poor horse killed for stepping on his foot. Even you were shocked that a man would kill a perfectly fine creature for a prick of pride and then . . . then while he is courting me, he seduced two of my women—"

"Two?" He questioned, then realizing, "Oh, for God sakes!"

"Aye, and poor Mayra is so daft, she didn't know what was happening till the man dropped his leggings. 'Twas like the raping of a child—"

"Listen you, sister mine . . ." He cut her off, the great wealth of his energies going into controlling his temper, rising as it always did when he confronted the only living person who could speak to him like this. "If you think I will let the affairs of state be altered by a virgin's fears—"

That was too much! "Virgin's fears? That is a lie, you know full well! Dear God, I will lay with your army to prove it! I decline for Lucerne! The man is shallow, witless, unendurable, and while he might put his nobility beneath God, 'tis elevated in his mind's eye, well above the angels. His only notion of justice is that of a lance or sword, his idea of righteousness for the people is the swift collection of his outrageous tithes. I will not marry him, Charles! I will not! Charles, Charles," she clasped her hands together as if in prayer, switching tactics in a breath, pleading now as her eyes went wild with the fear of it. "If you asked only for my lifelong unhappiness, I would give that to you gladly, you know I would, but, God forbid, what if something happens to you? Anne Marie is still without a child, and with no heir my husband will inherit the realm—"

"Stop it, I say! Enough!"

Nichole gasped, her hands clasping her mouth. He had expressly forbidden ever mentioning Nanna's prophecy—the night four years ago when the old woman announced to the full court that the man Nichole married would inherit the realm, she had seen it with her famous third eye. The auspicious announcement came before Charles's second wife died in childbirth with a stillborn girl and long before it seemed obvious that his third wife Anne Marie was barren. Everyone had believed it even then, and most still did, for Nanna's sight was as famous as the miraculous power of her medicines, potions, and ointments. Just as Nanna could cure headaches and hangovers, a child's fever or earache, infertility or overfertility, and every problem in between, the old woman could predict everything from the course of storms to the sex of the unborn—and all with startling accuracy. Nichole was Nanna's initiate in the old religion, and she had been taught all these secrets, not just the ingredients in the potions but the tricks of the prophecies. And none the least was this last.

Only Nichole knew Nanna had made the whole thing up, or so she had confessed "'Tis a goodly way to protect ye when I'm gone. If yer kinfolk all think the man ye marry inherits the realm, then the fools will be sure enough to pick only the very best man. No foppish blue blood old men fer ye." Nanna had laughed, always amused by the success of her ploys. "And did ye not see the look on Charles's face . . ." Nichole *had* seen the look on Charles's face, and though Charles claimed to think Nanna half senile and the rest of her ridiculous, from that point on he did not bother to hide his animosity toward the old woman. Like her mother . . .

Which tore her in two. For as much as she loved her brother, no one who lived—past, present, or future—could win Nanna's place in her life or heart. Nanna was an essential part of her, and in a way only the initiate could understand. She loved Nanna as much as her own mother . . . more even, for Nanna *was* more. Nanna had molded her very consciousness with the ancient wisdom and knowledge of the old religion, forming the very beat and pulse of her soul.

The explosive conflict sat between them, the fuse of Charles's temper running very short. He held his head in the gloved hand as he tried to control his anger. Yet as Nichole stared at him she abruptly understood that he had done this on purpose. He had waited until Nanna had fallen from her fever into the coma, waited until Nichole was too weak with her grief to fight him.

Slowly, in a tone made hard with the control he placed on it, he said, "My lords were right, I see that now. I raised you with too free a hand. I reap the consequences now, as it is finally time for you to do your duty to me and to Lucerne." She started to protest, but the velvet glove came to her mouth. "Nay, sister mine, I will hear no more. I will let the matter settle in your mind, and in time you will see the wisdom of my choice. You will marry the duke. I will force you if necessary."

Then, with those pale eyes shimmering beneath emotions she didn't understand, he turned from her. For one long moment she waited incredulously for him to turn back and offer the acquiescence he always gave her, until now. Dear God—

With a sudden flurry of yellow, Nichole swung around, running up the steep steps. The girl fled past the chapel, the sewing room, past the guard's rest and the servants' rooms. She reached the solar landing and turned down the well-lit hall to her outer rooms against the west wall that overlooked the lake. She pushed open the door and stepped in the dark space of the waiting room and through the door into the warm, soft light of her chambers.

Mayra rose at once, but stopped upon seeing Nichole's alarm. "Milady? What's—"

"Leave me, Mayra. Please . . ."

"Aye." Without another word, Mayra lifted her skirts and quit the room. The door shut. The silence rang loud.

Thirty-three candles lit the space of Nichole's vigil. The still September night air was warm, filled with the sweet, perfumed scent of the candles. Sparing no expense, Nichole had replaced the common wisps of rushlight made from tallow with sweet-scented candles of expensive beeswax. The candles surrounded the old woman in gold light where she lay so still on the four-poster goose feather bed under a blue satin comforter. Nanna's element was air, her color the blue of a summer sky and during the long hours of the seven-day vigil, Nichole had embroidered a blue velvet cap with beautiful birds made of gold and silver thread. The cap now covered the old woman's head and her knee-length white hair was neatly plaited with line-thin blue silk ribbons woven decorously through the long ropes.

Like a great centurion oak, Nanna had always had a tall, strong, and commanding presence, growing more beautiful with each year's passing. Yet now, with seven days of nothing but the broth and the ravishes of a fever that would come and go with the wind, the old woman looked small, frail, remarkably childlike, as if the Goddess's promised rebirth had begun before the last breath left her body.

A month ago Nanna announced she would soon be dying, that it was time. Just like that. She set about preparing for the passing, much as one might prepare for a long journey. Nichole was given a multitude of instructions, but the old woman had denied her the comfort of grief, for there was just too much to do: order had to be set to her treasured book of hours, the last secrets shared, recipes checked and rechecked, and Nanna's rather surprising fortune dispensed to the poor.

Within two weeks a rock had formed in the old woman's lungs, which brought on the fever. Nanna's life was made by air—and as fire consumed air, fire was her antithesis and so it was the fever, Nichole knew, that would take Nanna's life. Just as she had planned, the old woman at last fell into unconsciousness, where she had stayed for seven days now. "This way ye don't have to mourn over a still and lifeless body. Yet ye only get seven days, then ye can bury yer grief with my body . . ." Nanna felt certain the only good tears were made from the uplifted heart, from joy. Tears were, after all, a passive response to the world, changing nothing. One should either accept the tragic or change it, and crying signaled neither.

Nanna was also a stickler for the laws governing the art of numerology, and since the seventh day was the one of rest, transformation, change, Nichole had little doubt Nanna would leave her on this night . . .

This night when she needed her most! Nichole leaned against the door, staring through the flickering gold light to where Nanna lay, her heart still pounding furiously. Thoughts clamored one after another, piling to reinforce her conviction. "I will not marry the unjust man! I will not . . ."

A miracle took shape before her eyes, or so she thought as she watched the bright, haloed light forming over the bed where Nanna lay. Just as her mind rushed with wild ideas of miracles and enchantments, she realized the light was brought by nothing more than the hot sting in her eyes. "Oh, Nanna . . . Nanna!" She rushed to the bed, dropped to her knees, and with all the drama of a young girl's heart, she seized the old woman's still-warm hand in hers. "Nanna . . . Nanna, was my strength drawn from you all these years? Is that why I feel so weak and frighted a sudden? Nanna, oh, Nanna," she whispered, washed in an overwhelming wave of sadness and missing and fear, "I have lost him. I don't know what to do. I . . ."

For the first time since she had knelt alongside her mother's deathbed nearly ten years before, tears came from her eyes. Then it was like a dam breaking, as wave after wave of grief rose, crested, fell away only to rise up again. Each time she felt the tears finally subside, she desperately tried various tools to keep the wave upon the sand, to calm her emotions, but another wave would rise more powerfully crushing than the last, choking her, leaving her gasping and helpless and alone until—

The voice was neither weak nor faint but filled with outrage. "Mercy of angels, Nichole, do ye think I need all this light to die by? Beeswax, no less! Have I taught ye nothin' all these years?"

Through wide, blurred eyes, Nichole looked up to confront the darkly brown ones, and the shock of her young life! Apparently Nanna had made a mistake in her calculating or planning—which itself was a kind of miracle, as the old woman's mistakes, like the Goddess herself, were as rare as a summer snow. Nichole was too shocked to respond to the changed circumstances, and she kept wiping her eyes as relentless tears filled them. Nanna took the girl's shock into her consideration, giving her a moment's time to catch up. "Ye got my hand all wet and . . . and what is this on my head?" She reached up to remove the cap, and as she examined the beauty of the stitchery, emotion filled and changed her eyes.

The old woman found the girl's face and only then realized why she had come back. Normally Nichole's eyes were the blue of the deep waters of Lower Lake beneath summer sky, a tempestuous blue that reflected the girl's soul, her fervent passion for life, the wide scope of her heart, that included all of Lucerne—this rich land blessed with deep, clear lakes, thick forests, the ever-majestic presence of snowcapped mountains and, most of all, her love of the people . . . Into these eyes Nanna looked and yet what she saw confused her.

Nichole's senses returned all at once, swelling with sudden joy and excitement as she stood up, still wiping at her eyes. "I cannot believe you opened your eyes. I . . . I will call for Mayra and a tray—"

The old woman caught her hand, squeezing it, and

Nichole felt the weakness of her grasp. The fever had returned, too. "My child . . . my dear, dear child. My time is an hourglass, turned upside down . . ." She collapsed, weak against the pillow. The memory of the bright, warm light surrounding her receded like a dream upon waking, and now she was here again. "I kept hearing ye callin' and callin' . . . and now I see . . . Nichole, what has happened? The grief and sadness are mine . . . but this fear? Where goes this fear?"

In her desperation Nichole did not grasp the miracle of it. All she knew was that Nanna had awakened when this was not possible, awakened to tell how she should change Charles's mind. "He announced my bethrothal tonight. He waited till I was weak with my grief—"

The old woman grabbed Nichole's arm. "Who? Who did he name?"

"The Duke of Uri, Gustave de luc Froissart!"

"That bastard! He promised me . . . He swore—" Rage changed the old woman's eyes into something fierce and frightening and deadly. "Nichole, Nichole, listen to me, listen. You cannot marry that man, you cannot. There is far more than your marital life or the souls of your unborn sons at risk . . . far more. You must fight him—"

"I begged, pleaded, threatened, and he turned from me. For the first time he turned his back to me. I fear the worst! I fear he stepped from the reach of reason, the bond of my love. The Church is on his side, he will force it!"

The old woman's illness could not accommodate the surge of her emotions and she started coughing violently. Worried eyes watched the frail body shake. The fit finally left the old woman gasping, each gasp forming a word. "I should have given it to ye long ago. I should have foreseen he would betray me once I was gone, but I thought . . . 'Tis a bad omen to give this to ye, a very bad omen for 'twill bring a passel of terror, but I . . . ," She started coughing again, weak gasps for breath. "I have a weapon against him, a thing that will force him to your will. Nichole, Nichole . . ." She grabbed her arm and in all of Nichole's life, she had never seen Nanna more alarmed. "Are ye strong enough to go against the man your brother is on this? To save Lucerne?" Passionately, "Are ye, Nichole?"

Wide-eyed and alarmed, the girl nodded—slowly at first, but as she stared into the conviction burning in the old woman's eyes, ever more vigorously.

"No matter what he does or says, ye must resist. I see . . . he will put the fate of many in yer hands, but there must be a trick in this. Their fate depends on ye not just fighting Charles . . . but ye must also win." She closed her eyes, forcing her strength to rally long enough to explain. "Turn to our trust for comfort when the world turns dark. Know only that ye cannot marry that man, no matter what . . ."

The voice faded to wheezing sputters, and Nichole leaned over the bed, alarmed. She grabbed Nanna's shoulders, "Nanna . . . Nanna!"

The old woman felt her throat close as if it were a chimney valve. She could not breathe. The memory of the white light beckoned, threatening to overcome her senses, and so powerful no other soul could resist. Yet using all the strength of her great will, she pulled Nichole down to her mouth to ensure the girl heard her words well: "The paper . . . the paper . . . Yer father's blood, he knows not where 'tis. Get it, Nichole, get the secret . . . 'Twill ruin him, ruin . . . Nichole, where are ye? Put ye hands on the Bible . . ."

A warm, gentle wind blew in through the window and the light of the candles leaped at it, desperate to keep the old woman's soul in the room for the girl. Yet Nanna was of the air, from which light drew existence, and as the air swept and left the room, it took out the lights, leaving only half a secret, the darkness, and a young girl crying over the still and lifeless body of the old woman she loved.

A thick mist clung like angel hair to the base of Mount Pilatus, spreading a gray blanket of fog over the North lake country of Switzerland, where five riders rode at a gallop. No flags designated the Swiss canton of the riders, though the predominance of maroon and black marked them as being from the Lucerne Valley. Nor was there any sign of the highborn status of two of the riders, for none of the usual fanfare or entourage accompanied either Lady Nichole Lucretia or her brother, Charles the Bold, Lord of the Realm of the Lucerne Valley. This was a secret mission of the utmost importance and urgency and no one was to know about it.

Only Charles and Nichole understood the impossibly high stakes of the game being played, though it was now Charles's retaliatory move, and for his own reasons, he kept his young sister ignorant of their destination. Owing to her personal fortitude— "She might look like an angel but she rides like a man, she does," one of the men commented, unwillingly admiring her impressive riding ability—Nichole never once complained, not of their predawn departure, or of being denied the company of her ladies nor, indeed, even of the seven hard hours of riding. Still, none of the men were inclined to appreciate the courage and determination covered head to foot in a dark maroon cape that spread like wings in flight.

Pulling back on the hard-worked leather reins to hold the stallion back a pace or two, Charles caught a sideways glance of his sister. Nichole kept her back ramrod straight and, though aware of his scrutiny, she ignored it, staring straight ahead at the mist-covered land, the dew-laced leaves of trees and grass as if the common scenery held the fascination of an illuminated manuscript.

Nichole showed no sign of her fear.

As the horses galloped past the last village of the Vierwald region and headed north, Nichole at last guessed his design. The ill-fated region of Stan! Why, how strange! The horses thundered through an abandoned field, grass and bramble bushes growing where wheat should be, evidence of indigent soil and tired people. It was the only depressed region of the canton: the people of Stan were as poor as the crops here, too poor to support any industry. Nanna always said Stan was ill-fated, not because of magic or mystery or its distance from the protection of the Lucerne Valley or even, as most thought, because it sat beneath two black laylands, but simply because these poor people existed in the morning shadow of the great Mount Pilatus.

Nanna . . . Nanna . . . Nanna . . . Like a curse or a spell, the name appeared in Nichole's mind with every thought. Still, she gave no sign of her fear or the strain accumulating for the last three days since the old woman's death . . . accumulating like an avalanche racing toward a thunderous crash. Like her fear, she held tight to the reins as Tardian fought for the bit, uneasy and restless behind these men, more uneasy with the three stallions in the group. As Nichole skillfully managed her half-wild mare and took in the strangeness of her surroundings, she thought Nanna's words must be true. Ill-fated because of the shadow! Not because Nanna said it—God knows, the old woman was just as likely to lie as to tell the truth—but while mists in Swiss lake country were usually warm, the overcast sky above seemed darker and the mist thicker and colder here.

A feeling gradually penetrated Nichole's senses, and her gaze danced nervously about the landscape as the inner voice told her to be afraid. The steady pounding of horses' hooves became a backdrop for the thud of her heart as her gaze flew about the fast-moving landscape—nothing but swirling colors of green and grays. She tried to tell herself she was safe, that no matter how she threatened Charles, he couldn't, *wouldn't* hurt her. Yet it was as if she heard the screams of terror echoing through the land from the night, as if she already knew what he was bringing her to see . . .

Nichole had not spoken all day and she would not speak now, though through the thickness of her cloak, her very skin, she felt the anger in his gaze. She could feel it! Charles, Charles, I had to! I had to force this hand, for I cannot, *will not,* marry the duke!

At last the horses came onto a wide shepherd's path that led into a small country village and Charles held up a gloved hand as he pulled rein to stop. The dappled gray stallion raised hooves to the air, and the man upon the beast in motion looked a magnificent mythological sight: the tall, princely figure clad in a black velvet broad tunic, scarlet leggings, and fur-lined cape, the handsome face crowned by thick, rust-colored hair. Nichole's fear cried out in silence: Dear God what have I done in making him my enemy! My brother who I love more than anyone now . . .

The horses quickly rallied around Charles, and Nichole skillfully brought her mare into control, tightening the reins and calming Tardian's nervous dance. Charles sat atop his stallion directly across from her, his men gathered around. These were not the lords of Council, but Charles's own guards, men who, except for the newer face, had served her brother as long as she remembered. The newer man was Kairtand, shrewd and dangerous Kairtand, the great red giant at Charles's side, he with his watchful eyes, both silent and knowing. Something surely amiss around him . . .

"We are almost at the place, sister mine."

His tone sounded barely above a whisper, and yet the

world suddenly seemed still, as if time itself had stopped. She nervously cast her gaze about her, not understanding the furious pace of her heart, the quick, deep breaths her lungs demanded. The silence again. There was nothing save the profound quiet of a Swiss mountain mist, but this silence spoke to her and loudly.

"Death has been here," she said, as a way of explaining her fear. "*Mon Dieu*, I hear the cries of the dead in this silence."

A surprised brow rose. Charles should be used to her uncanny intuition, the intuition of the initiates. "That old witch served you well. Your intuition is keen. Death lies ahead in a place I will show you, a place that will change you, sister mine."

Nichole watched as he turned his mount away, emotions blazing in her eyes. What did he mean by that? Dear God, what were they doing here? The silence of the glen became a roar in her ears, warning her with the pounding of her heart and pulse, the quickness of her breaths, and the frantic search of her eyes. The grief of Nanna's death washed over her in force, leaving her alone as she never before had been. She must take care. 'Twas a deadly game of blindman's buff, one that, for Lucerne and the good of all, she had to win.

Once recovered, she pushed Tardian into the forest where Charles's men waited, leading the horse ahead of them to her place behind her brother, oblivious as always to the stares of his men. Nanna always said a man's brass stare falls dead in the air when you fail to see it. Which proved true once again as Nichole's gaze focused ahead of Charles and through the trees.

The men knew what lay ahead, so it was Nichole's cry that broke the silence. "There's smoke!"

"Aye, fire was set to this place."

Smoke rose, indistinguishable from the mist except at

blackened and charred foundations of what had once been houses. Tardian neighed angrily and reared back. The party stopped. Understanding her creature's fear as her own, Nichole leaned forward to speak softly into Tardian's ear, but the horse threw her head back, agitated, and refused another step forward . . . and even more when Nichole tightened the bit, kicking her boots to her side. Tardian would not have none of it, so terrified was she.

With an irritated curse, Charles came to his sister's side and took her bridle in hand, in this way forcing the creature forward. "What's wrong with her? Why is she so frightened?" Charles's gaze held a strange light. "You and your creature are the only ones among us not trained for battle. You do not need the sight of your religion now. Open your eyes and behold."

The words were said as they emerged from the forest at the edge of the village. Nichole froze instinctively, and for one wild moment her body knew before her mind understood the vision before her. Black smoke rose from many of the burned houses and shops, curling mournfully into the gray mist like the very shapes of ghosts. But that was not the focus of her vision, for in the center of the square lay a macabre pile of bodies . . . bodies of the townsfolk.

Nichole stared for one second, that was all. There were decapitations and mutilations and bloating carcasses, painted with an impossible volume of dark, dried blood. Greedy rats scurried on and around the pile, a vision drawn from hell. She drew in a shocked breath and, without thought, the instinct to survive caused her to gaze about: a desperate toss to the burnt houses beyond, where eyes riveted on the one remaining box of flowers left—but left, it seemed, only to make a point by contrast. For beneath the box of flowers a woman lay with her arms wrapped desperately around a child, a blanket of blood spread around them.

The breath in her lungs burned with the unholy taste of the terror here and she choked on it a split second before she saw the same horror in the red giant's gaze, as with efficient moves, this man Kairtand grabbed Tardian's bridle while Charles lifted her from her mount across his saddle where he held her as she wretched. As if to expunge the vision, she did not stop until she was weak and breathless and trembling.

"Charles . . . who . . . who did this?"

"The Basel Alliance. Jonpaul the Terrible himself rode here last night."

Jonpaul the Terrible . . . Jonpaul the Terrible . . . Her mind numbly echoed the name. She had always known it, everybody did. Until now she hadn't believed it, none of it: Lord of the hated Basel Alliance, Jonpaul the Terrible, a demon who rode through the countryside disbanding entire villages to hunt peasants for sport, a great monster of a man who, drunk on the devil's own laughter, could take down fifty warriors. Until now, he had always seemed like the dragons and tales of olden days, made only of myth and legend.

The air was unnaturally still and quiet, the echo of a thousand silent tears of innocent people who wanted nothing more but to live in peace and good will throughout the changing seasons of time. Nichole braced herself and, using all her strength, she forced herself to look upon the dead once more, pairing the sight in her mind with the name Jonpaul. So there would be war now, as this Lord Jonpaul the Terrible of Basel stretched the reach of his ambition after the Burgundy War to the lands of Lucerne—this dangerous enough, but even so much worse now with his alliance with Solothurn and Berne. A war. She tried to imagine not just one village sacked but the entire land of Lucerne and all her people in it falling beneath the swords of raging warriors who killed and raped and then killed some more . . . but she could not, for this image was many, many worlds beyond the scope of her imagination.

Terror seeped into her mind, seizing the whole of her, and, seeing this, Charles battled to keep triumph from showing on his face. "And now, my pretentious little sister," his voice sounded profane against the silence of the dead, "you see why it was wise to keep my army when so many wanted my men disbanded and sent home. I knew, Nichole, I knew the lord Jonpaul would never turn from us. There will be war soon and I will win it. I have the army of St. Gallen, but I want Uri." With vicious emotion, he continued. "I must have Uri, and you, Nichole, must get it for me. You will marry the duke!"

The words penetrated her terror to form a denial. 'Twas a kind of madness she would never be able to rationalize and she did not try to. Not now . . . for directly contrary to Charles's expectations, Nanna had warned her that he would throw the fate of many lives into the equation: ". . . but their fate depends on ye not just fighting Charles on this, but ye must also win."

She closed her eyes and covered her ears, the echo of Nanna's voice louder than the wails of the dead. Each word carved the conviction in her heart: she must fight him . . . she must fight him . . .

Then she only shook her head, and it was the boldest move of her life. The choice had been made long ago . . . no matter what, she could not, would not marry the unjust man. Bloodshed or no, war or no, she could not marry so more men might die. Even if to save the Lucerne she loved. "No," she whispered, "No, Charles—"

"You would dare!" His voice thundered above her. "You would dare! Lord Jonpaul can spread this ruin across our land, all of it, and you would dare say no to me? *Vertlucht!* Nay, sister mine, nay!" Charles's hands snaked painfully around her arms. "Nay! I say nay! My will be done. You will marry the duke! Paper or no, I know the place where you won't have chance to threaten me again. If you will not marry him to save Lucerne, then perhaps you will do it to save yourself from exile!"

Chapter Two

The late-afternoon sun slanted through the tall, arched windows of Dornach Castle, falling in streams to the square-cut marble floor of the great hall where the lords of the realm convened. The noise rose in noticeable increments throughout the evening, competing with the musicians serenading the gathering from the gallery above.

Few of the lords or ladies seated at the mammoth white-clothed table on the dais or the servants and pages rushing about to serve them noticed the fine melody of notes played by the English musicians. Nor did the lords and ladies pay any attention to the startling buffet of food spread before them—or certainly not the attention deserved by the bountiful plates and bowls of soup, lambs' heads, pork griskin, ox palates, fricasseed trout, various fruit and vegetable dishes, and French pie. With the exception of one or two of the ladies who whispered praise for the ingenuity of the chef's preparation of these dishes as they discreetly adjusted the stiff bodices of their gowns, all of it was ignored. The men might have been eating oatmeal and tack for all they knew or cared, their attention was so riveted by the heated argument. In typical Swiss tradition, the lord Jonpaul welcomed dissension and discussion on all issues— Especially this issue.

Interspersed among the men, the ladies managed to keep their own counsel, enthusiastically engaging in their own conversations and using the opportunity of the Council to renew friendships and exchange news. Yet knowing the discussion would last for several hours more, the subject far from being resolved, the ladies began leaving to check on servants and children or coalescing in smaller groups of twos and threes to discuss their own concerns. Unlike their men, the ladies had an unspoken agreement not to discuss this possibility of a war among themselves, as if voicing one's fears out loud would make it more likely.

The pretense of domesticity soon shattered as Lord Hans Wesmullar suddenly slammed his fist on the table, sending bread falling to the floor and an errant bird flying to the ceiling. The court of the great hall fell instantly silent. One servant dropped to his knees before he realized the outburst had naught to do with the wine he just spilled. Jonpaul's great Saint Bernard, Hercules, sat up, alert and warily watching for trouble. The musicians stopped on a high crescendo that seemed to reflect the passion of Hans's conviction, the color reaching his lined, weathered face, an ominous light in his bright blue eyes as he shouted, "I say enough! Enough!"

Despite the lord's fifty-three years, he was still a great show of a man, handsome and strong, as fearless in battle as Jonpaul himself and nearly as popular. While he was known for the impulsive reach of his sword, he was nonetheless viewed as a just and fair man and for any number of reasons, not the least being the prosperity of his lands and the city of Berne, the older man's lasting friendship with Jonpaul, and the balance his more conservative opinion provided against the excess of Jonpaul's reforms. His voice was weighed heavily by the council. "Strike the barbarians before they strike us again! Let me lead my men across Pilatus for a quick offensive!"

All gazes turned to Jonpaul. His Lordship's darkly intelligent eyes held Hans, but no one could tell what he was thinking, for the handsome features of his face remained impassive, expressionless. "Ah, a quick offensive." His rich voice sounded in quiet authority over the room as he appeared to consider this, a deception. "That would risk losing you, not just one of my dearest friends but your men as well, some of our best. And what is it we might gain?"

"Retribution!" The call swept the room in a chorus of ascension. "'Twould show the bastard that we are strong—"

"That we are strong," Jonpaul smoothly interrupted, wearily repeating the words with no feeling or inflection, as if this were the most common kind of banality. *The sky is blue, the grass is green* . . . "Do you imagine that he does not know we are strong, that he has any doubts after Burgundy? Who in the world could doubt it after Burgundy?"

The reference was to the great battle of Burgundy, an event that would live forever in Swiss consciousness. Since the beginning of their history, the Austrian kings had coveted Switzerland, King Ferdinand even more than his predecessors. For years, King Ferdinand had begged King Charles of France to join him in a final offensive into Switzerland, a measure King Charles refused until at last the hundred-year war ended and the last of the English Army were finally expelled from France. But then the French king faced a far worse threat to his sovereignty when the Paris streets suddenly swarmed with ten thousand professional soldiers with nothing to do but make trouble and court rebellion and insurrection. It seemed far better to send them across the border into Switzerland and bring those barbaric Swiss a measure of German civilization than to lose his crown. And with promises of rich rewards and booty, Charles of France sent his army across the border.

Charles the Bold of Lucerne, St. Gallen, Uri, and Zurich were the only Swiss states that did not send their men to join the lord Jonpaul Van de Birs of Basel, Lords Bruno of Solothurn, and Hans Wesmullar of Berne and their army of two thousand who were to meet and soundly beat the French-Austrian Army of better than ten thousand men in the famous battle of Burgundy. Two thousand Swiss men held the French back for nearly two weeks before a ruined French Army finally fell back, suffering losses of nearly ten Frenchmen to every one Swiss. Despite the decisive victory, the Swiss placed a heavenly value on each and every life lost, and it seemed to all a heavy price to make the Swiss warriors famous across the European continent and to ensure no foreign power ever dare attack Swiss soil again.

Most all of his court nodded agreement with Jonpaul's words, and as Jonpaul leaned back, waiting for the inevitable question, his gaze stopped briefly on Margarite, Hans's wife. Margarite was large with Hans's eighth child, a surprise in her forty-second year and a blessing she swore God sent to ease the pain of losing their firstborn son in the battle. She bowed her head, genuflected, and if this were not enough to demonstrate her gratitude for stopping her husband's apparent desire for a suicidal mission, she blew Jonpaul a heartfelt kiss. Jonpaul winked, a gesture that provided brief comfort to all the ladies watching.

"Then what shall be done about them?" Lord Bruno now stood, a dark-haired giant among traditionally tall men, as great in battle as Jonpaul and Hans themselves. Lord Bruno's canton, Solothurn, was the second largest in the Alliance and his opinion weighed accordingly.

More often than not, the issues debated by the council were dominated by the three lord's opinions: Jonpaul's idealism and Hans's conservatism mediated by Bruno's pragmatism, a perfect triangle. "The bastard's aggression cannot be left unchecked!"

The men all agreed, turning now to await Jonpaul's answer. Although Jonpaul had yet to pass his thirty-first year, he had been unanimously chosen as the Lord of the Realm of the Alliance after coming into his inheritance of the Basel canton three years ago, a decision celebrated every day since. It was not just that his innovative, highly unorthodox military strategy had become world-famous after the Burgundy War, or that his own unparalleled battle skill—praises of which were sung as far away as France and the German states—but the fact that his civil innovations had made the Alliance stronger and more prosperous than ever.

With the gift of wisdom aiding the wide reach and scope of his intelligence, Jonpaul was an enlightened leader of men. Jonpaul's uncle, Lord Jon Van de Birs foresaw the need for more than military knowledge in a leader of the people and shrewdly interrupted the boy's military training to send him to school. Jonpaul had studied the languages at Basel University—Greek, Latin, and Hebrew—making him learned in the areas of Roman law and history, the writings of the philosophers Aristotle, Aquinas, and Duns Scotus, among others, and this knowledge was used for the good of all.

Though his fame outside of the Alliance consisted predominantly of the many stories of his battle skills and heroism, within the boundaries of the cantons of Solothurn, Basel, and Berne he was known for his many popular measures and innovations. It was Jonpaul who had introduced the idea of the general assembly—or *landsgemeinde*—to the cantons, letting the people decide on all matters of jurisprudence. The Alliance's new military strength under Jonpaul's leadership also allowed him to fight many of the Church's more oppressive laws and tithes, while his arguments for doing so were so convincing and eloquent that Basel's Bishop Pol de Swquin not only presented the arguments to Pope Martin, but the Holy See had actually found itself agreeing with Jonpaul, if somewhat reluctantly. There were other things, too: The trade schools Jonpaul financed alongside the university were the first open door the lower classes had to the trade unions and merchant class, while his popularity among the lords also allowed him to introduce the set of laws that served to protect the common folk and peasants from undue hardship brought by a once brutal feudal system.

Presently Jonpaul leaned back, surveying the large room full of people. After allowing the lords to exhaust the other possibilities before presenting the risky venture, he at last saw it was time to introduce his plan. He needed agreement of one and all, but it could not be presented in front of the ladies.

A half dozen servants arrived and began clearing the huge table, leaving only the bowls of fruit and the pitchers of ale and water. "Adline?" Jonpaul addressed Bruno's wife of many years.

"Yes, milord?"

He cocked his head with a telling grin and asked, "Do I hear young Jon crying for you? And why yes . . ." he pretended to listen for distant sounds, "there go Nicholas and Hecktor—"

"My God," Bruno himself took up this game, " 'tis a virtual chorus of distraught babes out there!"

The ladies all glanced at one another, then rose amidst relieved smiles and laughter. Things could not be so bad if Jonpaul himself was teasing them, could they? None minded being banished either, for though the most interesting things were said in their absence, each knew they'd hear it in the quiet hours of the night as they lay with their husbands.

The ladies adjourned to the relief of the men, who were further spared the hour of endless goodbyes and curtsies. The musicians and servants rushed to follow, leaving only individual squires to wait on the lords, their stewards and their knights, and the half dozen representatives of the free cities, should the need arise. The hall grew quiet as Jonpaul then stood to his full height, like Bruno, an unusually tall man. He leaned his strong, battle-scarred arms on the table. "To answer your question, I say, indeed. Indeed the outrages must be stopped and I intend to stop them. Yet my plan is for peace, peace so rarely tried, so desperately longed for. I am tired of fighting and blood-letting. God knows," he whispered solemnly, "there has been enough. And a battle with the Lucerne canton would be a bloodbath—on both sides. They are, after all, our brothers, raised on the same land by the same mothers and fathers. Unlike our French neighbors, they have our same skill and fierceness, and who can say if they might not find their courage someday? And this makes me wonder if it is the men of Lucerne who provoke us into war?" The intensity of his gaze found each face in the way that he had, each man personally invited to answer the question. "Nay." He shook his head. "These men are like us; they long to go about their lives and work in peace. It is not the men of Lucerne committing these atrocities, but rather the result of one man's grandiose ambition."

Jonpaul's point was rarely made in any of the Swiss cantons and alliances, for the people of a given state had always been held culpable for their lord's actions. Yet once Jonpaul presented the idea, the men all aye-ayed it, though with some hesitation, not knowing where it would lead.

"I do not have to name him, for you know of whom I

speak. I have been asking myself what the tyrant wants? He already burdens his own people with the highest taxes in the Swiss cantons, tearing the heart and drinking the blood of his people as voraciously and viciously as a snow wolf. I hear it said that children—the very children of his own people!—starve after the lot he steals, these taxes of his. Where do these riches go? To pay his standing army!"

"What? A standing army still?" more than one of the lords questioned, no one understanding until Lord Bruno having discussed this with Jonpaul at length, stood to explain.

"Aye!" He slammed his fist on the table. "A standing army of a thousand still! A thousand men paid to wait! We kept the knowledge till now, when we were all gathered to do something about the menace brewing on our borders."

Disapproval raced through the men. This at last was news. It was unheard of in Switzerland to pay an army without a war or battle or threat! Men had homes and families, wives and children to support and protect, land to farm or goods to produce. Of all the countries in the world, the Swiss alone needed no standing army and never did. The Alliance, indeed all the Swiss cantons, disbanded men immediately upon their return home, for each and every man—the poorest peasant to the wealthiest merchants and the very lords themselves—could be counted on to return the very day a call to arms sounded. The idea of paying men to do nothing was an outrage, even more that a lord would need to pay men to protect their homes and families.

Jonpaul's own anger showed now as he continued. "And I ask you, what does that tyrant want with his standing army? Our tilled soil and rich farmland? The unsurpassed wealth of our harvest? Our trunks of gold and silver? The labor of our people? Our wives and daughters? Aye! Aye to all. This greed-crazed bastard would have all of it, and he will kill thousands of men to get it. Thousands, for, I—as you and each one of our men—will die a thousand deaths before we let that man claim an ounce of what's by right ours."

The collective agreement came in a loud chorus of ayes, and Jonpaul waited patiently for the quiet. When it came he said simply, as if it were now the obvious solution, "So I propose we wage war on Charles the Bold, that we destroy him and the menace posed by his greed before we take arms against the men of the canton of Lucerne. I am convinced if we destroy Charles the Bold, we will not have to war with the men of Lucerne."

The silence was broken by hearty exclamations of surprise as the lords digested what had been said. How could they destroy Charles without engaging his men, or for that matter, the Church? This concern was voiced by Ulrich, civic leader of Basel, who shook his neatly cropped head of pale-gold hair, his eyes questioning, uncertain, as if he had missed something. "Fine ideas, but how say you to destroy Charles without engaging his men—"

The hall trumpets sounded outside, interrupting Ulrich midsentence. Two pages pushed open the great wood doors as the hall servant stepped inside to announce the appearance of Kurtus, a man of Jonpaul's personal guard. As always, Kurtus arrived in the center of a whirlwind of energy, entering the great hall in muddied traveling clothes and with his arms outstretched as if fully expecting to receive thunderous applause. Though he stood shorter and more slender than most men, he was made of steel and owned a speed of reflex and a quickness of mind that put him on equal footing with the best warriors. Sometimes, such as in war, he took the world seriously, but now was not such a time as, with a mocking bow and a reckless twinkle in his lively blue eyes, Kurtus beseeched the lords not to rise on his behalf. The lords greeted the outrage with groans and, unwillingly, a few chuckles. The young Kurtus's mockery of protocol was famous, and what to do about it was often discussed. Only his favor with Jonpaul kept the solution offered by decapitation from coming up too often.

Seeing Jonpaul with a hand to his head, looking as if he was in the sudden throes of a gripping headache, Kurtus erroneously concluded it was less than perfect timing, but rightly saw not to waste any more of His Lordship's patience. His calloused fingers pushed through his dark curls, but a grin spoke of his success and, as he bent down to pet Hercules, he announced, "My mission was a success, milord. The wench you seek waits in the hall."

Jonpaul lifted his head with a grin, a reward in and of itself. "By all means, let us have a look at the girl."

Kurtus nodded to his guards. Two men appeared, dragging a bound young woman, the sight of whom brought muttered curses rising from the table as the lords tried to guess what this was about. This girl's hair had been cruelly shorn to the skull, ruining what was once surely a comely face, if a little plump, though it was hard to see past the discoloring bruise and swollen eye. Traditionally, no shears ever came close to any Swiss women's hair, and more often than not, unbound hair reached the knees or beyond. The current rage in the French court for short, cropped curls was shunned throughout Switzerland, causing shudders among the women's heads when the subject was discussed, for shorn or short hair was the most common punishment for women who committed a heinous crime to make the shame of it visible to all and was done only when no man would claim the guilty female. Also as part of her punishment her dress was ripped at the sleeve, her apron torn and stained, and her hands tied, all of which was most unusual treatment for a female of any status. No other nation of men was more protective or kind to their womenfolk than the Swiss. Unless she had committed the most grievous kind of crime, murder or thievery, this poor girl's treatment was incomprehensible.

Mayra looked terrified, and she was, her gaze darting from one unkind face to another. She hadn't believed the man Kurtus when he claimed to be the personal guard of the lord Jonpaul himself until the moment Dornach rose in the distance and she made out the coat of arms waving on the blue-and-green flags from the towers: the great horns of the forest Elch beneath crossed swords.

What she didn't know, what for the love of God she could not reason, was what they wanted with her. The court! She stood before the high court of the Alliance! Mayra of Interlaken knelt before the lords of the hated Alliance. Her mind kept turning it over but arriving at no clue to make sense of it . . .

"You are Mayra of Interlaken, serving maid to the lady Nichole Lucretia, are you not?"

The rich timbre of the man's voice held no hostility, yet Mayra's breaths grew enormous as Jonpaul came around the table to approach her. He seemed larger than life even then, with his unconventional height and steely strength, attired in clothes that seemed an austere expression of his unequaled status: He wore a green-and-black brigantine—the lightweight padded leather tunic reinforced with metal plates—and black suede breeches tucked loosely into tall boots. All very austere indeed. No kindness or gentleness played a part in the thick brows arching like wings over his dark gaze or in the scar that crossed his cheek and touched his upper lip on the perfect cleft that marked the dead center of a fine strong chin. That he was handsome came as a surprise, for he was not reputed to be so, but everything else pronounced his name loudly in her mind.

Jonpaul the Terrible.

The echo of his thick black boots on the cold stone floor reverberated in her mind's eye. The lady Nichole? Dear Lord, what could he want with her? What did the devil want with the angel Gabriella?

A hand lifted her face for an examination. Seeing the bruised eye, Jonpaul asked, "Kurtus?"

Kurtus looked offended, then slightly irritated. "Not I, milord. God strike the lecher dead who did. We came upon her as two others were beating her to the ground, apparently bent on a raping."

"I see." The information displeased Jonpaul, though no doubt the idea that she had been through much would surely aid his purpose. "Loosen your tongue, girl, 'twill go far easier."

"Nay." She bravely shook her head. "I will say nothing to you."

"You won't?" He pretended surprise at this. "My dear girl, have you heard nothing of my reputation?"

Mayra looked about uncertainly, as the question intentionally put in mind the famous atrocities of the lords of the Alliance. They were the fiercest warriors on God's earth; barbarians each, and the most terrible was the lord Jonpaul. He was said to have once killed fifty armed men with naught but his halberts and sword, and simply for sport. Even the Church was afraid of the unholy Alliance and the lord Jonpaul. The outlying villages lived in terror, for it was said that the lords themselves had a favorite pastime, a hunt that started with a dispersal of all men, women, and children into the forest and lasting until every last one of the peasants were killed. She herself knew a groom whose brother had actually seen one of the mass burial sights.

"Mayra, Mayra," Jonpaul's voice lowered compellingly, "surely you've heard rumors of the tortures we put our prisoners through? The only reason I'm giving you the chance to talk first is as a special favor to my servants. They begged me for rest. You see, it takes weeks of scrubbing to get bloodstains off this stone—"

Mayra's wide eyes swept the smooth stones of the floor, as if to see these stains before she caught her lip to keep from crying. "What can you want from me?"

"Some information, nothing more." Then with unfeigned gentleness, cleverly changing the subject as well as the tactic, "What crime made your lord turn you out unprotected?"

She kept her eyes on the cold stone floor where she knelt. Uncontrollable shivers shook her frame. She was a hairbreadth from hysterics, certain he would soon be killing her and wondering why it mattered now that she had nothing to live for. "I don't know. 'Twas all a terrible mistake, but . . . but, you see, last week the lady Anne Marie sent for me the day after . . . after—"

"After her husband banished the lady Nichole from his court?"

She hesitated but briefly before nodding.

"To silence you?"

"I don't know. At first I . . . I didn't know anything. Only that Milady Nichole retired from her brother's court, without word to anyone, and in the dark dead of night. I should have gone with her! I have been with her since last Michaelmas. She always sings praise for my service too, I must say and, and—"

"And what happened then?"

"Lady Anne Marie called me to her chambers. At first I thought 'twas to instruct me on how I was to follow Lady Nichole, but nay. She had two grooms there and she was upset, crying even as she accused me of the most . . . vile debauchery." Her look was one of horror. "I cannot even repeat it for . . . for fear of God's judgment, but I swear I never . . ." The next breath brought tears to her eyes and she was crying, still unable to believe all that had happened, overwhelmed that it had.

"You say you were falsely accused, Mayra. We want to believe you, but we need to know why? Why would Lady Anne Marie banish you from Court?"

A smarter girl would have seen the trick in this, but Mayra was neither known nor loved for her brilliance. Nichole often found herself defending the girl to her ladies and especially to Nanna—Nanna, who was impatient with any display of human frailty—defending her by pointing out that what Mayra lacked in sense she more than made up for in the size of her heart.

Mayra thus had no idea how she was being baited, or even that she was being baited. "I don't know . . . I don't know . . ."

"Let me help you. Something to do with the reason Lady Nichole was banished?"

"But I don't know why Milady was banished . . . I—"

"Mayra . . ."

The pronouncement of her name was a warning, one she fully understood. "'Tis true, 'tis true, I swear it. I don't know . . . she never said why. I thought 'twas 'cause her brother brought up her marriage again, but—"

"Marriage?" This was alarming. "Marriage to whom?"

Mayra hesitated uncertainly. She supposed they would find out sooner or later, and anyway Lady Nichole surely would not marry now. "The Duke of Uri."

Surprised murmurs rose through the room. That marriage would go far to align the two powerful states, and with Charles the Bold as reigning lord, the union would be against the Alliance. It went far to explain the escalation of Charles's atrocities.

"Go on."

The impatience in Jonpaul's tone scared her more, and Mayra looked uncertainly to the side. "There is nothing more to say."

"Will this marriage take place?"

"I don't know. My lady has been refusing all these months—"

"Refusing?" he questioned, incredulous. "Charles allows his sister to refuse his will?"

Mayra landed on the shores of truth at last. She, indeed no one, could ever explain Lady Nichole's stubbornness or obstinacy, the very extent of Lady Nichole's own will. "You'd have to know milady. Why, the last time Charles brought up the subject of her marriage, meaning to humiliate her, me thinks, the lady Nichole told him flat out that she would only be too happy to marry if only he could find her a better man than she herself! Aye, she did," Mayra responded to the confused, incredulous looks of her audience, then continued energetically, misreading their outrage for disbelief. "The lords and knights all hooted and howled when she said it, and more than one man stepped forward to teach her a lesson but then . . . then milady tossed her anlace at the boldest of them and swish,"—she whistled—"off went his ear! Just like that! She has a goodly aim for her sex and it did seem to prove the point."

"Aye." Jonpaul had heard enough. "That Charles's sister is a wild young girl in dire need of a man's backhand!"

"Mercy of God." Bruno did not believe it. "What do you make of a world where young girls are allowed to insult knights, tossing daggers at their face?"

Calse summed up the collective sentiment. "The Lucerne court is as civilized as rutting pigs!"

Still laughing, Kurtus pointed out, "Our mistake was in asking the men of Lucerne to the Burgundy War—'tis the warring women we needed to court!"

Hearty chuckles greeted that, and Jonpaul waited a moment before asking, "So what reason does she give for her refusal to marry the duke?"

"Well . . . er, because of the prophecy."

"The prophecy. Which one is that?"
"The one that says the man the lady Nichole marries will inherit the realm of Lucerne."
"Of course the lady would believe this—"
"Well, not at first, though everyone else did, but now that Anne Marie appears to be barren, the lady Nichole cannot take the chance, you see. She is like that, her heart and mind are on the people: She nurses them when they are sick, she feeds them when they are hungry, she gives all her allowance to alms for the poor, and she thinks the Duke of Uri would not do well for the people."
"You seem, young Mayra," Jonpaul neatly summarized, "to be telling us that this girl's whims and superstitions are dictating the highest course of the state?"
Groans and shakes of head expressed the lords' incomprehension of Charles's handling of his unconventional sister. Hans swore, "The bastard's wits are more addled than even we are supposing."
Jonpaul further questioned, "So did Charles send the lady away because of this refusal?"
Mayra nodded after a long pause. She did not dare look at his Lordship, but the silence grew and ominously so, until she heard, "You are lying. I will know why."
Her gaze shot up with a small gasp before she quickly shook her head.
"Listen girl, have you not wondered how my men found you? Why you were brought here? Either I have the miraculous powers of a seer or I have a loyal subject placed in Charles's court. Either way, I happen to know as a fact there is trouble there. Trouble that has to do with the lady Nichole. And I think you know what it is."
"No . . . no! I don't know anything more, I swear it!"
"Where is she?"
"I don't know that, either."
The look in those steely dark eyes stopped her cold, the

devil initiating the fall of Adam and Eve. Unarmed, he only held up his hand. Hans withdrew his anlace from its jeweled sheath on his belt, and tossed it through the air. Jonpaul's gaze never left her as he reached in the air and caught the knife's handle, his reflexes a miracle in themselves. As he examined the blade, he asked the lords, "Toes this time?"

A round of concurrence rose from the table until one of them said, "Toes never work with the women. They lose too much blood before they find their voice. Try the fingers first."

"I've always wanted to see the nose go myself."

"You've never seen the nose? Oh, now there's a sight! First the blood spurts—"

"No . . . no, I'll tell you . . . I'll tell you!" Mayra knelt before Jonpaul as if he were a god, and indeed at the moment he had the very same power over her life. She would have chosen death over the telling but not, dear God, not mutilation. "I don't know why Milady was banished, and that's the truth. She knows something, a secret or something . . ."

Mayra paused as fear worked into her face and choked her insides, bringing the rush of words tumbling out of her mouth faster than she could think to change them, "'Tall started with an argument about the duke, just after the old witch—er, Nanna, Lady Nichole's favorite, passed. Lord Charles came to Lady Nichole's chambers and there was furious arguing, oh 'twas bad, and I wouldn't have been easedroppin', really, but for an idea she would be a needin' me. I . . . I was scared for my lady, truly scared. She was not herself since the passing, no sleep or food, nothing but reading the Bible, page after page of the Bible. I wanted to help her and that's the truth. His Lordship cursed and threatened and said he would force her, but Milady—oh, you have to know her willfulness!—she remained calm like, as if it didn't matter what he said! Until she said—"

"Yes? What did she say?"

"Milady said she would not be forced to marry the duke, that Nanna had given her the secret as a weapon to use against him in this matter. Then suddenly the room came quiet until Milord said he didn't believe she really had this weapon and if she did, the sister he knew and loved could not use it to ruin him like that. Milady Nichole did not cry, but oh, her voice was heavy with sadness as she told him not one of her hours would pass without prayers that someday he could forgive her for this, but that God alone stood above her love of Lucerne and the welfare of the people and she just had to take the drastic measure."

Murmurs of amazement rose from the lords and, breathing hard and fast, crying Mayra said the last. "Lord Charles said threat or no, he knew how to get what he wanted. He said he'd take her to a place that would change her mind. And, and I suppose he did, for they rode out before dawn."

Jonpaul stared, knowing in his way, that she was telling the truth. Which made the next question the most important. "Where was she taken to?"

She hesitated, and after the space of a frightened pause she rushed on. "I . . . I didn't know at first. Charles returned by the next morning, but Lady Nichole wasn't with him. I was afraid for her life. I half thought he must have killed her, but no. Later I found out she was taken to the Abbey of St. Gallen to be held there as a prisoner until she agreed to marry the duke."

After a thoughtful pause, Jonpaul stepped behind the terrified girl and cut the ropes binding her hands, then instructed a wide-eyed servant to see her bathed, clothed, and fed, that from this time forward all would know she was wrongly accused and now under the protection his own household. Having been certain he would kill her,

Mayra fell over with gratitude, but the girl was already many minutes gone from Jonpaul's thoughts . . .

Silence came over the table as the lords watched Jonpaul turn his back to the room, his mind turning over the information, traveling across Switzerland to the castle of St. Gallen where a young lady was held prisoner.

"So, my lord," Hans rose to address Jonpaul, the Council in general, "does the lady Nichole own information that is a threat to Charles's power? Is that what this is about?"

"What could it be?"

Lord Bruno, ever the pragmatist, scowled. "Possibly no more than a foolish woman's gossip."

"Aye," Jonpaul agreed. "It could be nothing, an item of no use to us. Or it could be the kindling stick that lights a flame beneath our enemy."

"Well, how the devil do you propose to find out?"

"Obviously," Jonpaul said innocently, "we must fetch the lady Nichole from St. Gallen and put the question to her, which conveniently would keep her from that marriage as well."

"What?" More than one of the men rose upon the outrageous suggestion. A loud roar of dissension and disbelief rose in the room. "Have you lost your reasoning powers, Jonpaul? St. Gallen, the most heavily guarded abbey in the land? Protected by Charles as well as the lands of Uri! We would lose as many men as with a direct all-out war with the canton of Lucerne. 'Twould be madness to go there for the lady!"

"Aye, 'twould be madness to send our army to fight the standing force of the St. Gallen for a single girl. So we will not send the army. We will send one man and one man only. A single man who will penetrate the walls of St. Gallen and steal away the lady Nichole—with her secrets intact. That is my proposal."

"Impossible!" Hans stood again. "What man could

penetrate the forces of St. Gallen single-handedly?"

"Any man," Kurtus pointed out, but—"But what man could do so and keep his life? Now there's the question."

Jonpaul only laughed now. "And my lords, here is the answer." His bow put shock on the faces of the Council, more as he moved to the steel crown of horns, his famous steel bonnet. He kept a small fortune in guldens there, a convenience that amounted to a profanity against this symbol of a warrior's strength, but Jonpaul was ever eccentric. The bag of gold was tossed on the table. With a grin he addressed the men. "Fifty guldens gold says not only do I return with this lady Nichole but that I do so before the next moon."

Now the lords and men of the Alliance laughed, a great roar of laughter rose from the table and filled the great hall, a sound that was whole-hearted and gave unanimous approval to his proposal. Talk of which carried them through the night, until, many hours later, Kurtus added to Jonpaul's limited knowledge of the lady Nichole. He tipped his cup toward the money bag still on the table. "Now, milord, I do advise you to spare a coin or two for a dispensation. You will, I hear, be needing it."

"Dispensation, is one in need of a dispensation?" Father Ari pushed his way through the men. He smoothed the plain dark-green friar's cloth over his great bulk and searched out the faces. "'Tis you, milord? Why, bless the good luck! I offer bargain rates today!"

The men laughed at this, for dispensations were the Church's practice of abolishing a sin before it was actually committed, for a pretty price, of course. It was a source of many jests among the men, who, unlike the peasants, saw the straight line between the practice and the Church's treasury. There were no pretensions about Father Ari, and while he might sell one or two for a cup of ale and was a loyal member of the Church, there were no doubts about what he thought of the practice.

"Aye," Kurtus teased, "he will be needing one. For marksmanship aside"—he chuckled—"the lady Nichole is said to be a bit more than passing fair. Indeed, 'tis said the lass is more comely than Botticelli's Venus, and a good deal more real."

The men laughed when Jonpaul, after finishing his drink, said, "If that's the case, one dispensation just might not be enough."

"Not enough?" Father Ari questioned, only partially teasing. "From what we hear of your appetite, milord, nothing less than a papal dispensation will do . . ."

Chapter Three

An elaborate tryptic of the trinity hung behind the Bishop of St. Gallen, Kuno of Stoffeln, where he sat at a fine hand-carved oak wood table. Upon a red silk cloth edged with German lace and embroidered with gold thread lay the first course of his supper: beef soup, ribs of lamb, sturgeon, artichoke buttons, and stewed peas, all in all enough to feed ten. A favorite altar boy had the honor of sitting at the table with His Eminence, but the handsome boy paid no attention to the bishop or his extravagant feast, consumed as he was with a recent present of six mice in a gold gilt cage.

Four priests waited in the wings for the unlikely chance of gaining an audience with the bishop, who typically heard the concerns of his abbot only once monthly, and then with a bored air and an inclination to delegate. He was a hard and shrewd man, and despite his vocation and well-known scholarship in an obscure portion of Church law that dealt with the treasury and the dispensation of papal favors—the benefices, parishes, rectories, and archdeaconries—he exercised a disinterest in nearly all theological scholarship and debate. Let other Church dignitaries ponder how many angels dance on a pin or just what was meant by the words

I am that I am, he had better things to do. All of creation, from each sprout of a pea pod to the very words uttered by the pope himself, were predestined, unfolding according to His will, and since man could not know the higher reasoning of the Creator, there seemed little point in discussing it. "Charity?" He questioned the very suggestion. "Reflect: If God's penalties for past sins are poverty, disease, and suffering, then who are you to ease or alter, in any way interfere with His judgment? Leave charity to Christ and the saints . . ."

The converse was also true, he knew: his own ever-growing wealth and fortune were obviously the blessing of His reward for his good work. Obviously. Not that he had started out in life with God's blessing, quite the contrary. His beginnings were a good deal less than humble, having been born the fifth and last son of a poor Venetian farmer and his wife, a family separated from starvation by a mere acre of hard-worked soil, forever held at the mercy of capricious whims of seasonal weather. All he remembered of his father was that he was nothing more than the most pitiful beast of burden, undernourished and overworked, dying when Kuno was but eight, leaving him with nothing but the certainty that he, Kuno of Stoffeln, was meant for better things.

Yet having no wealth, inheritance, or noble lines, and unlike three of his four older brothers, he had neither the inclinations nor the physical skill necessary for mercenary service. There was only one avenue out of his father's life of hardship and toil, and that was through the Church. Entrance to the Church required a minimum clerical skill, the ability to read and write, but even the most modest education was as far out of reach for one of his class as a head crowned with jewels. For a year and a half, a determined young boy sacrificed food and often sleep to pay for a few hour's instruction a week, but his progress was not just painful, but painfully slow. Just as he began to see he could not go on much longer, the door to another world suddenly opened.

Owing to his boyish good looks—his dark curly hair, widely spaced dark eyes, and slight frame—he was introduced to a certain monsignor who was willing to supplement the price of his instruction for the pleasure of viewing certain unorthodox liaisons with other carefully selected boys. These favors also bought him a place at the monsignor's table, and for the first time in Kuno's life he not only had enough to eat but he viewed a wondrous world of wealth and opulence, a world where the silver knife set in his hand was worth more than a year's labor, where his every discomfort was met by a servant frantic to please him. It was like ascending from the cold, dark depths to the light above, like being pulled from a churning cesspool into sweet, perfumed air. It was the palace of his dreams. He did not intend to leave it.

The rest was easy. With the monsignor's help, he was ordained within two years and then began a steady climb up the Church hierarchy, a steady climb for which he was eminently qualified, for in these times, power and position within the Holy See was got by shrewd political alignments, clever maneuvers, and good old-fashioned bribes, skills which Kuno of Stoffeln fortuitously had in abundance.

The severe poverty of his earliest years were all but forgotten. Now in his fiftieth year, and despite a personal treasury many kings would envy, the security of his position as bishop, and an ever-increasing number of benefices, there remained a young boy terrified of being poor again. Nightmares and daydreams plagued him: dreams where his father battled a giant rat over a few crumbs of food to feed his family, of his mother crying when she lost the two babes born after him, of his own flesh wasting away on his frame, nightmares all about being hungry again. No amount of wealth could buffer these fears, and, in a way he didn't understand, it seemed the more he accumulated the more he was frightened it would be taken away.

It was not an entirely irrational fear, either. The only thing separating him from the impoverished masses was the power of the Church. While that power might be decreed by God, it seemed to Kuno to depend entirely on the armies of the Holy See. The winds of change blew across Switzerland and he felt the warning chill of it. He was afraid of the Alliance and the liberal reforms of this Lord Jonpaul of Dornach and his heretical attack on papal authority. A dangerous threat indeed, and Kuno was mobilizing his energies to wage the counterattack by corresponding with Rome and joining forces with Charles of Lucerne and, soon, with the hand of God, the Duke of Uri . . .

Presently, as Father Udo began serving generous portions of the beef soup into his gold-plated brass bowl, a raised, jeweled finger signaled commencement of the weekly reading of the tithes—the taxes got from each of his thirteen benefices and three craft guilds. With an embroidered cloth secured about his neck, a silver spoon set in one hand, he began to feast.

With a blind eye twitching uncontrollably, Father Rudolph read from a great long list of names and titles, the amount collected—in its gulden's value—following each name. The older priest knew better than to trust the archbishop's appearance of disinterest as the jeweled hand petted the boy's head, smiling indulgently. ". . . and lastly for the southwest of Appenzell, Schwyz—we have two bars gold even. From St. Gallen proper, we have first—"

"What, my son? Did you say two bars gold?"

"Yes, Your Eminence."

"There must be a mistake. The monthly tithes from Schwyz are two bars gold, and I believe forty-three gulden, unless I'm mistaken?"

A nervous shuffle of feet resulted from this unnerving reminder of the bishop's memory for numbers. "Well, no, you're not mistaken, Your Eminence. You see, poor Schwyz lost nearly two thirds of his land to a sudden flood of the—"

"You are sadly mistaken if you imagine I am interested in . . . ah, Schwyz's personal misfortunes. Failure to pay due taxes results in one year of indentured incarceration, and, as you well know, there are no exceptions—"

A commotion of running footsteps and raised voices sounding outside interrupted the proceedings. Outside the door two dark-clothed sisters desperately deplored the young lady to desist at once. "For fear of severe punishment, I beg you not to press this—"

The young lady ignored their concern as only the highest born could. The guard at the door to the bishop's chambers got only slightly more of her notice. "Milady!" The man managed to overcome his natural response to her appearance. "You can't go in there—"

"And you, my simple man, cannot stop me." She reached past him, but to her irritation, a broadsword suddenly dropped over the entrance. "Remove this obstruction at once!"

"Nay, upon my life I cannot—" He stopped as an anlace manifested from beneath a gold cloak. This was put to his face as she rather calmly told him, "I am not interested in the limits of your abilities. Now, grant me passage or feel the sharp point of my dagger across your sorry face!"

The sisters gasped, stepping back with the utter shock of seeing a lady behave so. The guard froze, mortified and only because, like many a man, he would easier die than combat with a woman. As she well knew. He reached the crossed bar on the door, lifted it, and pushed it open.

Like a gust of cool, alpine wind, Lady Nichole Lucretia

swept regally into the bishop's chambers. No one moved or spoke, the sight of her so struck the men. Against the dark cloth of the priests and the gray stone of the floor and the wood beams of the walls, she appeared as a burst of color and beauty. The dark-gold velvet cloak parted to reveal a stunning gown of creamy yellow and white beneath. Long, unbound hair fell in waves over that, which in and of itself was an act of rebellion, for all women were required not just to bind their hair but to wear a caul to cover their heads when standing before His Eminence. She forswore the necessity of a curtsey, too, and instead, those blue eyes swept the room, briefly pausing on each person as if to assess each potential consequence, dismissing them when she found none . . .

Until those eyes finally settled on the bishop. "You refused to admit me. Why, I wonder?" This was asked with a toss of the folds of her cloak over her straight back and shoulders. The unself-conscious movement revealed a low, tight-cut skin bodice, girdled under high, rounded breasts that pressed against the rich fabric with each breath. The view was all but hidden, though, for the riot of unruly dark hair fell in streams on past her waist. She was alluring and chaste, and more than one of the priests found himself trying to divert his gaze. "Am I to be treated as a common prisoner here at St. Gallen?"

"My dear girl—"

"Girl? Indeed not. I shall be addressed as Lady Nichole Lucretia. Thou shall do me honor to remember it."

The roomful of men gasped at her boldness, for she pushed too far. And really, she was a girl, unmarried and only ten and seven as well! Yet the bishop remained impassive, giving no visible response to her outrageous conduct, past the barest hint of some small amusement. "As you wish, my lady. The point, it seems, is that you are interrupting the business of the day."

"The business of the day?" A single brow rose

delicately, a pretense of surprise. "And what, pray tell, would that be?" She approached a nervous Father Rudolph, then peered into the book he held in his hands. "Your collection book, of course. I should have known. Indeed, all the poor people of St. Gallen and Appenzell know the holy business of Your Eminence is the collection of taxes and tithes, your great, long lists of numerous fines and penalties. The door to heaven doth open, but only at a king's price! Dear Lord, but one hardly comes across a farmer who can afford to feed his family let alone provide shoes for the children against the winter. I've begun to wonder if you do not demand even the hides of carcasses for your precious tithes."

Father Rudolph quickly genuflected, deploring, "Milady, by all that's holy here!"

"By all that's holy here?" She turned back to the archbishop, her eyes daring him, flashing and as wild as her tongue. "Don't tell me you are fooled by this man's ecclesiastical pretense? There hasn't been anything holy here for over a century! Certainly not since Your Eminence bribed Saint Jacob de Murs into fooling the pope to anoint him to this lofty position!"

"Enough!" The bishop's swarthy face reddened noticeably, his fury seemed to well up like wind caught in a sail, finally pushing him up from the chair to his feet. "Enough!"

Nichole stopped, for she had indeed said enough. Father Rudolph gasped "Blasphemy!" under his breath, this while genuflecting to ward off the girl's profanity. Nichole felt the swift beat of her heart in the silence that followed, as she waited for his response with a calculating eye.

"I would remind you," the bishop pointed his finger and each word came slowly, weighted by his fury, "that, regardless of your status here, I have the authority to see you properly chastised for these insults—dismemberment of that tongue for its boldness would be only the beginning! You, young lady, would dare vilify my name with God's own church—"

Suddenly he stopped, staring with disbelief. She was baiting him! The girl had purposely orchestrated this sordid little scene! Baited him to see how far she could push, to see . . . See what? How badly Charles and he needed her? How much she could get away with here? To make absolutely sure he could not punish her? Yes and yes, and curse that blue blood of hers! The intelligence of the Medici and the courage of the Swiss, no other female he knew would have dared.

The bishop sank slowly back into the chair, diverting his gaze in an attempt to control his temper. The girl thought him little more than a pawn in her battle with Charles, though the convincing emotion she put in her little speech left no doubt that not only had she meant every word but she had enjoyed humiliating him in front of the audience.

She would be made to pay for this . . .

Seeing his enlightenment, Nichole swung around and began pacing, focusing her sight on a small statue of the Madonna and child hidden away in a tiny alcove behind the altar. The Christian form of the Goddess. 'Twould do no good for them to see her alarm. She had meant to get locked away in the dungeon until her brother was forced to come to settle her punishment, but no, they must need her badly. Very badly indeed. For words that would warrant a death penalty from anyone else, she would have got nothing more than a tongue lashing. She could hold out for a year of Sundays and they still would not let her go until she relinquished. What to do? What to do . . . ?

"My mercy runs thin. Now," Kuno finally spoke in a voice much changed by her trick, "is there anything else you want?"

Escape! Her heart and mind screamed that magic word, an intonation, a wish, an imperative. Yet if there was no possibility—

Have faith! 'Twas that she felt so afraid of this trap. What if there was no way she could escape? How long before she succumbed to her brother's demand? She closed her eyes and calmed the wild rush of emotions, yet instantly the scene of the village Stan appeared again, and again, she could not escape it. Doubt brought her night terrors, and little wonder, too, for what would it or anything matter if she lost Lucerne to the beastly actions of Jonpaul the Terrible?

Hope rest in her faith! Faith that not all the lords of the Alliance were not one with Jonpaul. Faith that they could see the reason in negotiating before war brought its ravages to the land. Faith that Charles could be made to at least try to reach past the terror of Jonpaul's power to a more moderate and just presence that surely must exist within the Alliance . . .

"Yes, indeed there is something else. Now that I've an idea of how much you and my brother need this marriage, I will speak frankly. I will not rest my doubts. I need to be allowed to correspond with him . . . Charles. He alone can help put my doubts to rest. I've come to see that you arrange it."

Kuno was just about to laugh out loud at the audacity of making *any* request after her sordid little scene when the very oddity of the request set him wondering. Strange, now that he thought on it, Charles had expressly forbidden any correspondence. Why? As a matter a fact, he seemed as concerned that no quill, paper, or messenger service fall into her hands as he was that she not escape. "Not only must you make absolutely certain her feet never leave St. Gallen, but make certain none of her words leave this place as well. Absolutely no contact with the outside world . . ." Odd, too, that no women came with her. There was something here, something Charles was afraid of . . .

"Impossible," he moderated his response. "Your brother specifically mentioned you be denied these things. At least until you agree to the marriage contract."

Here was the play of power, the razor's edge she walked upon: Charles could keep her shut away from the world indefinitely, making her a prisoner the rest of her life. She would never have a single visitor or be allowed to correspond in any way with the outside world and would thus escape the threat of the paper.

The paper, the paper, the paper . . . How she had wracked her tired mind over this thing that promised to bring Charles to ruin. What could it be? ". . . your father's blood will ruin Charles." What did that mean? The answer lay in the Bible, and just as soon as she escaped from this purgatory, she intended to continue the search until she uncovered the secret. Just the pretense of knowing there was a secret had got her far, very far, and perhaps her fate was to use this lever to make Charles at least attempt to reach past Jonpaul the Terrible to stop his threat of war! ". . . the fate of many rest in your ability to fight Charles on this . . ."

For now she had no other ploy than to try her last threat: "I will never marry the Duke of Uri! I have told him a thousand times, no less. Never! So now what?"

The archbishop picked up a carving knife and began tearing off healthy portions of the roast pig, in control again. "We shall have the pleasure of your company at St. Gallen indefinitely, milady." The call of her bluff had cost her much; he'd hammer the nail through her heart. "And know this as well: Should you try to escape, you won't get far, I promise. Also, any man who aids such an endeavor—through fault, neglect, or actual intent—will be put to death by way of dismemberment. A terrible way to die, I'm told." The effect of that last statement was so severe that Nichole's face drained of its high color and her fists curled with impotent fury. "And now my lady Nichole Lucretia, having neither the time nor inclination to entertain a misbehaving young lady, I will ask you to take your leave. As it is, I've endured your company long enough."

The rebellious blue eyes shimmered with the heated passion of her antipathy. Yet she was helpless. For now at least, she was helpless. With a regal sweep of her skirts, she withdrew. The doors opened, she turned down the corridor, heading toward the open air of the courtyard. The two sisters fell in pace behind her. Two guards followed them, guards that would never be more than a shout away. She was at last her brother's prisoner.

The midnight bell rang as the distant horn of a shepherd in her sleep as Nichole dreamed of yearly sojourns with Nanna up to the crowning peak of Mount Pilatus. The trip took two days of arduous climbing up shepherds' paths through the heavily forested mountainside. Springtime sun slanted through the thick, leaf-green trees, shading the world like light through emeralds. They stopped at clear mountain springs to ease their thirst and cool their feet, where they broke bread and cheese while Nanna told stories of the old days long ago before the Christians, when the forests were filled with the great Elke, and magic and mysteries of the Goddess were celebrated . . .

These stories carried them through to the die kampfzone, where the forest stopped and the snow-patched pastures of the goatherds began. Their goal lay beyond at the very crown of Pilatus, the place between heaven and earth, a wild kingdom made of light and silver rocks, green grass and wind-filled silence. The reward stretched below as far as the eye could see in the vista of the entire Lucerne Valley, a vista so breathtakingly beautiful as to be painted by God himself: Lake Lucerne resting in the hollow of green mountains, dozens of villages, and the city of Lucerne itself. There, far below, were her father's three castles and four of Lucerne's churches and the main road that wound through the forests to pass through the wall-walk over the lake and into the city villages, branching off to tiny specks that were individual chalets and farmhouses . . .

How she loved that yearly sojourn!

Dream-spun memories interrupted these happy scenes. "Why does my father dislike me so?" Nanna would not lie. Unlike her mother and brother, she would tell the truth. Sure enough, upon hearing her question, she grabbed Nichole's arms as if needing more than her wide-eyed attention.

"'Tis his mistake, not yours. Ye must always believe that. Yer father is led only by ambition, and a great ambition it is. I suppose he regrets yer sex. He wanted an heir."

"But . . . but my brother is heir."

"I know . . . but I suppose one son is not enough for such a man." Strange images danced through her mind, glimpses of things past and forgotten, until the voice of her father's steward sounded in her mind again as he spoke with harsh urgency to her father: "I saw it today! With my own eyes. As we came upon the forest elk. I downed the buck and told Charles to see that the creature was killed, then I left him to it as I went after another. I came back nearly an hour later and I found him . . . Dear God. . . ."

"I am afraid of him!" her mother cried. "Yes! 'Tis true, I'd swear I was mad if not for Nichole. Nichole is mine, and as I remember each minute of her birth from my body, I feel her with every breath I take, as if a part of my heart lives and breathes in the child—"

"Stop! Stop it, I say! I'll hear no more of these unnatural sentiments for our son. Your son! Do you hear me? Charles is my heir!"

"No . . . No . . ." Nichole turned in her sleep, her dreams turning bloodred as she saw the sacked village, a glimpse drawn from the future, and heard her mother crying, "'Tis all too late now: The darkness waits . . . I feel it. Nanna did this, 'tis her doing and all to take my flesh and blood from the salvation of Christ our Lord . . ."

"I'll never marry the duke! Never! Jonpaul . . . Jonpaul the Terrible rode here last night . . ."

The last words seemed to wake her. Opening her eyes, Nichole lifted on her elbows to stare across the darkened room with wide, cautious eyes, suddenly as alert as a titmouse in a moonlit field. The quiet of the night was broken by the song of nearby bullfinch, the hum of crickets, and the more distant banter of the guards at the tower outside. A gentle breeze blew through her open window, rhythmically lifting the canopy over the bed where she slept. The fire still crackled in the hearth.

Night terrors again. With a sigh, she fell back against the pillow. After two fortnights of close inspection of all possibilities, she forced herself to accept the idea that there was no escape from the St. Gallen Abbey. Like a fortress, 'twould take an army of five hundred to penetrate these walls. While she was allowed to take walks outside, two guards accompanied her at all times and forbade ventures any more than a few hundred paces from the walls of the fortress. Any man aiding her would be put to death, he said, and God knows she believed him. She could not risk asking for help now.

What if she did agree to the marriage? Perhaps that would change her circumstances, giving her the opportunity to escape before they made her sign the marriage contract. She'd have to be clever about it and—

A slight creak in the floorboards shot her gaze up. She

stiffened imperceptibly, suddenly aware of what had awakened her. A footstep . . . then another. She caught a cry and held perfectly still save for the undetected movement of her hand and the sudden pounding of her heart. Reaching slowly under the pillow, she touched the cool metal of her anlace . . .

The footsteps stopped at the foot of her bed. The dim light from the hearth cast a huge shadow over the quilt she lay beneath. Her hand tightened around the dagger. There was the sound of a rapid intake of breath, the footsteps coming around to the side of her bed, leaning over—

Nichole bolted up and swung her arm, stopping the thrust of the blade at the throat. A sharp breath sounded in a queer whistle. "One move more and I will slit—" She abruptly made out the winged wimple of a sister. "A sister of the cloth? My God, what?"

Sputtered gasps of fear came from the woman—older, she saw now—and for a long moment Nichole stared at the unlikely form of her assassin, if indeed the woman was an assassin. "What are you doing here? What do you want?"

No words came from the terrified woman, frozen, it seemed, with the uncertainty of her fate. Her neck remained arched, poised to feel the sharp point of the blade cutting her throat. Nichole made no move to ease her fear, as her eyes adjusted to the dim light and she made out her shape. She looked a large woman, well into middle age, but it was hard to see in this light. There was something vaguely familiar about the regular features, the large nose, and the wide-set mouth. All of which, like her size, seemed unusually masculine for a woman, as if celibacy had stolen her femininity bit by bit, day by day.

Nichole thrust the knife harder, a hairsbreadth from piercing the skin. "Speak! I command you!"

The woman only shook her head, slightly, then with more assurance. Nichole grabbed the woman's upper arm and, careful to keep the knife positioned at her throat, she came off the bed. She led the woman over to the hearth to see better. With her free hand, she took a kindling stick from the hearth's ledge, struck it to a candle, and brought this to her face.

"Why, I know you!"

Nichole's wonder banished all trace of her own fear, the knife lowered a bit. The woman's eyes widened dramatically as they followed the movement. In the instant, she jumped back and, taking Nichole by surprise, she spun round and rushed from the room, scrambling to open the door.

"Wait!" Nichole rushed after her. She reached the door and flew into the hall, but too late. The dark skirts turned down the corridor and she was gone. For a long moment Nichole stared at the eerily deserted hall before she slammed the door and slumped to the floor, her mind spinning over the strange visit.

'Twas Katrina, she knew, 'twas Katrina, the wife of Kristonsen, her father's best friend and one of the best soldiers in all of Lucerne. Kristonsen had died some many years ago in one of the minor border battles with Basel and the Solothurn long before the Alliance. She could not have been much more than eight at the time, but she had a vague memory of the ladies gossiping that Katrina had not properly mourned the passing, gossip that had stopped when Katrina decided to move her household to the small, outlying town of Sursee. As far as she knew, Katrina had never been heard of again . . .

Only to show up nearly ten years later as a nun of the Abbey of St. Gallen. Why, how strange! A nun who had snuck into her chambers like a thief in the dark dead of night! Why? What was she after?

She would find out on the morrow.

* * *

Tall, thickly forested mountains rose on either side of the narrow, mist-covered valley of St. Gallen. A two-story, four-foot-thick stone-enclosed wall comprised the fortress of St. Gallen, which surrounded the monstrous church itself, with its high towers and arches and obscene gargoyles. Next to it were the stone and wood-beamed abbey and rectory along with the stables and barn. The township of St. Gallen lay in the hallow some long mile away, hidden now in the mist. Now, in the early fall, the fields had been harvested, the soil tilled, and presently dried grass was being shorn to keep livestock fed through the upcoming long winter months.

Nichole stood beneath a lone tree a hundred or so paces outside the fortress walls. Normally she loved the mystical quiet of a Swiss morning beneath a blanket of fog, but now, waiting to interrogate Katrina, the utter silence unnerved her. She closed her eyes, listening to the lull of the river nearly a mile and a half away.

How strange she felt! She just felt so . . . on the edge of discovery, as if something momentous was to happen. She supposed it was. The sisters of the Order of St. Martin would pass by at noon and Katrina—or Sister Mary Teresa—would be in the procession. It cost two guldens to get that information, another gulden to bribe the guards into letting her come outside the fortress walls for a morning rather than afternoon walk. The guards sat several dozen paces away. One man sat on a bench with his long legs stretched before him and his head resting on the back of the wood bench in an apparent state of rest, while the other leaned on a propped-up knee, watching her every movement. At the toll of the bell they would switch places, she knew, for apparently they felt watching her required only one man's attention, though four guards slowly kept their paces, watchful as well on the fortress walls.

There was no escape from this place . . .

Nichole kept her gaze down the green slopes, where somewhere in the mist the sisters toiled to barricade the sides of the river, where it often flooded. The arduous task would not be finished until springtime, so the poor women would have to labor through winter like common beasts of burden. It was unusual work to give women; the bishop knew no shame. The thick fog prevented sight beyond two hundred paces or so, and all she could see really, the only movement down that way, was a field-hand pushing a wheelbarrow piled high with bales of hay up to the fortress.

Wringing her hands, pacing, Nichole idly watched this man's progress, not taking any real notice until she saw how badly the poor man limped. For the love of God! Even cripples toiled like beasts of burden here! She wondered what childhood ailment or battle had made him a cripple until . . . she noticed the limp seemed exaggerated, perhaps even contrived. No doubt to get out of more work. Well, she for one did not blame any man of St. Gallen that!

How tall he was, too, she noticed, not knowing why, past having little else to observe. He did not look common, either—far from it, she saw, as he came closer—not with that thick crown of dark blond curls falling over and around a red headband, and the . . . why, yes, the bearing of a king and the hard-worked muscles of a knight! How extraordinary he looked. Even with that scar on his face, there was something about him . . .

The man stopped about twenty paces away to wipe his brow, though this did not seem necessary. She noticed the sleeveless, loose-fitting tunic, belted with metal-studded black leather and tall black boots. Not common fieldhand garb! A leather-wrapped pole hung from his belt, and something else, too? What was that? He wore no common leggings, either, but rather suede breeches disappearing in his boots, not inexpensive, either . . . He must have a rich relation or something . . .

A dark gaze abruptly penetrated her awareness. Well! How dare he stare at her like that! A thin, dark brow rose and she swung around, presenting her back to the disturbing gaze. It must be her blue silk gown, worn with a matching blue velvet head cloth that completely covered her head, falling behind and over her dark-blue cape and crowned with an expensive gold headband—all of it so fine as to attract attention from common folks. No doubt, the man had rarely, if ever, viewed a lady this close.

To her surprise, he rolled the wheelbarrow toward her, passing directly in front of where she stood. She cast a quick glance at the guards, only to see their disinterest in the man's proximity. One still slept. "A good day to you, milady." He bowed slightly, very slightly, as if not wanting to tax himself overmuch and somehow—she did not know how!—he gave the perfectly ordinary greeting the mocking edge of sarcasm.

She barely nodded in acknowledgment and turned away again, until she realized he had laid the wheelbarrow down and then had sat under the tree, her tree. She swung back around. He rested his long arms on bent knees, leaning against the tree and looking as if he had not a care in the world, that was, if one did not notice a certain alertness in his gaze. She ignored a dazzling white smile to demand, "What do you think you're doing?"

"I am easing the ache in my back."

"Must you rest here?"

He looked around. "I see no better place. Would you deny a poor man a moment's rest?"

The dark eyes—a forest green, she noticed—held hers, somehow daring her to object, and for a long moment she could not turn away from the unfathomable depth of intelligence and strength there. A tingling raced up her spine, a warning. Just as she was certain this was no ordinary man, certainly not a poor one, the first bell of noon broke the morning quiet. Eleven more bells rang in close succession, then a medley of the churchbells, but she had already turned away, staring down the incline for the sisters, the strange man nearly forgotten . . .

Until he ventured, "What is it Milady waits for?"

She turned back around, his audacity in speaking to her met with a look of incredulity. "I do not believe I granted you to leave to address me?"

The question was a demand, one that triggered an arched brow, the barest hint of an amused grin. "A thousand pardons, milady. I see I've overstepped the humble boundaries of my station. Forgive my breach of conduct."

Again those eyes. Not just the way they settled on her and seemed to pierce the very cloth of her gown to reach her skin . . . but they kept moving to the tower where the guards walked, the men at the bench and the mountains behind—

She released her breath all at once, realizing her imagination as well as her tension soared in these troubled times. "If you, my good man, will forgive my temper . . . I fear the tension of my days get the best of me. I wait for the sisters. I'm told they come this way."

The apology surprised and pleased him, though Nichole failed to notice as she turned away again, seeing the sisters moving up the hillside in the far distance. At last!

"'Tis your beauty, milady."

What was that? She heard wrong, of course. "Pardon me?" she asked as she turned around again.

"Your beauty. You see, it made me forget my place." He grinned as he twirled a long straw in his finely carved mouth, a disarming gesture, especially with the bright laughter in his eyes. "A great beauty it is, too, fairer than any my eyes have seen. I had been warned, but I wasn't expecting this—" His hand motioned to her. "Like a radiant sunrise, your beauty, milady, is an enchantment. A beauty sung by poets everywhere, I'm sure."

A radiant sunrise? Enchantment and poets? She stared in a dumbfounded stupor. No one, not the highest lord in the land, had ever addressed her so freely. The idea that a fieldhand found the unprecedented boldness to comment on her appearance left her speechless—speechless and tongue-tied, betrayed, Jonpaul saw with laughter, by a beguiling blush rising fast on her cheeks.

As if his impertinent words were a great jest! A beauty like a sunrise indeed! No ordinary fieldhand here! Just as she was about to give him a tonguelashing he'd not forget, she realized the sisters were marching through the gates. She forgot the strange man as she quickly scanned the two rows of darkly clad women. It was hard to tell; in the same dress they each looked like the other, but—

"Katrina!" Spotting her, Nichole dashed into a run. Katrina stopped, froze, then quickly rejoined the line as if she might possibly escape further notice. Too late. Nichole reached her and grabbed her arm, jerking the large woman from the line. Startled, the sisters in front and behind stopped, staring wordlessly.

"Go on, my good women!"

The woman remained dumbly mute and unmoving. With a natural air of authority, Nichole snapped, "Go on, I say!"

The others moved on, passing them where they stood. Nichole turned to Katrina. Only her face showed from the wimple, a white caul that looked like two great wings lifting ludicrously into flight. Her eyes lowered with fear as she shoved her hands into the folds of her habit. With the light of day, Nichole saw the harsh and bitter lines that had ruined the once-comely face. Deep lines fell from the corners of her mouth as well as her eyes, giving the impression of a perpetual frown. It was impossible to imagine laughter on this now-tragic face. "So it is you," she first said, taken aback by the changes brought by the years. "You do remember me, don't you?"

The questioned received a slight nod, nothing more.

"What were you doing in my bedchamber last night?"

Katrina said nothing.

"Was it to see me after these many years?" When she nodded, Nichole's tone softened. "Oh, but why would you come in the dark middle of the night like a thief? Did you think I'd not admit you?"

The question got no reply, but briefly solicited the woman's eyes. For one brief moment, Nichole saw those eyes and looked upon a soul, ravished with bitterness and hatred. Nichole took an instinctive step back. "What has happened to you? Why do you look at me like that?"

There was no reply, and it occurred to her the woman had yet to say a word. Nichole's hand snaked around the woman's arm, imploring: "Speak to me! What is wrong with you? What has happened to you here? I can help—"

This last met with a moan of a wounded animal, a sick sound from deep in the woman's throat, and she opened her mouth. Nichole gasped, froze as she stared at the severed tongue. Bile rose in her throat. She shook her head, slowly, then adamantly. With unmasked hatred, as if Nichole herself had done this to her, Katrina pulled away. Only Nichole had yet to release the arm she held and, feeling it tremble, instinctively wanting to help somehow, she clasped it tighter.

Katrina's free hand emerged from the folds of the habit . . . Perhaps to strike her. Nichole would never know, for suddenly she was staring at the disfigurement of the sixth finger. She had never seen one such before, but Nanna was in the habit of cursing it often, this mark of an ill-begotten life that many swore belonged to Satan himself. With horror and bewilderment, she slowly lifted her eyes with the question . . .

Only to confront Katrina's hatred again. She snatched her hand away and turned, running to the open gates of the fortress just as the sounds signaled the noontime changing of the guards. Thoughts spun like a child's top as Nichole tried to make sense of what the sixth finger meant . . .

"Milady, I beg a favor."

"What?" Startled, Nichole swung around to see the tall man. Her eyes looked up into the center of his chest. He was a good foot taller than she, she realized in some distant way, noticing, too, he had a perfect cleft on his chin. "That," Nanna once told her, "'tis the mark of unnatural strength. Beware when ye see it, girl . . ." Breastplates were sewn into his tunic and one arm was behind his back as if he hid a present there for her. She half expected a rose to be thrust in her face, a token of this man's ridiculous infatuation. No such thing happened, though he was laughing, and up close she saw the remarkably straight white teeth, the intensity of his dark-green eyes. The odd observations registered but dimly as her mind remained firmly fixed on the horror she had just seen. She could hardly think. "What favor? What do you want?"

"You, Nichole. I want you. From the first moment I saw you." She heard the words and froze. He stepped forward, and with the shock of it all, she braced her hands against the hard muscles of his bronzed battle-scarred arms so that the small of her back arched dramatically. "One kiss to send me into battle."

Nichole never heard the last over her startled scream, a scream that ceased as his mouth came over hers and hard. Her first kiss and it was a grave offense. To touch her in the most innocent of circumstances could easily land a death sentence, but to steal a kiss in the smack middle of the day with guards watching was a good deal beyond madness. As was this kiss! Rage surfaced in a furious rush of emotion, a hot swell needing the outlet of her lungs but stopped by the hot intrusion of his tongue and she couldn't breathe—

The guard's first screech pierced Jonpaul's ears and he looked up at the exact moment the guard stepped over the invisible line drawn by his mind. A halbert, shaped like an ax with a spike at the end, spun through the air and struck the bonnetless guard's head. The man fell to the ground without a sound. In the moment the other guard drew his sword, Jonpaul tossed a baselord. The startled scream swung Nichole around, but she never saw the guard grab his abdomen just above the thigh where the knife hit its mark, inflicting a debilitating but nonfatal wound . . . for as the guards from the tower shouted the first alarm, and bows raised and aimed, Jonpaul swung her over his shoulder and ran. Ran with the speed of a racehorse. The least of his concerns were her frantic demands to cease or the small fists furiously pummeling his back, for Jonpaul had just received the full attention of the army of St. Gallen.

The chase was on.

Chapter Four

She couldn't believe this was happening, she just couldn't! Dear God! Each bounce knocked the wind from her and she couldn't breathe. With all her strength she pounded furiously on his back, screaming, "Stop! Stop! You'll never get away with this!"

She might have been a sack of potatoes for all of his response, the way he ran with wind's speed. Still pounding, she lifted her head. The world bounced menacingly, but she managed to see the commotion on the fortress walls. They had not even gotten off the wall-walk yet! Dear God . . .

Visions of arrows flying at him terrified her, the idea that she would be hit in the fire scaring her senseless. Redoubling her efforts, she pounded harder, screamed louder, frantically trying to stop him. Gritting her teeth, she twisted up and around, caught a handful of his hair. Nails scraped his scalp, and with all her strength, she yanked his hair. She heard a brief grunt before she struggled to reach up again . . .

Retribution came swift. Without stopping or even slowing, he seized a long pole wrapped in leather from his belt and smacked her bottom hard. She cried with a sharp pain that went right through the cloth of her cape and skirt. Again. She collapsed with the pain, only to feel the next jarring step smash her ribs into his shoulder. She gasped for breath. Dizziness washed over her in waves, and just as stars and blackness swirled about her head, he threw her to the ground.

Nichole landed on her back hard against the grass and dazed, gasping, she sat up. Stars swam round her vision as he worked to untie the lead of a huge black stallion, the last thing on earth she would ever sit upon—especially as it was outfitted for battle and speed, minus any heavy armor. "Nooo" sounded weak against the frantic pounding of her heart as she struggled to get to her feet.

A dark brow rose at the astonishing speed of her recovery; a smile followed. That one smile terrified her more than any one thing in her life, though she did not stop to contemplate it as she was on her feet and running, running before he managed to turn the steed around.

Jonpaul let her go the distance as he removed a baselord—the shorter lance—and a halbert, and holding both in one hand, he kicked heels to Zermatt and gave chase. With skirts lifted to her waist, she ran faster than she ever had, a pace fueled by the desperate idea he would kill her, the instinctive fury to escape that. Her foot caught a stone and she stumbled. Her desperation miraculously caught her fall, but, jarred, she released her breath in a pain-cry . . . another as hoof beats thundered behind her, but still she was running, running through the high grass to reach the trees beyond . . .

The hooves thundered in her ears. The huge steed appeared as a shiny black cloud, a darkening at her side. He leaned over and she screamed as, like the iron claws of the mystical gwythaint, he swooped down upon her. The air squeezed from her lungs as he swung her up into space and over the saddle. A magician's trick with the devil's own strength, she could not believe it had happened except she was settled neatly in front of him with her right leg hugging the horn. There was no time to think, for the gods gave the beast wings and they were flying.

The wind whipped her face, bringing moist tears to her eyes and blurring the landscape—nothing but a retreating swirl of green and brown colors. Her head bounced against a metal breastplate in his tunic, jarring her thoughts, though his huge body seemed to completely envelop her, nearly absorbing the severe jostle of the impossible speed of his horse. The anlace! Yet she couldn't reach the hidden pocket up her sleeve . . .

Jonpaul gripped his prized mount with all the strength in his legs, giving Zermatt full rein for a blazing speed. He just might escape with not a drop more blood spilled. One hand rode the reins, the other still held the weapons, and in between sat a young lady, a treasure of beauty worth many, many times her weight in gold.

Fear seized the whole of her, her body was rigid with it. Small hands revealed her desperation as her nails dug hard into his forearm. A small trickle of blood ran from one of the tiny wounds, but he didn't notice, not when they might soon be joined by warring men . . .

The speed of their flight seemed to increase, when this was not possible. They were going to die with a fall, she knew, and shut her eyes tight. Fear choked her, but the wind whipped her face, and though her scream had no voice, she felt it from a deep well of terror inside, a terror that could not grow more, or so she thought until she opened her eyes again and through blurred vision she saw a deep gully, a deadly trap no horse could bridge.

Nichole swung round to brace against his chest, while his arm came around her as much as this was possible and he leaned forward, bringing her with him. The great beast leaped in the air, his long legs stretching like the wings of a raven. An impossible jump, his back legs hit air and he slipped. Dirt flew, but Zermatt refused the fall, pushing against the sharp angle of the gully's side until he pushed his weight up and they were flying again.

Relief came as a swirling nausea and breathlessness, for it was not over yet. Within the next minute they reached the river. He turned the horse, galloping into the water to race with the current downstream. A cold spray of water leaped to life on either side. She stared with wide-eyed incomprehension at the river stretching into the mist, a vision from a dream. Why, dear God, did he go this way?

Because water left no tracks!

It suddenly occurred to her that a fall in the water might hurt but would not likely be fatal. In that instant she swung off. He cursed, trying to catch her but too late, she was ever quick. She slipped like water under his arm, dropping to her hands and knees with a splash.

The icy cold water reached her thighs. She lifted her head just in time to hear his loud, spine-tingling curse. The horse reared high in the sky, his hooves crashing angrily back to water as Jonpaul swung around to see the direction she took through the trees. He turned his mount to give chase, but, dear God, for a girl in wet skirts, she was fast.

Sunlight just began to lift the mist, falling in streams through the dark forest of towering pines and birch trees. Wet slippers crushed the needles underfoot as she raced for her life, her breaths coming in small, frantic pants. She was nearly hysterical with terror, not thinking, only running and running. Trees took the shape of night demons, their branches becoming gnarled arms reaching out to grab her. One caught her cape and brought her to a hard stop. She cried as she tried to disentangle it and, once done, she turned—

She stopped dead in her tracks. She never heard him, he was just there, manifesting from the lingering veil of mist. Watching from maybe twenty paces away, he sat majestically upon the great black horse looking every bit like some forgotten Greek god. She did not know she was shaking her head, but abruptly she swung round and started running. A sharp whistle sounded loud in her ear, and smack! Wood cracked, and she found herself staring at the halbert stuck to the tree directly in front of her.

A whisper of the wind would have made it her skull.

"One step more and I'll knock you senseless."

Her breaths came hard and fast. She stood perfectly still, staring at the halbert. The sound of hooves crackling the needles as he approached might have been the roll of death drums. Rage piled upon her fear. She lunged for the ax. Two hands seized the handle and, with all the force of her strength, she pulled and pulled until—

Until she heard the sound of his soft laughter as he watched this. "Should I lend a hand, milady, or is this, ah, a declaration of your independence?"

She swung around and met his gaze, pressing against the trunk of the tree. Her lungs burned, breaths came in huge gulps, and her eyes were alive, wild with fear. Sunlight glinted off the metal of the anlace in her hand. "Aye, independence bought by your death!"

She did not point the dagger at him; she was not a fool. Few men she knew could fight this man, no woman had a chance. So the sharp point of the dagger lay against the shiny coat of Zermatt's neck and, as Jonpaul saw the nature of this threat, all humor and amusement disappeared. He whispered a command to Zermatt. The great beast might have been a statue, he held so perfectly still.

"Death, which I think I shall soon see!"

A wound to his horse would leave him on foot, chased by all the men of St. Gallen. He'd have no chance. The cleverness of the move was well beyond any woman he knew and most men, too. He would not underestimate her again.

Nichole held the dagger with firm assurance as her

mind raced over this sudden opportunity. Should she risk forcing him off the mount? Then she might use the horse for her own escape! Or should she just hold him until the men found them, a safer measure for sure, but what would she have then? Nothing. She'd still be trapped at St. Gallen, still a prisoner. With his horse she might be able to get away! Here at last was a key to freedom! Just as soon as she found out who he was and for whom he acted.

"Who you are?"

A wicked gleam came to those dark eyes. "Your worst nightmare, no doubt."

The dagger turned once in her hand, a warning. "Do not provoke me! Believe me, I know how hard one must thrust a knife to pierce the creature's flesh! Now, whom do you act for?"

"I act for no man, milady."

She paused, considering this. 'Twas a lie, she guessed. This man must be her brother's enemy, *her* enemy. But who? Who would do this and why?

The horse shifted his weight nervously. Jonpaul leaned over and whispered in his ear again. The great beast snorted, then held still again.

She noticed the ten or so halberts jutting from his saddlebag. Two lances, too, both short. The madman had prepared to fight the army of St. Gallen single-handedly! Why, he must be mad to risk his life for her, and why? "What do you want with me?"

A brow rose, a strange smile followed. "What do I want with you?" He repeated the question as he took in the sight of her: the determined look in the magnificent eyes, framed with coal-black lashes and the thin arch of her brows, the pert tip of that nose, and, dear Lord, the red of that mouth, the long lines of her neck, and the rapid rise and fall of her breaths. The better question might be how could blood fill his loins when he was about to be charged by the army of St. Gallen? Though even now, he knew, far more than her physical beauty, it was the fierceness and courage of her spirit—uncommon in men, even rarer in women, impossible in one her age, and it made him suddenly chuckle. "I begin to wonder myself."

She hardly understood this. "This gets me nowhere. You must be mad! I say, get off your horse. Slowly now. One false move and I'll wound your creature."

Too slowly, he made no move to obey.

"Did you hear me? I said get off!"

He still made no move to obey.

"What do you wait for? Do you doubt my courage?"

"Nay." He smiled softly, "The marvel of your courage is plain. I'm only trying desperately to think of a way to disarm you without hurting you. Perhaps if there was more time . . . I am sorry—"

She never knew what hit her, his boot struck her so fast. With all the restraint he knew, life exploded from her lungs and blackness swirled and swirled as she fell back side to the ground. Instantly he was at her side and, from the depth of the blackness, she heard whispered words of an apology, a jostling and then a chuckle, the devil's laughter roaring through her and she was terrified . . .

He lifted her mercilessly small weight to his arms and, seeing the anlace, wanting a memento, he bent down and retrieved it. Zermatt pranced nervously as he felt his master's weight again, but as Jonpaul gathered back the reins, he heard the distant sound of horses and men. The chase. Nichole tossed her head back and forth, coming to quickly. The situation crashed into her dazed consciousness and, with it, the sound of the pursuing men. She opened her mouth to scream, alerting the men as to where they were, but his hand clamped hard over her mouth. "Oh no you don't, Nichole. No screaming now."

His single hand blocked the air from her lungs and, like

a drowning person, she gasped frantically as both her hands came over his one. He moved swiftly. The reins were dropped. The great horse danced a circle with this freedom as Jonpaul reached into his saddlebag and withdrew a cotton scarf. This was tied around her mouth and knotted in back. She was trying to shake her head with the single word "no" when a heavy rope twisted quickly, effortlessly around her hands. Forced forward, the rope was then tied to the saddle horn, making her hug the horse so as not to fall when . . . if . . . he could no longer hold her. He reached forward, grabbed the reins, and checked his mount. Swinging around, he leaned over and, as if he were Arthur pulling the sword from the stone, he effortlessly retrieved the halbert from the tree.

Forced into the awkward position, Nichole tried to catch her breath. Though she couldn't turn around to see, he kept himself and the horse still to listen for the sounds of the chase. It must have split: one distant sound behind the approaching thunder of horses pounding through the river.

Someone must have seen them! Dear God, please turn this way! She cried out, but with the cloth in her mouth, the cry sounded muted and weak, surely not audible at a distance. She struggled with the rope binding her hands but this, too, was useless.

Admiration came to his gaze as he saw the extent of her determination, her absolute refusal to give up. "Easy, love. I might yet get out of this with no blood spilled."

He slowly let the horse pick his way back through the forest. Tense with fear and apprehension, Nichole never knew if he meant her blood, his, or both, but it hardly seemed to matter. It never occurred to her that he would suffer a care for the blood of St. Gallen men, for all she could think of was that he would not get away with this, he could not! An army of men was out looking for them. He was just one against a hundred! She would soon witness his death, probably never even knowing who he was or acted for—

Horses trampled through the forest. War cries broke the sanctity of the forest quiet. Two mounted men burst through the trees. Jonpaul dropped the reins. A halbert swung through the air, swung by his left hand and caught by his right, the movement used to gain force as it swooped in a circle to spin through the air, landing across a man's chest, this as Zermatt rotated in a circle for the next throw as more men trampled into the glen. He was hopelessly outnumbered, but the odds transformed him into something monstrous and menacing and impossibly fast moving, as again and again like the swift turns of a windmill, his left hand fed a halbert to his right, which spun it with savage force through the air.

One saw the poetry of his motion only from a distance. In the shock of it all, Nichole saw only a landscape of glittering colors, flailing hooves and horses, wild movement, the chaos and madness that was war. She screamed as a halbert flew at them a split second before it was struck down midair, while simultaneously Zermatt leaped to the side and allowed him to swing the short lance in a vicious parry. Swords clanged a half dozen times before Jonpaul seized the advantage, and Nichole heard the blood-curdling cry of his opponent, his blood obscuring her vision . . .

Within minutes, four more men lay wounded on the ground, their horses rushing from the blood-soaked ground. No man, not now, not ever, lived to penetrate the ten-foot invisible circle Jonpaul drew around himself. No lance, sword, or mace touched him without penalty. The magic circle in his mind. Like Nichole, he used to feel each wound he gave until his reflexes and speed grew faster than his mind could accommodate, but now he neither thought nor felt, only acted: he threw, swung, threw until only three men remained . . .

Four halberts left, then three as he knocked a man who fled the terror of the glen. Cowards got no mercy, though Jonpaul rarely threw fatal blows. A large red-haired soldier swung from behind a split second after a resounding clap as Jonpaul caught his broadsword in his right hand and swung round to parry the deadly strike of the soldier's mace. Nichole screamed, but Jonpaul ducked, caught the chain in a clamor around his sword and, with a queer twist and inhuman strength, he sent it back. The mace smacked the soldier in the face and, with an agonized cry, the man went down, clutching his face and blinded by his own hot blood.

Nichole drew hard, fast, gasping breaths, her nostrils flaring with the thick scent of spilled blood as she closed her eyes to the terror surrounding her, but as her hands were tied, she could not block the moans and cries of the wounded sprawled around the glen. The frantic thud of her heart echoed the repetition of Oh my God . . . oh my God . . .

Letting the last man flee, Jonpaul swung off his horse. He quickly retrieved three bloodied axes from the ground. With one in hand, the rest were set back in the saddlebag before he mounted Zermatt again, swinging up behind Nichole.

With the hot sting of blood in his eyes, the red-haired soldier struggled to sit up. He wiped at his eyes with his shirt, frantically groping for his own halbert. His hands found it. With blurred vision and a bad aim, he threw at the retreating back of the warrior whose name he had now guessed. The whistle of the ax swung Jonpaul around only to feel the wind brush his thigh and smack—

The razor-sharp edge of the blade sliced neatly into Nichole's leg before dropping to the ground, her cry piercing his ears. He stared at the sliced skirt as her blood rushed out over the cloth. He never understood what happened to him in that moment, though it had happened one other time as he watched his uncle killed at his side in battle. A murderous rage rose swiftly, surely, an inhuman thing that could effortlessly kill the next twenty men he saw—only now it was directed to the red-haired devil lying gasping on the ground! Zermatt swung around with instinctive knowledge of his rage, pranced quickly to the fallen man, while Jonpaul's broadsword manifested magically in his hand. This was raised to a thrust into the red devil's chest—

The single word "no" came as a muffled plea, so loud in her heart and mind Jonpaul was made to heed. His gaze focused hard on the plea in her terrified eyes. His raised arm hesitated between mercy and death until his eyes fell to her wound, where blood soaked through the cloth. For a moment, time stood still, and like a god he was as he waited, waited for mercy to overcome the rage pounding so hard and fast in his chest.

Nichole did not trust his ability to find it. With heroic measure that he'd never forget, she suddenly closed her eyes and braced against the searing-hot pain of her severed leg to use the last of her strength to kick Zermatt's side. The great beast reared high in the sky and, with an angry neigh, his hooves returned to the ground in a gallop and they were off.

Jonpaul slipped his broadsword into its sheath, while taking a knife from his belt. He cut the gag. Nichole drew sweet, gasping breaths of air, but the world began to recede into gray colors, undulating with the hot, stinging throb in her leg. Tears blinded her from the wind or pain, she did not know. She felt faint . . .

Giving Zermatt full rein once the direction was right, Jonpaul managed to withdraw a wound cloth from the saddlebag, which he pressed against her leg. Her world exploded into bright red colors as he held it there hard, even as Zermatt raced against the wind. She cried against the pain, frantically pulling at the robes binding her arms like a chained animal. The pain; she couldn't bear a second more, she was weak with it. Strong arms pulled her close to stifle her struggle as he kept the cloth to her wound.

She went wild to escape the pain, but he kept her helpless to move. "Please . . . Nooo—"

"Don't fight me, love," he called against the wind, yet she never heard. She collapsed, conscious no more. He did not release his hold, though his relief felt heady. Watching as she bore that pain was as hard as seeing it inflicted; he'd rather climb Mount Blanc again . . . twice.

Saints in heaven, who was this girl? Wild as a fallow doe, as courageous as the maid Joan herself, and with that girl's own saintly heart, and all in a package more lovely and tempting than the opened gates to heaven. She looked so pale and small now, and how strange! This unsteady joy and relief in the feel of her slight, steady breaths against his arm!

Who was this girl?

The Alliance included the lands of Basel, Solothurn, and Berne, all lying south of the Rhine, far west of St. Gallen and Zurich and northwest of the Lucerne valleys. Jonpaul's destination lay ten miles to the northwest, four thousand feet up into the Bodensee mountain range. A fair-sized cave waited there, stocked with enough supplies to last until the chase was given up for lost and the men turned back. As it was, he expected the other larger group of men who had ridden west to soon realize their mistake and double back to catch him.

While he might take ten men down, he could not take thirty or more. The only hope was in outrunning the arrows of the crossbows, and for that Zermatt was eminently qualified. No horse in all the St. Gallen's stables could outrun him, even with an added hundred or so pounds. With any luck, they could reach safety not long after nightfall.

Sensations piled: the dull throb that was Nichole's leg, the jostle of the gallop, and the thunder of horse's hooves. She shivered with furious chills. A great warmth waited just behind and she leaned into it, trying to wake enough to make sense of it. She opened her eyes to see the world flying at her. She jerked to full awareness, throwing the chills off as she did so. "'Tis you! 'Tis still you and—"

Against the wind a chuckle sounded in her ear, sending a curious tingling down her spine. "You weren't imagining I'd give you up after warring with ten men to keep you, did you now?"

With sudden vehemence, she cried; "You still won't get away with this! You'll never get away—"

"But I am, Nichole, I am—" He spoke too soon. From behind came the sound of the pursuit. They were spotted. Human shouts rose weakly above the running hooves of thirty or more horses. Jonpaul turned around to see, knowing how close the horde must be if heard above Zermatt's gallop. A great cloud of dust and grass rose in the far distance. The climb ahead would put them closer, close enough to take aim.

"What are you doing?!"

It was a dangerously weak cry, for he had pushed her full over the horse, shielding her body from the arrows with his own as Zermatt raced up the hill.

"Arrows, we are about to be fired upon!"

"Nooo . . ."

The captain of the guards raced a good half mile behind the group, having lingered longest at the scene of mayhem the blond giant had left in the meadow. He alone knew the orders, and when he saw the men stop, rallying the horses in circles to take aim with the crossbows, his shout was an impotent whisper against the wind. He kicked spurs to his mount, but the beast already gave him all he was worth.

Crossbows were drawn tight as the captain's voice sang over the wind. "Hold fire! Hold fire! The lady cannot be risked! Cease fire at once!" Only two arrows flew, both falling short of the rapidly disappearing target.

The thwarted attack gave Jonpaul a necessary advantage, and he lifted back up to feel the wind whipping his face. Braced for arrows, certain death . . . she didn't understand. "Why . . . why are they not firing?"

"It seems I am not the only one who wants you alive."

"Of course . . . Of course, her death might be a good deal worse than her abduction, she suddenly understood. She tried to lift back up, but the effort cost too much. She felt his strong arm circling her, drawing her back to his chest. Her leg felt like numb throb now; she had the terrifying idea it hung by a thread of her flesh. She tried to form words, to look at it, but the world receded again. Darkness swirled and swirled and she remembered no more . . .

The sun began its descent beneath the Bodensee Mountains, melting the blue sky into violet. Because darkness came late at summer's end, only three, maybe four, hours of light remained in this memorable day. In the far distance, cotton clouds gathered around the lofty snowcapped peaks. At last the lengthening shadows provided relief for Jonpaul's windburned skin. Zermatt pranced at a goodly pace, picking his way up through the rugged forest-lined hillside, a half mile or so from the bank of the Thor River. The rush of water sounded loud even from the distance. Another two miles. Alone, Jonpaul would have long since dismounted to stretch his legs and set his horse free, his anxiousness to see Nichole's wound tended making him keep at a gallop had Zermatt not been long since spent. A run now would ruin the creature, if not permanently, at least for the long journey back to Basel.

At last Zermatt crossed the small tributary, rushing on its way to reach the mother water of Thor, and turned off to the right. The cave sat above a deep pond of water, hidden behind the waterfall that fed it and surrounded by a thick forest of trees. No one would ever find them here.

After gathering Nichole in his arms and dismounting, he carried her up and around a small hill of boulders, then around the edge of a ledge twelve or so paces above the pond. Stepping behind the waterfall, he went through the tall, narrow opening to the cave.

With luck, she wouldn't wake.

Yet she did wake, as if her consciousness needed to take stock of her changed circumstances. She opened her eyes to see shadows dancing over darkness. Her pulse leaped to life as she struggled to sit up. A fire crackled and danced against a dark wall . . . that was all she saw. The thick bed of fur beneath lent the first clue that her surroundings were not drawn from her imagination and, slowly, the terrifying circumstances filtered into her dazed mind. Made of packed earth and boulders, the cave opened to a bedchamber-size room, narrowing to a tunnel of darkness at the end. The tallest point looked maybe twelve feet. His saddlebag rested in the corner. The sound of water nearby and the light of day still streaming through an opening brought the realization that she was in a cave with water just outside.

Water . . . She would kill for a cup of water. A fierce thirst burned in her stomach and made her look anxiously about her. Further inspection granted her wish. A huge cask of cool water sat at her side. With an eagerness that bordered desperation, she lifted it to her lips and drank greedily. The sweet moisture wet her parched throat, sliding into her stomach. She kept drinking until she felt herself swimming with relief until—

The dangers seeped into her mind.

He must have brought her here! He must be outside somewhere! Dear God, how had he escaped the army of men in pursuit? And her leg, she didn't feel anything past a dull burning, nothing, as if it were no longer there. A small cry came as a gasp. She was afraid to look.

Gathering all her courage, she tossed back the fur cover. She slowly lifted her skirts, the end on one side caked with dry blood. She stared at the bloodied leg, and, after several long seconds, she discerned the actual wound. A five-inch gash on the outside of her left leg an inch or two above her knee.

Surprise brought her thin brows together. 'Twasn't so bad! Honestly, for all the blood and lack of sensation, she had been imagining it was severed, barely hanging by thin threads of flesh. This was nothing. Well, almost nothing.

The sight of it gave her courage. She looked about again until her gaze settled on the saddlebag. With effort not to use her bad leg, she crawled like a cripple. Dizziness washed over her in waves. She waited a long minute to catch her breath, then continued the struggle to the bag. Once there, more dizziness washed over her. She fought to overcome it, long enough to seize a halbert and her . . . anlace!

How kind of you to retrieve it for me!

With weapons in hand, she crept back to the furs and collapsed breathless onto her back. With the dagger in one hand and the broadax in another, she threw the fur back over herself.

Tension seized the whole of her, interrupted by an occasional shiver of fear. Little wonder at her fear, yet with luck, she could turn this nightmare into fortune. The only thing separating her from freedom was his death.

His death, dear God, forgive me. She had but a chance. If she could just land the ax against his neck when his back was turned, when he least expected it . . .

"Ah, what a fine friend you are, Zermatt," Jonpaul whispered in the beast's ear as he presented the horse with a shiny red apple. Zermatt's teeth snatched it greedily from his hand and he laughed. "There is no better." The horse neighed and nodded his fine head. Lifting the saddle, Jonpaul strode around the incline to the ledge. Just before the waterfall, he set the saddle down, quickly pulled off his belt, broad tunic, and then his boots before diving into the cold, clear water beneath the fall. A cleansing swim before he tackled that wound! The water replenished his energies, cleansing his skin of dirt and sweat, at least enough to dress Nichole's wounds, he was sure. He swam for several seconds directly under the waterfall before diving under and emerging on the other side. With an agile leap, he climbed out onto the rocks, walked around, and retrieved his things before he emerged in the opening to the cave.

He set the saddle down, seeing she still slept, thank God. Stitches were so painful—the worst part of battle, Hans always said—that after every battle the fortress walls filled with the screams of men, followed by hours of moans. He'd put her through too much already. God knows, her bountiful courage and fortitude would be taxed enough when they finally reached Basel . . .

Two buckets of water and fresh cloths waited near where she lay. A medicine basket sat near the foodstuffs in the back of the cave. After lighting three torches, he got the basket, found the needle and thread, and, with effort, he worked to thread the needle.

Carefully pulling away the cover so as not to make a sound, Nichole sat up, then waited for the maddening dizziness to pass. How weak she was! Now or never, though, for there would be no chance once he discovered the missing weapon. Tapping her last reservoir of strength, she stood to her feet. The dizziness intensified with sharp, stinging pain, washing her in momentary blackness. With wide eyes focused hard on where he knelt, and ignoring the pain, she leaned against the wall, steadying herself. Not making a sound, not even daring a breath, she silently came behind him. Small beads of perspiration lined her forehand and her hands shook with the weight of the ax as she raised it—

The task was as easy for one of his sex as childbirth and "Jeezus!" he pricked his finger, swearing out loud. Like a call that triggered an avalanche, the ax came down, came down with her weight as he turned and, with lightning-quick reflexes, rather effortlessly caught her up in his arms. It took a good long moment for him to overcome his surprise to realize just what had happened. A clean miss. He looked behind him to the halbert lying on the ground, then back at the girl in his arms.

Dark brows lifted as he studied his prize. How on God's earth did a girl—woman—come by such courage and determination, this idiotic though admirable idea she could fight him? What trick of parentage paired those masculine qualities with this beauty?

Yet her unlikely position made him say; "I like my women eager, love, but this"—and suddenly he was laughing, laughing with the relief of a hard-fought day, "this goes too far."

She stared at the play of light and shadows over the strong features of his face, her own thoughts racing over the utter courage and outrageousness of his conduct as she wondered what manner of beast was he: He had not just stolen her beneath the very light of day but also beneath the guard tower and her guards, single-handedly battling over ten armed men, wounding or worse every mere mortal man who came within three-foot radius of his person—and then, then he had outrun an entire army of men! An entire army of men! The mere thought that he had conceived of such an outrageous deed filled her with a blind rage; the idea that he had actually gotten away with it to laugh at her now brought the rage trembling through her. Her entire being throbbed with the dull pain in her leg, ignored now to raise her fist and smack his face hard.

Which did nothing but banish the light of laughter from his eyes. "My God, you are a witch, child!" He grabbed her hands in one of his and, for all the strength there, it was a gentle hold. Unlike his words. "Listen up, love. You are mine now, a possession. Don't make me enumerate the countless ways in which I might hurt you. Let it suffice you to know that your each breath is at my mercy."

She frantically searched his face, confusion mixed with fear. "You said you would not kill me!"

"There are things plenty worse than death. Especially for a woman."

Unfeigned shock lifted on her face. Wise to the ways of the world, she knew only one thing worse than death for a woman and the idea of what he meant came as a great shock indeed. "Now you will rape me?!"

She didn't understand his changed expression upon hearing that question, but some inexplicable amusement followed. Only because for all the valor and fierceness of her spirit, the blunt question and the utterly incredulous and desperate way it was put made him know he held a virgin in his arms. Unbelievably innocent, the only thing more surprising was his disappointment.

She misunderstood his emotions, and the idea that he might indeed rape her produced great panic. She would not go down without a fight. With a small cry of denial, she twisted to escape his arms, while a raised fist hit the rock that was his chest, returning, but only to be caught. "Easy, love, easy," he cautioned as he stood up to carry her to the pallet, trying to keep his thoughts focused on getting the leg stitched, especially necessary if she kept insisting on these taxing measures. "You are weaker than a kitten from blood loss and pain, you can't fight me now. Save your strength. God knows, you will be needing it."

As much as the words, the solemnity of his changed tone alarmed her more. Her thoughts raced. She didn't know she was shaking her head, her eyes glaring with horror and hatred both as he brought her back to the pallet. As soon as he turned back to retrieve the thread and needle, she carefully placed the dagger in between two of the furs. Then she sat up, her gaze as watchful and mistrusting as a mother cat stalking a rat.

Returning, he knelt by her side. He reached a hand to her but she recoiled as from the hot touch of fire. "Don't touch me!"

His gaze went hard, his own dagger manifest instantly in his hand. "You are becoming more troublesome than a bout with the pox. I will remove your clothes with a decent hand, leaving your only undergarments intact. Or maybe I shall rip them to shreds and shake them from you, a thing I guarantee you'll regret when it keeps you naked before my eyes for the duration of our time together. Now which is it?"

Those blue eyes filled with emotion, and breathing hard and fast, and not from her recent exertions, she paused but briefly before unclasping her cape and setting it neatly at her side. Then she swept the cloth of her headscarf from her back and wordlessly presented him with the neat row of buttons. Which he deftly unbuttoned, slowing some as he saw more and more of the untouched white skin of her slender back beneath the cotton chemise. Even her goddamn backside was enough to rouse a blind man.

Once done, she paused with her back to him and her arms crossed over herself, resting on her shoulders.

"Please . . ." She heard a shuffle and assumed he turned away. Trembling and feeling faint with weakness and dizziness, she pulled the gown from her shoulders and then, with some more effort, from her legs. This was set over her cape. Her hands lingered on the straps of her chemise. Dried blood caked it to her leg, but it had to come off, she knew. She grabbed her cape from beneath the gown, and with one hand holding this over herself, she pulled the thin cotton off her shoulders and down to her waist. With care, she lifted it from her skin before pulling it over her wound.

Only then to turn back around and see how he stared at her. She frantically searched his face, but he was not looking at her eyes, rather the whole of the delicate lines that drew the temptation: the thin lines of her long neck, the straight angle of her shoulders and thin arms, the tease of her full breasts pushing up against the arm that held the cape to her. He reached in slow motion to her head. She gasped, caught his hand to stop him, but with a surprised look, he took her small hands in one of his, then reached his free hand to pull the gold band from her head. The long headscarf that hid her hair followed.

Because of her fairness, he had been imagining a pale blond color—not hair like a midnight sky, rich and thick, dropping to coil on the fur where she sat, startling against the ivory skin and the blue eyes.

He cursed out loud and released her hands, reminding himself she was trembling with pain and a hairsbreadth from fainting. He got the first cloth and, careful to circle the wound itself, he dipped it in water and began cleaning the blood from her leg.

Trying to ignore the dull throb that was her pain, she made him the object of her study, searching—and rather desperately—for a sign of his weakness, a weakness she knew had to be there and one she had to find. The shadows lengthened and torchlight danced over the bronzed skin and gold hair. He was handsome, and devastatingly so. He wore the red sweatband around his head like a crown, his wet curls carelessly falling over this, accenting his fine large nose and the thick brows arching over the startling intelligence found in those eyes.

Yet one would never think he was handsome, his strength so overwhelmed all other impressions. He radiated strength, a raw, physical thing, manifesting in his unconventional height, the hard muscles encasing not just his arms but his long legs and the wide width of his chest as well. Athletic veins created a curious map on his arms, moving like snakes as he worked. All these athletic pronouncements lay beneath trophies he wore as battle scars, for numerous scars marked his arms. An angry red gash went from his shoulder down, disappearing in his breeches. The highly touted mark of the mace wound scarred his side. After seeing his unparalleled battle skill today, Nichole could only wonder how he possibly had got even one scar, let alone so many. She would not have been surprised to learn nearly all his wounds were got before he had even reached his twentieth year.

All in all, she knew this about him: He had done what no other man she knew could. He had abducted her from beneath the entire army of St. Gallen. She would never have believed it if she hadn't been the victim. Thinking of this, watching his movements, she saw he had a familiarity with the cleansing of wounds, no doubt from his experience in war. She herself knew both the old and new medicines. Nanna had seen to that.

She also knew he frightened her to the depth of her soul. She would have to kill or maim him to gain her freedom, and that made her regret her sex more than she ever had before. Despite the astronomical odds against her, she knew she would defeat him—and only because she had to—or die in the trying. Before she did that, though, it would help so much to know who he was and what he wanted.

"My mind runs in circles around the question of whom you are. Will you tell me now?"

The wound had opened and bled again from her ridiculous attempt to put an ax in his back. The resulting mess put anger in his voice. "You don't need to know that now."

"'Tis only fair that I know who you are!"

He looked up briefly, irritated. Curse it all, an angel's voice on top of all else . . . "Get it straight, love: My handling of you will not, *cannot* be fair."

The words brought a rush of panic. "Dear Lord, I am weak from hunger and exhaustion and blood loss. I can do nothing to you now! Why won't you tell me?"

"For that very reason, love. You are too weak. I'll not frighten you more tonight."

She searched his face frantically, trying to determine if he had said that to terrify her more or if he could possibly mean it? She still hadn't decided when he tied a cloth tight around her wound.

In a voice weak with pain, she offered, "If you bury the needle in hot ash and say two psalms, 'twill take away the sting."

He might have known. His eyes focused on her with hard interest. "You are an initiate in the old religion?"

She couldn't determine his response to it. The Church used to be tolerant of the old religion, condescending to its practitioners and their traditions and celebrations of nature. Some of the more wonderful holidays were even incorporated into Christian holidays, so that the winter solstice feast became the Christmas celebration. People everywhere, even the priests, valued the initiates for their medicines and potions, as well as their famous skill in midwifery. She had spent most of her life studying with Nanna. She knew potions and cures for every imaginable ailment and many unimaginable—all of these carefully put first to memory, then practice, and, last, to her treasured book of hours.

Yet in the last forty or so years, the cardinals of the church had decided the rites of the old religion were blasphemous, and the practitioners witches. Witches! Just over twenty years ago, at the last Council of Bishops at Basel, two initiates were burned at the stake. Unbelievable in these days of enlightenment! Because of her mother, she was not just a Christian but a rather devout one. Nanna tried to tolerate this, emphasizing the similarities between the old and new religions as well as the difference between the laws of man and laws of God. The two were forever separate in her mind, so she embraced nature as the living manifestation of God, a worship that demanded only a heartfelt reverence for all life on earth. Her heart, like Nanna's, sang with the songs of the old religion.

She studied him intently. Not knowing who he was or where he came from, let alone his opinion of the subject, she could hardly confess. Needless to say, she did not relish the idea of the stake.

Jonpaul reached a hand to her cape, drawing it from her knees. She watched his reaction as he stared at the thin line on her left knee. It was a common mark of the initiate, left from one of the more minor exercises, whereas two razor-thin lines were drawn on both knees. The right knee received the white light of the initiate's healing powers—and if one's light was pure and strong, it disappeared—whereas the left remained untouched.

His thumb slowly smoothed the small mark. He must have sensed her hesitation, for he said, "My own mother was an initiate." His lips curved with a boyish kind of smile, one that took her wholly by surprise. "You'll find no danger from me for those practices, things that amount to old wive's tales and foolish superstitions, innocuous potions and hand-holding at birthing times."

Hand-holding at birthing times indeed! What arrogance belonged to his sex! Men, Nanna always said, are all alike. The only reason they were given different faces was so they'd know which house to return to at night. Well, if he meant to insult her, he wasted his breath.

Jonpaul watched her curiously, bemused by her apparent restraint as he washed his hands, then stood to fetch some food for her. He came back with an apple and bread and set these on her lap, then sliced some cheese and handed that to her. She hesitated, not having expected anything from him.

"If you're hungry, eat now, before the stitches. You won't be able to afterward."

It was good advice. She felt starved and weak from the wound and no doubt she'd need all her strength in the next few days. Yet with her mind turning over the most important question, she hardly tasted the food, though she greedily devoured the bread and cheese until the last bite of cheese fell from her hand and, with a pained gasp, she grabbed her leg. Warm blood trickled over her hand. He knelt at her side before a word could be said. "Hold still now, this will hurt." She braced as he tightened the tourniquet, then placed the wet cloth over her wound, cleaning it again. She bit the inside of her mouth to stop her cry, tense as the sharp, stinging pain seized the whole of her leg. Once clean, he looked up to see this. Her face went white. She gripped the fur, her small knuckles turning white and blue with a valiant effort not to cry out. The stitches would be worse. "I could knock you out. You'd feel nothing."

Dizziness echoed the pain, but she managed to shake her head. "No . . . no. I am strong."

She was indeed strong, but he was not and with a soft curse, he said, "I just decided I wasn't asking." Before the words had even penetrated her pain, a fist lightly touched her skull and, mercifully, blackness claimed her once more. Within the half hour he had finished the last neat stitch. A week or two, no longer, and the leg would be as good as ever. The torchlight danced over her pale skin, a troubled expression marked her lovely face even in sleep. That hair created a dark circle around her head. Not knowing why he might want to torment himself but compelled nonetheless, he lifted the cape that covered her unclad form.

The sight caught his breath and fueled the pace of his heart. He might have been suddenly running as he stared at the beauty caught in firelight. Like a conjurer's trick, the picture was drawn from the far recesses of his imagination, the living, breathing embodiment of his desire. She lay perfectly still on her back, the firelight casting a golden color over the flattened though still round and full mounds of her breasts, tempting beyond reason, curving dramatically to a painfully small waist and, dear God, the beckoning flare of her hips, the narrow tuft of dark hair, and the impossibly long legs, the whole of her nothing but softness and curves. As he stood there staring, the passion and desire to possess her physically, a heinous crime, put fire to his blood and heat to his loins. Unexpected and definitely not wanted, the quickness and force of his body's response were alarming, to say the least.

Lady Nichole Lucretia was indeed in trouble.

Chapter Five

Visions filled Nichole's dreams, merging and changing against the landscape of sleep, ending at last when she saw a distant hillside where an ugly old woman stood waving her hand from far away. A hand marked by the sixth finger . . . the sixth finger . . . Nanna trying to tell her something, gasping and choking . . . then, as she looked upon the burning ruins of the village of Stan, bright red blood soaking her vision.

Breathless and panting, Nichole bolted up. Noonday sun streamed through the opening in the darkened cave, and as her eyes swept her surroundings, for one wild moment she didn't know where she was . . . until at last her eyes came to settle on a pair of black boots to the side, then lifted over the suede breeches and a scarred chest to his handsome face. With hands on hips, he stared down at her and, dear God, she must be dreaming still to imagine concern on his face.

Trying to recover, she gathered her hair and pulled it back, smoothing it with her hand as her eyes, still wide and enormous with fear, danced around the cave. He groaned, drained the last of his water, and looked away, irritated with the extent of his lasciviousness. He had never been a man "cock led," as his men so gamely put it, and the extent of his desire seemed unmerited by her beauty alone—lovely as the girl was. Aye, what he knew of her spirit was indeed a wondrous, winged thing, but what he felt was physical, raw and definitely earthbound. He didn't understand the irrationality of it. He could not, would not, indulge it. Lying with her would be a disaster. A virgin, no less.

Yet here he was, spending half the morning watching her as she slept, imagining all manner of scenes: those eyes darkening with passion, the taste of her lips, and the feel of her breasts, parting her thighs and the sweet mercy of sinking into her sex . . .

He tried to temper his thoughts. "A nightmare, love? I wonder what monsters play in your sleep?"

"None, I can assure you, that are worse than the monster who stands before me now."

A quick grin transformed his face, but there was something else—the way he stared. She became conscious of how she must look and, nervously, she clutched the fur tighter about her breasts.

"You kept calling for Nanna?" He remembered her servant had said Nanna had been her favorite, that she had recently passed. Wasn't that the one who made the prophecy, too? "Who is that?"

Still dazed, the mention of Nanna's name brought a distant look. "A soul very dear to me . . ." She thought of Nanna's deathbed for the hundredth time, the secret shared in Nanna's last moments, a secret that took second place in her mind at the moment to escaping.

Third place if the Basel Alliance declared war. Still fresh and raw in her mind, the memory of the poor people of the village of Stan struck sudden fear in her heart, and now with this man and his abduction, she was likely to suffer night terrors the rest of her life, as short as that might be.

"If looks could kill . . ."

"You, sir, would be quite dead. Where are my clothes?"

"I hid them."

He hid them! She frantically searched the surrounding area to ascertain the truth of it. She had to have her clothes. "You'll give them back?"

"Not immediately."

She took this in and, confused, unable to hide the edge of desperateness from her voice, "Oh, but why not?"

"Why should I?"

"But I can't go anywhere without—"

The amused light in his eyes stopped her cold. "Exactly. You won't go anywhere without them. The alternative is tying you up—which, by and away, I will do if I have to. After watching your heroics yesterday, I'll take no chances." Those blue eyes widened with fury as he headed toward the opening, "Keep the fire going. You have free rein of the cave. I warn you though—don't take so much as a step outside."

"Wait! Where are you going? You can't just—"

Yet he did. He left before she could mutter another cry of protest, of which she had many . . . many . . . many! She fell back against the furs, her head spinning in desperate circles over her situation.

Fear made her heart pound and her hands go clammy as she stared at the opening. She tried to hide them, determined not to let him see her fear. Who was he? What, dear God, what did he mean to do with her?

It must be ransom, it must. If that was the case, he had no idea how lucky he was! Her brother would have to pay him what he asked. He would have to. Of course she would not tell him how desperate her brother would be to keep her safe and alive. Charles, dear Charles, how frightened you must be for me . . .

Dear Lord, if she could just survive to escape this man! Then she could make her way back to Lucerne. Charles's relief would be a great surge she'd use to her advantage. It would soften his heart at least long enough to listen to her. Perhaps she would not even need the leverage of the paper—or whatever it was. Aye, it made perfect sense of a sudden: Charles would be so happy to have her back, safe and alive, he would agree, if not to forget the marriage altogether, then perhaps to postpone it long enough to find another avenue to save Lucerne from the threat of Jonpaul . . .

She had to escape!

She felt for the dagger. She'd have to pick the moment carefully. If ten warring men could not take him down, she'd have no chance unless she took him by complete surprise—when he least expected it. She'd have no second chance. Horror filled her eyes as she thought of killing him . . . even this beast . . .

She had never killed before. The most sacred tenet shared by both the Christian faith—so dear to her soul—and the old religion was a reverence for all life, the belief in its sanctity. She alone seemed to understand the commandments. How many times had she argued with men that no clauses specifying the exceptions sat beneath Thou shalt not kill? Only now to find an exception herself . . . and if there was just any other way . . .

She washed her hands, face, and her wound, briefly admiring his neat stitchery before, she combed her hair using her fingers as spikes. She pulled and lifted it back into an unplaited tail, using only a strand of that hair to hold it, a trick Nanna had taught her. Wrapped in a thick fur, she stood up. Slowly, carefully, she applied her weight, testing her strength. The wound throbbed with the exertion, but she ignored this. First she would find her clothes, if they were in here . . . then she'd search for another weapon.

But the only worthwhile thing she found was his last

apple, which she ate to spite him. She hoped he missed it. There was cheese, bread, and potatoes, two sacks of these, enough to last for over a week. He had removed his weapons, too, ever thorough in his perniciousness. Light streamed in from the outside, and she turned toward it. The sound of running water told her a waterfall fell nearby. How she would love to bathe . . .

Wrapped in a fur, she cautiously stepped to the opening. Two more steps put her outside, where she took in the wonderful spectacle of nature before and above her. From the rocky cliffs a thousand feet above, a small waterfall dropped into a wide, clear pond. A forest of pines surrounded the inviting pond on one side, while the other side opened to a meadow of green grass edged by more trees. Boulders were interspersed throughout the meadow. The air filled with the sweet redolence of pine, while the sky was a wide arch of summer blue. She drew a deep breath—

A shrill whistle sounded against her ear, and she screamed in a gasp as the arrow hit its mark a hairsbreadth from her neck. She froze. Only her eyes moved in a frantic search of her assailant and she gasped when she saw him.

The Swiss were not known for modesty, especially Swiss men, and unlike other people of the Continent, the wealth of lakes and rivers in Switzerland made cleanliness coveted and bathing a daily activity. Nichole had seen hundreds of naked men and yet, for some reason, the magnificence of his unclad length as he lay casually on a boulder across the way caused a sharp intake of breath, a curious constriction in her throat, none of which had anything to do with the fact that an arrow flew past her ear.

The bow rested in his hand, another arrow at his side. She noted his marksmanship, but then she had already witnessed more than enough of his battle skills.

"Mind my words, Nichole. Back inside."

She hesitated for but a moment before she opened her mouth to complain. Before a word was said, a second arrow flew, landing exactly opposite the first on the other side of her head. With a startled gasp she ducked back inside only then to endure the humiliating sound of his laughter.

After a while she came to sit at the opening of the cave, where the sun fell to the side of the waterfall in a pretty rainbow of colors. From here she viewed the other side of the pond, where tall water reeds grew in profusion, jutting like spears from the mossy bank of the meadow. The reeds reminded her of one of Nanna's more improbable stories, and she closed her eyes, washed in a sudden wave of grief and missing and longing for the old woman . . . Nanna, who granted her last wish and gave her the means to choose her own husband! Just the pretense had saved her thus far and, with will and cleverness, she would escape not just this man but the unpleasant fate of marrying the Duke of Uri.

This man must want something from her brother, something worth more than his life, though no doubt he had operated with the assumption he would live to reap his reward. What was it? This must be a means to blackmail her brother for something. But what? She would go mad with not knowing!

Oh, Nanna, how do I escape now? What should I do? What can I do?

A rustle of movement warned her he was returning. With effort, she stood up and, leaning against the side of the cave, she held the fur tight against herself. As he stepped inside, the world retreated into darkness, his tall frame eclipsing the light of day.

How he stared at her! She felt his warmth and half expected to hear his heart beat, he stood so close. His nearness triggered an irregular beat of her own heart and made her forget to breathe, only to realize it with a small startled gasp.

As if her beauty wasn't trying enough, the moment made her appear vulnerable—a deception, he smiled, knowing her that well at least. Not willing to imagine what he might do with her consciousness of him, he forced himself away. Relief washed over her as he did so, and she turned toward the sunlight, drawing an even breath and trying to slow the curious pace of her heart. He held two good-sized bass, neatly skinned for cooking, and set these with potatoes through rods to place over the fire. "Are you hungry?"

"Always." She told him the inconsequential truth. Nanna always said she had the appetite of a man, and sometimes two. She started to ease her weight onto the pallet and he was there, a hand under her arm.

"Easy . . ."

She tensed with his touch. He started to turn back away, but her hand on his arm stopped him. The light touch went through him like a lightning bolt and his gaze dropped to the culprit and her small, smooth, utterly feminine hand, yet neither weak nor uncertain. She withdrew it quickly, as if she saw the mistake in touching him. "I am mad with wondering! Tell me who you are, where you've come from, and what you want?"

The cold light returned to his eyes, and he turned away, kneeling before a stone he used as a table, where he deftly began slicing cheese. "All in time, love. You'll know soon enough."

"I want to know now! Are you keeping me for ransom? Is that what you are doing?"

"Ransom?" The idea seemed to surprise him. "Ah," he chuckled. "A good idea if only there was a man who had a treasure equal to your worth."

How his eyes lit with laughter as if she, this whole situation, was a great amusement. Even when he seemed solemn, that light gave the devil away. She took the cheese he offered. "But I tell you I have no worth."

"A lie or an incredibly naive statement."

"I mean, I have no worth if you mean to extract ransom from my brother. I can tell you now he'll never pay."

"Another lie. I've no doubt that if I wanted ransom, I'd get it."

The way he stared at her, it was as if he knew that for a fact. "How long do you mean to keep me here?"

"As long as I want, love."

Her eyes shimmered with the emotion of that. Slowly, vehemently, she said, "You'll never get away with this, you know. They won't give up looking for you. While you might battle ten men, you cannot fight an entire army."

"That depends. Which army are we talking about?"

If he was only joking, she might have been only indignant, but while there was some amusement in his statement, he clearly meant it. She fell silent, watching as he turned the fish and potatoes, striking a casual pose—one long leg outstretched, one bent, his arm resting on that as he poured water into a cup.

A tension built in the silence. She tried to steer away her acute consciousness of him and each of his movements and the way he stared at her. A fluttering hand brushed back her hair, and when he smiled at her motion, she diverted her gaze. Why did he watch her like that? It scared her, she could not help it, and it made her think he meant to . . . to—

She wanted to tell him she would die before she'd let that happen and she would, she truly would if he made one false move to her. Yet, despite the barbaric boldness and outrage of his abduction of her, his speech was not just educated but each word, it seemed, spoke of his intelligence and wit. What was it Nanna used to say?

"Watch out for the very best warriors, girl, for great skill comes only with the shrewdest minds . . ." She remembered the first moment she saw him, knowing even then he could not be a fieldhand, the way he teased her . . . "It's your beauty, milady," he had said and then, then, as he planned to steal her from the light of day, he had kissed her.

Two dark brows lifted as a hand went to her lips, which she lightly traced with her tongue, as if to soothe the nerve-tingling memory of his audacity. His movement brought her gaze to him, for he fell onto his back with sudden laughter, "Dear God, get me out of this!"

Confusion lifted on her face. "Get you out of this? Are you not the abductor? Don't you have the choice?"

"So I've always thought," he said, still laughing. "Only I've just now become a fatalist. Here, let's find a distraction." He sat up again but with effort. He took the rods from the fire and handed her one. If she weren't so hungry, she might have tossed the hot metal stick in his face. Even with her hunger, she might have if she weren't so frightened of his retribution. Ignoring her obvious emotions, he deftly sliced some more cheese, handing this over with stale bread.

If only she knew who he was and what he really wanted! She didn't know and couldn't think, not with his silence as he studied her while he ate with all the intensity of a lion about to dissect and devour its prey. Numbly she began eating the food, too, but did not taste it, still willing her emotions back and back until she heard: "So, Nichole, I've been told you refused to marry the Duke of Uri?"

She nearly lost a mouthful of water and, looking back, she carefully set the cup down and just as carefully asked, "How do you know that?"

He shrugged, finishing the last of his fish. "It's common knowledge, is it not?"

Considering court gossip, she wondered if it might be. It also told her that he had access to the going-ons and intrigues of her brother's court . . . which could mean he worked for someone within the court. But who? One of her brother's men? A plot . . . A plot, but for what? What did he want?

He took up the bread and cheese. The amusement shone only in his eyes as he pointed out, "Why did you refuse? The duke is your equal in title, he is rich, and many of my ladies, I remember, found no fault with his appearance."

"Your ladies?" A delicate brow rose as she accepted another slice of the bread and cheese that he offered.

It was the closest he came to giving himself away, but Nichole misunderstood, and simply because the pairing of this man with nobility seemed, at the very least, absurd. "Your ladies must be simple peasant girls, for they alone have the freedom to consider a man's title and wealth, a simple vanity like appearance to be a measure of worth." She stiffened, though, as it suddenly occurred to her, "You're not . . . dear Lord, you're not in service to the duke?"

He shook his head, smiling at the eloquence of her words. "Nay."

"Do you know him?"

"Aye. I have met him."

If they were to converse, she would turn it to her advantage. "Oh? Where was this?"

"Different places."

This was useless; he disclosed nothing. "Well, what was your impression of this man you think I should marry?"

"Quite the contrary. I don't think you should marry him."

"Why not?"

"I'd best not say. I'd hate to shade your impression of a

man who might be your future husband."

"You are jesting, I hope. Even you yourself cannot imagine you would shade my opinion on such a weighty subject?"

He was teasing, though he might not have been. Kurtus was fond of saying if they could only harness the escalation of women's heartbeats and breathing when Jonpaul walked in the room they could turn the Rhine back to Germany and flood the barbarians. Indeed, nearly all women catered to Jonpaul's every word, especially his opinions of fancy, which often brought disastrous consequences to court. Not long ago he had complimented Lady Maeves's red velvet dress and by the week's end half the females in Basel were wearing red. For months the city streets looked like poppy fields from afar. Then there was the time upon Jonpaul's return from the French court that a gathering of ladies begged the news of the latest fashion. He couldn't think of any, or any he favorably regarded except for a new, musky perfume worn by a number of the ladies with whom he had bedded. "'Twas quite enticing," he had said, then teased, "or it would have been, if only it could make up for the irregular bathing practices of the French." It had taken the merchants only a week to fill the rush of orders, but for months the perfumed scent of musk so permeated the halls of Dornach that a petition circulated among the townsfolk to change the city's name from Basel on the Hill to Brothel on the Hill and, even a year later, jests to that effect were not only made but still laughed at.

Nichole obviously regarded the idea of him influencing a young lady's opinion as a jest and that made him smile. "I suppose I can't influence you. It seems your mind is quite made up on the subject anyway."

"Aye," she nodded, supposing nothing could be lost by talking to him, though not naive enough to imagine much could be gained, either. "My mind was decided the very day I met him."

Jonpaul remembered what her maid had said of it, but he was interested in her own words. "What damning fault did you see in him?"

"He is cruel, prideful, and vain—an unjust man if ever one walked on the earth."

His brows furrowed in an effort to understand, "He didn't hurt you, did he?"

There was a curious intensity in the question, one that she didn't understand. "No, not me personally. Yet I discovered the sorry truth even as my ladies and I watched his entourage enter the courtyard. First he shouted meanly to his underlings, which Nanna always said was the surest sign of a black heart, and I believe that. Then, then as he dismounted, his horse reared and came down on his foot. He screamed, and I remember my maids and I tried not to laugh and without much success until . . . until he ordered the horse slaughtered for the infraction! I think even my brother was surprised that a man would kill such a fine creature for a prick of pride. Well, that did it for me, and while, of course I could never abide that kind of cruelty, I told the groom he might keep the horse if he just kept it hidden until the duke left and pretended he did the terrible business. There were numerous other things, too, none worth the mentioning, but I knew then he was no one I might consider for marriage."

"A small but telling incident," he agreed when he saw she had finished. "God knows you can't have a man killing someone every time his . . . ah, toes get stepped on."

"You may think it's humorous but I don't!"

"Quite the contrary, Nichole. I don't either. I'm full aware that your brother has no heir, that his third wife appears to be barren, and that if . . . when he dies, the man you marry will inherit the realm of Lucerne. The well-being, perhaps even the lives of many, might very well be put in the hands of the man you marry."

She read his sincerity and sighed, wishing her brother had the same understanding. "My brother and his lords, indeed everyone, make my marriage into a matter of political convenience. What man has the highest price, the biggest army, the richest tithes? My opinion weighs less than . . . than a lone ant lost on his trail."

"Ah," he said, and he was smiling, "few, if any, high-born ladies have a choice."

"Aye, 'tis true," she nodded as a sad light came to her eyes. "I've always known my sentiments would not matter on the choice of my husband, that love is a most distant dream, but somehow I know, too, that the man I marry, if he were kind and wise and generous, if his heart and mind were on the welfare of the people, that I would come to know a love—maybe not a poet's love, but a good and strong love nonetheless and that I—"

The amusement in his eyes brought an abrupt self-consciousness and she stopped, only to feel a twinge of horror. What was she going on about? What lunacy made her speak so to him, her abductor?

She misinterpreted his patient smile, the amusement and emotion in his eyes as he watched the regrettable self-consciousness work its way into the two bright stains on her cheeks. "Don't stop, love. I'm fascinated. Really."

"You are baiting me!"

He never denied it. "Aye, but only to discover what allows you to put your judgment above your brother's. What makes it your decision?"

She searched his face, but the sudden complexities there hid everything and revealed nothing. He could not know . . . know anything. "Only my will."

Somehow his eyes said he knew she was lying and that frightened her as much as his next words. "Will is nothing without the power to enforce it."

She stared, just stared, and fear and tension built in her silence as she tried to assure herself he could not know, that his questions were asked in ignorance. No one knew but Nanna and Charles and now herself, and she only pretended to know. Yet there was no escaping his threat. Suddenly it sat between them, waiting like the count to thunder after the strike of lightning. She could feel it.

She was a means to an end for him, and whatever he wanted, she knew with sudden certainty, he meant to hurt her getting it. She drew a shaky breath, and it came as a shock to feel how afraid she was. She was completely alone and defenseless. Her only chance was to use the dagger while he slept, but as she tried to imagine that liberating scene, it seemed impossible. She felt so weak and tired from the blood loss, her heart pounding with just this effort to digest food, yet alone fueling the strength necessary to kill a man. Not just any man, either.

Her fear produced a plan, far-fetched but she didn't have much else. "I want to bathe."

She did not think he'd agree, which was only the first of many obstacles she would have had to overcome, but he surprised her with an easy "Why not?" Until he came to her . . . Her eyes immediately filled with panic, a panic increasing dramatically as he bent down and lifted her to his arms, mindful of her leg but not at all of the fur that covered her. This slipped to the floor as her long hair swung over his arm. She could not protest with her fists, for her arms were used in a rather desperate and futile effort to cover herself.

"Don't look so alarmed, love," he said as he carried her into the afternoon sunlight and behind the waterfall. "The pleasure is not new."

"While I slept?!"

Her outrage made him laugh. "Your charms would tempt a saint, which we can both agree I'm not."

To say the least. "Put me down. I can walk!"

"Not well. I would if I thought for a moment you wouldn't try to run on your leg the minute my back was turned or my eyes were diverted." Which was not going to happen with her unclad beauty not just before him but actually in his arms. The extent of his desire was becoming alarming, if only by the ever-increasing effort used to stop it by dwelling on the menace it would breed in the future. The last thing he needed was a personal investment in her.

He set her at the water's edge, chuckling with the speed with which she disappeared into the depths. A good swimmer, he saw, watching her smooth, strong strokes carry her out to the middle. He sat on the barren boulder, content to keep a watchful eye on her as well as the landscape.

After he had led the St. Gallen guards to think he left in a different direction, it seemed unlikely the chase could follow them here. Still . . .

Nichole's heart pounded furiously, though she took care to maintain a pretense of bathing. Treading water, she ran her hands through her hair, dipping her head in and out of the water, until she spotted it . . . across the water where the edge of the meadow met the grassy banks of the water, those tall water reeds growing in healthy abundance. She would need only two breaths to reach it . . .

Like a mermaid she was, he could not watch her a minute more. Nor was the tightening in his groin helped by the sun's warmth on his skin. He was beginning to be more than irritated with himself and, with a curse, he stood up, stepped out of his breeches before diving into the cool depths of the pond.

He emerged in deep water and, treading, he scanned

the surface for her. And waited. Within the two long minutes, alarm worked itself into his face. Within the next minute he swam to where he had last seen her, still expecting her to emerge any second. Then he started diving, his mind filled with thoughts of her wound somehow opening and her fainting dead in the water, the utter foolishness of not minding her helplessness . . .

Reaching the reeds, Nichole surfaced for the sweet bite of air before going under again. Submerged, she blindly grabbed a reed from its weak hold under water. This was put to her mouth. One good blow cleared the hollow tube of water. She began breathing through it, and in this way she would stay submerged until he decided she had drowned . . . Nanna had taught her the trick long ago as they waded knee-high in the weeds looking for a male crawfish, one of the thirty-three ingredients used in the coveted love potion. "I knew a man once who was caught red-handed in Lord Sarum's bed."

"In Lord Sarum's bed?" She, with a ten-year-old's wisdom, couldn't understand why anyone would want to sleep in that old man's bed. Senile ole' Sarum had lost his wits with his teeth, and he reeked of foul medicinal potions, pounded raw liver, and the cabbage fed to him each day in the hopes of reviving a sense of reality. "This man was just sleeping?"

"A bit more, I imagine. That vulture was too old even then for his young wife, but, anyway, this young fool escaped into the lake. Just disappeared. They assumed he drowned there until the next day the washing women saw a ghost under the water breathing from one of these here reeds. For, you see, they are hollow tubes . . . useful for any number of purposes."

Having used the trick many times in water games with friends, Nichole was not surprisd by how well it worked. She could stay submerged for hours, she supposed, save for the chill of the water. Yet she'd find the strength to stay at least until nightfall when he, too, gave her up as dead. Then in the cover of darkness she'd emerge and run—stumble—down the mountain . . .

With each minute passing, exitement began pounding in her overwrought heart. It was working! He would be looking for her body now, thinking she had gone under! Soon he'd know she was dead! Dear Lord, keep me safe here . . .

If only she knew where he had hidden her clothes . . .

After a methodical, herculean search of the entire bottom of the pond, Jonpaul leaped out of the water, his heart hammering like a savage drum. Knowing each second was one too many in passing, separating her life from death, his gaze searched from above, a gaze that at last scanned the area of reeds, then doubled back to see the dark hair floating on the surface before he dove back into the cool depths.

Just as she was certain of victory, something grabbed a handful of her hair and yanked. Before she had time to think or fight, his large hands came over her arms and she was pulled swiftly from the water. She forgot the reed hanging from her mouth until her sputtering gasps dropped it to the water.

Upon seeing her alive, he felt a swift, powerful surge of inexplicable joy and relief, a thing far surpassing any predictable response. He tried to excuse the feelings and did, turning quickly to the question of how it was possible. Then his gaze fell to the water reed floating nearby.

Anger emerged in the instant. "Damn you, girl! I thought you were dead! Dead! Each word lashed at her like a whip to the face and he stopped himself from shaking her senseless. In a breath he lifted her up and tossed her over his shoulder, bringing her quickly out of the water. The next breath gave voice to her own outrage and wild emotions of having come so close only to be caught again. Small fists hit his back for all she was worth . . .

Which was nothing. Less than nothing. He ignored it, her, everything, as he carried her quickly back to the cave, planning to tie her up and save himself the trouble of any more of her idiotic escape attempts. He swung her down to his arms and then lowered her to the fur. He meant to get up for the rope, but in the instant his senses riveted to the vision before him, everything changed.

His weight rested on his arms, positioned on either side of her head, and time ceased, as he stared down at her and she stared up at him in turn. The dark hair was a thick, wet rope trailing off to the side, pulled from her face to reveal the delicate lines of her vulnerability and sudden fear. My God, she was temptation itself. Her eyes seemed like light-filled gems, and few men, certainly not he, could resist the confusion there. Tiny dots of moisture covered her forehead and rose-flushed cheeks, the impossibly full mouth, sliding, he saw, from the long arch of her neck and beckoning voluptuousness of her bare breasts. The compelling beauty of her nudity sent the drive of his desire soaring and soaring, well past any boundaries of rationality and will . . .

As if the world had suddenly slipped away and there were no warring fractions or opposing nations or different sides. The only thing existing was the play and promise of desire. "Dear Lord . . . Dear Lord." He spoke slowly as still he stared with the heated passion of his desire naked and plain in his eyes. This gaze brushed her wet skin with its heat, and she was shaking her head as the curves of his fingers came to her forehead to gently smooth back an errant strand of wet hair. A single finger traced a line around her mouth. Confusion filled her eyes. She didn't understand, even less when he said in a whisper, "Like Eve before the Fall, you are, or Venus in a star-filled night."

The words made no sense to her, even less the intense warmth in his bright eyes, darkening now with things she didn't understand. For, despite the impossible tender touch of his hand, her mind was immobilized by the terrifying idea he would strike her. She was still shaking her head, a negation of the idea she would feel the repeated strike of his hand and her helplessness to do anything—anything past begging for a mercy she never imagined him giving . . .

Until she looked down from the handsome face to see the hard, waiting staff of him. The sheer size and threat of him brought a scream, but one caught in a gasp. Her eyes shot back to his face. The knowledge of what he was about crashed into her mind.

The anlace! The anlace was buried in the fur beneath her. She swallowed once. If she just lay still and pretended she was somewhere else, and let him have his way for a minute or two . . .

Jonpaul was mindful of her fear and his need to banish it. He would not take her against her will. Never that. Or, not if she were a virgin.

The thought allowed him to harness the pace of his desire. He gently caught her chin, studying the pale, lovely, and thoroughly frightened face. "Aye, you feel its power, too." He laid a finger over the place on her neck where her pulse fluttered wildly, then traced a line to a place above her breasts where, beneath the lightest caresses of his hand, he felt the swift force of her racing heart. She gasped, feeling a tingling rush along the path of his fingers and, catching her lip between her teeth, she forced herself still. "Yet you are afraid? Nichole, you know I would not hurt you?"

She nodded slowly. Despite her resolve, she was rigid with her fear. The dark-green gaze seemed like two magnetic pools as he studied her, unhurried now. "I must know, love. Does a virgin lie beneath me? The confusion and fear in your eyes says yes . . . and yet—" a finger traced a line over her mouth, "there is something else in these eyes. Are you, love?" The question was whispered against her ear. Tiny shivers erupted and she could hardly think above the pounding torrent of her blood. "Tell me, Nichole, for no matter how hard it would be to move from you now, I would not want to take that gift."

She slowly shook her head. Deception increased the fear in her eyes, but her mind was so firmly fixed on the anlace, she missed the change on his handsome face. A kind of joy filled him, perhaps better named as relief, for while he knew well that unlike men, women rarely attached easy sentiments to their lovers, a virgin would be so much worse. He could not do that—or he'd like to think he'd have the strength necessary to put distance between her and the rage of his desire, but he knew even then he was dreaming . . .

More as he let his lips brush hers, once, and as he lowered his weight to her, he felt the shock of it going through in such force as to steal his very breath. The incredible pleasure of the mounting sensations spilled into his body: the cool brush of her wet skin, her soft, full breasts against his chest, the softness of her skin as intoxicating as a scent of lilacs and summer sun, the rapid rise and fall of her breaths, and the very beat of her heart made him close his eyes and count against his sudden weakness.

The touch of his hard body felt like a bolt of lightning, and she ignored the tingling sensation of her breasts against the shock of his hard, hot staff on her belly, a shock igniting a virgin's terror. She instinctively began to twist away from him . . . it . . . the threat it posed, but she stopped instantly. The movement shot a queer heat through her limbs, changing her perfectly solid muscles and bones and flesh into something quivering and weak and frightened, more frightened when she saw his knowing gaze upon her. "Easy, love . . ." The words were whispered and felt as much as heard. "I will not hurt you. Never . . ."

Yet she still shook her head, confused and scared, just scared, her mind tumbling in its confusion of untrained senses. Then his mouth hovered just over hers, warming her lips, caressing them with his breath before . . . She gasped, which he used to his advantage. He gently lowered his lips to hers, adding a sensual pressure until, with surprise, still no small amount of confusion, she felt the shocking sweep of his tongue. Her thoughts spun like a ball thrown afar and then they were gone, gone, gone . . . banished by a swirling sea of bright warm colors bursting beneath closed lids—reds and oranges and golds of a radiant sunrise, colors that faded only when his mouth finally lifted from hers.

She drew a shaky, gasping breath. Oh, no . . . oh no. The magnitude of her mistake was dawning, yet the dawning awareness could hardly overcome the place her consciousness was riveted to: every place his body touched hers. She felt hot and shaky all at once. She couldn't think, and then he was kissing her again and she was sinking . . .

"Love . . . Love." He broke the kiss but kept his mouth dangerously close, and she sensed his smile within the rich timbre of his words. "Are you teasing me with your tongue?" The question was asked as he gently caressed her mouth with his lips, an invitation that brushed her lips with shivers, then her cheeks and forehead, the petal-soft lids of her closed eyes before returning again to her mouth. "Here, I'll show you . . ."

A definitive "Ohh . . ." made him laugh, the warmth of his amusement sounding against her ear with a rush of hot shivers, as shocking as the idea he could laugh now.

"Shall we try it again, love?"

His thumb drifted over her cheekbone, moving to her lips. A gentle pressure urged them open. As he was kissing her, drinking from the sweet taste of her mouth, his curled hand rested against her neck where he felt the beat of her pulse increasing with his. His hand slid over her shoulder, caressing before, light as a feather, he let it drift over the curves beneath him. She broke the kiss, gasping and confused, just confused. Had she a thought it would have been simple: Oh, Nanna, you never told me . . . for previously unknown serums were heating up in her body, gathering with each second's passing and in the most unlikely places, making it impossible to remember her name let alone to overcome the practical logistics of reaching for the anlace. And then, then, how could she . . .

She felt the warm scrutiny of his gaze as he said with a coherency she envied, "My God, you taste like the light of sunshine, you feel like its warmth." He lifted partially up. His gaze followed his hand over her side to stop beneath her breasts. That hand slipped over her flattened stomach, then back again and again. She drew a sharp breath, the curious tingling alight in her loins, growing, it seemed, making her want to twist and writhe. Then his hand swept over her breasts.

Lightly teasing, the palm of his hand tested its softness before drawing erotic circles first over one peak, then the other. She gasped, instinctively arching into the sweet fire of these sensations. A groan of his own pleasure was lost beneath the furious pounding of her heart, the sharp sucking of her breath as she felt a rush of warmth between her thighs—"Oh . . . please—"

The erotic sensations were too new and too frightening, yet the changes in her breathing told him when he found the right movement, and before he could hear her protest he was kissing her again.

With effort, she finally managed to tear her mouth from his, meaning to cry or scream or beg, she didn't know, but the sound came out as only sputtered gasps for breath, sweet breaths he caught in his mouth as his lips caressed her upper lip, gentle kneading the treat, forcing her to share the very air he breathed.

The only thing she could think to do was to try to save herself. "Oh, please. I think . . . I think I want to stop."

The words sounded strangely weak, even to her ears. Her eyes were closed tight as if to shut out what was happening, and so she only sensed his smile.

"Stop? Why in heaven's name would you want to stop?" He kissed her lips, softly, sensually before starting a trail down her bare neck. Shivers, lit by fire, she felt a thousand shivers and more when he whispered against her ear, "I don't think I can, love. I don't think I've ever wanted a thing, anything, even my life, as much as I want you at this moment."

Indeed the only thing that might have stopped him was a contemplation of those words and their truth, but he didn't stop. His mouth returned to kiss hers, his tongue gently teasing hers until she gasped. This time his kiss was unhurried, slow and tantalizing, more as his hand tested the curve of her waist, before he went on to explore the delicately voluptuous curve of her hip. He spread his fingers, luxuriating in her softness as he cupped her buttocks to pull her tighter against him.

It felt as if her blood had vacated her head for her lower extremities, then rushed around to meet the touch of his hand and body. More as his lips left her mouth to press an unhurried trail along her neck. The brush of a day's growth of beard was a curious tickling on her most sensitive skin. She lay there gasping, feeling faint and helpless, as if being filled with fire but . . .

His lips found her breasts, her nerves went wild. Light as a feather his lips coaxed the exquisite peaks to tight buds. Chills erupted in force and there might have been a weak whispered no, no, but all denial was lost, meaningless against the swift currents he filled her with as the caress of his hand, the gentlest massage over her abdomen, caused the pounding of her heart to drop to a roar in her loins . . . a pulsating warmth that seemed to want to writhe and grow until somehow he would know how to bring her to rest . . .

Then as he watched passion change the lovely flush on her face and form, brightening it as his gentle whispered words carried her with him, he showed her how that was done. She arched her back dramatically, not understanding at all and scared senseless by the gentle fan of his fingers over her sex. Over and over again until she felt hot, feverish, shaky. A moltenlike pleasure grew and spread there. The breath quickened in her throat and his, but she managed a muffled cry before his lips found hers again. Terrified by this edge of ecstasy, beneath the intoxicating warmth of his lips, her will struggled up from the depths of passion to produce the liberating idea that her arms were free.

The dagger lay just beneath the fur cover . . .

Nichole's hand curled around the edge of the fur, just inches from the dagger but his kiss slowly dissolved her will into his. Then he was whispering things against her ear, gently biting the sensitive lope. Gasping, feverish, and terrified, she tried to steal her mind from the hot shivering pleasure to reach the knife . . .

One inch more—

Yet as if he knew his fingers renewed the gentle stroking of the moist softness between her legs.

She couldn't reach it, but— "No . . . no . . . Please—"

"Yes and yes," he replied as he dragged her into another long, hard kiss. She swooned beneath the gentle pressure of his lips, the intoxicating taste of moist warmth, and as he deepened the kiss she forgot. Forgot who he was. Forgot the dagger. Forgot to breathe. Forgot everything as she swam in a dizzying sea of pleasure . . .

She had to stop this! She had to! Desperately she tried to tear her mouth from his, but he misunderstood this. The sensual pressure of lips changed, and as she felt his tongue slide over hers, exploring every height and hollow, even as he parted her legs . . .

His own pleasure pounded through him, voiced in whispered words of passion she could not now understand as she felt the smooth, hot pressure of him sliding back and forth between her sex. She was gasping for air, dizzy and flushed and not understanding at all the sudden throbbing fear that made her blindly fling her arm, groping for the knife.

She felt it beneath the fur. She tore the fur away. Her fingers curled tightly against the handle. Seized with a mindless terror, she raised it and, with all her strength, she thrust the dagger into his back—

The dagger stopped time itself. It ceased, froze as the sharp, searing heat of it crashed into his consciousness. There might come a day he would laugh at the shocked emotions rocking his body, but it was not now. Not now. He looked into the terrified pools of her eyes to understand her intent. Murder, and the only thing that came between her and her goal was an aim that put the dagger into the hard bone of a rib. She saw the first moment of his disbelief as he was reaching instinctively behind to grab the knife. Like a lion's teeth on a thorn, he ripped it from his flesh and flung it across the room.

Until that moment she hadn't perceived the extreme gentleness he dealt her; she never felt the tenderness revealed with each touch of his hand. She saw it now and only because it was gone. What replaced it made her shake her head and futilely, desperately, claw at him, suddenly fighting, fighting not for her virtue but for her very life.

He ignored his pain. He ignored her cries as he caught her hands and pinned them hard to the fur. Naked terror changed her eyes. "Oh, aye, you have reason for fear now. And I will see it increased ten fold before I even begin to release my hold on you."

"No! No!" She twisted desperately beneath his iron grip, and, breathless, she cried, "I'll make you kill me before I let you rape me!"

His body was rigid with the potent, deadly mix of his desire and fury, poised above hers with its imminent threat. "I don't think you understand," he said in a voice made cold with far more than anger. "The very word means you don't have a choice." And he joined her to him, and forever more, they would be joined.

Chapter Six

Night had fallen at the Castle of the Lower Lake, where the ladies waited for the men to return in the hall of feasts and servants rushed about to light the lamps and torches. Outside the doors, Anne Marie waited until the last minute to appear. "A pretty dress makes a pretty girl," her mama always said, and though Anne Marie had reason to doubt this, she nervously glanced down at her new dress, hoping, always hoping. The Paris-made gown was lovely. The dark burgundy velvet circled her like the petals of a rose. It had a low-cut, elaborate bodice of woven gold flowers set on contrasting pink silk, long silk sleeves tightly buttoned. Matching ribbons were woven into her short dark curls, which were lifted and pinned to hide the short length.

Genuflecting once for strength and clutching her rosary beads as a lifeline, she at last stepped inside. She forced a smile, though this was far from genuine. Murmurs and whispered surprise rose as the women curtsied and moved to grant her a place among them. Their appreciation gave her a brief measure of courage. She prayed Charles, too, would be pleased.

The appreciative murmurs died quickly as the collective attention of the women turned immediately back to Nichole's predicament. Nothing, certainly not Anne Marie's excessive regard for costume, could distract them from Nichole's shocking refusal to marry the Duke of Uri and Charles's response to it. Ann Marie was deaf in one ear and she didn't hear Annette whispering what her husband had told her just last night. She misinterpreted the silence and hastened to fill it. "Do you ladies not feel a chill in the night air already? A bad sign here, I am told, a prelude to a bitter winter . . ."

The comment did little more than reinforce the general opinion that Anne Marie's company was a good deal less than scintillating, that she seemed to somehow always miss the point. It was not just her deafness, either, a secret Anne Marie hid from the world, it was also that if she lived to be a hundred she would never master the languages here. One language was not enough for the Swiss. The court normally spoke a German dialect that seemed to have nothing to do with the high German she had learned in the convent. Sometimes the language was laced with French adjectives and verbs, all wrongly placed and, then, if that weren't confusing enough, all of sudden and for no apparent reason, perfectly normal people were speaking a harsh English, the King's English, too, not the more common tongue some of the sisters at the convent had spoken.

Anne Marie's comment received a nod or two, that was all. She would always be a sore point with the ladies, for when Charles began searching for his third wife, he left Lucerne for the distant fairy-tale land of the French court. She stood at least a head shorter than the other women, and where they were fair-skinned, she was dark. "She even looks French" was heard often enough, and "French" was synonymous with "diseased." Yet Anne Marie was the daughter of Jean Fouquet, Seigneur of St. Goblain, of Assis, of Montmirail, and Lord knew of where else, the Viscount of Meaux, and while love was normally not considered a good reason to marry, Charles had imagined he fell in love with the small, voluptuous convent-raised girl, who, before her father had introduced her to Charles, had never talked to a man outside of her family. For three months, Charles had imagined himself wildly in love with the shy fifteen-year-old-girl. Anne Marie knew the exact dates of the only time happiness saw its way into her life. She also knew the exact hour his love left . . .

Swiss women were wholesome women and proud of it and, unlike the French, they did not need a daily change of dress or whore's tricks to keep their men, and they looked down upon those who did. Despite Nichole's defense of Anne Marie—"You mistake shyness for airs and coldness. Can she help it if she is French? Can she help it if her parents send her those beautiful gowns? Oh, aye, she is a bit awkward in company but if you would just treat her with a measure of kindness . . ."—Nichole's insistence was the only reason they forced smiles and when, from out of the blue, Anne Marie offered comments on the weather, they managed to hold laughter back until she left.

Presently the ladies forgot Anne Marie altogether as the far more serious subject was resumed and, with the air of scandal and secrecy, the whispered exchange of words had an unnatural speed and urgency. "'Twas Nanna's death, me thinks. The poor girl is in a state of shock. She can't see past her grief, there it is—"

"Wouldn't you just know that old witch's passing would cause all this trouble—"

"Old witch? How can you speak so of that saint? You, of all people! Why, who among us does not owe a child's life to Nanna? That old woman's company might have been less than pleasant, but, Lord knows, she more than made up for it—"

"Well, true, but a saint? Really—"

"The point is that Nichole will come to her senses soon—"

"She'd better! She went too far this time. Who really can blame Charles for keeping her at St. Gallen?"

The mention of her husband's name brought gazes turning back to Anne Marie as the ladies waited a moment for her to join in the defense of Charles's dictates, but Anne Marie could hardly think of what to say. For one wild moment she imagined they were going to guess her part in the rest of Nichole's misfortune—the banishment of the poor maid Mayra—and she held her breath, praying the attention would leave her . . .

The other ladies were quite accustomed to her inability to lend anything to a gathering and they quickly moved on. "St. Gallen though? Such a terrible, dreary place." Lady Yvonne went on urgently. "I can't see young Nichole there for long, nothing but women in wimples and men in cloth, and the bishop . . . ! Why, Milord once told me he . . ." She whispered the juicy gossip to the other ladies, who appeared quite shocked by the information.

"The one thing everyone can agree on is that Nichole is smarter than ten others together! I just know she'll come to her senses! Milord says she has to—it's the perfect match for Lucerne—"

"Oh, but don't you remember how afraid you were to get married? I didn't sleep for weeks before my wedding day—"

"That's not what Nichole is afraid of! Don't you know: Nichole is not afraid of anything except marrying the wrong person. 'Tis the old woman's prophecy—" She stopped, realizing the blunder too late. The prophecy foretold that Charles would not have an heir, that Lady Nichole's husband would inherit the realm, which of course was the fault of Anne Marie.

Anne Marie's eyes filled with the humiliation of it. Two bright stains spread across her cheeks. How they must hate her! Everyone blamed her for not providing Charles with the heir he so desperately needed. Everyone hated her for it, everyone but Nichole, Charles's wild young sister, whom everyone loved . . .

Nichole, Nichole, forgive me! He made me do it, he made me. I am not strong like you . . .

The ladies would have been surprised to know no one was more distressed over Nichole's banishment than Anne Marie. As a matter of fact, the only time Anne Marie ever raised her voice to Charles was when she was told of his sister's banishment. "Oh no, Charlies, *mon Dieu,* you can't mean it!"

"Ah, you, too, my love? Is there no one who hasn't fallen under my sister's spell? I'm surprised you have in you—"

"Nichole just needs time—"

"Time?" His voice filled with disgust and loathing, "Well, she'll have plenty of that at St. Gallen."

"There is a problem of her maid, though. I don't know how much the chit heard, but I can't take the chance. Now let's see if I can make you good for something after all. I want you to . . ."

When Anne Marie heard this, she shook her head, retreating, but Charles caught her arm, squeezing until she cried out. Like all men, he was dangerous when he drank, but this night seemed even worse. Still, she tried to dissuade him. "Not Mayra! Please, Charles, the girl is dear to Nichole—"

"You, my little rose, will do as you're told!"

Forgive me, Nichole, forgive me . . .

It was always Nichole who came to her defense, whose smile and interest could set her at ease and banish her awkwardness. Since the beginning, Nichole saw past her shyness and extreme self-consciousness, the layers and layers of beautiful clothes she hid behind, to see into her soul and its suffering. Only Nichole seemed to understand how hard it was to be taken from one's home and family, even the familiarity of one's language to be set among a country of strangers, who decided at a glance they did not like her and never would. Only Nichole offered hope when it was clear her marriage would not be blessed with children. "Nanna believes the fault to be Charles's and if Nanna believes it, 'tis probably true. That's why this potion doesn't work. The very worst thing you can do is dwell on it, for the preoccupation alone can prevent conception. Nanna doesn't know why that's true, but it is. Then again, perhaps it is God's way of saying you are meant for other things . . ."

The ladies had, of course, resumed the heated conversation, dismissing the slight as they dismissed Anne Marie. Anne Marie felt her heart slowing as she remembered Nichole's practical advice on winning the affection of these ladies: "You have only to believe in yourself, the basic goodness God entrusted in your heart. I believe Nanna is right. She says your shyness is the result of shortsightedness, that your trouble is that you dwell on your faults so long and hard, each is magnified in your mind tenfold. Well for heaven's sake, stop doing that! Toss your attention outside yourself! And try spicing their affection with a little flattery, too. This always works—women warm to flattery like flowers to the sun. 'Yvonne! Your boy grew half a foot since the last we saw him' or, 'Annette, your hair is the envy of the court,' 'Margarite, your sweet butter is tastier than any I've ever had,' and so on . . . You will see how they come around . . ."

Oh, she had tried. Once. Arriving on a conversation about hair, she perked up and with enthusiasm offered, 'How pretty your hair is, Annette, the envy of the court . . .' only to abruptly realize they had not been talking about hair but rather air, the foul air coming from the lower well . . .

Of course it all might be different if Charles cared for her, if he didn't hate her, too. She could survive anything if she had not so totally and completely failed him. If only he didn't make her feel as if she wasted the air each time she drew breath . . .

A great clamor of spurs and boots sounded at last and stopped the conversation as all gazes turned to the entranceway. Charles appeared, followed by a dozen others. Servants rushed forward to take bonnets and unlace the mail.

The men appeared red-faced and furious, still many hours later arguing about the latest report from the village of Stan. A peasant had just arrived, who had witnessed the mayhem and slaughter there, yet lived to tell the story. The old man had not seen any colors and numbered the men less than the previous reports, but still the description paired the name Jonpaul with Satan on each man's lips. Until these unrelenting border atrocities, the lord Jonpaul had been a much touted warrior and, for some, even a hero. The wild success of the lord's military strategy and battle skill as he led the Swiss defensive in the battle of Burgundy was much heralded, and if it weren't for detailed descriptions of what he did as he turned his victorious army to Lucerne to make Charles pay for courting King Ferdinand and not sending the men of Lucerne to the Burgundy War, he would have been a hero even among the men of Lucerne. Until now few had actually believed the stories of the secret atrocities of the lords of the Alliance. The evidence was mounting though. The lord Jonpaul's Burgundy success put him in mind to think he might take Lucerne, too, and by force, unheard of among Swiss nations who had for centuries argued about borders but who otherwise lived in relative peace together. To murder innocent peasants—simple farmers and womenfolk and children—was truly incomprehensible. It made no sense, and no one would have believed it, if not for the growing pile of dead.

The knights and lords tried to quiet the talk in front of the ladies, though half of them were so worked up, an immediate call to arms would be heralded. Charles would have them wait the winter, however, to retain the duke's army through the lady Nichole's marriage, to use the winter to better train the men. "Soon, milords, soon enough . . ."

The ladies felt the tension but looked confused, for they had been spared the details of the atrocity. That something terrible had happened was on each hard face of their husbands, though, written in anger and, less apparent, fear.

Charles was the exception. As he held still while a servant removed his mail leggings, he caught Anne Marie's eye. Her heart leaped and she suffered a moment's confusion, too—a different kind—before she nervously lowered her eyes. He had not looked at her that way in over a year!

A wave of his gloved hand stopped the argument and silenced the men as he came to where she stood. "Anne Marie, you look lovely tonight." He drank her perfume. "A most refreshing change from the muck and curses of my men . . . like a rose waiting to bloom."

The compliment warmed her cheeks and she forgot to breathe for a long moment, she forgot to breathe. The next thing she knew they were being seated, the lords and ladies taking their places at the table. A servant rushed to drop a cloth on her lap. Charles himself poured her wine and kept his hand possessively entwined with hers. As in the beginning . . .

No, don't hope. Not now. Charles could be a loving, even kind, husband when he chose, when he wasn't drinking. When he was pleased with his men or the way events had gone. Still, she was hardly aware of the food being served, the conversation on all sides about Swiss valor and how for hundreds of years the Basel, Solothurn, and Berne cantons, like Lucerne, always managed to work out disputes without bloodshedding, that Swiss never went against Swiss, but Anne Marie could hardly follow this as Charles leaned over and lightly kissed a sensitive spot on her neck, then whispered promises . . .

The messenger, Heinz Meier, sergeant-of-arms for St. Gallen, rode the fastest horse at a breakneck speed across the lake, into the city of Lucerne, and out onto the main road that wound through forests and farmland along the Lower Lake to finally reach the well-traveled road leading up to the Castle of the Lower Lake. He flew through the open gates into the courtyard, jumping off the mount even as he reined the horse to a quick stop. Two grooms raced to catch the horse, for the lone rider was already running to the main doors.

Excited servants raced ahead to lead him through the corridors directly to Lord Charles. The doors were open for the coming and going of the many serving the table, and Meier almost tripped over a small woman carrying a full urn of Madeira through the doors. Before he could even be announced, "Milord!", he dropped to a bow, raising quickly as silence dropped like a curtain over the people at the table.

Charles stood slowly to his feet, his brows drawn together in anticipation of some bad news.

"I bear unbelievable tidings from St. Gallen. The lady Nichole has been abducted—"

Shocked gasps and cries interrupted him.

"The army is searching as we speak—"

"What?!" came as a demand and not just from Charles as many of the lords and men at the table stood, too. From the ladies came more gasps and shakes of head and exclamations of "dear Lord" and "my heavens" and "no, not Nichole!"

"Abducted?" Charles could hardly understand what it

meant, let alone how it could have possibly happened.

"The lady was taken at noon today. She was taking the air when a lone man approached, apparently disguised as a fieldhand. The man landed a halbert and lance against her men as he carried her away. He was gone before the call to arms could sound. There was a chase. Eleven men finally met the warrior and . . . there was fighting . . ." Meier hesitated with this part, hardly able to believe it himself.

Charles could not now speak, as the implications raced through his mind and seeing this, Lord Victor Schumacher of Sursee shouted with his own anger, "Yes? Eleven men met the warrior and . . . ?"

"Eleven men lay wounded, two are not expected to see the sun rise, the rest . . ."

"Yes? And this beast?"

"The warrior, they say, was not hit."

A hushed silence came over the room, broken at last by the lord Victor again. "You are trying to tell us that one man," he held up a finger, "one man stole the lady Nichole from the light of day beneath the army of St. Gallen?"

"Yes, milord. He rode away on the fastest horse any had ever seen. The search continues on the eastern slopes of the Bondensee Mountains, where we followed the trail. They might have been found by now—"

With violence, Charles threw the goblet to the floor of Meier's feet. "Or she might be lost to me now! God, how could this have happened?! One man against the force of St. Gallen . . ." Then, with bright madness and uncontrolled fury in his eyes, he abruptly realized. "'Tis ransom! My God—"

Meier swallowed his fear to interrupt. "I think not, milord. The men who fought say the warrior was a great blond giant, who except one, no one any had ever seen before. The man used halberts, spinning them through the air as if touched by magic, missing not once. He swung one halbert that knocked another back to lay a wound upon the sender. No one ever saw fighting like this, except one man. Milord, he is saying, they are all saying now . . . they are saying the man was Jonpaul the Terrible himself."

A shocked silence answered this announcement until, shaking with rage, Charles screamed back, "Of course the goddamned cowards say the name Jonpaul! They might have said Satan himself, for what other excuse have they for losing my sister to a single man? A single man! Fates on earth, I can't believe this!"

A waved hand finally dismissed the ladies. "Get the women off" was whispered. The women were all shocked, confused, desperately worried for a girl most all of them loved. More than one of them had fallen into tears as they were quickly ushered out of the hall. Anne Marie was almost too distressed to move until the gentle hand of her maid lay on her shoulder to help her out. Anne Marie paused at the door, though, and motioned for silence when her maid protested. She had to hear all of this, but all she heard was the call for arms, ushered in a voice that could not hide her husband's sudden desperation, especially as it held these words: "I will get my sister back alive or every last one of my men will die in the trying . . ."

Nichole crouched against the wall near the dancing light of a torch. She held herself in a tight ball, in a futile effort to stop trembling. The long, dry hair tumbled over the fur she held tightly against herself. One bent finger was in her mouth as if she needed something to stop herself from crying. The pale skin still held a bright flush from the brush of his beard, and while she was far beyond the help or comfort of tears, her eyes looked wide, luminous, made of the very firelight they reflected. She was trying to think long enough to save herself.

He leaned on the opposite wall, watching her from the

dark shadows that completely hid him there. At some point in the endless passion and play of his revenge, she must have fallen asleep in his arms and only to save herself from being used a single time more. Less than a minute after she woke, she scrambled as far away as the cave would let her, where she now crouched to control the violent trembling. As she was beyond tears, she was beyond shock. Every inch of skin, every nerve and fiber of her being felt used: stroked, aroused, fanned, finally rocked with a thing too violent to be pleasure, then mercifully soothed but only to be stroked again. She was weak from it, her consciousness fragmenting and threatening to crumble into a hundred pieces if she did not figure out the only thing that mattered now.

"I must know who you are."

The whispered voice revealed the world of pain she was in, though having inflicted it, he had no illusions about its magnitude. Those first few moments, the sweet mercy of his penetration rocked through him, mind, body and soul. He felt the tightness of her sheath, the rip of her maidenhead. The shock of it mobilized all his strength to control the demands of his body long enough to look in her terrified, pain-filled eyes and realize, dear God, she had sacrificed her virginity for a desperate chance to escape. The knowledge changed everything and yet nothing . . .

"I . . . I saw you fighting. I saw you in battle. You must be famous . . . Aye, your skill would be sung across Switzerland and beyond. So," she clung tightly to this first clue, using what little strength that remained to her to focus on it, "I would have heard your name spoken at Lucerne before . . ."

She frantically searched her dazed mind for the names of men famous in battle. "There is the terror Wendt from Austria, but you . . . you are Swiss. There is a celebrated hero Rudolph of St. Gotthard, but, but I heard it said that he died in the battle of Burgundy."

"Nichole . . ."

She turned to the quiet sound of his voice. It was an attempt to touch her again, to reach out and pull her back to the place where he had kept her prisoner: the surging melting heavenly bliss of an intimacy so deep, so complete, so whole that by forcing it upon her warring, frightened soul, he had transformed heaven to the cruelest kind of hell. "No, love," he had said at one point, seeing her demand and knowing what she wanted without her words. "Oh, no. Despite everything, I cannot, will not regret what I took from you. Like regretting your very next breath, it's not possible . . ."

The fall from grace. Nanna had warned her what would happen long ago: "Original sin is a place heavy with knowledge and weighted with tears, 'tis, a great weight . . . very much like getting old. While one might mourn the passing into this place, what one loses to get there, one cannot regret it. You will see, Nichole, you will see."

So it came to pass.

Nichole closed her eyes and remembered the cold winter nights after her mother died when she felt lonely and sad, and when it got too heavy to bear, she'd sneak into Nanna's small room alongside her own. Somehow, no matter what time in the middle of the night she appeared, Nanna was still up, welcoming her with wise, sad eyes that understood everything without words. The old woman took her into her arms and, as she lay her head on the old woman's lap, Nanna would stroke her hair the whole night long, singing sad, haunting lullabies in Romanesch, the old language that they both loved until at last she'd fall asleep.

Nanna, I miss you . . . I miss you . . .

"I remember it said . . ." She opened her eyes and spoke in a voice soft and faint, heavy with this sadness. "Who else . . . who else then? Peter of Calis? But . . . but he would be old now and probably dead, too . . . There is Jonpaul the Terrible from the hated Alliance, but you . . . you could not be him . . ."

Only the whisper of his voice begged the question, "Why not, love?"

"Why not . . . why not?" She stared off into space and slowly shook her head, not even considering this a possibility. "Because God is not so cruel. Jonpaul the Terrible is like no man alive, not . . . not even you. He is twice as high as most men and three times as wide and the reason he is called Terrible is because of his facial deformities. They say at least half the men he slays die, not from his sword but from the fright of seeing him."

There came a weighty pause. She tried to think of other names until she heard: "Do you believe that, Nichole?"

"Believe what? Oh. No." She shook her head, trying hard to keep focused on this. "Of course not, but 'tis nonetheless said. Since the battle of Burgundy, the world has been afraid of him, the reach of his godless ambition. Common folks say it to explain the hellish sadism the man spreads across the country. 'Tis meant as metaphor, just as the Medusa—that mere mortals are not able to look upon evil incarnate directly."

He stiffened as he heard this, searching the wild young girl crouched in the corner as far away from him as possible, trembling, trying to ignore her pain long enough to guess his name. A name paired in her mind with hellish sadism and evil incarnate. Dear God, if only this was a poor jest. Braced, he said quietly, "I've never heard those things said about him before."

She turned to peer into the surrounding darkness, compelled, for reasons she did not understand, to see him. "You give yourself away at last. You must not be from here or anywhere near here."

"Nay, 'tis that I know those things aren't true."

"How . . . how is that?"

"I know him."

"You know who? The lord Jonpaul?"

"Aye."

"Dear Lord, you're not . . . you're not his man?"

"No. I am not that."

A thing, terrible and alarming, crept into the cave. Like a chilled, bitter wind, she felt suddenly cold and afraid. A violent shiver shook her and she tried to see but could only find darkness, shadows dancing like demons over the darkness where he stood.

"You have seen him then? Is he . . . is he—"

"This monster of your imagination? Is he twice as high and trice as wide as other men? Is he like the Medusa or evil incarnate? Nay," his whispered voice filled with a curious intensity, "he is only a man, love, like all others."

The shivers intensified, she felt suddenly as cold as death, weak and feverish. She clutched the fur tight about herself, the name of her brother's enemy echoing through her mind. For a moment blackness swirled like a tornado in her head, bringing her to the vivid memory of the village Stan and, knowing but not, she cried out, "You are wrong . . . you are wrong. My brother took me to a village, and with my own eyes I have seen what this man has done. With my own eyes . . . I saw the simple common folks slain, mutilated, and maimed flesh piled into a bloodied mountain. There was a mother . . . a mother holding her child—"

A small cry escaped her, and she clutched her mouth to stop the words, as if to banish the memory, the idea, the certainty, and her eyes grew wide, more frightened than she ever had been as he emerged from the darkness to lift her up. "Nay 'tis not so, Nichole!"

"Thy own eyes have seen it! You know! You are . . . Your hand, these hands that hold me now as I stand, that have touched kisses to my lips and changed the very beat of my heart, these hands saw a sword pass through a mother's heart as she clung to her—"

"Stop it! Stop it!"

The fear and terror of it choked her, blinding her to his own alarm as he demanded, "Did your brother tell you 'twas me, the hand of the Alliance upon that village?" When she wouldn't answer, he repeated "Did he? Answer me, Nichole! Did—"

"Yes! He knew 'twas you, Jonpaul the Terrible. In all the world there is only one man who would have murdered like that—"

"Why would a man take a girl to see such a scene? A young girl? Why, Nichole? To show you why you must marry a man you hold in contempt and loathing? To show you why he says he kept a standing army of one thousand men? An army that he means to join with another?"

Shock registered briefly over her fear. "No . . . no," she was gasping, "you can't know that!"

"But I do, Nichole, I do. I know more, too: I know that the men of the Alliance have never plundered a village of common folks, and I know my lance has never touched a woman. And since it wasn't the men of the Alliance, then who did kill those innocent people? Who, Nichole, who? There is only one answer, and *he* did it. The reason he had those poor people slaughtered was to show a young girl—"

"No!" She covered her ears with her hands and closed her eyes, shutting out the litany of lies. "'Tisn't true. You're lying . . . you're lying!"

He forced her hand down. "Nichole, think! Think—"

"Think what? That my brother slaughtered his own people? Or think that the man who can slay women and children can also lie? I don't have to think long on that, for I know . . . I know! Oh, God, oh, God, kill me now as I stand, because if you don't, if you let me live 'twill be with a vow to spend each and every day to the godly purpose of seeing you dead!"

Jonpaul held her tight by the arms, staring down at the rebellion bright in her eyes as she stared up at him. Yet those eyes changed as she searched his face. She slowly shook her head, frightened even more when she saw what he was about and, with a soft curse, he damned the quickness of her mind.

"How can you know? I don't know how you can know?"

"Does it matter?"

Those eyes frantically searched his face, choking on her fear, rising, mounting with the rush of her conclusion. "What do you want from me?"

"The threat you used against your brother. I want to stop him before he draws the Alliance into war."

"I'll never tell you," she said in a frightened whisper. "Never."

"You will love. I'll make you. I have to. Thousands of lives lie in the balance."

"As if you care! If I believed that pretense, you wouldn't have to force me to tell you, but I don't and you will have to kill me before I ever utter a single word that will help you claim the forest lakeland."

The intensity in his gaze blinded her. For a moment she couldn't see and she was shaking her head, a negation of who he was and what had happened and, most of all, what was going to happen. He would have her tortured until death became a gift he gave only in return for her secret, and the thought of it made her dizzy, sick with fear. Her knees collapsed and she was vaguely aware of being caught in his arms and lowered to the fur pallet.

"Listen to me, Nichole—"

Jonpaul stopped, frozen for a split second before his hand came over her mouth—hard. Her eyes went wild with fright as she imagined him trying to choke the life out of her but no, he held perfectly still, listening to the night a second or two before his arm slipped under her and he lifted her to the opening of the cave.

The waterfall drowned out all sounds. He listened, straining to hear, but no sound rose above the hammer of their hearts and breaths. Jonpaul slowly eased his hold on her mouth but kept her backside against his long length. The greath warmth of his body could not offset the chills racing through her, a small measure of her enormous fear, he knew.

"He won't give up, you know," she whispered passionately. "You can keep me here for months and months and he will search until, as God is merciful, he finds you."

The words slowly worked a measure of alarm on the handsome face as he released her. She would have felt considerable relief seeing his alarm, no matter how small, to know that he could be afraid, but she didn't notice. She felt an urgent need to cover her nudity, for his gaze felt nearly as dangerous as his touch and, as soon as his hands left her, she dashed to the fur covers, then retreated to the safety of the shadows where she watched and waited.

Jonpaul the Terrible . . . Jonpaul the Terrible, she could not believe 'twas him, the man who had emerged from the noble lines of Dornach to change the world and threaten peace for all time! The nephew of Jacob Van de Birs, lord of the realm of Basel, Jonpaul had inherited Dornach and the wealth of the Basel trade routes maybe five years ago before his elevated position allowed him, against the most overwhelming odds, to battle and soundly beat the Austrian King Ferdinand.

She knew the recent history well, she had lived it. St. Gallen, Uri, and Zurich were the only Swiss states who, on Charles's orders, had not sent their men to join Jonpaul of Dornach, Lords Bruno of Solothurn, and Wesmullar of Berne and their two thousand men who were to meet the French-Austrian contingency of better than ten thousand men in the famous battle of Burgundy. Like the rest of the world, Charles saw it as a disastrous cause, for those states were as good as gone before the battle even started. He knew which side would be victorious. Thus he attempted to negotiate with the Austrian king for the independence and sovereignty of

Lucerne, St. Gallen, and Uri, leaving Zurich to fend for itself. These negotiations slowed as word of the battle reached Lucerne, finally ceased altogether with the incredible news that the French soldiers had turned back after suffering losses of nearly ten men to every one Swiss, losses that gained them not an inch of Swiss land.

Although she was only fourteen at the time, Nichole remembered the fear of those days. All of Lucerne waited for Jonpaul the Terrible to turn his army east to Lucerne and bring Charles to his knees in retribution for not sending his army to join the Alliance, for running to beg mercy from Ferdinand, the enemy of all Swiss. That's when the "Terrible" came to be attached to the lord Jonpaul's name as each day brought stories of the terror spread by his army as they headed toward Lucerne. Drunk on the heavy taste of blood and victory, Jonpaul the Terrible and his men left a trail strewn with bodies as they raped and murdered, pillaged and plundered each country village in their path . . .

Only to learn that the full force of St. Gallen and Lucerne waited for him on the border. Fighting Frenchmen was one thing, meeting an equal number of their fellow Swiss countrymen quite another, and Jonpaul at last knew fear and wisely turned his army home. Until now she had never believed Charles and the few lords who saw a constant threat from the Alliance, a threat fanned with continuous hostilities along their common border. "Aye, the lord Jonpaul is terrible, for sure, but he'll never dare to try to take Lucerne!"

It was the popular sentiment of the lords of the Council. Only Charles had understood the threat of the Alliance. Only Charles had understood that Jonpaul the Terrible's ferocious ambition would not rest until he had taken Lucerne. Only Charles had wanted to keep the standing army. Most of all of the other lords had disputed the wisdom of the measure.

Charles had been right all along, and now she had ruined everything by refusing the marriage that would make Lucerne strong enough to fight this man. Nanna, did you know that? Nanna, did you mean for me to sacrifice my people and my land—

The Goddess who never makes mistakes . . .

"I think you are right. I had imagined the search to be short, given up for lost at the end of a week, two at the most. Yet Charles will be more than desperate to have you back, won't he?"

It was all Nichole could do not to cry out as he came to where she knelt. He, too, knelt, watching as she pressed against the wall of the cave, looking as if she fully expected to be beaten or worse.

Quietly, with as much control as he had left, he offered her the bargain, one he was now desperate for her to take. "Love, love, let me end this terror shaking through each of your tired limbs, no doubt seizing your very soul. I want so badly to grant you freedom and set you on your way home, now, this very night. End it now, Nichole, for you are right. 'Twill only get worse from this point on."

She stared at the strange compassion in his eyes, alarming, for it seemed to mean that even he would feel bad for what he would put her through to get the secret. She could not answer, though, and when he saw this, he seized her arms again. "God, girl, trust me—"

"Trust you?" Incredulity and the great wealth of her antipathy nearly overcame the fear pounding in her heart, shining in her eyes. "Trust you to make me regret my next breath? To show me other tortures worse than death? I do," she nodded, "I do, and still it won't make me turn traitor to my brother. You would ruin my brother to take Lucerne. You know there'd be no standing army without him, that Lucerne at last would be vulnerable to your lust and greed and thirst for power—"

"You are wrong, Nichole! Wrong! 'Tis your brother

who threatens Switzerland with war. No one from the Alliance wants war—"

"Then what was the poor village of Stan? Practice for a maying? Your way of making Lucerne feel at ease with the way of our neighbors? A gesture of your good will?"

"Do not tap my patience with you." Jonpaul pulled her sharply up, his voice rising dangerously. "It is thin to break as it is, and I've no wish to stop and teach you manners tonight, not when so many lives rest in my ability to convince you, an admirable, though misguided young girl that her brother has spawned the litany of lies and for his own malicious gain. 'Tis his greed and lust and thirst for power, 'twas your brother who pillaged that village and, God knows, 'twasn't the only time he sent mercenaries to plunder the outlaying villages—I have had to put my knights on the border townships to stop him. And I will stop him, love, I will. And if what you know will bring Charles down and keep the Alliance and the forest cantons from war, then God, girl, you can believe I will get it out of you." He paused, studying the pale, thoroughly frightened face, before adding the last, "And, love, the only choice is whether I get it by force or reason."

A cold, numbing dread swept upon her and she was shaking her head. From some distant place in her mind she marveled at the deceptive sincerity he hung on every word, no doubt the envy of Satan himself, king of all deception. Yet slowly the measured words came to her.

"I don't know what you're talking about. Even if I did, I would choose death over the telling to you, the most hated enemy of all Lucerne."

He studied her a long moment before saying, "God, I curse your courage, girl. So be it," and he released her. He moved to the other side of the cave and, as her mind filled with images of tortures and terrors and things worse than death, as she expected to have to fight for her life at any minute, she watched with confusion as he reached up to a ledge hidden in the upper shadows. He removed the neat pile of her clothes, washed and folded, until he tossed them to her. "Get dressed, love. We will ride to Dornach tonight."

Swift, uncertain relief left her shaking as with confusion she picked up the clothes. To Dornach? Tonight? Her confusion vanished beneath a sliver of hope. They would never make it, never! These mountains swarmed with the army of St. Gallen and surely they would be caught—

She hurried into her clothes, her heart pounding tiredly, more, when next she looked up, and saw ropes in his hands.

"I did say it got worse, didn't I, love?"

There was no point in fighting him now, for she needed to save her strength. The battle had, after all, just begun.

For six long hours there was nothing to see, dark shapes changing and moving like ghosts against the dark night as Jonpaul kept Zermatt at a dangerous pace, letting the great beast pick his own way in the northwesterly direction toward Basel. A light rain fell. The ground was slick and wet beneath Zermatt's steady hooves, but the beast, by miracle or magic, never once stumbled.

Exhaustion and wind kept a sting in Nichole's eyes, while cold and fear kept her trembling, shivers that were lost beneath the severe jostle of the ride. She could not swallow with the gag in her mouth. No torture could be worse than the thirst burning in her parched throat. Fragments of pain shot from all parts of her body as well: her bloodless legs, the soreness where he had touched her womb, the dull throb of her wound, a severe ache in her shoulders and lower back, and the icy numbness where her hands were tied to the saddle horn, the burn from the ropes binding her wrists. Each was a demon she had to fight back and subdue, but none was more menacing than the thirst . . . the burning thirst . . .

At last exhaustion chased her consciousness away. Darkness stretched its fingers in every direction. Danger hid in the corners, fear choked her insides, and she was running, running for her life until suddenly he stood in front of her. "Father!"

Rage so changed his face, she screamed, trying to back away, but he caught her by the arms and started shaking her, "You are nobody, nobody! A female—"

"Nooo, that's not true . . . 'tisn't true! I am strong—"

"Strong enough? Strong enough to save my place? Are you, girl?"

"I am! I am! I'll never tell, never!"

The rage vanished from his face with macabre speed, replaced by a smile. "Run along then," and he was laughing at her and she was running, running, chased again. Then he, Jonpaul, emerged from the darkness to surround her. His unnaturally strong hands came around her throat and he was choking her, then shaking her. He was killing her, she couldn't breathe—

She woke minutes later, gasping. The gag choked her, thirst burning still in her throat. Small beads of perspiration laced her brow and she felt feverish, trembling, breathing hard and fast, harder still when she saw the changed landscape.

The first sliver of gray light stretched across the land, and though she didn't know where they were, the rocky hillside and the wide arch of vision told her they had passed out of the Bodensee mountain range into the flatter land of the northwest. No one had seen them through the darkness and rain. An hour more, two at the most, and they would be in the border country of Basel, out of the reach of the search.

The imminent danger heightened her senses. She had

to slow him down, for each minute lost was one more chance the army had to find them. She cried out. The sound was muffled, but with all her remaining strength, she twisted, as if desperate. Jonpaul pulled the gag from her mouth and she drew gasping breaths before she managed the single word, "Water . . . water, please."

Zermatt slowed from a fast lope to a trot, tensing her as her brain rattled in her skull and her bones bounced against the saddle. "My cask has long been empty. Until my country's line, I don't want to stop—"

"But I am so thirsty!"

"A thirst with malicious intent, perhaps? The same intent that made you hide your innocence and welcome my touch as you plotted how hard to thrust a dagger into my fool's heart?" He kicked Zermatt back to a lope. "No doubt your thirst can wait."

Anger gave her voice above the wind and jostle and speed of their flight. "Shall I die for my deception? Was not bending me to your will for that eternity punishment enough? Losing my innocence by your rape—"

He heard that word and reined Zermatt to a quick halt. The great horse lifted high in the air before his hooves crashed to the ground, and the world stood still as Jonpaul took her chin in hand and looked into her eyes. "Rape?" he questioned. "For a moment, no more, and made by a fury of your own making. Not an excuse but a fact. Look at me." She met his eyes again, an exchange made by their shared memory and as intimate as it. "Aye, love, innocent no more, you know better than to call what passed between us by that name. No matter how hard or badly you might want to, you can't change it now any more than you'll ever be able to forget it."

Those words sparked a bright mutiny in her eyes and a strange light in his, but as the heat rose on her cheeks and, with a mind on his retribution, she dropped her gaze to the saddle horn where her hands were bound. She did not like being called to testify like that. She would like to say in her defense that whatever passion she gave him was wrought by his clever, skilled hands and even that, dear Lord, would not have been gotten had she known then his name.

Zermatt passed from standing still to a lope in seconds. A chilled morning wind washed her face and set her teeth chattering. She might not have gotten water, but at least she bought a minute or two. The hours without sleep, the rigors she had been put through on top of the hours of the severe jostle of this ride were beginning to take their toll, all so much worse with the stress and strain of her fear. She did not resist when Jonpaul pulled a fur from behind and placed it about her shoulders as he brought her closer against the warmth of his body. Accepting kindness from him was the least of her crimes and she was fast reaching the point where she would trade her life for a mouthful of water and rest—her life but not the secret.

Never her secret.

The landscape flew past at a dizzying speed, unchanging save for the placement of the scattered pines and rocks and the lightening of a gray sky's new day. The rain became a drizzle, then stopped altogether. Still no sign of anyone or anything, though Jonpaul kept his gaze ever watchful.

Zermatt carried them up over a gradual incline. At the top a vista stretched before them, no more than a wide, huge carpet of meadow. A forest of pines grew on the edge of the meadow. A number of rabbits looked up, locked their gaze for a moment, then disappeared into the forest. Jonpaul turned Zermatt up to go around it rather than maneuver through the trees, a measure of his boldness. As they neared the upper edge of the forest, she heard the sound of running water. Nichole turned to see a small trickle of a stream carving its way down the hillside and into the forest. For tense seconds, she was afraid to beg but more afraid not to . . .

Jonpaul took one look at the all too real agony in her eyes and cursed himself for having caused it. He hadn't known and, despite what she might be expecting in his hands, he knew at least it would not be physical in nature. Zermatt stopped near the water's edge and tossed his head to get rein enough to drink himself. Jonpaul dismounted, filled the cask, and returned to her. As her hands were tied to the saddle horn, he mounted again and, holding her in his arms, he tilted her head, at last answering her agony.

Nichole finished over half the cask. No Dutch candy ever tasted sweeter than this water! She was gasping with relief when his hand struck her mouth hard to stop her scream. Terrified eyes followed his to see the lone rider atop the mountain staring straight down at him. The unmistakable red hair formed his name in her mind: Kairtand!

Anxiety transformed Kairtand's face and he threw his gaze to where the others rode, less than a quarter of a mile away. He looked back, but Jonpaul had already brought her gag up and seized the reins, pulling Zermatt up and into a run in the same second. Nichole threw her gaze as far back as possible, catching the briefest glimpse of the lone rider, still and unmoving as he watched Jonpaul carry her away. Her mind spun in a whirlwind of confusion before bursting into a red-hot sea of rage, rage that had no vent until some six or seven miles later when Jonpaul finally pulled the gag from her mouth again.

"Dear God, may He have mercy on his black soul! The coward! He was afraid to fight for me, for Lucerne! Afraid! He let you carry me away! How could he? I just don't understand . . . how—"

Jonpaul was laughing, he could not help it. "It's my luck, love. I am blessed."

"The devil's own," she cried, but her voice was lost in

the wind. Within the next hour, everything was lost as they at last passed into his land. Her heart sunk beneath the weight of her doom, and if she had any strength left, it would have been used in tears. A thousand hopeless tears . . .

The first signal that she was all but through came when he cut the ropes binding her hands. She rubbed the sores there, gently coaxing blood into her icy cold hands. The sun broke through the clouds, but by this point she was too numb with exhaustion to feel its beckoning warmth. They passed one village after another, each larger than the last, until finally they crossed the Aare River at the first township of Olten.

As Zermatt pranced into the town, the call sounded on the town's horn to herald Jonpaul's arrival. Excited faces appeared in flower-lined windows. Women, men, and children rushed out the doors of thatched-roofed houses and shops to wave as they passed. Holding her head high, Nichole stared unseeing ahead, not glancing at any of the kindly faces who excitedly called to wish their lord well. Though her cheeks were flushed and two red smears underlined her eyes with exhaustion, she was dressed as a highborn lady and her beauty was plain, all of which incited the idea that she must be the lord Jonpaul's new bride.

Neither Charles nor her father ever received such a warm welcome from the townspeople, especially free townspeople, unless coins were tossed ahead of time. Nichole was trying to reason this through. Was he making them wait for his coins . . . ? Yet no one seemed to be expecting coins tossed, for they waved from windows and doorways. A group of young boys was chasing after Zermatt now, and even they seemed more concerned with the weapons showing from the saddlebag. How did the people even recognize him? He wore no coat of arms on his mantle, and, normally, chevaliers, especially the grand seigneurs or lords, traveled with an entourage of banners and people, at the very least a squire who led the war-trained horse behind their masters. He had none of these things. Yet the people knew him.

At last they reached a stable, where he was greeted by an army of servants desperate to do his bidding. Jonpaul was ordering a fresh mount and giving instructions for Zermatt's care, when a cobbler, with tools hanging from his belt and a mismatched pair of boots in hand, shouted out, "The lady, milord! Do say there will be a wedding to celebrate soon?"

Nichole braced, frightened, as she expected Jonpaul's harsh hand to come down on the man who spoke so freely to him. Nothing happened, though. Jonpaul only grinned as he lifted her to the ground. No other woman he knew would have made it this long, though still he had to hold her weight, she was that weary. There was a gentleness in his arms and an amused light in his fine eyes as he replied, "Does milady look like my bride-to-be?"

A man's voice sang out from the crowd:

"Cupid has aimed,
The arrow flies true,
At last our great lord,
Is given his due.

A beauty she is
A sight to behold.
Her hand rests in his,
Forever to hold."

Jonpaul laughed with the others and said, "I know that voice. Step forward man and let me have a look at you." A tall, older man stepped through the now-large crowd. "I thought I heard a familiar mocking in your voice!"

Jonpaul laughed, remembering the man. "You rode at my side during a part of the great battle. Tom, is it?"

Before the man could answer, the attention was diverted by a pretty young woman running to the crowd, her three traditional plaits swinging like ropes with her flight as she held a treasure in her neat white frock. Breathless and smiling, she dropped a curtsey before Jonpaul, then held up a large bundle of foodstuffs.

"My oldest brother entered the trades because of you, milord. My father sends this modest token of his gratitude: 'Tis the best cheese in all Switzerland, our finest sausage and sweetest wine, my own mother's warm bread."

"Ah, your father's gratitude is reward enough but," he accepted the package, offering up a dazzling smile, "the gift is welcomed."

Wide-eyed, Nichole watched as Jonpaul touched his lips to the poor girl's hand, nearly dropping her into a faint! The starstruck look in her eyes left little doubt she'd be reliving the scene for years!

The girl was only the first of his many well-wishers. Nichole listened with confusion as Jonpaul bantered with the crowd, sharing news of Basel and Dornach while offering congratulations on everything from good crops to new babies, declining, it seemed, a dozen offers to dine as two grooms worked quickly to remove the saddle and bags from Zermatt and put these things on a fresh roan-colored stallion.

Nichole could hardly believe what she was seeing. That Jonpaul would condescend to talk with the common folks. That they would offer him food! Never in her life had she heard Charles pass a single word to his people—even an order would come through another. She had always been scolded for it herself, while the many common folks she graced with conversation or a visit had to be sworn to secrecy . . .

Yet suddenly the swelling audience took up a shout for her name. The man Tom's loud voice broke above the others. "Are we looking upon your new bride, milord?"

Jonpaul scanned the anxious faces of the crowd, made a decision, and, to her absolute horror, he laughed at the idea. "Nay," he said. "Here stands our forsworn enemy and my war prize. Thou looks upon the lady Nichole Lucretia of Lucerne."

Like a bad omen, the name changed the mood of the crowd in the instant. Awed, disgruntled whispers rushed like wildfire in dried grass through the now-swelling crowd, repeated with curses and hatred. Nichole took one glance at the angry sea of faces and her body went rigid with fear, blood pounding fast and furious through her.

"She's far too fair to be that dog's sister—"

"Too pretty to have been sprung by a pig's loins—"

"Now the bastard will have to show his face to men, to get back his sister!"

"Never! A coward only hides—"

"Tom, give the lady your song!"

This last cry was taken up until Tom, more than willing to oblige the crowd and seeing a nod of approval from Jonpaul, leaped up on nearby bales of hay. Jonpaul could not have asked for a better show and, pleased, he held Nichole against his long length, a precaution in case she thought to bolt as she heard what his people thought of her brother. Tom first dropped a bow to Jonpaul and then with his next nod, he began:

"The great horn sounded
From valley to crest.
The French wolves were baying:
Swiss freedom or death!

With halberts in hand
the lord Jonpaul doth rise

'I'll greet these French dogs
With my own deadly surprise!'

Bruno, Wesmullar, and Calse, too,
Gathered men and their swords
And the Swiss we did march
To the great war of the worlds.

Though hopelessly outnumbered,
The numbers were skewed
For each Swiss sword
Took ten French to hew . . ."

The audience burst into laughter and cheers and grinning, ear to ear, Tom waited a moment before continuing his song:

"The Swiss, we are fierce!
With thunder and lightning
The French bellies we pierce
Till those men were running

Like rats in a fire
Those French turned hightail . . ."

Nichole could hardly listen. Not that she didn't understand the people's pride. She did, yet she knew the path this song would take. She knew and braced, tried to shield herself, to steel her emotions, but—

"While brave men were mauled,
And fires did burn,
One lord, he did crawl,
the quaking Lord of Lucerne.

Belly up on his back

And knowing no shame,
He begged mercy of kings
'Swiss freedom's my bane!'

Trading Swiss to our enemies,
A traitor's fate he doth earn,
He threatened Swiss souls,
At the stake he should burn!"

Humiliation burned on her cheeks as at last the hateful song ended to the wild cheers of the crowd. For a long moment emotions clamored so hard and fast, the torrent drowning out the cruel jeers. Desperate, unable to bear a second more of their taunting cries, she covered her ears against the attack of sound. Jonpaul forced her shaking hands from her ears, whispering, "I think you should hear what the good people think of your dear brother, love."

As the crowd quieted, Tom shouted to her, "Bring that honest song to the coward your brother is, milady!"

Jonpaul passively let the crowd take shots at her—to a well-defined point. While Nichole knew better than to try to answer a mob's cries with reason, as her heart was pounding and the taunting jeers grew, the lilt of her frightened voice cried out with abject desperation to redeem her brother's name, "He's not a coward, but as brave—"

It was as far as she got. "Oh, aye, 'tis a brave man who turned belly up to war tyrants invading his country," Tom spoke for the crowd and with plain masculine scorn. "If left to your brother's brave hands, we'd all be kneeling to the French kings!"

The crowd cheered. Against this deafening noise, she saw Jonpaul's satisfied smirk. Curse him! She knew what he was about! He did not fool her! He fanned the people's hatred as a butcher feeds pigs—preparing them for the sacrifice of their lives for his war to get Lucerne. Red-faced and livid with rage, she foolishly, valiantly, tried to reason with them. "Wait! Wait! Hear my words. No one in all Christendom knew the Swiss force had a chance! No one! If you people had any honesty in your souls, you'd admit that you fought fully expecting to die a martyr's death!"

"A better choice than kissing King Frederick's arse!"

When even Jonpaul found himself chuckling at that, the happy crowd took up the Swiss National Song and it was beneath this happy chorus that Jonpaul mounted the fresh stallion. He leaned over to lift her in place before him. To the wild well-wishing of the crowd, he waved goodbye and, at last, mercifully, they were off again.

Dornach was less than a five-hour ride away . . .

Chapter Seven

Father Ari looked up from his ledger to see the boy sitting with a distant light in his large blue eyes, staring out the tall open window to the courtyard below. With a sigh, he rose, moving to where the boy sat. The boy's discarded quill left a smear across his otherwise neat page of Latin text and, seeing just how neat the letters were, his graying brows rose. Remarkable considering the boy was only six! While education normally did not start until the seventh or eighth year of a boy's life, young Gavin had been pushed into six or seven hours a day of private tutoring. His father had been forced to concede this to the boy, and only because he had finally caught his son copying whole pages from the Bible by candlelight, he had been that desperate to learn how to write.

It was generally agreed that Gavin's mind was far too active. An early start on his education was thought wise, mostly because books seemed to be the only thing that kept him out of trouble. And he was constantly in trouble. Those few times Gavin wasn't actively seeking trouble, trouble, like a faithful friend, sought him. The two hundred or so souls who lived or worked at Dornach and the five hundred in the supporting township outside of the castle begged for a couple of hours a day respite from the "terrible Dornach rapscallion" as he was fondly referred to.

Yet young Gavin had already mastered numbers and he was reading Latin like a lad twice his age. Boredom was a constant threat, taxing Father Ari's considerable resources. It had been kept at bay this last month when he repeated lessons in Greek, then at night by learning the constellations—Gavin had his father's fascination for astronomy. Today, though, all the lessons were lost to the dreams of boyhood.

Gavin's gaze was fixed on the high-curtain-wall, the walk-run over the chapel across the courtyard, where his men were lined up, bows strung and arrows flying at the rushing attack of the combined force of Ferdinand, Charles the Bold, and the King Charles of France! Aim, true men! Curse all! Forty soldiers suddenly lifted a felled tree, running to ram it into the castle gate. "Hasten to the hot oil bins!" he cried as he took down four, now five, of the armored men with aim so true, his arrows slipped between the cracks in the mail—

Father Ari waved a hand in front of the boy's face. Guiltily the lad brought his eyes around, then rolled them upward with a mischievous smile as if to say, Oh no, here comes trouble.

"Gavin, what see you out that window?" He looked down to see a kitchen maid running toward the kitchen with fresh-drawn water, some geese squawking nearby, a couple of grooms leading two horses across to the stables. "Ah, I wager I know. 'Tis your father, am I right?"

The boy shook his head, but Father Ari was looking for a sign of the hunting party due back soon, in hopes of getting some venison for supper.. Then he pushed his hand through Gavin's golden-brown curls. "Well, just because the lords have returned to wait for him doesn't necessarily mean he will be arriving soon. Could be weeks more, you know."

Gavin shook his head, adamant, his blue eyes suddenly cross. That was too long!

Father Ari sighed, motioning with his head toward the door. "Oh go on, be off with you. God knows Latin can wait for the morrow."

With a happy smile the boy jumped up, grabbed his crossbow, picked up his arrows, and raced through the door. "Don't go bothering the kitchen maids or the—" He stopped realizing too late the words were wasted, for Gavin couldn't hear a thunderclap an inch from his ear. He was sadly quite deaf, which was at least half the trouble.

With his arrows strung on his back and his bow in one hand, dagger in his other, Gavin raced down the hall of the solar chambers above the hall, fighting menacing enemies all the way. Ten men lay slewed along the staircase and he was attacking the captain of the guards as he burst outdoors into his mother's abandoned herb garden. Yet here he stopped instantly. With reverent solemnity, a straight back, and tilted chin, he quietly passed the small orchard, the five dovecotes—where doves had once roosted the year round. The white doves of peace, his mother's much-loved pets that had left for grief the day she died. Or so people said. Others, like his father, said 'twas only these cold winters of late that keep the birds away. Once his father said if his mother's soul ever visited Dornach, 'twould be in the form of one of those lost doves she had tamed and loved . . .

Once past the outer fence, he raced to the kitchen. Smoke rose constantly from its elaborate chimney since the lords of the Council arrived back to wait his father's return. He burst through the door. The room was crowded, a number of people busy preparing food: Kily, the grand steward of the kitchen, stood poised with knife in hand over a whole side of beef that lay across the table, two maids prepared a pair of plucked geese for spitting, carrots and cauliflower were being chopped, at least three maids rolled and pounded dough. A song stopped as people turned to see him there, greetings were called and smiles offered, and all the women began telling him what could and could not be had at the moment, what would be good for him, what would not be. Not a female in Dornach didn't try to mother the motherless boy. Between his status, the missing mother in his life, and his deafness, the unruly boy's every indiscretion was forgiven, if not forgotten entirely, and there was no person more loved in Dornach than the wild young boy.

Gavin smiled—shyly—pretending to watch their lips as they spoke. Yet with his back to the table and his hands behind his back, he slipped two still-warm pastries into the uplifted edge of his tunic, just as Honore pointed a spatula at him and said these words: "Anything ye might be wantin' to hold ye over before supper—a piece of fruit or a handful of the rice puddin', anything save the pastries behind ye—"

The last words were said to his back as he raced out of the kitchen and ran for his life. Across the yard, he next appeared in the smithy where a pastry was traded to the mason's son, Peter—in charge while the older Peter napped—in return for temporary possession of his father's old baselord. Within the next half hour, young Gavin led a group of boys around and around the wall-walk that circled Dornach, waging a war against the older village boys and a war unto death, as the strict codes of chivalry demanded.

Sometime later he waved goodbye to the last of his friends, who wasted several long minutes trying to communicate to Gavin that his maid was calling for him. Gavin could tell his friend was raising his voice louder and louder still, as if this might help, and it was moments like this he hated not his deafness but his mute tongue, his inability to shout back, "Let her hang herself, I'll come when I want!" Instead, with wondering eyes, he waited as the lad finally gave up and, in frustration, left. Then he stared over the wall-walk to wait for the hunting party's return.

Dornach Castle, the grandest in the land, was built on top of a mountain overlooking the wide-open valley of Dornach and its township. One side of the mountain fell in a gentle slope of cleared farmland all the way down to the village and township beyond. The main trade route leading to Basel carved through the base of the valley, and on a clear night, like tonight, one could watch the lights in the houses, lit one by one as dusk settled into the muted brown and gold shades of fall over the green hillside. The other side fell much steeper, dropping from the wall-walk in places over a hundred feet to a steep hillside of thickly forested land. A few beeches scattered in between a pine forest as thick and dark as the black forest, the place of mystery and adventure that he loved.

Tonight, though, he stared down at the village far below to watch the main road. The trees stood still as the wind died, but the air held the coming winter chill and, as he was searching for the North Star in the violet sky, he missed seeing the lone rider fast approaching until a movement of failing horse's hooves at the gate caught his eye, and when he saw that, he was running.

Nichole felt confused and disoriented, not having slept or eaten since the morning yesterday, exhausted from the ceaseless tax of this long, nightmarish ride on top of all other terrors. She felt as if she couldn't breathe, then suddenly as if she were breathing too heavily. She kept falling into a cold sweat, then shivering with chills. Consciousness became so fragmented she had no idea sleep had won at many points since leaving Olten, and so she missed seeing not just the many villages along the way but the entire free city of Basel. The only consolation to her utter misery was that for now, at least, she was too tired to be afraid of anything. If given the choice between saving the world or a piece of ground that wasn't moving, the choice would have been made by toppling over . . .

Yet as Dornach Castle rose at last in the distance atop the mountain, a curious tingling came over her. She straightened up as her irregular breathing slowed, deepened. Her heart kicked in with fresh blood. She felt as if she woke suddenly, not just refreshed but with curiously heightened senses.

She must be hallucinating. While dark claimed the land, Dornach's square-shaped curtain-wall rose too high in the clear violet sky and its nine rounded towers projecting from the curtain-wall at regular intervals were too many; the castle was simply far too large. Those few people she knew who had acutally seen Dornach happily reassured everyone the lord Jonpaul's largest castle was a good deal smaller than the Castle of the Lower Lake, smaller even than her brother's smallest castle, Montrose, and that Dornach was a dismal stone-gray centuries-old keep, no bigger than a house really, complete with an offensive moat so foul one smelled it for miles in all directions. Yet this Dornach was enormous, at least three times larger than the castle at the Lower Lake, its wall twice as high, and there was no old-fashioned moat or keep.

The horse galloped through the wide-open gates and to her side Nichole caught sight of a young boy running fast to meet the horse and rider. "Gavin!" Jonpaul called with a curious softness to his voice as he reined in the tired mount, dismounting before the horse stopped to open his arms and receive the boy. Round and round he swung the boy in his arms, laughing, finally stopping to greet the blue eyes with more laughter. "Gavin! Two weeks gone and it looks you've grown another inch or more!" He ruffled the boy's curls and, with a grin that spoke of a heart-pounding love, the boy did the same to Jonpaul's curls. "How fare you? Has Ari been battering your brain with his Greek?"

Gavin nodded vigorously, collapsing in his father's arms as if dead, and Jonpaul laughed. "That bad, I see. Well, it only gets worse, Gavin Van de Birs. What page have you reached?" Gavin motioned with fingers. "Forty-two!" Jonpaul whistled, and just as he was going to ask about archery instruction, young Gavin's gaze turned to see Nichole.

Still sitting upon the horse, she remained unmoved by Jonpaul's fatherly affection until the most piercing blue eyes she ever encountered turned to her. Indifference vanished, melting with a curious meeting of mind, as if she knew every thought passing through the boy's head. Both curious and confused, Gavin stared at her and saw in the ever-darkening light the exhaustion that rocked her, the red lines underneath her eyes, and the threat of doom hanging over her head. He saw the rip in her dress, the chill in her hands, and he looked a long time at the sores at her wrists where his father had bound her hands.

He stared at the most beautiful princess in the world, a young princess his father had saved or captured or stolen . . . then abused. His father, whose stern voice had been used only once when he had tied Betty's plaits to a tree and left the girl for the ants to eat, meaning to come back in a bit to rescue her but somehow forgetting until nightfall when a search party was underway. His father, who said the measure of a man was not his skill in battle but his treatment of his dependents, that only the most gentle hand could ever be used on a woman and then only to help or comfort her.

Breathing hard suddenly, his eyes shot to his father

with the accusation, a demand for an explanation.

Knowing his son's mind well, he said crossly, "You're too young to understand yet, Gavin."

Then he dropped the boy to his feet, just as the horn sounded thrice signaling the return of the hunting party. Grooms rushed out. Watching for the hunting party, the guards posted in the tower wall-walk finally noticed who stood in the courtyard as well and the horn was raised again to signal the lord Jonpaul's return.

Within minutes the entire world seemed to be rushing into the courtyard. Thus forgotten, Gavin was able to return his gaze to Nichole. She still sat on the horse, with her back straight but her beautiful eyes hidden beneath lowered lashes, oblivious to the world, as if her body was there but she was not. A valiant attempt to protect herself from the unkind scrutiny of dozens of strange faces! For the lords Bruno and Wesmullar, their squires, Kurtus, and his father's steward, Mickeil, the falconmaster Rob—all rode up a fast trot, a dozen barking dogs behind them. A half dozen grooms ran behind them, carrying the two felled deer, bags stuffed full of fowl and hare. There was a herd of horses, clamoring, shouts and cries, back slapping and general chaos as the dust settled and the court of Dornach beheld Jonpaul's prize, the lady Nichole Lucretia.

The masculine noise sang loud and felt deafening. Nichole didn't know what was happening. Laughter and cheers and questions flew at Jonpaul. "No trouble! None past what the lady herself gave me. And that was enough," he swore, then laughed. "They should have sent her out in armor; 'twas far easier fighting the army of St. Gallen than the girl . . . Nay! There is more courage and determination in that one hundred and so pounds than in an entire army of warring men. She has neither slept nor eaten in days. She is weary beyond exhaustion and that will serve us well. Tonight . . . Nay,

I won't let her rest . . ."

Thoughts clamored furiously through Nichole's tired mind. The next thing she knew, someone, a man's hands came to her waist, not a groom but a knight by his tunic and mail leggings, the traditional belt and spurs, and he lifted her to the ground. "Can you walk, milady?"

She nodded, her heart pounding furiously, more afraid than she ever had been, certain they would be killing her soon. Tonight, he said . . . tonight—

"This way, my lady," Kurtus motioned toward the inner courtyard where a large group of men and lords entered through the doors that led to the great hall. She did not see the ladies peering with intense curiosity behind them. She took a step, stumbled, and before Kurtus could catch her, Gavin was suddenly there. With all the strength of his lithe six-year-old body, he held her arm, guiding her reluctant feet to the hall. Meeting those eyes again, the boy's concern caused a sudden stab at her heart and threatened at last to cause tears. A wavering effort held them back.

Nichole felt the sudden warmth of the entrance hall and saw its splendor, magnificently decorated with flags, the Van de Bir coat of arms and colorful tapestries, and lit by the bright light of fine brass torch flames. The man led her through doors, down a hall past an inside serving kitchen, a buttery and waiting chambers and she knew not what else, finally past a door to a small, barren sitting room where she was led to a bench. Somewhere along the way she lost Gavin's kind face. The man withdrew wordlessly and the door shut, then bolted on the outside, and she was alone.

The quiet felt worse than noise as it brought with it a painful ringing in her ears, the curious unnatural sound of the hard slow thud of her heart. Her skirt was damp on one side where her wound must have opened again, but she ignored this, for it seeming inconsequential beneath the anticipatory strain of what would happen. She closed her eyes and tried to think how to save herself, but she could not hold a thought above her fear. Time slipped from her and she knew not whether an hour or minute had passed when the door opened again.

Nichole spun around, fully expecting to see Jonpaul, with his lords and executioner in tow. Yet it was his boy, Gavin. He slipped inside, shutting the door behind him. Carried in the skirt of his tunic were two apples, a leg of goose, a slice of cheese, a wooden bowl, a large cask, and a clean white napkin. Pity and fear rested in his eyes as he set these gifts before her. He carefully poured water into the bowl, wetting the napkin and holding this out for her to take.

The most sincere thank-you ever expressed passed unheard, so set was the boy's eyes on the tremble in her hands as she removed her headband and cloth, and he saw the thick black hair that took him, like his father, by surprise. She took the napkin and began wiping the dust and dirt from first her face, then her hands and neck, scrubbing for several long minutes, then splashing the remaining water over her face again. Once done and, with wisdom beyond his years, he handed her the water cask.

She drank her fill, and with a transparent need that brought both a question and condemnation to his eyes as he wondered if his father kept even water from her. He held up the goose leg, but she shook her head. She did not eat of the flesh—no initiate did, but she had no appetite in any case. Yet Gavin insisted. He picked up the apple and put it in her hand, then brought her hand up to her mouth as if he spoke with action and not words. She tried to shake her head, but those eyes implored her, and for reasons she couldn't understand, she complied, and only to ease the boy's worry.

Nichole gasped and turned frightened eyes to the door when some long time later the door opened again and there stood Jonpaul. He wore clean clothes, a rich dark-blue tunic belted at his waist, loose black breeches, tall boots, and his hair was wet. A strange light came to his eyes when he found his boy sitting at the girl's side, their hands tightly entwined.

"Gavin—"

The boy suddenly jumped up, and placing himself between Nichole and Jonpaul, he withdrew the baselord from its sheath. Nichole heard Jonpaul's sharp breath, and for one moment she stared with incredulity and disbelief before she thought to save young Gavin the beating of his life. She reached out for him but caught a sharp look from Jonpaul that stopped her. Only then did she see the admiration and pride worked on Jonpaul's face as he studied his boy, for he knew full well the courage it took to overcome the fear of this measure.

"Would you fight me to save her, Gavin?"

The boy nodded, his face a remarkable thing, much older and wiser than any six-year-old boy's should be.

"Gavin . . . do you not know me well? Would you question my judgment so rashly?"

Gavin hesitated, pausing as the question came to his eyes.

"Aye, she has known a harsh hand from me. Harsher," his voice softened as his gaze lifted to Nichole behind him, "than you can know. She is the sister to Charles of Lucerne. She knows a secret that will save the Alliance and even her own people from war. She knows a secret that could save thousands of lives. I must know what this secret is. I must do what it takes to win the secret from her. Gavin," he knelt before the boy, taking the baselord from his unsteady grip as the blue eyes searched his face to see the truth, "she will be safe as soon as she tells us."

Nichole covered her face in her hands and Jonpaul used this moment to silently reassure his son, who, after a long glance back at Nichole, left the sitting room.

Jonpaul stepped in front of her. His strong, warm hand came to her chin, bringing up her face to study her fear. He could only wonder at her eyes: fear dancing in them with the uncertainty of her fate. She could not last much longer, he knew. With little or no food or water for two days now, wounded, bruised, her innocence stolen by force, and after that ride few men could have made, she could not possibly last long. "Nichole . . . Nichole, it's not too late to save yourself."

She shook her head.

"What if I told you that I, this lord of terror and evil in your mind, have no stomach for the means and methods commonly used by the lords of the Alliance, that I would remove myself from your interrogation."

She searched his face, her eyes frantic. "I don't believe you. I—"

"It's true, love. I won't be there."

It was the truth she suddenly saw. Anger momentarily overcame her fear as she cried, "And you call my brother a coward? You who cannot bear your own tortures? You are despicable! Despicable!"

Jonpaul caught her hands as she started swinging like a wildcat. He held firm, gently adding pressure until her energies dissipated—everywhere save her eyes. Those gems were bright and furious, filled with her loathing. "I have warned you. So be it." While not normally melodramatic, his last words seemed suddenly appropriate: "May God be with you."

Two guards appeared in the door. Jonpaul stood up and stepped to the side. Wild with fear again, she hesitated. The thought that they would put hands upon her brought her up and, with more dignity than she knew, her skirts swept the floor as she left on unsteady feet to meet her fate.

The guards led her down the hall, past an open screen and into the great hall, dimly lit. Her eyes swept the high arch and wood beams in the middle of the hall, then the enormous hearth, Flemish tapestries, and stone-cut murals—this floor made of marble squares set over stone ones—before finally settling on the shape and forms of her torturers.

A father of the cloth, donned in plain robes, studied her intently as he spoke to the knight, the man who had escorted her inside. Over a dozen other knights crowded around the dais where their lords and stewards sat at a long-white-clothed table. The lords were distinguished by embroidered coat of arms on their velvet-ermine-lined surcoats. They looked in the dark light more terrible than she had imagined men could look: their eyes were cold and their faces were mean, etched by cruel lines and looking as if they might devour her on sight. Her knees buckled under, a small cry escaped as she stumbled. The guards' hands came to her arms and she was led before the dais, then made to kneel before them as her cloak was removed and her hands were tied at the elbows behind her back.

Quiet came over the hall. She lowered her eyes, unable to bear the brutal scrutiny of so many men. A feverish blush rose over her as quiet came over the hall. Her hands went clammy and her breaths came fast. It seemed they stared at her for a too long time before one lord at last stood to begin the interrogation. Her gaze shot up briefly. The lord looked like a great beast of a man, with a round face, dark hair, a beard, and a voice as gruff as a bear's roar. He wore a gold mantle, an elaborate black coat of arms embroidered across his chest, and an ermine cape hung across his shoulders by a thick gold chain. A dark, narrowed gaze pierced her skin to measure the pounding of her heart and she swallowed—

"Here kneels before the lords of the Alliance the lady Nichole Lucretia, sister to Charles of Lucerne. Milady Nichole Lucretia, do you know whom it is that addresses you now?"

Nichole held perfectly still and made no response. She'd not condescend with a word or nod, so much as a gesture of acknowledgment.

Lord Bruno glanced up at the man hidden in the shadows of the upstairs gallery. Jonpaul had to remove himself from these proceedings simply because he could not trust himself to keep the necessary control or emotional distance, a statement Bruno rightly took to mean far more had passed between the two than a goodly ride through the Swiss mountainside.

Lord Bruno turned back to the guard and nodded. A whip cracked against the floor an inch from Nichole's person. Her gaze jerked up with the fright, a hot wave of alarm washed over her, and Lord Bruno was made to see what Jonpaul meant when he said, "Eyes as wild as a wood creature, more beautiful than jewels . . ."

A word of advice, milady. Save your strength for the harder questions. I put the question to you again: Do you know my name?"

She hesitated but a moment before heeding the wisdom of this advice. "I know not your name."

The melodic lilt to her voice, so heavy with fear, would have softened even the harshest men watching had they not been bound by the conspiracy. Her fear would work to advantage, the more the better—this was the point.

"I am Bruno of Solothurn, member of the Alliance of Swiss states. The people of Solothurn have recently suffered a series of attacks by a band of warriors sent by your brother, Charles of Lucerne. Warriors, who have swept upon a country village there—"

"No! 'Tisn't true! I know that's not true—"

"Your belief in the truth does not alter its light. So far this has happened three times and we," his voice rose ominously, "will suffer these atrocities no more." He paused, letting her measure the words before starting up again . . . Which she did, as wildly she wondered if, like Jonpaul himself, Lord Bruno sacrificed his own people to make it appear that Charles was provoking the Alliance into war . . . and if that was so, dear God, how could one prove it?

"It seems, milady, your brother would draw us into war. To win this war he needs the army of Uri to join the combined force of St. Gallen and Lucerne. So it seems he proposed a marriage to get this. Yet we understand you refused on the surprising grounds that you, a girl of ten and seven, found the presumptive arrogance to find fault with the Duke of Uri's moral character and refused the proposed marriage. The thing far more astounding was that Charles apparently conceded the right of refusal to you. In all of Christendom, it is forbidden for an unmarried female—be her noble or of the servile estate—to presume to pass judgment on the dictates of her guardian or the 'moral character' of her superior. The hightest penalty for the heresy, excommunication and anathema, separation from the faithful, would, and my God, should, have been immediately decreed. It was not, for in your possession, you have the means to threaten your brother, to cripple his movement and promise him ruin."

Bruno paused as the hall filled with unkind commentary on this presentation of her crime and intrigue. Blood pounded in her head, color rose on her pale face, but her eyes stayed fixed on the ground as the hall grew silent again. How could they know? A spy? But no one knew save Charles . . .

"So, Lady Nichole Lucretia, we will ask you once: Will you save yourself and tell us willingly what comprised this threat?"

She shut her eyes tight, breathing hard and fast but not venturing a sound. Here at last was where the questions got hard, too hard to answer and, dizzily, she was reasoning if the pain was so great, beyond her imagination and therefore her ability to endure—

The whip cracked again in front of her, jerking her upright with a small cry and setting her trembling. "You will answer the question."

"How can I? I will not publicly defend my personal relations with my brother Charles . . . just as I am not guilty of a heresy against his good name, just as thou accuse my brother of the murder of peasants when I know . . . I know 'twas thou, the lords and knights of the Alliance who committed these crimes in the desperation to force Lucerne into war. 'Tis all a fabric of deception and clever lies—"

The whip cracked so close to her face, she felt a slash of hot air before Bruno's voice thundered across the hall: "Believe, I will not tolerate such an outburst again. Now, answer the question: Will you tell us what comprised the threat that bent Charles to your will?"

"Nooo," she cried in a whisper, her eyes shut as she shook her head. "I shall die before I utter a single word that might help the Alliance win Lucerne."

"Death is not an option. Yet. We shall employ the far more barbaric means: a piece of your flesh for every three minutes of your silence until you discover the wisdom of speaking—" He stopped, took a long draught of ale from a gold goblet, and, in that space, as if it were a signal, the men began wagering monies on how many minutes before she spoke out.

She caught her lip to stop a cry and closed her eyes to shut out the barbaric conversation she simply could not believe, so much worse when all men had laid their wagers. The lord Bruno asked the men, as if carving a carcass, "So what goes first? Ears this time?"

"Not the ears," Lord Wesmullar objected, then laughed. "Women use that particular organ so little, hardly a motivating sacrifice—"

The men laughed until another interruped. "Yet is she not the lady who had a hand at mutilating a knight in her brother's court? And was that not a ear that the sorry knight lost?"

That's not true! That's not true! She wanted to tell them that it wasn't true! On her brother's dare, she had thrown her anlace and it cut a lock of Enguerrand's hair, but it never touched his skin. He was her brother's knight and her friend and 'twas a jest, for 'twas Enguerrand's instruction that taught her how to toss the dagger in the first place and everyone, especially Enguerrand, had laughed . . .

"There's a measure of irony, a poetic kind of justice—"

"Ah, too much blood! Toes work far more expediently. I wager the lady won't lose more than three toes before she finds her voice—"

The hall erupted back into chaos as wagers were now made on how many toes she'd lose before she found her voice, each wager accompanied by descriptive recountings of similar experiences. Wide with this horror, Nichole's gaze jerked from one voice to the next. An agrument rose between two lords and a steward over how many lost toes would make her become a cripple. A knight sent a squire running to make sure there were hot coals still in the kitchen, to make sure they had that means of stopping the bleeding once she spoke. Lord Bruno stopped his argument long enough to congratulate the man on his foresight!

One by one the men stopped as gazes followed Bruno's to where Nichole knelt. On one leg now, she had brought one foot forward, where she struggled to edge her slipper off her foot, struggled with an effort that stole their breath. Finally a mercifully small bare foot, profound in its courage, extended outward for the knife. She fully expected to feel the cold sting of the blade and there was no doubt in anyone's mind of this fact; trembling like a leaf caught in wind, a hot flush rose on her face and she caught her lip in her teeth and kept her eyes shut tight to stop from crying out when the shock came.

Bruno's gaze shot to the gallery where Jonpaul stood, leaning against the wood boards of the wall, his gaze riveted to the sight few of them could believe. He could not see Jonpaul's face but he didn't have to, for he knew what would be writ there. He saw Jonpaul's hand gripped a dagger that had been thrust violently into the wood beams of the wall behind him, an attempt to control emotions and keep himself passive in this, when every strained fiber of his being called to him to end Nichole's agony, emotions Bruno himself understood all too well.

With her eyes closed and her head down, the silence was a great roar in her head. Tension gripped her with the certainty the first cut would land any second. She waited and waited . . . Waited . . .

"A courageous move, milady," Bruno said quietly in a voice much subdued. "But, alas, a foolish one, for it seems clear that torture would be pointless. So be it."

Not understanding, Nichole opened her eyes with confusion to see Lord Bruno conferring in whispers to his squire, which man quickly left the room. She lowered her eyes to escape the scrutiny of her prosecutors as they conferred in lowered voices, her eyes frantically searching the cold floor around her, not understanding anything. What unholy torment now? A new torture? Did they know the waiting was the worst? That she might bear anything if only it came quickly?

At last the squire returned. He held a bundle of cloth in his arms. The sounds coming from the bundle said it was a babe there, and she froze, riveted with sudden tension as the child was set before her. She stared disbelieving at first. Pale and pink, large blue eyes, and a head of downy gold hair, the baby could be no more than three months old to the day. He sucked on a cloth dipped in milk and honey as he wriggled in the binding cloth, staring with wide-eyed fascination at the torchlight against the wall. The cloth dropped from his little mouth and his gaze went sidewise to find it again, finding Nichole's face instead, and smiling at this new pleasure.

Nichole's lungs could not draw hard or fast enough to accommodate the sudden insurgence of breath. Darkness swirled even before she heard Lord Bruno say, "A bastard lies before you, son of a milkmaid, I believe. You profess to care about the murder of peasants. You will prove it now milady."

The swirling darkness stopped as her gaze riveted to the guard bending down with a knife held in both hands poised above the child. "No! No! Dear God, dear God, have mercy! Mercy! 'Tis but an innocent—"

"Believe me," Lord Bruno put violence and anger in his voice, "if it saves us from war, I will sacrifice as many peasants as it takes for you to answer the question!"

The great man's face was an exercise in masculine determination, a will she paired with evil, and she knew he meant it. She felt dizzy and sick. He would kill the babe to make her speak and keep killing . . .

Nichole caught her lip to keep from crying, hesitating precious seconds in a desperate, futile effort to find a way out. She could not even tell herself that over half the children who survived childbirth died before they were five anyway . . . and so many more lost their lives later by war or disease . . . and the child's blood would be on their hands, but she couldn't . . . she couldn't bargain with a single life. 'Twas only God's place to do so. "Every child is the Christ child, every woman his mother, the virgin . . ." Nanna always said, and she was right, she was always right. The moral code of her religion was absolute; she could no more keep her silence than she could thrust the dagger herself, and yet—

The guard raised his arm. Nichole screamed, struggling with the ropes that bound her arms as she rushed with the terrible words: "There is a secret, a paper written in my father's blood or about my father's blood, I know not which. On my woman's deathbed, those words were given to me to use in hopes of preventing the unwanted marriage proposal. 'Twas all so faint . . . she was choking . . . She said this paper could ruin my brother, that I might bend Charles to my will with its threat. Yet I do not have this paper, nor have I seen this paper, and my woman died after telling me to put her hands on the Bible where it must be hidden—"

As she stopped midsentence, the lords, the entire room of men, and Jonpaul in the gallery—all stared in an effort to determine if this could possibly be the truth. But then she looked shocked, the lovely face blanching white of a sudden. She had freed her arms and her hands circled her neck, a gesture of horror as the enormous blue eyes frantically searched the room. For she realized the mistake as she uttered that last word. They wouldn't believe her! 'Twas too farfetched! She had no proof! They would kill the babe anyway, to make certain—

Dear God, no! She panicked, felt a swift surge of terror and, with wide eyes, she searched the faces of the men watching her. Everyone was talking at once. Jonpaul leaned on the banister now, until Lord Bruno caught his gaze, and an understanding passed between them. "What is the nature of this paper?" Bruno asked, but knew, like Jonpaul, it seemed certain she did not know and had never known.

"I don't know!"

"You don't know? You say the woman died before she disclosed where the paper was hidden or the revelation on the paper?"

"Aye. Aye . . . !"

"How is it that Charles was threatened by this empty

air? And God, girl, keep thy eyes on the child as I measure the truth of what I hear!"

Nichole rocked back on her knees, terrified and desperate to make them believe her. She couldn't breathe again, and weariness swept through her like a powerful potion, but she struggled wildly to overcome it, these men, and this trial long enough to save the babe . . .

"I . . . I told Charles Nanna had told me the secret, that I would use it if he forced me into this marriage. He said he didn't believe me, that even if I did have this paper, he knew my great love for him would stop me from ever using my knowledge against him, and he was right . . . he was right, he was right. I could not in truth hurt him . . . until now . . ." The room seemed to blur and the shapes on the faces changed, swelling hideously like a disease on a wound. She closed her feverish eyes but only to see the great Lord Bruno thrusting a lance through a mother and her child, laughing hellishly, the face becoming Jonpaul's. Her eyes flew open and frightened, breathless, she cried, "He took me to the village Stan to show me where thou . . . thou had murdered the poor people and set fire to the crops and homes! I . . . I should have married him . . . May God have mercy . . . I shall never live another moment regretting . . . regretting . . ."

She didn't know what she was saying. The room spun viciously, colors whirled like a child's top, and through this dizzying scene, she saw the guard raise the knife over the child and she screamed, struggling to her feet to throw herself over the child—

From somewhere above Jonpaul leaped in front of her. He came toward her, calling her name. "No . . . no, please." She shook her head, the child, save the child . . . She watched his face change with alarm and she thought, she thought—

The room turned first gray, then black and blacker

still . . . and the last thing she remembered was the guard and the child and a knife . . .

One long stride and Jonpaul caught Nichole in his arms as she swooned. No one at first moved as they stared at her head draped over his arm, following Jonpaul's gaze over the long dark hair to the floor, where the ends brushed a small red pool of her blood.

"Let us see this precious blood well spent . . ."

Chapter Eight

Billowing clouds pushed against a violent sky and shadows lengthened over the forest-lined meadow at the bottom of a small valley, where an enormous maroon-and-gold tent stood out among more than twenty other tents. Two flags bearing the coat of arms for Charles the Bold of Lucerne flapped in the gentle breeze on the opposite sides of the opening to the tent, marking the camp headquarters. Horses lined up at the very edge of the meadow. A huge orange bonfire leaped viciously in the center of the camp, surrounded by a half dozen smaller fires. A number of men swung axes into downed trees, gathering the necessary firewood to last the night. A cart piled high with fresh supplies lumbered on its way into the camp. Groups of foot soldiers began returning in twos and threes, wearily seeking the short rest period allotted at the end of a hard day.

For men rode into camp at a fast lope. Atop a black mare, a red-haired soldier wore a white bandage over his face and chest, while his right arm rest in a sling. Another one of the riders wore a bandage around his head. They rode up to Charles's tent, dismounted, and gave their horses over to the groom as they waited to be announced.

They were admitted at once, the flaps were drawn back

by two pages, and they stepped inside . . .

Shadows danced on the maroon backdrop of the tent, orchestrated by the bright torchlight marking its four corners. Maps, dotted with small finger-size red flags, a wine cask, and three goblets covered the tabletop where Charles stood with Anton Dirr, the captain of the guards, Lords Victor Schumacher and Phillips at his side. The finger of his gloved hand pointed to the place on the map where he would have the search concentrated on the morrow, along the Thor River's easternmost banks, thirty miles outside St. Gallen. As the two wounded soldiers entered with his squire, all conversation ceased.

The pale-blue eyes lit with antipathy as he contemplated the two men. Not what he expected. With their own eyes downcast, the wounded men knelt and waited their punishment. Both had the hard edge to their faces and the well-exercised bulk of muscles that separated the professional soldiers from others, and the severity of their wounds was undeniable, even in this light. "So you are the men who met the beast?"

The red-haired man nodded. "Aye."

To him Charles said, "I'm told you lost an eye for your trouble and will probably lose use of that arm. Is that right?"

"Aye, milord."

Charles studied him for a moment more before he swung down into a chair and lifted his spurred, booted feet to the table. Picking up his wine goblet, he said in a passionate whisper, "You should have lost your life."

He let the two men shift uncomfortably; it was the least they deserved. "So I am further told the both of you are under the grandiose impression 'twas the Almighty Lord Jonpaul the Terrible that you fought?" His lips curled with an amused smile, the gloved hand stroked his mustache menacingly. "I will hear this dubious evidence personally and mind you, man, I would as soon kill you as listen to a lie. So what say you?"

Composed and unshaken, the red-haired soldier looked over at the man. "He has seen the man before. His eyes recognized the lord from memory."

"Indeed . . ." Charles turned to the other man. Dark-haired, of medium build—totally indistinquishable if not for his head wound and a tattoo of the Fraticelli sect printed over a terrible scarred arm. Odd that a soldier would be a believer in that ascetic idea of Christianity, taking a vow of poverty and renunciating the material world. "And where could you have met the lord Jonpaul?"

"The battle of Burgundy, milord."

"Indeed! And how is that, when no soldiers from either Lucerne or St. Gallen were dispatched to the Burgundy war?"

"My brother-in-law, the good man Francisco Datini, convinced me to join the just cause. I fought in the fourth regiment with all men of Basel, led first by the lord Jacob Van de Birs until he was killed, then by that great man's nephew, the lord Jonpaul himself. As I was in the front lines of the great war I saw the lord many times until I myself was hit by a baselord across my arm."

The lords behind Charles exchanged disbelieving glances. If the man fought in that war he might well be a traitor, spitting up lies to save himself. The same thoughts occurred to Charles, and after finishing his drink and holding out his goblet for more, he demanded, "And so you say the man was Jonpaul?"

"Aye. There can only be one of the likes of that man. As I came upon the lord, I was startled with the shock of it, but my loyalty went to the lady when I saw her hands tied to the saddle horn and a gag in her mouth. There was the briefest moment of doubt but the next thing I know the halbert I threw at him was coming at me in the head.

No one else in all of Christendom and beyond could throw a halbert like that."

The man's admission of a moment's hesitation revealed an undeniable honesty and, staring at the man, gripped with sudden tension, Charles came slowly to his feet. He leaned over the table, his weight braced on his arms as his gaze shifted to the red-haired soldier. "And you? What say you?"

"I have not seen the lord Jonpaul before, but neither have I seen the fighting I saw that day." The red-haired man seemed to stare off at the torchlight as he remembered, still shaken after all these days. "He was tall and blonde, and his eyes were like a forest at nightfall, darkly green—"

"Aye 'tis the right color of the lord Jonpaul's eyes."

"He rode a black stallion better trained than ten others—"

"That is Zermatt! The lord Jonpaul's famous horse!" the other man interrupted again.

"Aye. The lord moved faster than an eye could follow, unholy speed. One after another, the men fell. When I came into the clearing, men were already spewed from one side of the small glen to the other and the man's arms swung in repeated circles like a windmill—I don't know how the halberts left his hands. I was the last to reach him and the only one to get close. I had a mace in hand and charged behind him, and I swung." The soldier's arm lifted in the air as if needing to demonstrate. "Yea! But as if he had eyes in the back of his head, the mace hit his lance instead of his head. With a queer twist, he swung it back to hit me in the face. I went down blinded by my own blood. I reached for a weapon at my side and sat up and swung with all my might as he started to leave the glen. He turned the horse around and came back with his lance raised and meaning to land me a death blow, but the lady—may the holy Virgin keep her safe!—she kicked the beast to save me."

Silence descended when at last he finished the story, the hushed sound broken by the flags flapping in the wind, the muted sounds of the camp settling down for nightfall ouside, horses neighing and men talking, the distant rush of a nearby stream and Charles's brief consideration of the preposterous story. "Yet he wore no colors, right?"

"Aye," the soldier admitted.

"And he wore no bonnet or mail?"

"Aye again."

"Even the goddamn horse had no armor!"

"Aye, to give the beast speed for the chase—"

"Whatever I say! Jonpaul, the devil, ghosts and goblins and demons in the night. Excuses, excuses! Sons of Satan." Charles's pale eyes narrowed. "But there is more muck in this tent than the deepest ditch at Castle of Coucy. 'Twas an impostor you fought! A mad, lone warrior who got it in his mind to risk life and limb on the slim chance of getting me to pay ransom for my dear sister's safety. I have heard of such schemes before—"

"Aye . . ." Philip nodded, always agreeing with Charles. He was a small man, effeminate and given to books and histories, ill suited to his position on the Council, but as the sole heir to Interlaken, he was Charles's right-hand man. "Stealing nobility happens often in places like the holy land—among the devil's infidelities, men who commit barbaric outrages as frequently as the pope prays. And, besides," he wondered, "why would Jonpaul risk his life to abduct dear Nichole? Venus herself would not merit the trick—"

Victor shook his head, seeing the truth and frightened to the depth of his soul. Frightened for Nichole, for, "the lady Nichole is as dear to Lucerne as Venus was to Zeus and God's teeth, not just by the light of her beauty or the power of her charm. The lady Nichole gets us Uri and Uri keeps us safe from the Alliance! 'Tis plain—"

Victor stopped, and just as Charles was about to lash out, all gazes turned to the opening where the man of Charles's guard, Reinard, appeared. There was something frightening and strange about the tall man, his iron strength and quiet manner, but more and more Charles came to depend on him. No one thought of his unnerving presence now, for without pretense of formality he came right to the point. "The men on the west boundary are reporting a rumor that puts the lady Nichole with the lord Jonpaul in the township of Olten on way to the Castle Dornach."

Those words were greeted by a heady silence in which the tension built and built until with all his great strength and, as if it were his enemy's heart, Charles struck a knife in the dead center of the table before it was kicked over, and a blood-curdling call for the death of Lord Jonpaul sounded loud and long in the still night air. Reinard looked down at his boots, where he watched the dark red wine spread like blood over the map of Lucerne Valley and the lands of the Alliance . . .

The rich timbre of his voice whispering at her bedside pulled her up from the depth of the darkness. "See, Gavin? Did I not say I'd keep her safe . . . ? Nay, her wound opened again. I did not see it until it was too late, but we cannot wake her now, she needs her sleep badly. Aye, she is beautiful. Smitten, are we?" He chuckled, warm and untroubled, laughing with his boy. "Like father, like son. I would not deny you her attention, but know this: she is mine, Gavin. Mine from the first moment I laid my eyes upon her. She is my prize . . ."

The voices vanished and she saw the rose again, the red rose surrounded but untouched by the blue flame. Nanna, Nanna what does the rose and the flame mean? "Oh, let's see, well, 'tis an ancient test of true love, ye must have heard about it . . . No? Well, it used to be done on the marriage day, but I haven't heard of it for many years now. The common folks have no faith anymore . . . A man, hopefully your husband-to-be, gives you a single red rose. This you stick in the blue flame of the fire . . . No, no, you see, the red rose is made of love, so a single red rose means true love. The blue flame is the hottest part of fire and hence the most destructive. Fire is of the physical world, and beneath it is the flame that devours souls and separates one from all things holy . . . So the dream means your true love will be tested by the world, but will remain untouched . . . Oh, for the love of Eve! Wipe that dreamy look from your eyes, girl! The only being worthy of your love is God. No man will ever deserve the gift, I can tell you that now and save you your heartaches. Mother in heaven but youth is wasted on the young . . ."

The rose never burned but faded as the flames leaped and danced over the village Stan, the fire spreading, orange flames leaping into the sky, and she ran, trying to escape and running. The sky darkened with smoke and she looked up, frightened. Run . . . She had to escape, but suddenly the angry flames sprang in front of her and at her sides and she screamed, trying to escape the heat—

A cool, wet cloth came to her forehead and she heard a whisper gently coaxing her into a deeper sleep. "Easy, love . . . easy . . ." The fire vanished and she felt herself sinking, sinking . . .

A long time later she opened her eyes, greeted by the still night air and darkness edged with a faint, soft light.

She lay upon a four-poster bed, firmer than most and twice as large. A thick, dark-purple comforter covered her, made of a rich satin, while her head rested on soft, flouncy, goose feather pillows. The dark-green-and-purple velvet canopy drapes were parted, opened to the spacious chambers. A dark wood chest rested at the foot of this enormous bed. Directly across from the bed was an enormous tapestry, but 'twas too dark to distinguish its shapes. A matching dark wood chest rested against the stone wall, and above that hung a tapestry, too. There was a torchstand alongside, but no fire, an ewer and basin on top of the elaborate hand-carved chest, a fur mat on the floor. She looked to the other side and saw a thick bearskin carpet spread before a huge, hooded fireplace. Then she saw where he stood at the window . . .

The shutters opened out and he stood beneath the light of a half moon. Jonpaul wore only cotton breeches, tied at his waist, nothing more. One arm leaned on the stone wall, a bent knee rested on a stool as he stared at the window. Haloed by moonlit blond curls, the handsome face held the thoughtful look of a man contemplating the world he had made. She felt far too tired to panic at his presence or the certainty that he had put her in his bed, far too tired to think of all that had happened to her and what it meant, past the immediate concerns.

"Milord . . ."

The melodic sound of her voice, faint with weariness and sleep, drew his gaze. He took a sharp breath and then seemed to brace, as if expecting to feel the sharp point of her claws and he would have, he really would have if she had an ounce of strength to put to the effort. She tried to sit up, and when he saw this, he stepped quickly to the bedside to aid her effort. With worry and fear in her eyes, Nichole took his hand, squeezing it tightly, or so she thought. "The child! Please, is the child—"

He took a long moment to know what she referred to and for good reason. "Oh, aye, the child is resting in his mother's arms, no doubt sound asleep."

She fell back against the pillows with relief. The child was saved. Bless the Holy Mother. Before she did anything else, she would find that child's mother to tell of the heavy price paid so that her child might live—a child whose life would be henceforth charmed, surely meant in service to the charity of all.

The waiting women had plaited the dark hair into ropes as thick as his fist; one trailed off the side of the bed to nearly drop to the floor. Her pale skin held a beckoning luminosity in the light and seemed nearly the same color as the thin nightdress. The strings that gathered the gown at the neck were untied as if her breaths had been so shallow the women were afraid to inhibit her breathing. The nightdress barely covered the soft swell of her breasts, a tease to which he was particularly vulnerable. Unable to stop the impulse, a gentle hand came to her forehead, where his fingers stroked her hairline. To his surprise she made no move to draw from his touch. She closed her eyes again as if soothed. Yet when she opened them, absorbing his nearness, perhaps the pity in his gaze, there was fear and uncertainty as she relived the interrogation. "I am, I fear, too tired to fight you . . ."

"Ah, I am willing to wait."

Nichole took this at surface value, not understanding the intensity of those words, for there was an immediate concern. "I badly need . . . I need to find the *garderobe.*" She was praying that unlike the Castle of the Lower Lake, Dornach had the more modern lavatories, rather than the foul midden in the middle of the courtyard, for she would not make it that far.

A tender smile changed his face, softening the harsher lines there as he leaned over to lift her up. "Come, I'll help you—"

"No, please, if you will just show me."

"Not a chance. Your stitches tore and opened again. You won't be able to walk for some time."

She felt the stiffness there as he spoke. The wound was hot to the touch, but more than anything she was just too weary to argue with him. As he lifted her up, and moved through wide double doors into a hall, she saw she wore a nightgown, thin and made of cotton and her hair had been plaited by someone. All in all, it seemed to suggest they would not be killing her tonight, which was no surprise. After all, she had given them everything they wanted. Perhaps he would even let her go now . . .

He carried her into the *garde-robe,* larger than any other she had seen, which amounted to two, and both of these had been on her one trip to France some two years ago now. Everything seemed larger at Dornach, and, "There is a carpet here—"

"The men of Dornach are famous for a goodly aim."

The jest shot startled eyes to see his laughter. Which seemed too unlikely. After all they had been through, all he had put her through, after being battered and wounded, put through tortures and threatened with death, after all this, here he was teasing her in the *garde-robe* in the middle of the night . . .

With hands on hips, his tall frame stood in the doorway, waiting. She abruptly realized he planned to watch.

"Oh, please—"

He had to catch his lip to stop an amused grin. "Love, I am no stranger to you, and you can believe I'm not about to risk having you topple over in here to save you a bit of modesty."

Necessity stopped her rebuttal, though his words made no sense to her and she was still turning them over in her head when she finished. She stood up, dropping her nightgown, when a frightening dizziness came over her.

She tried to take a step but—

Jonpaul caught her fall and swung her back up to his arms. She grabbed her head to stop the spinning, suddenly breathless. "I am so faint . . ."

"I'm not surprised. You've lost enough blood to put down a man twice your size." He brought her back to the bed and then poured a pink liquid from a pitcher into a tall glass. This was pressed into her hand. "Drink up, love."

She peered into the glass, hesitating. He would not poison her, she felt fairly certain and she felt more thirsty than a Venice messenger. The liquid tasted deliciously of late-summer strawberries, eggs, warm milk, and spices. She finished the whole, but as the smooth drink settled in her stomach, she came to feel how bad off she truly was. He took the glass from her just as another wave of dizziness washed over her, settling with a bone-shaking weariness. Opening her eyes again, she found that both her hands held tightly to his thumbs for support as he strong, warm hand enveloped hers. She did not remember reaching for his support and she studied the contact with disbelief as she fought to overcome the profound exhaustion at least long enough to ask the pressing question: "What will you do now? I am trying to remember all I said, but . . . but the Bible—" Wide eyes shot to him, but he was studying the hands in his. "Will you try to steal this from Lucerne?"

"You searched the Bible three days for this paper and found nothing, am I right?"

Alarm lifted in her eyes. "How can you know that? I don't know how you know these things?"

It was a cry, rather desperate, too, but he would not upset her more now. "Rest now, love . . ."

"No, please." Sudden hope gave her a moment's strength. "The information is useless to you, is it not? I can see in your eyes . . . All for nothing! Will you have an escort take me home now?"

The question seemed to surprise him and she saw the familiar laughter reach his eyes. "Give you back to your brother so that he can force you to marry the Duke of Uri? That cruel, vain, unjust lecher, the infamous slayer of poor beasts? Give you to him?" He shook his head. "Not as I draw breath, love."

Those blue eyes filled with emotion as she listened to this, regretting every word she ever said to him, regretting not having married the duke the first time she saw him, regretting most of all the very breath Jonpaul drew into his body. "You mean not as long as you covet Lucerne and my brother's realm! You'd hand me over on a silver platter if my marriage wouldn't join Uri to Lucerne and make us strong enough to resist your unquenchable, unholy thirst for power—"

The words cost her much, for her body was simply unable to accommodate the fury of emotions, and dizziness washed over her in force again. Using all her strength, she pulled herself up from the imminent darkness long enough to hear: "Wrong again, love. If there were no Lucerne, no Charles, no threat of war, I would still not give your hand to another man for marriage."

She didn't understand these words. She tried to ask him, but suddenly her weariness began pulling her from his voice and presence, the solar and Dornach—the entire world turned upside down. The last thing she thought she felt was the gentle caress of his lips on her forehead. "Ah, love, if you only knew how much I would risk to keep the right . . ."

Nichole always had a fanciful, rich imagination. Her imagination had been fed from the earliest age, for among many other talents her mother told stories better than spinners' spun cloth and Nichole's life was replete with these fanciful tales. Then, too, women of noble birth were often better read and versed than their male counterparts and simply because much of a boy's life seemed to be taken up with the warring arts. Girls had more time to study. Nichole was no exception. Among the traditional Bible stories and allegories, Nichole had read the epics of Brutus, Greece and Troy, of Alexander and Julius Caesar, of Charlemagne, and how Tristan and Isolde loved and sinned and, if pressed, she would admit to her share of coarser stuff, the *fabliaux* or tales of common life, the bawdy and scatological. But among all the tales she read or heard, her favorite was the Arthurian legends, King Arthur and the knights of the round table, the dawning of the Age of Chivalry, where the words "right makes might" were uttered for the first time and laws superseded the judgment of arms, where for a short space of time, Arthur, so wise and deserving, more noble than any man since, ruled Christendom.

She kept a treasured picture of Camelot in her mind, an enchanted image of how she imagined that great castle to look, and when she first saw the tapestry that hung opposite the bed in the light of day, it seemed as if the artist had shared this fanciful vision. The tapestry showed a grand and airy castle set against a green and leafy hillside, an enchanting vision indeed and not just because of the use of modern dyes and the resulting splendid colors but the very scene itself and its details. The castle looked modern but must be ancient, built in the olden days when peasants labored entire lifetimes for their lords. Nine imposing cone-topped towers, surrounded by man-size battlements, jutted up to a blue, springtime sky. The guesthouse alone, alongside the enormous wood gate outside the wall, looked twice as large as the Lower Lake's old keep. The stone-and-wood roofs of the chapel, the towering furnace of the kitchen, and soaring cornices and towers of the solar chambers all topped the massive stone wall. The castle of her dreams!

Nichole looked around. An older woman was asleep in a chair. She threw back the covers and slipped from the bed, and ignoring the stiffness in her leg, she cautiously approached the tapestry where she viewed the enchanting scene up close. Lords and ladies were riding, picnicking and hawking, groups of peasants mowing, milking, and harvesting the fields. So detailed, she could see each green leaf on the trees, the individual bulrushes along the marshy banks of a small fishing pond where two boys fished, a rosy-cheeked maid peering idly from a flower-lined windowsill in the solar tower, the ribbons on the ladies' cauls lifting on the breeze, the purple-and-green colors of the guards . . .

Purple-and-green colors, Dornach's colors . . .

Colors that turned gray as sudden dizziness and breathlessness swept over her again. She turned back to the bed, but before she took a step, the gray turned black and, much like a child's rag doll, she slipped quietly to the floor. Madeline, the older woman, woke to find her there and immediately called the guards . . .

A servant entered the solar study where the men convened to light the torches as Jonpaul read the carefully composed letter twice, then passed it to Kurtus at his side. He looked across the table at Hans, who had penned the letter. "By God, that should do it."

"Aye," Bruno agreed. "Assuming Charles does believe she has this paper, it just might work. At the very least," he added as he poured spiced wine into his goblet, "we have prevented the lady's marriage—"

"And without the army of Uri," Hans finished, "I doubt if the coward will press any further."

They were all aying this when the door opened and

Bruno's second oldest son, Williams, Jonpaul's squire, entered, a strange fear working on his young face. It was the common practice among the nobility to send sons into another lord's service as squire where the boys would learn the martial arts and other aspects of the chivalry code. Young Williams suited Jonpaul well. The boy was quick to learn, bright and hard-working, if a bit too eager to risk life and limb in his service, much to the consternation of his mother, the lady Adline, and the amusement of his father.

"Milord, you are wanted in the solar chambers. The lady took a fall—"

Alarm immediately lifted on the handsome face. The other men exchanged glances as Jonpaul quickly left the room with young Williams. "There it is again," Bruno motioned as the door shut behind him. "Did you not see that look? The very same look as when the lady fell faint and we saw she had been bleeding throughout. The man is in love with her, I say . . ."

Jonpaul returned less than a half hour later, still cursing. "The girl might be smarter than ten others, but she is certainly senseless. There she was sprawled out on the floor in a dead faint. No doubt the result of another harebrained attempt to escape in the middle of the night, dressed only in a nightdress and with not enough strength to lift a cup let alone—" He stopped abruptly, noticing the interested gazes of his audience. What the hell was this? His gaze narrowed, "What goes here? Why are you looking at me as if I were a—"

"A cock with his head cut off?" Kurtus supplied.

Hans almost lost the sip in his mouth as the men roared with laughter. Jonpaul tired unsuccessfully to keep his emotions from showing, knowing it was best not to ever encourage Kurtus. "Let's get on with it. Have all signed here?" he asked as he took a candle to pour wax in his seal, the elk horns over his family's coat of arms.

"What about the Bible?" Bruno asked. "Can you get it?"

"Aye," Jonpaul replied as he sealed the letter. "Not that 'twill do us a passel of good. Nichole is, as I say, smart and clever, and I've no doubt that if it was there, she would have found it. Still . . ."

Father Ari stood up, and as the men talked, he pretended to examine the neat row of illuminated manuscripts before he interrupted. "There is another point to all this. Have any of you thought about the Church's response to the lady's untimely abduction?"

"God's teeth," Kurtus swore, "but I have now lived long enough to hear Ari refer to the Church with neither curses nor his hand held out for coins."

The men laughed at that and Father Ari quickly hastened to explain the uncharacteristic remark. "The world be a hard enough place without your humble servant here bringing up unpleasant subjects but, alas, I feel, sirs, you are all overlooking a future problem. With Kuno at Charles's side and with that man's well-known papal influence, you can be sure the Church will not view the matter of the lady Nichole's abduction lightly."

"'Tis true." Hans folded his arms across his chest. "No doubt Charles will turn to that fat crown to put pressure on the papal train."

"Ah," Bruno scoffed. "What the devil can those old men do to us?"

"Aye," Jonpaul, too, scoffed at this. "The Church is as impotent as a gelded yearling. 'Twill take months for them to respond to the initial report of Nichole's abduction." He chuckled at the thought of the game that would be played. "Then no doubt in a couple of months, we will receive an inquiry to ascertain if the accusation is true—"

"An inquiry tempered by the calculation of the tithes they collect from our lands and free cities," Hans added.

"Aye, and I will write back that it is not true, that the lady Nichole was gracing our court with her presence when winter set in, prohibiting her return. Another three months will pass as they attempt to explain this to Charles, and he in turn attempts to set them straight. Another inquiry will be made, and so on. Dear God, but 'twill be two years of polite correspondence before they take a single definitive step—"

The trumpet sounded outside and Jonpaul stopped as the horn sounded twice, then three times. The men all stood as a page opened the door to make the announcement in the event they hadn't heard the horn inside. "What the devil now?" Bruno said as he followed the others out. The lords met two of their stewards in the hall and all quickly descended the three staircases, passed through the entrance hall into the darkened courtyard. Over thirty other men were rushing into the courtyard as a lone rider, wearing the black-and-white ribbon of alarm, rode up at a gallop to stop before Jonpaul.

Jonpaul didn't recognize the man until the horse stopped and he lifted the salad—his steel bonnet. "Vasco!" he said as one of his sergeants-of-arms swung off his mount to drop in a quick bow.

"Milord, there's been an ambush outside of Rarburgt. Three knights dead, your friend Otto among the three. This note was attached to that good man's dead body."

"No," Jonpaul whispered as he took the note. Otto had been his uncle's squire, eventually one of his more heroic knights, a man who had taught Jonpaul the lancing paces as well as horsemanship. He was also one of his closest friends. Not Otto, anyone but Otto, Jonpaul was thinking this as Williams raced to fetch him a torch. Hans put his hand on Jonpaul's shoulder and Jonpaul gripped the large hand tightly for support. Williams returned, and with torch in hand, the surrounding darkness suddenly lit with fire and Jonpaul read the note out loud:

"Three knights dead every sunrise that you keep the lady Nichole Lucretia, sister to the signator Charles the Bold of Lucerne. War if the lady suffers any harm or humiliation or harshness in your hands."

The note was signed by Charles's hand, his seal of two crosswords over a stone tower burned in the side of the paper. Jonpaul raised his arm and crushed the paper in his fist. "Never!" His voice sung in quiet authority in the still night air even as he signaled the trumpeter to call for arms. "Not a single man more shall meet the blackguard's sword with his life!"

The trumpets blasted, a sound that would call every able-bodied man within a three-mile radius of Dornach. A roar of agreement met the words. The lords called for the immediate attention of their squires, archers, and sergeants-of-arms—except for Dornach's, all captains of arms remained always at their courts. Men soon began pouring into the courtyard, with boys and dogs underfoot, and within the hour over a hundred men were gathered there as over and over the situation was explained in rushed whispers and excitement.

"Holbien!"

"Here, milord," Holbien, the captain of the guards at Dornach, stepped forward.

"Gather, my knights. We will ride out tonight. To arms!" The crowd raised swords to the night sky. Bruno promised thirty more knights not presently at Dornach, Hans promised forty. The rest of the men would come from the cities and townships. "You, Ramon," Jonpaul ushered the orders, "you are to take two men to ride to Sursee with our own message to Charles, and you, Clives," he pointed to one of his sergeants, "take five men to Basel, Olten, Rarburgt, and Argau, to give the call to arms. I want one hundred and fifty men more to join the knights patroling the border by this night's end. Groups of ten with three men on watch at all times. From one end of the Alliance to the other, no mile shall be unguarded."

A deafening chorus of aye-ayes greeted this, and Jonpaul finished with: "Let us meet this vow with our own: Not one life more!"

Nichole watched from the solar chambers at the wide window that looked out to the courtyard, transfixed with horror and fascination by the chaos and shouting below. She held tightly to the windowsill, steadying the slight tremble in her hands and severe weakness rocking her mind and body. Madeline, the kindly waiting woman, after discovering she could not stop the lady, stood close behind to catch Nichole's fall in case this need arose.

Standing on the scaffold, Jonpaul still shouted orders as his mail was being fitted over his brigantine with his squire's help. Many of the faces surrounding him were now known to her: the lord Bruno, who had interrogated her, the great beast of a man who murdered innocents without remorse, the friar who had watched him threaten the babe's life and many, many others, too, all faces drawn from that nightmare she would never forget—including the man who talked to Jonpaul now, a knight from his personal guard.

"Me?" Kurtus questioned, outraged, "a watcher of women? What heinous crime or deed have I committed against thee to deserve this punishment?"

"Kurtus . . ." That was all he said, and the rising lilt to his tone brought Kurtus in check. Williams brought Zermatt around and Jonpaul mounted, tightening the reins on the beast's dance as he waited a moment for the others to mount. He looked to her not human, rather like some terrible warring god, Zeus or Mars himself, and for the first time she could imagine the great force of his swooping upon the village Stan to unleash maelstrom of murder and mayhem . . . Just as Madeline murmured in a dreamy voice, "Is not he the most handsome man in all Christendom?"

Nichole's breath caught and she swung around, giving that woman a look so sharp, Madeline instinctively drew a pace back and vowed never to mention the lord Jonpaul's name to her again. Nichole turned back around, her eyes hot and glistening with the outrage. The familiar dizziness came over her again and she gripped the sill, closing her eyes until it passed. "You lost enough blood to drop a man twice your size . . ." he had said, and she believed him now, for she was literally too weak to stand for long. With effort she returned to the scene below, barely able to hear the words.

". . . Father Ari will help you. The women have instructions for her care. But mind you, Kurtus, the girl is a wild thing. Give her free rein within these walls, but not a moment of solitude. And I mean *not a moment!*"

Hans and Bruno joined Jonpaul at his side. Jonpaul's gloved hand raised with the signal to march. The knights followed him and the foot soldiers followed behind them. A dozen boys too young for service would follow the procession for miles until one by one they turned back. Nichole saw young Gavin in this group and she felt her heart leap with a queer emotion. What was it about this boy?

More men joined the procession outside the courtyard, and as Nichole watched the darkness swallow them up, Jonpaul would have been surprised to hear her prayers joined to his; "Please, Holy Mother, not one life more . . ."

"What's this?" Madeline did not understand. "Crushed tomatoes and carrots? Vinegar and hashish seeds?"

"Aye." Nichole leaned back against the pillows, almost

too weary to respond. "And some ergot. Brown eggs will help if you have them, but none of these should have the red dot. 'Tis a common potion to make one's blood stronger. Have you not used it before?"

"Milk and honey—"

"Nay, tomatoes and carrots, hashish seeds, ergot and egg. Trust me."

So it began. Nichole orchestrated her own recovery, which seemed to her to be painfully slow, though the white light made her leg heal to a hard scab. For four days she did nothing besides shocking the kind waiting women at every turn but eat and sleep. It was not just that she was extremely particular about the preparations of her meals and these potions of hers, but she absolutely refused to even look at any flesh. It was not that the initiate was actually forbidden meat, but in order to partake of the flesh of any heart-beating creature that draws life from air, one had to go through a ritualized series of prayers and thanksgiving, then the rather lengthy rite to stop the dead animal's spirit from entering the body physical and disrupting hard-earned harmony. Nichole never found it worth the energy, and to do so now would be impossible. Then, too, she knew well that after so many years, her body would refuse to digest flesh, more so in her weakened condition.

The situation caused an uproar in the kitchen until the kitchen mistress remembered Their Lordship's mother had also refused to eat flesh of any kind. She got out a dusty set of recipes her own mother had served to that great lady, and with sudden respect and zeal, she began serving Nichole these tasty meals.

There were other things, too. The young lady refused to allow Dornach's physician into the room to look at her. In the course of her long training Nanna had made her read every word of the physician's books and Nichole could and often did recite dozens of erroneous treatments to anyone who would listen. It was not just that with few exceptions their treatments didn't help, but many of them actually hurt. Two popular practices, bloodletting and trepanning—the opening of the skull to relieve fluid pressure—often brought fatal results to the ailing patient. One called a physicain as one called a priest, when all hope fled. She still had plenty of hope left. Not only did she fully intend to recover but she fully intended to escape long before Jonpaul and the men of Dornach returned.

The waiting women were kind. He must have spoken with them. They treated her as if she were a visiting dignitary rather than an enemy or prisoner. They told her about poor Mayra, that she was now serving a rich merchant's widow in Basel, claiming she had found happiness there. This explained much, of course, though she didn't understand the story about Anne Marie's banishment. Something was wrong in the telling, for Anne Marie would not do that . . .

The women seemed most anxious to please her, never once mentioning her predicament. The exception was Kira, the youngest. Though she was polite, she was also quiet and hardly ever spoke directly to her, taken as she was to staring out the window or studying the different art effects in the spacious, sunny room.

Nichole could often read a person's character from their looks, the intuitive gift of the initiate. Kira was a pretty girl, if not beautiful. Thick, curly brown hair that fell to her shoulders crowned a pixie round face and large brown eyes. She wore bright, pretty dresses, a different one each day, and often plaited her hair, wrapped it like a crown around her head, or simply tied it back. Rouge gave her a deceptively innocent air, as if she were a blushing maid. But she was not, for her eyes told the story, revealing the passions that ruled her. Kira, Nichole saw, would know no moderation. She would love this and absolutely hate that, everything would be felt in the extreme—which included her animosity and resentment at serving a lady of Lucerne. The girl had lost her husband-to-be in the Burgundy War, and no doubt the antagonism owed itself to the fact that Lucerne stayed out of the Swiss effort.

The other two women were kind and generous, and obviously forgiving. Madeline was an older woman, who was still quite attractive, and mostly because of the humor she brought to everything. She spent a good deal of time outside with the man Kurtus and the guards, jesting and laughing the afternoons away over a game of cards or chess. Bettrina, too, the wife of Holbien, Dornach's captain of the guards, was kind. She was a pretty woman who was expecting her first child, and like all first time mothers, she could think of little else—Nanna always said the first child steals your mind long before they take your life. It put Nichole in an awkward position, for those few times she was up and working on her macramé rope—to escape, in the likely event he put guards at the gate—she found herself talking with Bettrina about childbirth, trying to set her fears at ease.

"You must stop fretting. You will have an easy time of it, I can tell."

"Oh? How can you?"

Kira, who was examining a gold-gilt mechanical clock on the chest, turned around as if she, too, would like to hear this.

"Well there's three things that are bad signs. Too slender or too fat and you are neither. Space of the hip bones is important, too, and I can see you have nice wide hips. I can also tell by your fine complexion that you have a goodly balance of blood, the bile and phlegm. Rest assured, your time will be easy."

"Hmm," Kira said. "Only the Almighty knows whether or not a woman's time will be easy, and even when a woman is so huge like Bettrina, I hear the pain of it makes death welcome."

"Hush now!" Nichole ordered sharply, and just as Madeline had learned, the look she shot to Kira could bring up an advancing army. Kira took the reprimand with surprise and some embarrassment and she turned back around. "God knows, of course, but so do those who have been trained in midwifery. I studied with the best and my eye is good. I can tell just by the look of you 'twill be an easy time. And, while of course there is some pain," she cast a reproving glance at Kira's back, "there is tremendous joy as well, and for most women this joy is so great and pure, it completely overwhelms all else."

Nichole purposely made it sound like a religious experience, knowing that expectation shaped experience. Bettrina blushed with excitement and smiled, reaching out to squeeze Nichole's hand. Nichole forced heself to smile back, but 'twas these very moments that brought dark thoughts darting blindly like bats in the night through her mind. Of course she knew better than to blame these women for their lord's crimes, but did they lay with a man who had plundered the poor village of Stan? How could they be so ignorant of the evil that existed here, rampant like a disease? Could it remain hidden by that huge wall that separated a man's work from their women's?

Nichole and Bettrina talked for some time, Bettrina questioning her and Nichole freely dispensing Nanna's imparted wisdom. The midmorning meal was served—oatmeal and sugared blueberries, bread, jam and butter, eggs and fruit and upon finishing all of it, weariness washed over her like a disease.

Strange voices visited her as he slept. Women's voices near the bedside, and she tried to open her eyes to see the faces, but she could not, as if her eyelids were alive, independent creatures, not fully under her control, and it was maddening . . . so maddening . . .

"Did not I tell you she was as fair as a warm spring day?"

"Why, she is pretty indeed! Look at that dark hair, she must have Italian ancestors—"

"They say her mother was a Medici, daughter of the Viscount of Milan, Bernado Lucchino de' Medici . . ."

"Aren't they joined to the House of Savoy?"

". . . midwifery? Three months too late for me. I had Francis . . . she nearly did me in with . . ."

"Be quiet, Kira! Milord says she is not to blame for her brother's warring . . ."

"Do you think 'tis true . . . I mean about his hand? You've never heard? Oh, dear . . ."

The hand . . . the hand . . . the hand . . . Suddenly she saw the distant hillside again where the ugly old woman stood waving her hand. A hand marked by the sixth finger. Nanna was trying to tell her something, gasping and choking and then the blood, bright red blood soaking the vision of the burning ruins of the village Stan . . .

A small hand squeezed hers so hard it woke her and she opened her eyes to see Gavin sitting at her bedside. A smile lifted to her eyes. "Gavin!" Yet the boy looked pale and his eyes were large, hot with worry. She looked behind him to see the flowers thrown about the floor, Bettrina bending over to pick them up. She did not see Kira watching with interest from the other side of the bed.

"You had a terrible nightmare, tossing, and crying out in your sleep," Bettrina told her. "You gave us all a scare. Young Gavin even dropped the flowers he picked for you."

"Oh . . . did I give you a scare, Gavin?"

The boy nodded. Few people could understand just

how scared he was, too. Foremost in his mind was the connection between sickness, lying in bed and death. In the partial way memory works, he recalled vividly every time someone was put to bed and died, like his mother, while he forgot the far more frequent, though less dramatic times, of recoveries. For reasons he did not quite understand, the thought of Nichole's death, the mere thought of it, felt like a great stabbing pain in his heart, a potential devastation he would have trouble recovering from.

Nichole brushed back a dark blond lick of hair from his forehead, seeming to sense this. "I am feeling very well now. Do you know why I'm recovering so quickly?"

Gavin shook his head.

"Someone has been putting flowers at my bedside every day. These flowers have so brightened my spirits that my leg is much better and my blood is stronger." She realized as she spoke she did feel better, her weakness disappearing, replaced by the heaviness of lying about in bed for so long. "Why, Gavin . . ." She looked suddenly surprised as if it just occurred to her. "Don't tell me? 'Tis you who brings me these lovely flowers?"

Rosy color spread across his cheeks and he nodded, his mind stuck on the joyful idea she would be well again.

"Then I shall press a blossom between the covers of a great large book to keep it forever. Did I tell you ladies, Gavin is my defender? 'Twas Gavin here, who moved to save me on my darkest night. With more courage than Lancelot, he drew a baselord twice his size against the most fearsome knight in all Switzerland!"

"Oh, indeed!" Kira interrupted, unable to bear Gavin's obvious adoration a moment more. "The stories you spin. As if the boy doesn't have enough problems without getting a head full of notions about knighthood and vainglory deeds . . ."

Madeline reprimanded Kira sharply, not understanding at all what thorn pricked the girl's sense to say something so mean, even if it might be true. But Nichole listened not at all as she took young Gavin's gift from Bettrina, savoring the sweet scent of edelweiss. The last. 'Twould be winter soon . . .

Gavin had the maddening habit of rarely letting his gaze fall to people he did not like, and in this way he eliminated them from his world as effortlessly as closing a shutter on a cold draft. For all he cared, Kira might not be in the same room, yet he "saw" every word Nichole said and her praise set his young heart beating like the wings of a lark in flight.

". . . well, all his problems and here she is filling the boy's head with stories and giving him—"

"'Tisn't a story, Kira." Nichole finally thought to interrupt the argument. "Gavin did draw a baselord against the most fearsome knight in all of Switzerland, did you not?"

Gavin nodded vigorously.

"And what problems could you mean, Kira?" Before Kira could tell her, Nichole looked suddenly alarmed as if she guessed. "Oh my, don't tell me—you are off like so many other brave knights to meet the terrible three-headed Dragon of Navarre? No? Oh well, but you have heard of him, have you not?"

A shake of his head assured her he had not.

Then Gavin discovered something even more wonderful about Nichole, and that was she told the best stories. The ladies of the Lucerne court depended upon Nichole to get the children to bed at least two nights a week when they would all gather in the hall for the treat. Nichole had hundreds of stories to draw upon, too, but there were three or four favorites the children demanded to hear over and over again and one of them was the story of the terrible three-headed dragon of Navarre. The adults were hardly immune, either: Bettrina and Madeline soon found themselves listening as well, chairs were drawn up to the bed. No one noticed the door open and Kurtus and the two other guards hanging in the way, their cards forgotten despite the two guldens on the outcome. For it was a most fanciful tale of lost kingdoms and brave knights, princesses and dragons, and Nichole had no idea how well she told the story until finally—

"... the dragon saw he had lost the battle, and knowing he was about to be slain, he opened his great mouth in a mighty roar. Brave Galahad raised his sword, and with all his strength he sent it across the tooth made of jewels! His sword sliced it neatly in half, and as the dragon lifted into the air, thousands of diamonds, emeralds, pearls, and sapphires and rubies fell like raindrops to the ground."

Gavin clapped his hands with the others and Nichole laughed, finishing with, "And what do you think our good Galahad did with all those jewels?"

Gavin shrugged, knowing, of course, but unable to reply.

"I bet you can guess, can you not?"

Of course he could. Galahad brought the jewels to the king, who surely rewarded him with the fair princess's hand. He didn't understand why she was waiting for him to speak or why she was staring at him like that. Nichole's gaze shot suddenly to Bettrina. Gavin turned to see her speak.

"Oh, milady, young Gavin doesn't ever speak—he's dumb, you know. You didn't know? Oh, aye. The boy's deaf, too—"

With alarm, incomprehension, Nichole's gaze came back to Gavin, "What can you mean by that? You can hear me, can you not, Gavin?"

He shook his head.

"But then, how—"

"He can tell what is said by how lips move," Madeline supplied. "No one can reason how he does it. 'Tis a miracle, most suspect, a gift God gave him to make up for it."

Nichole could hardly believe it was possible. "Is it true, Gavin? You hear nothing of what is said?"

Gavin nodded, but Nichole could hardly believe this. How very strange! Nanna had made her read the book of Sidrach, the descendant of Noah to whom God gave the gift of universal knowledge, and in that great, large book, it is said the language of the deaf mute was Adam's, that of Hebrew. Clearly, this was not so for Gavin . . .

Seeing how carefully Gavin measured her response, though, Nichole, like the boy's father, pretended it was simply a small obstacle he had learned to overcome. "Why, Gavin Van de Birs, you must be the smartest boy in Switzerland then!"

Gavin knew not to agree with such praise, even if it was probably true. He shrugged as if to say, Ah, well . . .

"When did you fall deaf?"

"Oh, he was born that way," Madeline said.

"From birth," Bettrina said at the same time.

Nichole saw only Gavin now. It simply could not be true, otherwise he would know only Hebrew. "That's not true, is it, Gavin?"

Madeline shook her head, "Oh, but it is—" Madeline stopped, shocked when Gavin shook his head. Sensing something important here, Kurtus stepped quietly inside and said, "But that can't be true. I remember the first time milord realized it. 'Twas soon after the boy's mother died—bless her soul—and he was still in swaddling clothes."

"Did his mother die of influenza?"

"Why, yes—"

"Gavin, do you remember the last time you heard?"

He nodded.

"How old were you?"

He held up four fingers and the audience gasped. Four years old and he was— "How old are you now, Gavin, nine, ten?"

Nichole knew her boys and the idea that she thought him so much older brought pride swelling in Gavin's little chest, revealed in an irrepressible smile. He held up six fingers, though.

"Oh, you look far too strong and tall to be only six!"

Kurtus chuckled. So Jonpaul was not the only Van de Birs in love with the lady . . . his son was as well. Gavin, who never gave a woman a moment of his bright-eyed attention before, but then Kurtus did not know many men who could resist this lovely girl's charm.

Nichole paused a moment, trying to keep her disappointment from showing. Nanna had a miraculous potion for ear afflictions, but it would not work after so much time. It was two years since the last time Gavin had heard . . . the damage was no doubt irreversible by now. Still . . .

"Milady, how could you have known that?" Bettrina finally asked.

"Oh . . . those who have never heard words, those born deaf live in a world so vastly changed from us, they never learn any but the most fundamental means to communicate. And it is said that in their hearts they know Adam's language, Hebrew. Gavin is only six years old, but he understands everything that is said. He could only have gone deaf after he already understood the language—"

"That can't be." Madeline just couldn't believe this. "The boy was no more than a year and a half then and he didn't speak a word—"

"Children understand language long before they start speaking. No doubt he didn't lose his hearing until his mother's influenza settled in his ears, and it was off and on until then. Now I bet you were swimming when your hearing came back the last time, right?"

He shook his head.

"Climbing a mountain then?"

He nodded, pleased with how well she could guess things. His father and Kurtus had taken him on a long trip up Mount Zermatt, after which his father had named his war-horse . . . He looked to see Kurtus standing there. He made a triangle with his hands.

"Me?" Kurtus asked and then guessing, "Why, he must mean the trip up Zermatt. Jonpaul and I took the boy, but, oh God, I remember now. It seemed all of a sudden Gavin got excited about something. He jumped up and down and kept pulling on his father's shirt—"

"He wanted to tell his father what was happening," Nichole said, her voice marked with sympathy. "Was there a great popping in your ears?"

When he nodded, she said, "Oh, I bet that hurt a bit?"

He shook his head, shrugged. It was so exciting to hear his father's voice he never minded the pain.

"Gavin, do you still sometimes hear popping in your ears?"

He shook his head. That was the last time.

"What does it mean?" Kurtus asked.

Nichole did not tell him. If Nanna had lived her life at Dornach instead of Lucerne, she would have no doubt saved the boy's hearing. Now it was too late. Of course she would at least try the procedure—as difficult as it was to do, as difficult as the potion was to concoct. That is, she would have if she had her book of hours and her chest with her. She was at last truly Jonpaul's prisoner, a young lady who would be escaping in a day or two, and if God is merciful, a young lady who would never have to see this chamber or these people again, especially Gavin's father again—his father who was her forsworn enemy, a great warring man who slaughtered innocent people and preyed upon war to feed his greed.

Nichole looked up at the tapestry across the bed. The only thing more difficult to believe than the idea that the lord Jonpaul had anything to do with this most beautiful castle was that the wondrous young boy at her side had been made by his flesh. A strange sorrow washed over her and it came as a shock to feel a sadness from the idea she would not likely ever know Gavin better.

Chapter Nine

"If a man traveled twenty-five leagues a day without stopping, he would reach the stars in seven thousand one hundred fifty-seven and one half years." Father Ari stated the fact with authority, tutoring Gavin outside the doors to Jonpaul's chambers. Kurtus needed time off in the mornings and the only other person Jonpaul trusted to watch Nichole was himself, which Father Ari would not have minded at all if only the proximity to the lady Nichole wasn't have such a curious effect on his student. The boy's eyes wandered to the closed doors yet again and Father Ari sighed, wonder if it could possibly be the bath. The lady Nichole had ordered a bath and the great, large tub had been rolled inside and filled. While he himself was of an age to know the attraction of three women sitting chest-high in soapy, scented water, Gavin was only six—Gavin, who had wanted to know just last week why God ruined the world by making girls, too?

"Gavin . . ." Father Ari leaned forward to catch the boy's attention. "Gavin Van de Birs, am I wasting my precious breath? Pay attention or I'll switch to Latin verbs . . . All right then, as I was saying, if one sat upon a star—which would be impossible, for the stars must be hot like the sun in order to emit such light, so if one did not burst into a human pyre, one would surely burn their breeches . . ." Father Ari paused, chuckled, slapped his knee, then waited for Gavin to laugh. Waited in vain. Playing their ubiquitous cards nearby, Amherst and Frederick even chuckled, but not so Gavin. A ridiculous, dreamy look seemed permanently etched on his face, a look he was simply too young to have. "Well, if one did sit on a star, though—and one dropped a rock, 'twould take over a hundred years to land on the earth. There it is, the lesson for today: Never underestimate the power of a pretty maid on six-year-old boys . . . Very well, I am done. Deal me a hand, will you?"

Gavin ran out to fetch Nichole some fresh flowers and Kurtus joined them some time later. All went well until a playing card dropped to the floor from Father Ari's long green sleeve. An argument ensued, reaching near fever pitch as Amherst accused Father Ari of cheating and Father Ari maintained the errant card was no more than a good-luck charm. "Aye, it does look like a regular playing card, but I assure 'twas bought by my grandfather from a bishop in Avignon and for a pretty price, separated from the very playing cards used at the last supper."

Kurtus and Frederick nearly fell over with laughter, but Amherst, who was losing, growled, "Oh, aye, and the lucky card just happens to be a wild card?"

"One could hardly count on luck from a deuce? Even if it were touched by a disciple—"

The door suddenly opened, and with a walking stick in hand, favoring her good leg, Nichole stepped into the hall. Dressed in the mended and washed rich blue gown and cape, she looked like the very princess in the lively story she had spun, lovely and regal. And that hair! Drying now, the dark hair was plaited many times, each braid doubled into a shoulder-length loop around her head like an elaborate caul. Apparently she intended to go somewhere, which of course was impossible. With a smile, Kurtus went back to the dice game. "Not a chance, milady. Jon would have my head if I let you go running about Dornach."

"Make that two heads," Father Ari added.

Nichole straightened, raised her chin. Kurtus noted the sparkle in her eyes, but he had no idea what it meant until she said, "While I'm sure your heads bring you each a measure of comfort, however small, neither means anything to me. I want to be taken to the mother of the child whose life I saved. I think you owe me this."

Kurtus came slowly to his feet, looking maddeningly sincere when he asked, "Child . . . What child?"

"What child?" Nichole repeated, wide-eyed, incredulous, outraged. "Dare you ask me that? The cold-blooded callousness necessary to even pretend not to know what I'm talking about is enough to lift the hairs on a demon's neck!"

Kurtus looked at her as if she spoke another language, as confused as the half-dozen people watching. He glanced at Father Ari, who could always be counted on to explain the inexplicable, but that man only shrugged. "A thousand pardons, milady, but—"

"I am talking about the child you were going to murder to make me talk!"

"Oh, that child!"

He was smiling. She stared with disbelief. She felt she had entered another world—hell, perhaps. Created by people who were such brutal and vicious killers, they had lost all natural, human sentiment. An innocent child meant nothing to them, a mother and her children meant nothing to them, an entire village of unarmed innocent people meant nothing to them.

"God's own teeth but I had not a clue as to what you were talking about. Well, now you want to see that child again?"

She nodded, no longer trusting her voice to speak.

"Take her . . ." This was Father Ari, pretending to examine his cards.

"Jon would not—"

"Take her," Father Ari repeated louder as if it were only a question of making himself be heard. It would be best for everyone if they got it over. No doubt even the lady would be relieved to know the truth.

"Ah, well." Kurtus pointed his finger as if to emphasize his words. "I warn you, milady, you won't like it if I do. Just don't blame me, for Christ's sake."

She searched his face for meaning, seeing only the unnatural amusement. "What do you mean? Milord told me the child had been left unharmed."

"Oh, aye, not that . . . But, very well. If Milady wants to see the child, it's easy enough to arrange. Just step down the hall and to the stairs." He motioned with his arm. With a final, cold look, Nichole turned, and appearing remarkably unencumbered by her bad leg, she passed down the hall. Bettrina and Madeline exchanged confused, uncertain glances before following behind.

Kurtus led the way, passing down the hall, then down the wide staircase to the second landing. His gallant attempt to aid Nichole's passage met with a stone-cold glare. Sighing, he led the way through the brightly lit window-lined corridor. Nichole heard a maid singing in the courtyard below. Singing! The women here seemed to have no idea of the world they lived in, just as gay and sunshiny as you please—

Suddenly Kurtus stopped before massive double doors where two pages waited outside. Nichole watched with confusion as Kurtus spoke to one young man. "The lady Nichole would like to call on Lady Adline, if it's convenient to be received."

The boy run a bell rope, opened the door, and slipped inside. Kurtus turned back and offered her a huge smile.

"I don't understand?" Nichole asked. "What would a

milking maid be doing about the solar apartments?"

"I can't imagine," Kurtus said.

When he said no more she asked, "What are we doing here?"

"We are waiting to be admitted to Lord Bruno's chambers."

"But why? If you think I need that man's permission—"

The doors were thrown open and the page announced that the lady Adline would be happy to receive the lady Nichole. Kurtus swept his arm and confused, suspecting mendacious intent, Nichole swept into Lord Bruno's chambers.

She stopped in the doorway, staring into the sunny and spacious outer room. Three tall windows opened to the courtyard, where the maid's lovely voice lifted to fill the room with her melody again. Rich, elaborate carpets covered the marble floor where various children played: a little dark-haired girl with a doll and carriage, two boys with toy soldiers lined up on opposing sides, and a pretty, older girl, who sat alongside her mother with an illuminated manuscript on her lap, all in all the very picture of domesticity.

Upon seeing Nichole, Lady Adline rose to greet her. Nanna would have approved heartily, for the lady was large, enormous even. "Now Nichole, there goes a woman meant to bear and nourish children . . ." Lady Adline topped Nichole's fine stature by a good two inches and, while not fat, her tall frame was cushioned voluptuously from her head on down, volumes that seemed barely contained in the tight-fitting day dress of green, gold, and cream. She had fair, light-brown hair, prettily fixed around a round, animated face, and dark eyes, smiling now as if Nichole were a friend. "What a surprise!"

Nichole dropped a stiff, brief curtsey even as she

interrupted. "My pardons. There is a mistake here." Angry eyes turned to Kurtus. The wife of that beast Lord Bruno was the last person on earth she cared to visit and he knew that, she knew he knew that. "What is the meaning of this? Do you purposely mean to torment me?"

"Torment you?" He seemed quite shocked by the idea. "God's teeth but I'd rather slay the terrible dragon of Navarre!"

"Then I ask you what is the meaning of this?"

"Meaning of what, milady?"

"I asked to be brought to the child—"

"Aye."

"Well?"

The oldest girl, Jeanne, rose, disappearing into the adjoining room.

"Well what?" Kurtus asked.

"What am I doing here?"

"Why, you just articulated the point—you came to see the child."

"My child?" Lady Adline smiled, pleased with the idea.

Nichole began to suspect the man Kurtus was daft. In any case, she had enough of his senseless game and turned back to the confused lady. "Again my pardons. For some inexplicable reason—"

Nichole stopped midsentence as the older girl returned with a babe in arms. For a long moment she stared, knowing, but not. With confusion, a tingling of alarm, she stepped slowly to the smiling girl, who dropped her own curtsey. "My youngest brother, milady. Named after our lord Jonpaul . . . Would you?"

As if a bouquet of flowers, Jeanne offered the child up to Nichole, yet the pretty young lady—the one, Jeanne knew, that everyone was talking about—appeared quite shocked, frozen, it seemed, as she stared at the brother. Jeanne watched the rosy color draining from Nichole's face and though her mouth opened to speak, she didn't. Tongue-tied to boot. "Milady, is something amiss?"

Nichole's gaze snapped up to the girl with a look that could have turned Sodom to stone. Then she swung around, and to the shocked gasps of the women, she marched out of the room, so fast even with her stiff leg that no one could go after her.

Kurtus could not follow her, for he had some explaining to do, explaining that would cost him much. Lady Adline heard the story and remembered her husband had asked for their youngest boy to be brought to the great hall that night . . . She and Nichole had much in common. As Kurtus watched the lady's face redden with anger, he remembered Bruno saying, "Whoever said 'twas a man's world, does not know Adline. I'd rather fight a hundred warring men than my own dear wife—and I'll tell you this: I'd have a hell of a lot better odds of surviving a hundred warring men than that good lady . . ."

Once he had Adline properly worked up and outraged, he made his way back to Jonpaul's chambers, leaving a string of curses down the hall only to discover the women, guards, and Father Ari gathered around the great, wood doors.

Nichole had barricaded and bolted herself inside and would not now open them. Kurtus pounded on the door, deploring, "Open up, milady. Come now, aren't you glad to know that you are not among murderers of children?"

Nichole picked up an expensive porcelain vase—imported from Turkey—resting on the wood chest. With all her strength, she threw it against the door, shattering it into a million pieces.

"Oh, for God sakes! Listen, woman! Milord had to get that piece of information by any means he had, short of and I quote him now: 'harming so much as a hair on the lady's head!' Now all Lord Bruno did was use your own ridiculous opinion that the men of Dornach—men who have wives and children themselves, mind you!—were these murderers of women and children. By God, when you fainted Lord Bruno told Jonpaul that if he ever put him through something like that again—"

There was another crash and Kurtus jumped, then froze with alarm. "Oh, God, not his mechanical clock!"

Father Ari's thin brows rose. "Tsk, tsk." He shook his head and sighed, dismayed. "Ah, well, 'tis just a clock. Jonpaul is bound to get over it. Some year. The enormous and inexplicable pleasure he got from taking it apart and putting it back together . . . Well, he was bound to tire of that. Some year. After all, Princess Ann Marguerite gave it to him, did she not? And, Lord, we all know the fool he made of himself over that lady! Well, 'tis best forgotten, I say—"

"Ari . . ." Kurtus wondered if suicide might not be the best course, it certainly would be the most expedient—

The trumpet sounded outside. Kurtus heard it but didn't really, as for a long moment he refused to believe he had that kind of luck. "Oh, God, he will kill me. Milady, please. If you have any mercy in your heart, open this door—"

When the next object crashed against the door, Kurtus wisely saw to shut up and exit. He would toss the problem to Jonpaul himself and may God have mercy on her soul! "That's it. I give up." He turned away to greet Jonpaul in the courtyard, Father Ari falling in behind him. Bettrina and Madeline tried various means to gain entry to the chamber, but at last they, too, gave up as the sounds of excitement eventually lured them away.

It was the chanciest coincidence that kept Kurtus, Father Ari, the women, and servants from explaining the situation to Jonpaul for several hours more. This, Kurtus kept telling himself, had nothing to do with the unexpected success of their mission and plot and

Jonpaul's resulting exuberant mood. The men rode in, laughing, patting each other on the back, greeted with flowers by the women, children, and servants. More people arrived from the village to celebrate. Cups of sweet wine and cakes were passed around, and it took the scouting party nearly an hour to dismount and disband. Then it took another two hours for Jonpaul to dispense instructions to his household, to arbitrate the dispute between the local farmers and Basel city merchants over fall prices again; to tell the Naples representatives in no uncertain terms that no men from Basel or Dornach would leave for mercenary service at any price; to decline the invitations from the impatient envoy of the lord of Coucy and get the unpleasant man on his way back home and to give new orders to the masons. Finally he dismissed everyone and headed up the stairs to change for supper. "So," he said with an anticipatory grin, "you say she seems fully recovered?"

"Indeed," Kurtus said.

"Has she been a great lot of trouble?"

"To say the least."

Jonpaul laughed. "Ah, she is a wild thing for sure. Well, now that I'm back, I can set her free to go about—"

"I don't think she has a mind for going about just now—"

"Oh?" They turned down the hall and came upon Amherst and Frederick. Jonpaul gave his greetings before moving past them, missing their nervous exchange of looks with Kurtus. "Yet, if as you say she is recovered . . . ?"

Jonpaul went to lift the latch on the door only to discover it was bolted on the inside. He knocked. Nothing happened. He knocked louder. "Kurtus . . ."

"Since noon now. She wanted to see the . . . ah, child she saved. So I took her."

Jonpaul searched Kurtus's face, coming to all the right

conclusions. "What did Adline think?"

"That it would be a very long time before Bruno felt the comfort of his bed."

Jonpaul chuckled, then removed his baselord and slipped the blade in the crack between the two doors underneath the latch. He lifted it to the top and opened the door.

Kurtus braced. "I should warn you—"

Too late. Jonpaul's boots crunched broken glass and he looked down to see the remnants of his treasured mechanical clock among the other debris. His gaze lifted, then riveted to the culprit.

Nichole stood twenty short paces away in front of the tapestry and behind the large tub of water. Like Diana in the hunt, her hands and arms held a bow, armed with an arrow ready to fire into the dead center of his chest. Kurtus started in, took one look, and instantly ducked back out with the loudest stream of curses to ever sound in these halls. Curses that ended with, "Christ, it's got to be Gavin's!"

"Aye," Jonpaul said.

"Shut the door behind you, milord."

Jonpaul did, slowly, then leaned his great height against the doorframe, his hands behind him.

Nichole swallowed slowly, her heart suddenly hammering. The dark blond curls created a halo around the disarmingly handsome face, the barest suggestion of a smile making him seem all the more menacing. His tall frame was clad in loose-fitting beige breeches, a plain forest-green brigantine belted at his waist, and moccasin boots. The common clothes accented his uncommon strength and the viciousness of his fighting swam dizzily in her mind. A forest-green sweatband sliced across his prominent forehead, making his eyes seem darker. She felt his dark gaze holding hers, swallowing her down into their depths and she remembered Nanna saying, "Eyes are but looking glasses to the soul . . ." and "Evil has layers and layers of depths, its surface is always a deception . . ."

Dear Lord, how his eyes were like that!

A deeoy like his kisses. Kisses begun with a devastating prelude, a gently built crescendo that demanded and got her surrender before blossoming beneath a passion she never imagined, never could have imagined, an unholy passion that made her writhe and twist and cling to him, and never want him to stop—

Her next breath brought a hot swell in her chest and she felt the heat rising on her cheeks. How could he do this to her? When she knew! She knew all about his cleverness and deception! Just as he wore the two elks on his iron breastplates and belt buckle, the same elks carved into the door he leaned against, the elk horns seen throughout Dornach: the ancient symbol of the fecundity of life on earth, life protected by strength. He on the other hand, he did nothing but destroy!

"Tell me what happened?"

"Will you put that down?"

Despite the lively interest in his darkly green eyes, he seemed maddeningly unconcerned about the imminence of his death. She was sorry for this; she would like to see him suffer. "Only with your death."

"You will kill me now?"

"You are surprised, milord? You might have been bluffing with Lord Bruno's boy that night, you might even have been bluffing about knives and bleeding and things worse than death. You might have laughed yourself silly over my gullibility. But I assure you, milord, I am not bluffing you now."

He hardly listened. Only one sense was working, and it was visual. Her eyes were hot and wild and more beautiful than stars in a velvet night. And her hair, too, braided and looped like ropes, catching and reflecting the late-afternoon light streaming in through the windows, shimmering with each breath and slight movement as if each strand were an alive thing . . . Memories of their time together flooded his consciousness, laying the naked beauty of her unclad form to the ground and taking those lips beneath his—

With considerable, vexing effort, he tried to steer his mind back to the immediacy of the situation, the idea she meant to kill him. He could not be alone with her! There it was, and the idea both irritated and amused him . . .

"You deserve worse," she was saying, "but I am counting on hell to serve you just punishment. And even if Nanna is right and there is no such place, at the very least I will be saving countless lives from your treacherous hands."

He heard the melodramatic words but was pondering another question, as he wondered about her beauty and its effect on him. Beauty alone rarely shaped his desire, but her beauty paired with the rest of the package seemed to act like a tonic, altering the beat of his heart and changing the amount of oxygen his lungs needed . . .

"Did you hear me?"

"Oh, aye." He would not laugh, no matter what, he would not laugh at this. "Well, now," he tried to be reasonable about it, "you know the people of the Alliance would not take my death lightly?"

"Aye 'tis my death, too, I know. At least not in vain. I only pray that God forgives me."

To her surprise, this made him smile. She could tell he tried not to, which somehow made it worse . . . then even worse as he said, "'Twould be terrible indeed if we both suffered eternity together."

He might be joking but the idea alone made her pause. Surely God would understand. Like the maid Joan, she had to do this to save the innocent. Nanna believed hell was an illusory place imagined by religious men: hell, the underworld where the damned hung by their tongues from trees of fire, the impenitent burned in furnaces, unbelievers smothered in foul-smelling smoke—nothing but black waters of an abyss where people sank to a depth proportionate to their sins, the place of hideous eternal tortures where all men were naked, nameless, and forgotten. "Oh, Lord, child, they just made it all up. How else could they explain to the simple folks what life without God or the Goddess would be like? Aye, even Dante. Have ye ever met a single soul that lived above all the Christians sins . . . ? Neither have I and I tell ye this, too many people die for it to be that terrible . . ."

Still . . . To be there with him!

Tiny beads of moisture manifested on her brow, but she knew better than to linger over the question. She must get on with this. "What happened? The people were celebrating as if it were the Feast of Fools' Day?" The Feast of Fools was Nanna's favorite holiday, the one day before Christmas when everyone was allowed the wildest heresy, as all the people gathered in the streets to make fun of and parody the church. Her question, though, with all its worry, sounded like a plea. "Why?"

"There have been no more assassinations since your brother received my threat."

Those eyes frantically searched his face, trying to understand. "What assassinations?"

"I thought you would know. Your brother killed three of my men and said he would kill three each day I keep you."

The information was a shock to her he saw. She hadn't known and he would have preferred to keep it from her. The next long pause filled with her pain, broken at last with her whisper, "May God be merciful . . ."

She tried to tell herself that it was his fault and not hers but, somehow, in the queer way the mind measures and thinks of such things, she produced the tautological idea that three men would still live if she had not . . . "I am afraid to ask, with what did you threaten my brother? My own death? Did you tell him you would kill me?"

He shook his head. "Nay, love."

"What then?!"

"With a letter that said we had the paper, that you had given it to us and that we would use it if there was a single more death upon our borders."

For a moment he imagined tears filled her eyes as she searched his face to determine the truth of it, but the emotion changed to disbelief, then, with wind's speed, anger. Fury trembled through her and her face flushed as an arrow suddenly flew through the air. It hit the stone of the doorframe, a hand's space from his face, before dropping to the ground. By the time his gaze found her again, she had another arrow in place.

"You are lying! He'd never believe that. And he could not be blackmailed like that, I know he couldn't. Whatever the secret is, it cannot be so damning he would turn belly-up to you!"

Something dangerous came into his eyes as he paused to measure his response. He hadn't believed Bruno when he said Nichole truly didn't know what was written on the paper, but he saw now Bruno had been right after all. "You know, Nichole, until this moment I didn't believe you truly didn't know what the secret was. I see now you don't. You must wonder, though, do you not? What could be writ on a paper that could bring your brother to his knees?"

She had wondered, endlessly but to no end. She had no idea what it was, what it could even possibly be. "Whatever it is, I can rest assured you will never in fact get it. You will never be able to use it against him."

"I will have my hands on the Bible inside of a week."

Nichole's mouth pressed to a hard line, her anger returning in force. She didn't believe that, though so practiced in deceit was he that, he said it as if it were a fact . . . Something was wrong, for he was too calm. She wanted to look behind her but of course 'twas impossible that someone should be there. She had only to aim in the dead center of his chest between his breastplates and he would be quite dead . . .

"I am not stupid, milord."

"I would never accuse you of that," he said with feeling.

"Indeed? Even a simpleton could see that your hands could never touch the Bible, and for any number of reasons, foremost among them is that you will be quite dead before darkness sets in this room. You will be dead just as soon as you answer my question."

"Love . . ." he chuckled at the understatement. "You have my full attention."

"Before I ask, know your answer will not save you. You, milord, are doomed no matter what you say. There is nothing to gain by continuing your litany of lies. Is that understood?"

He nodded, the strangest light in his eyes, and somehow it made the bow waver in her hands. She quickly righted it. His nonchalance had to be a bluff, she was not duped. Inside he would be frightened. Just get on with it . . .

"I want to know, I want you to tell me . . . what you are . . . what you do. The people of Dornach, Basel, and the whole of the Alliance, these people are innocent. As innocent as lambs for the slaughter. They don't know you, do they?"

"Quite the contrary, I believe they know me well."

"A lie! They don't know you! There would be peace with Lucerne if not for your darkly evil raids on the borders, raids you do in the dark dead of night without anyone knowing. Even the lords of the Council, Lord Bruno and Wesmullar, they don't even know, do they?"

"I'd be interested to know what makes you think that?"

He saw it was the right question. She did not want to tell him. She bit her lip, a gesture of uncertainty, then cast her gaze momentarily to the side and looked suddenly confused, perhaps even frightened.

"I don't know," she confessed, but this was her own lie. She *did* know, and that was the problem. ". . . 'Tisn't here, this evil, the weight of it, the oppression it brings to people. Madeline and Bettrina, the servants, and even the man Kurtus, even him, they are all untouched by it. And then when I saw the lady Adline my intuition spoke so loudly, a great dizzying ringing in my ears and I know, I know she is a kind and decent woman. There is a light about her soul and she could not love her husband if he . . . if he participated in the destruction of Stan, even if she was ignorant of it."

He remained still, his gaze fixed and unwavering as he was remembering his mother's uncanny intuition, like Nichole's. The practitioners of the old religion used it as others use their sight. His mother's gift was so celebrated, she was often asked to mediate for the accused. One time a young man was accused of the raping and killing of a girl—an extremely rare crime in Switzerland, one that carried a penalty of death by torture. Everything pointed to this young man's guilt: the girl's blood was found on his clothes, he was the last to see her the night of her death, and a furious argument between the two over her rejection of his marriage proposal had been heard by a half-dozen different people. Yet his mother had only to walk into the high court to know he was innocent. "This man is innocent and wrongly accused, this I know. His execution would be the same crime you mean to revenge." That was enough for his uncle, and despite the protestations of some high-ranking people, he let the man go. Two weeks later there was another rape of a girl, and though she was badly hurt, she said a terrible demon haunting the forest had done it. Everyone assumed the girl was incoherent, suffering the ill effects of what had happened to her, until the search party found a mad Frenchman, crazed and deranged, living off roots, berries, and small wood creatures . . .

About his neck was the murdered girl's bloody shawl.

Remembering countless other incidents, Jonpaul guessed the rest and said softly, "There is more."

Nichole slowly shook her head.

"You intuition, love. What does it say about me?"

She shook her head, emotions changing her eyes as she cried, "That you are a danger to me! That your deception is so deep and so clever and so thorough, it deceives me! It deceives everyone. Your ungodly ambition for Lucerne makes you do these things in secret. Only I know the truth! No!" She instinctively jerked back as he stepped toward her. "Don't step to me—"

Yet he ignored her, certain she wouldn't . . . "Nichole—"

A swoosh sounded, and smack! The arrow hit dead center in chest, between the two breastplates. He swore as he caught the arrow at his chest and, "Jeezus, that hurt!"

Nichole went very still, save for the hard knocking of her heart. Her breath caught in her lungs, expelled in a sudden gasp of fear as she saw him holding the arrow that should have felled him and left him dead in a pool of blood. Then she shook her head, backing up as she imagined all manner of supernatural possessions to explain this phenomena.

"Dear God, you are possessed!"

He was rubbing the point on his chest, but seeing she apparently believed this made him burst into laughter, "Possessed only by a mad young lady bent on my murder.

That is, I believe, the second time you've tried to kill me."

"The third's the charm" was all she could think of to say as she hit the wall, pressed into the farthest corner of the room. He started toward her. She shook her head in abnegation of the sorcery just witnessed, and her eyes were wide with this fright until suddenly they dropped to the arrow in his hands.

"But . . . how—"

"About a year ago, Gavin, who's a fair hand at the sport, took to shooting apples off his friend's head. Well, thank God he never once missed until one day came a rival of his, an older boy who often uses his deafness for jests. Then suddenly my little tyrant put that boy's arm in a sling. The women of Dornach saw it as a warning, and though the men refused to alter the boy's arrows to humor a woman's fear, they soon found"—he chuckled—"just how cold an empty bed gets in the winter. Needless to say, the ploy did not take long to work. So now, until a boy is fourteen, he can only use arrows with points made of blunted acorns. Like this," and he held it up.

Nichole searched his face. "You knew the whole time . . ."

He nodded and, like her, said nothing. Words were meaningless suddenly and not because she was recovering from the certainty of witnessing murder or a heady, near violent relief that it didn't happen. The relief, swift, potent, intense, caused a piling of confusion. She couldn't think why she felt this surge of heady relief, but then she couldn't think at all, not when he stood before her and reached a long arm to the wall behind as he stared down. She felt a heightening awareness of everything, and all at once: how very near he stood, and the warmth this brought her was as if she just drew against a raging fire on a winter's day, an awareness of the clean, masculine scent of him, a scent made of musky spices and horses and hard-worked leather. She was aware most of all of how alone they were and the effect of this: the slow, hard thumps of her heart, a tightening knot in her stomach, and sudden breathlessness, a telling rush of color to her cheeks.

The arrow dropped unnoticed to the floor. A handsome smile illuminated the emotion in his eyes and told her he was fully aware of the piling of sensation his nearness brought her, that this amused him. His free hand came to her face where he traced a light line around her cheek.

"If you kiss me, I'll die."

The melodrama made him chuckle. "An empirical proposition," he said, and the rich deep voice lowered. "You know what empirical questions call for, do you not?"

She found it impossible to answer. Impossible when his finger toyed with the nape of her neck, moving in feather-light strokes up to the sensitive spot behind her ear. Hot shivers raced up her spine. Impossible when the heat of his gaze penetrated the velvet of her gown to alight on her skin.

Frightened, she suddenly ducked under his arm. He was ever quick. The iron bar of his arm lowered like a guillotine before slipping around her waist and pulling her against him.

Each and every nerve in her body greeted this intimate contact with a thing best described by its opposite, chastity. She started to push away, but, he gently pulled her even closer.

The pulse in her throat jumped furiously as blood rushed to her head. She felt pinpricks of pleasure erupting from every place his hard body aligned with hers, an embarrassing tightening of the tips of her breasts where they pressed beneath the hard muscle of his chest, drawing tight against the constraints of cloth. Her fear expanded like a cloud on the horizon to fill all of her . . . but for all of it, she could not move.

Once, when she was a little girl, Nanna had made her watch the mesmerizing effects of a snake's gaze on a tiny, winged creature. "Be warned," she had said. "There will be a man in your life who can do that to you . . ." And here he was at last. She was trapped by the mesmerizing effect of his eyes, the fires of the passion there. It kept her still and unmoving, even as he said with warmth and humor, "Let me kiss you, Nichole . . ." His lips brushed her forehead and he closed his eyes, teased by the faint lavender scent in her hair, "and afterward you can tell me it was worse than dying."

He lowered his head, brushing his lips against hers with an unhurried, gentle tease and she gasped. Then his hand tilted her chin slightly, and as if indeed it were a test, he pressed his warm breath and moist lips to first her neck, then along a tender curve to her ear until he heard another small gasp, felt the tremble of shivers and knew her pulse raced nearly as fast as his.

He pressed the advantage. His lips came to hers with the gentlest pressure and, Dear lord, she tasted like late-summer strawberries, sweeter than life itself. He tilted her head back even farther and widened his lips like a man dying of thirst as his tongue delved into the incredibly sweet moistness. He groaned deep in his throat, the sound dying in their joined mouths. His hands slipped up and down the slender curves of her back, teased to distraction by the cloth, wanting to see, feel, taste her bare flesh against his—

The kiss broke so he could look to see where her raised knee was repeatedly trying to aim for a higher point, but was fortunately hindered by her skirts. A frantic pounding sounded from the door as well, Kurtus cursing in the hall. She was breathing fast and furious. His gaze fixed on her upturned face, though, and he studied the confused mix of emotions there: fear and fury and an unmistakable flush of desire. With sympathy, he said, "Remind me to teach you how best to ward off a man's attack."

"I'll show you the trick on my own!"

That made him laugh and, dear Lord, how laughter changed his face. "Why, my beautiful young lady, dare I hope for some more practice sessions? No? Then let's take care that we don't find ourselves alone again? Hmm?"

Those forest-green eyes sparkled suddenly with mischief and she stared aghast. The way he said that it was as if it were her doing! The idea that he believed this chased away her fear, leaving only anger in her eyes. Too late, he didn't notice as he went to the door to answer Kurtus's frantic pounding. He opened it and Kurtus stumbled in the room, barely catching his fall over broken glass.

"Jeezus! I was just about to break down the door—"

"It is a good thing you didn't. It seems these rooms are too small for the both of us. Escort the lady to new chambers on the east side."

A hand went to her throat and she suddenly could not breathe, her head spinning like a child's top over everything he had said. Sick with the sudden idea it was true, she rushed to him, grabbing his brigantine as if needing even more than his full attention. "Jonpaul, you said the Bible . . . You said . . . How could you get it?"

"Perhaps I can't. We shall soon see." He only wanted her out of here now. His body had yet to realize the changed circumstances, and it was hard enough without her reaching to him, the lavender scent driving him to distraction . . .

He could tell she didn't believe him, which mattered not at all. At last she lifted her skirts and turned away.

Kurtus opened the door, but then she stopped in the way and without turning asked, "Tell me what you think it is?"

"Why, there is only one thing it could be: a legal document that disputes Charles's rightful inheritance to the realm of Lucerne."

With her back to him, she stood for a long moment in the doorway. Then, with the slightest tremble set to her hand on the doorframe, she disappeared. Her thoughts rushed fast and furious as her feet carried her quickly away. He could not get the Bible, he could not. 'Twas a bluff he made, his entire being was made of tightly spun deceptions and the horror of it lay in the fact that she alone seemed to know this.

Charles was desperate to get her back! She herself was even more desperate to get back, desperate to tell him she never had that paper. And the lord Jonpaul surely doesn't have it! She had to escape, just get past all these guards at the gates and on the battlements and walk-wall . . . All she needed was a veil of dark and a good long rope . . .

Gavin left to watch the armorers in back and Nichole graced the large, kindly man Peters with her full attention as he pointed out the various weapons kept in perfect working order in the storage room in back.

Peters was confused but pleased with the lady's interest. No lady he knew showed the slightest interest in the smithy, not even his good wife—least of all his good wife, he smiled as he wiped the sweat from his brow. The great fire leaped and grew in the unhooded stone circle, fanned by an enormous bellows, and it was hot. The smithy was a place where rivers of perspiration fell from a man's frame as the fire had to reach temperatures that would melt the metals used to mend and make bolts, arrows, helmets and swords, cooking utensils—all the necessary metal repairs of Dornach.

"Our smithy is not so big!"

Pride made him smile at her, indeed, he could not help it. She was a comely maid, for sure, especially with the fire putting a pretty blush to those cheeks—

"And you shod all the horses of Dornach?"

"Just the castle, milady. There be two smithies in the township."

"What about the horses out in pasture? Are they kept shod, too?"

"Oh, aye. Never know when one might be needin' them."

To this Nichole agreed. "Indeed. One never knows. Tell me how many armors do you employ here?"

"Two, except on Fridays, like today. Today I have three to repair the chain mail . . . which," he looked to the back where the men were working, "I better check on. A moment—"

"Oh, by all means."

"Have a look around if you want," Peters called back.

Nichole did. Fully recovered now, she was ready. The macramé rope snapped with her weight; she needed a real one. By the time the kindly Peters returned with Gavin moments later, she protested that they simply could not interrupt his work any longer and bid him goodbye. As her hands were occupied beneath her cloak, she could not take Gavin's hand. The boy hardly minded as he rushed to join his friends in the game of stone-throwing popular among the boys of Lucerne, too. Nichole returned to her chambers, having seen all of Dornach she ever cared to . . .

Nights had fallen into a predictable pattern. Tonight was no different. Bettrina left to be with her husband at night. Madeline slept with her in her new chambers, a lovely, airy room with two tall windows overlooking the courtyard from one story above . . . Only Madeline never slept at night, or rarely. As soon as Nichole retired, Madeline slipped out the door to join the two guards at her door in their card and chess games, their cups of ale and laughter.

Darkness swept the room where Nichole sat on the bedside. She had asked Madeline not to make a fire, claiming to be too hot beneath the thick goose-feather comforter, that she kept waking each night hot and perspiring . . . which was true enough—only the heat had nothing to do with the comforter and everything to do with these terrible dreams of Jonpaul that plagued her sleep—dreams not of his terror or strength, not of the iron hand with which he held her, but of his passions that dark night in the cave—

No, don't think of it—

She tried to concentrate on the surroundings, the danger waiting ahead. The room was dark without a fire. Outside she heard Madeline chiding the luckless turn of the cards' touch. The bedcloth was fine, finer than any used for bedding at Lucerne. It ripped effortlessly in her hands, neatly shredding into nice long strips, but she suddenly stopped her work, thinking on it and wanting to stop but—

Too late. The memory of last night's dream was suddenly, maddeningly there, of his tongue leaving the sensitive points of her breast to circle her belly, and circle and circle until the hot budding swell of her sex made her cry for him, and she heard his laughter, laughter that made her bolt awake. Hot and feverish she confronted first the empty, dark room, then her body's altered state. Breathless, she reached between her thighs to ease the discomfort and—

There were apparently many things Nanna had neglected to tell her: like just how to get rid of that dark need. For instead of easing her discomfort, she had made it even worse and worse, and even now if she but thought of it, a curious tingling, then tension, sprang there. She twisted uncomfortably, and with sudden renewed vigor, she tore the sheet to the end. And again and again until it was in shreds . . .

Shreds she quickly tied into knots.

Once done she quietly rose. Bettrina had got her a pretty day dress of a soft forest-green cotton. The dress had long winter sleeves and a low bodice, and an embroidered flower apron went with it. She had protested the kindness but the woman had insisted and she was glad. For her blue velvet gown was too good to be worn for every day.

With excitement now, Nichole dropped her night-dress, and with only the brief, scanty undergarments, no bindings, she pulled the dress over her head. She hurriedly laced the front, not bothering with the apron, before gathering up her cloak, the neat coil of rope under her bed—which she hung over her shoulders—and then the long, tied strips of sheets.

The only way out was over the battlements. She might try leaving directly through the gates, but something about the efficiency of Dornach and her people told her Jonpaul's guards, unlike most others, could not be counted on to pass their watch in sleep. The battlements were different, for the guards were posted there to watch the routes leading to Basel, and as no one traveled at night, they had nothing to watch. They would surely be with cards or dreams, and even if they weren't, 'twas a moonless night and darkness would make her invisible.

She tied one end of the sheet tight to the bedpost, the other end she swiftly knotted around her waist. Several minutes passed as she tested the strength of the knots before she stepped to the window and pushed it out. The courtyard was deserted, nothing but dark shadows and hushed quiet. Even the courtyard chickens roosted. The distance was a good twenty feet, and her fear upon judging it spoke ill of the next drop from the much higher walk-wall. How much easier it would be if she could slip past the guards at her door to climb the three flights of the solar that led directly to the walk-wall, but at last that was impossible . . .

Courage made her swallow her fear. She climbed onto the windowseat and turned around. Back first and bent, she eased her form out the window. Not looking down for her life, her gaze focused on the rope of sheets in her hands as, with her heart hammering, she slowly eased her weight onto the rope until she felt the taut pull. Step by step she lowered herself. The small black boots kept part of her weight on the crevices of the large stones that made up the solar. Her hands were squeezed tight on the sheets, and with heightened senses, she listened for a rip . . .

The ground came as a surprise, a happy surprise. Breathless, she tried to unknot the sheet at her waist.

Oh, curse the blasted tremble!

She clasped her hands together in frustration. The strain of her weight had tightened the knot and she could not untie it, trembling like a leaf caught in wind. She bent for her anlace, slicing it in two, then cutting the belt it made at her waist. She never paused, for the time clock started running. How long before someone, anyone noticed the long white rope hanging from her window? She could not guess, but surely not long . . . Not long. She needed at least an hour to get over the battlement and catch a horse, and at least that much to get a good deal more than a head start over the pack of wolves he'd put on her trail . . .

With any luck!

Nichole raced across the courtyard. The walk-wall completely surrounded Dornach. Stairs led up to any of the nine towers, but these stairs were inside various buildings: the great hall and solar, the kitchen, the smithy, the piggery, the stables and chapel. She could not risk entering any of these. The only open staircase was behind the smithy across the yard and this staircase would not lead up to the shortest point on the wall, thankfully not the highest—that would be over a hundred foot drop!—but regretfully not the shortest, either.

Nichole reached the tall staircase, and with a furtive glance behind her, she raced up. She slowed at the top, trying to hear over the pounding of her heart and gasp of her breaths. No sounds came to her. Then—

Distant voices sounded to the left. The sound came from a quarter away around the wall-walk, at a place overlooking the hill leading down to the valley and the roads and the township. Far enough away, indeed. Cautiously she climbed the last stairs and reached the battlements, peering over. A forty-foot drop. As near as she could guess, the rope was thirty feet. Maybe more. A ten-foot drop was nothing for a girl who had spent much childhood time climbing many hundred of trees, she tried to tell herself . . .

Maps spread across the great hall's long table. Jonpaul pointed to each marked spot on the southwest pass through the Italian Alps where he planned to build the trade posts to facilitate the growing trade between the Italian states and Basel. The Basel merchants who gathered around him were not just impressed but excited. Trade would double if they could assure safe passage through those treacherous mountains, triple if all the posts were built . . .

"Milord, when could these be finished?"

"By summer's end for sure. Perhaps sooner. Sooner still if I could spare the extra men patroling for that cursed band of robbers at our throats—"

The door opened suddenly and the captain of his guards, Holbien, entered unannounced. The man was smiling. "Pardon, milord, but you asked to be informed—"

"Aye. Now?"

"As I speak. Though I fear we were a little late . . ."

Nichole forgot the rest of the miserere. The rope cut into her waist and her arms ached. Frantic eyes looked back down. Not ten feet but a good fifteen, more if she faced the truth. She couldn't; the truth would make her scream for the guards. She might not hurt herself, there was a chance. She had no choice. Now! Just do it—

She would, she swore she would, if only there were not those large rocks and small boulders littering the dark ground below. If she hit one of those rocks—

No, don't think of that.

She closed her eyes. Gasping for breath, panicked, she let go of her right hand to take the anlace from her mouth where she held it by the handle. Thinking of Charles and freedom and all the reasons she had to do this thing, she put the knife to the rope.

Muscle spasms in her other arm made her release the rope and she cried as the rope at her waist caught her full weight and her body swung into the wall . . . not hard but enough to hurt. Small beads of perspiration laced her brow and it hurt . . . it hurt so badly . . .

Probably not nearly as much as when she finally cut the rope and dropped fifteen . . . *No, for God's sake do not think of it. Just do it!* With a hot rush of panic, she put the knife to the rope—

There was a sudden jerk.

For one wild moment she imagined herself falling, then, "No . . . no," she cried as a guard pulled her swiftly up. Caught! A guard had caught her! Wild with more fright she looked up thirty feet to try to see, but the guard stood on the other side of the four-foot-thick wall at top. For one wild moment she flirted with the idea of cutting the rope still, but up and up, she was halfway up now and even if by some miracle she survived the fall, she could not get far now—

She grabbed her anlace tight. If it be but one man she had a chance still. The rope felt as it were to break her in two at the waist as he pulled her up too quickly, too quickly for one man! Tense, scared, a final, hard tug brought her over the top and with a breathless gasp of surprise . . . "Jonpaul!"

"Nichole!" He mimicked her surprise as he reached under her arms and rather effortlessly lifted her over the wall to sit there on the wide ledge between two battlements and why oh why, Nichole had to wonder, would she prefer to face the perils of a forty-foot drop to the rocky ground than the laughter in those eyes staring down at her?

"Kurtus is right. Fishing is a fruitful pastime!" There was no response and he watched for a moment, seeing the shivers tremble through her. "Are you chilled or just frightened?"

Her heart hammered so hard she could not for her life speak. He unclasped his fur-lined cloak, swung it from his shoulders, and placed it around hers. "Frightened I see. For good reason, too. Had you thought of it at all, love," he now warned when this was not necessary, "you would have known that a broken neck on my wall would have only been the beginning of your problems."

She hardly heard. The warning was inconsequential after just surviving the terrible fall to her death. Her blood still pounded wildly with the terror of hanging twenty feet over her death. "But . . . but how did you know to look?"

She meant it as a rhetorical question, an expression of disbelief, but he said, "My man Peters is ever scrupulous about missing weapons and ropes, though he naturally accused Gavin. Luckily I can always count on my boy's honesty, and then I had only to wonder who at Dornach might want to steal a rope. The guards had wagers on who could spot you first and my mistake was the assumption they would spot you before your foolish hide ever came close to dropping over this wall . . . and so help me God, girl, if you ever pull a brainless stunt like this again I will personally turn your backside over my knee and beat you sound—"

"Beat me? As if I'd submit!"

Jonpaul stared at the sharp point of her anlace at his throat. Like the strike of a snake his hand caught hers. She gasped in pain as he held it. Remembering the last time he felt this knife, a bemused look came to his eyes. The memory was not in any way associated with anything unpleasant. Still, he pried it from her tense fingers, his hand large and warm over hers. Still holding her one hand tight, he tossed the anlace over the battlement some goodly fifty paces into the forest.

She went rigid, alarmed by the danger shining in the dark eyes as he stood suddenly close. His nearness was a threat, one she felt fully in the whole of her being as he brought her hand behind her back, a move that forced her close and stopped her instinctive withdrawal.

"You little fool. I would have sworn you might remember the consequence of fighting me from the last time. A man subdues a woman in a timeless way, love, and unless you want to find yourself backside to the ground with my full attention, you will stop pitting yourself against my will."

"Never! Never! Not until your bones are ashes and your deeds are but distant memories of horror—"

It was as far as she got. Quicker than she could even start to regret the perversity of her rebellion, his knife manifested in the air, and for one wild moment she imagined her throat feeling its point. With swift assurance he sliced the rope at her waist, and before she grasped his intentions, he lifted her to the air and, like a time before, threw her over his shoulder. Deaf to wild cries of protest and indignation, he turned to the stairs.

Jonpaul stopped but briefly at the place his guards watched, and shouted over the idiotic litany of her threats, "Fetch the rope and keep two men on the northwest wall. If they ride tonight, it should be from the west."

Nichole cried with rage, helpless and maddened by it, the idea that he would stop to pass instructions when she was vowing to kill him. It seemed so unfair! She went wild with it as he carried her swiftly down the stairs and through the courtyard . . .

The doors to the great hall stood open. The men gathered there stopped the conversation as they suddenly heard, "I swear I will kill you! You'll never be able to stop me. I hate you . . . I hate you—" and on and on, fading as Jonpaul brought his baggage up the staircase to the third floor, down the hall and through his chamber's door.

With the small, tight fists still pounding on his back, he stopped to shut the doors. The slam silenced and alerted her. She went suddenly still just seconds before he marched to the bed and dropped her unceremoniously on her back. Then he leaned over her and braced his weight on his long arms, positioned on either side of her head. He did not touch her, he did not have to, not with the very devil in his eyes as he feasted on her sudden fear at last, the alarm in her wide blue eyes, and the outline of the curves he knew so well from dreams, but only once in fact.

"Provoke me now, Nichole. I will welcome it."

He would, she had no doubt he would. Or no doubt a raping would kill her. The threat made her face squarely the terrifying fact that she stupidly, senselessly, was provoking him, that something about him, everything about him, made her do this. Yet she could not fight him and win . . .

The weight of her helplessness appeared in a transparent veil in her eyes, though her lingering courage forced her to meet his gaze squarely. The surrender of will came in a silent shake of her head, one of the hardest things she ever did.

Jonpaul had an idea of how hard the concession was for her, almost as hard as his. "I will not warn you again." He straightened. "Leave me." In a compelling whisper, "Quickly, love."

Quickly, silently, she complied.

Chapter Ten

Tension distorted the weathered, wet faces of the sisters at the levee where they worked frantically in knee-high mud to build the dike. In sympathy for the impossible task, a half-dozen townsmen and some of their sons came out to aid the effort to stop the river from flooding their hard-worked fields. Having began early in the season, the rain fell unceasingly in torrents for three days now. There was no respite in sight. The sky appeared like a starless night, darker than gray by shades and full of Thor's own thunder, lightning, and a howling chilly winter wind.

Katrina's hands were raw, red and bleeding, save for her terrible marked finger. That never changed or altered or slowed its continuous feeding of rage into her body, a substance so powerful it kept her immune to the bone-deep weariness, the back-breaking aches and pain, a chill that went deeper than flesh. The other sisters managed by fear—fear of the heavy hand of doom, the end of the world marked by the imminence of Judgment Day at last.

It had happened some three hours ago. Lightning had struck an enormous tree some twenty paces away from the levee. The green steeple burst into flames that eerily, briefly, lit the world in unnatural colors of red and orange. The sisters who could, screamed, then all of them had fallen to their knees in a litany of wails and prayers at the ominous portent of doom. Everyone had briefly returned to the warmth of the rectory for a last confession, so as not to die in a state of sin, before returning to this levee. Though normally few of the sisters were ascetic—those practicing exaggerated piety by mortifying the flesh—Katrina had seen more than one of the sisters kneel down and pick up pebbles, placing these sharp little rocks in their boots as if the mud, rain, chill, and back-breaking labor was not enough self-abasement to assure God of their contempt for the worldly sphere.

The felled tree still sizzled and smoldered nearby.

The sound of horses' hooves in the distance brought Katrina's eyes up briefly to see the half-dozen riders galloping toward the gates of St. Gallen through the sheet of rain. Thick wool cloaks draped over man and beast alike, hiding their colors. She returned to her work. A familiar tingling along her spine, like an extra sense, brought her eyes back up. She came slowly to her feet, shielding her eyes from the rain to see, before she suddenly broke from the dark-clothed group to run to the fallen tree in order to watch the riders as they passed.

A squire rode ahead with the banner she knew so well: the Lucerne colors. Her gaze riveted anxiously to the man behind the banner. It was him! It was Charles! Charles . . . her mind screamed the name as an invocation, a desperate prayer—Charles!

On the flailing hooves of a roan-colored stallion, Charles the Bold raced toward the place she stood. Katrina's heart stopped and she did not breathe, for a long moment she did not breathe. It was only the blink of an eye. As the stallion and rider passed, the man turned his head, briefly taking in the dark-clothed woman standing near the still-smoking tree, drenched, hands clasped in prayer or plea or both. For a brief moment she saw the recognition in his eyes. Then it was gone, his gaze as dark and empty as hollowed holes to hell. Mud splattered on the cloth of her skirt as the riders passed.

The weight of the past sunk Katrina to her knees and she raised her eyes to the sky where they said God was. For a long time rain washed her tears into the wet, muddied ground where they might never have existed at all.

Grooms rushed out in the rain as the riders galloped into the courtyard. Charles dismounted and shouted orders, even as he made his way up the stone staircase to the forebuilding, his men rushing behind to keep up. Commanding vitality and energy, more with the deadly fury seizing the whole of him, he threw his sopping-wet cloak at a waiting woman, shouting for warm ale to be brought to him and his men, a table set, and, "Now," he said, gloved hands on hips, "Where are you, Kuno? I fear I need you badly . . ."

Morning light filtered in through the window alcove in Nichole's room where she sat on a stool, a writing block on her lap, a quill in hand, and the ink jar on the window seat as she furiously scrawled letters to home. He said he would send them after he read them. So be it. She had no means of protest, just as she had no escape. At least for now. Surely, if she were trapped at Dornach for a year the means to escape would someday present itself, but for now she had nothing as far as escape went but—

Charles would not let her perish here, he would not! Somehow he would find a way to get her back. No matter what she did or how she threatened him, he would not abandon her to Jonpaul. He had already tried, after all, the desperateness of that measure presented the proof, the absolute certainty that he still loved her, that he would go to any lengths to get her back. Of this she felt certain . . .

Yet how long would it take?

For even now homesickness sat like a weight in her heart. She missed her women and all the other ladies. She especially missed the children. Each face seemed suddenly dear to her. She missed her creatures, especially Tardian, and she missed, so strangely, her things: the peace of her familiar chambers, the window overlooking the lake where she often sat to watch the changing seasons of color. She missed her trunk, her book of hours, and all her instruments and alchemy. She missed everything . . .

A commotion sounded in the courtyard. She set her block aside and stood up to look out. Unfamiliar men rode in on horseback. Chickens flew in desperation to escape the galloping hooves. A fat sow scrambled away with indignant grunts. Nanna had taught her the trick of seeing into the creature's mind, of viewing the world from their small, dark eyes. These tricks were as enlightening and helpful as they were fun and over time she became better at it even than Nanna. That fat pig's distress was the result of her belly, heavy with a late-season litter . . .

A wagon followed the men, its cargo covered by rain canvases. She saw Gavin and the other children running to greet the party. Children . . .

The children of Dornach, each with happy, carefree hearts, quick to games and quicker to laugh. Like the children of the Lucerne. If the children of Lucerne met the children of Dornach a-picknicking, there would be no result but the joining of their laughter and games whereas if the men met, the result would be bloodshed and war, and why? At what point did they change and why did they have to?

Once Nanna had pointed out a simpleton by the roadway, and in response to her expression of sympathy, Nanna had said, "Save yer sentiments for some soul that needs it, girl, for that is the luckiest one in all Lucerne—the simple folks alone will never lose their child's heart . . ."

" 'Tis so true, Nanna," she murmured out loud.

The thought lifted her melancholy mood as it led her to him. 'Twas all his terrible fault! There would be no war if not for the reach of his ungodly greed. If only she could find proof! She was absolutely convinced that the lords Bruno and Wesmullar had no idea of Jonpaul's terrible ambition, of his darkly evil raids on the borders that made it appear her brother threatened the Alliance, all to foster the people's hatred in preparation of war. If only she could explain this to her brother and the Council, that it was not the Alliance but only one man. One man only!

The commotion came to her door and, startled, she turned to the door. Bettrina flew inside, took one look, and pushed the door open farther. A wide smile sat on her young face as guards lifted something into her room. "Oh, my . . . your trunk!"

Nichole froze, just froze, staring at the impossible as it was set beneath her bed. Dark-blue eyes shot up where two other men brought in another familiar trunk, her clothes trunk. Kurtus and Madeline bounced sprightly into the room.

"Here you go, milady!" Kurtus waved an arm, "Compliments of my lord Jonpaul."

Bettrina was excitedly exclaiming the fortune, anxious to see Nichole's gowns and stopping just short of opening the trunks herself.

Nichole could not move, she did not dare to move as her mind raced over the implications. Somehow the lord Jonpaul had got her trunks. Somehow his men had gained entry to the Castle of the Lower Lake to steal her trunks. How? There would be dozens of guards and people and—

She abruptly rushed to her trinket trunk and lifted the lid. Inside were all things dear to her: her smaller chest of four rows of silver containers of various sizes, each filled with rare and hard-to-find herbs and medicines, marked in the familiar black, Greek symbols. There were a dozen tools, small and large, all polished silver, too: her roller, incision knives, pocket instruments, crooked and straight needles, pins, then bandages, tape, thread, her lucky honing stone . . .

She reached to part the lining of the trunk lid. Inside was the most important thing she owned, her treasured Book of Hours lying on top of Nanna's book. Like Nanna's blue book, her green velvet book, four inches thick, contained the recipes of every potion Nanna had known and the method of every operation Nanna had taught her. She held it against her chest as she tried to reason it through. It was impossible! Unless . . .

Unless he had spies within the ranks of the Lucerne guard. Why, he must . . . But who? The familiar faces of dozens of men raced through her mind but none could possibly be traitors . . .

"The Bible!" She turned to Kurtus. "If he got my trunks, he must have gotten the Bible, too!"

"I wouldn't know about that, milady," he lied.

Seeing the lie, she searched his face. Kurtus was ever clever. "Where is he?"

"In the stables with the others."

Nichole flew from the room.

"But your gowns! You didn't even open . . ."

Jonpaul gathered around the stall with the other men where Sorro treated Bregenz, Bruno's stallion. A scowl appeared on his face as the small, dark man began the incantation. A worthless song, he knew, sung for show just like every other worthless remedy of his kind. And this man was not just any surgeon, either, but reputed to be the very best in all of the Alliance. His type did not normally condescend to treat the horse, but he did so now as a special favor to Bruno—a very expensive special favor.

He could not blame Bruno. God knows if Zermatt took sick, he, too, would no doubt find himself courting the surgeons. Again. This despite the wealth of his experience with these tricksters. Not long ago he had courted every surgeon between France and Austria, paying outrageous sums for their bags of poor tricks: the vile poisons and bloodletting and leeching and empty useless charts, and he might still be paying them, too, had not that dream warned him of the danger.

Bless you, Lisollette . . .

Finally finishing the chant, Sorro turned to Bruno to explain the astrological chart. Jonpaul turned away in disgust only then to see who stood in the wide-open doors. The daylight shone behind her, outlining her form with an otherworldly light—a light that contradicted his every feeling for the girl; for while these feelings were many and intense, they were definitely in the earthly realm. She spotted him and came quickly forward, and with a curse and a chuckle, the arresting fact presented itself again: He could not even look at the girl without a jolt of hard, hot desire . . .

A serious intent showed in her eyes as she came before him. He looked disarmingly casual standing there, leaning against the fence post, twirling a long piece of straw in his mouth. He wore suede breeches and tall suede boots, a sleveless tunic, a thick black belt from which hung a hunting knife and a halbert. As innocent as Judas. The halbert reminded her of the battle she had seen which brought animosity into her tone as she forswore the necessity of a greeting and came right to the point. "I need to know if you got the Bible, too?"

"What Bible, love?"

With amusement he watched her small fists clench the folds of the plain green day dress tight, her effort to control her anger. Normally she did not meet his gaze for any length of time, he knew, as if she understood the danger, that she might, if she looked long enough, see the truth there, but not now. Those blue eyes shimmered with antipathy as they met him squarely.

So he would not tell her. Like Kurtus. Perhaps another tactic. "I see. Perhaps then you might explain how you got my trunks? Do you have spies, milord?"

"Spies, love?"

"I think you must and, still, I just don't see how 'twas done?"

"Do you honestly believe my men are so brave that they might risk their lives to sneak two trunks past an army of guards and God knows how many servants? And for nothing more than to give a girl some pretty rags?"

"But then how—"

"I only asked for them. I sent a note some time ago." Incredulousness changed her face and he watched her struggle to believe this. "Why, love, you don't think your brother would deny you the simple comfort of your possessions, do you?"

"Well I—" She stopped, trying to reason it through. Of course her brother would not deny her the trunks, unless it meant cooperating with Jonpaul—cooperating for anything, but then . . . then he must have! Spies or no, as he said 'twould be impossible to sneak from an army of guards. "Then that means you don't have the Bible after all!"

A maddening grin spread over his face. "What Bible, love?"

Using all her strength, she managed to refrain from slapping the grin from his face and only because the memory of that terrible night was still fresh in her mind.

"You have been twice warned . . ." Still, she stared for a long moment before her gaze dropped to the halbert hanging from his belt. She had witnessed his battle skills, a miracle she would not have believed had she not seen it with her own eyes. Nanna's warning never to underestimate the very best of the warriors came to her mind. He was clever, cleverer than anyone she had ever met, and when she thought of the extent of his deceptions—

She met his eyes again. He was just too cocksure! She could not take the chance. If he had gotten the Bible, then she would find it. She'd start the search tonight.

Once settled, she started to turn away but stopped, noticing the gathering behind him. Cautiously she approached the stall. Jonpaul came to her side, confused by her interest. Then, as she took in the scene before her, he saw the sudden emotion blazing in the lovely eyes. "Do you have a fondness for horses, love?"

"Aye," she said, but no more.

She recognized the disease at once. The stallion's head hung low. There was no shine to his dry coat, a bad sign, as bad as the creature's labored breaths. She suddenly spotted the surgeon, recognizing his purple ermine-lined cloak and gold spurs—by law only surgeons could wear purple or gold spurs—and swiftly she sought and found the angry red mark where he had already done a bleeding.

A pail of blood sat at the creature's feet.

She could not save the beast, she just couldn't . . .

With effort she turned away.

Sometime toward the midnight hour, Nichole cautiously threw back the thick quilt. Bare feet slipped on the cold stone floor. The soft sound of Madeleine's slumber rose and fell. Otherwise, all was silent. Dressed in a thick cotton nightdress, Nichole tiptoed to the door, opened it as quietly as possible, and cautiously peered out. A chilly draft of air swept over her, the nights were becoming cold now. The single guard—she forgot his name—sat in his chair, his head bent in sleep as well. She crept silently past him.

Two shiny red eyes seemed to hover midair, but Nichole knew that cat, always sleeping on his favorite resting place on the bench beneath the window near her room. He meowed as she approached, and Nichole leaned over to rub his neck, quieting him before she continued down the darkened hall. Distant voices rose from the main hall below with a late-night card game. She stopped to listen for Jonpaul's voice. She made out the voices of Kurtus and Father Ari among other indistinguishable voices, but not his. She knew Jonpaul woke before dawn, so in all likelihood he was sound asleep.

She was counting on it.

The study doors were open. This was the first place she would search. The Bible would either be in the study or in his chambers. She slipped through the door into the darkened room. The red embers of a dying fire glowed from the corner of the room, which meant the room had been used tonight, perhaps to study the Bible for its secret. She made her way to the hearth, felt for a kindling stick, and struck it. The dim light revealed the candelabra on the desk. She lit three of the candles as much as she dared.

An hour later, after searching every nook and cranny and drawer, she determined the Bible was not in this room. It must be in his chambers then . . . She blew out two candles, saving one. Taking a deep breath, she left the room, cupping the candlelight and heading up the stairs to Jonpaul's chambers.

Voices came behind her as she reached the top of the stairs. She ducked down the hall, blowing out the candle, and the words of Kurtus and Lord Bruno disappeared down the lower hall. She drew an easy breath, then silently crept to the great wood doors at the end of the hall.

With her heart pounding, she gently pushed open the door, slipped inside, and shut it behind her. The room was dark. A single candle burned on the tall stand across the room—the common practice was to leave one candle lit during the warmer summer, fall, and spring months when no fire was necessary. She made out the outline of his sleeping form beneath the covers in the huge bed.

'Twas danger, she knew. She could never sneak away during the day with all the people around her. There was just no other way and, besides, she knew many of his habits. No one slept less than Jonpaul and so no doubt those few hours a night he did sleep, 'twas a very deep sleep he found. She'd make not the smallest sound, either . . .

The Bible would be in one of the two trunks. Like all wealthy men, one trunk would hold documents and the other clothes. Not knowing which was which, she silently moved to the trunk against the wall. Kneeling, she lifted the lid, stopping as it made a loud creak. Her gaze flew to the bed to see if it would wake him yet he did not even stir.

This was his clothes trunk, the lesser possibility. She felt over the neat stacks of various clothes, just in case. Tunics, brigandines, pants, belts. Nothing. She got up, leaving the lid open rather than taking the chance of letting the noise wake him. Quietly she tiptoed to the other chest against the wall—

Footsteps sounded outside the door. Nichole ducked against the shadow of the wall and held her breath. The door opened, and when she saw Jonpaul her gaze flew back to the bed, as if to verify the dual vision, only to now see the form in the bed was much too small to be Jonpaul.

Dear Lord—

She pressed hard against the wall, not daring to breathe. Hold still . . . just hold still . . . Jonpaul sat on the edge of the bed to remove first his boots, then his belt, finally his brigandine. This was tossed over the bench. Suddenly he looked up, alerted. His gaze circled the room, passing the place where she stood, but then riveting back to it.

A warm chuckle sent the hairs on the back of her neck rising. "If it is you, Nichole—"

The sentence was never finished, bless the small mercy. She froze, swallowed as he came to her, her mind not quite comprehending the horror of the situation until he stood in front of her. His amusement shined like a beacon in the darkness. She could see it! The blood vacated her head in terror. Every instinct screamed to run, which she certainly would, if only there was somewhere to run to . . .

She felt his intense scrutiny even through his amusement. "Why, I can hardly believe this." He chuckled softly. "I can't believe it."

Oh, believe it . . .

Then curiously, he glanced back at the bed. "Nichole . . ." he whispered still. "You should have told me—"

"What?"

"'Tis an awkward situation, to say the least. If I only knew . . . For, love, you can't imagine my disappointment."

This made no sense to her. If he only knew what? That she would sneak in his room to see if he had the Bible, then to steal it back? What did he mean by that? She looked about her for the clue. Of course he wouldn't kill her, but if he banished her to her room or, dear Lord, if there was a dungeon here—

Why was he staring at her like that? Her heart still pounded furiously, more as he reached a gentle hand to her face. The warm brush of his fingers sent a chill racing up her spine and she forgot to breathe, nervous and scared . . .

"The next time you feel . . . ah, amorous inclinations, give me but a hint? You definitely have first place with me . . ."

She searched his face, confused but only for a moment more. "Amorous . . . inclinations?" She drew a shocked gasp, her eyes widening dramatically. "Why, you think . . . You think—you bastard—" and she raised her open hand to land a hard slap to his face. Jonpaul, ever undaunted, caught her hand just inches from his face and, restraining her force, he brought it gently against his skin, as if she meant a caress. Anger made her hand as hard and cold as ice and fury trembled through her, staining her cheeks crimson.

Laughing, "Come now, no need to be angry! If you had given me the slightest indication that you'd be seeking my bed—"

"Seeking your bed?" she cried, but his fingers quickly came to her mouth, and with a glance at the bed, he indicated his concern for the sleeping lady, but her mind was firmly fixed on the idea that he thought, that he might somehow believe she—

Oh, Lord, the idea was too terrible! He didn't really . . . He couldn't imagine—

"Nichole, what else might I think? Here you are in my bedchambers in the middle of the night, dressed . . ." His gaze raked her gown again. "Well, I best not dwell on how you're dressed . . ."

Yet he was dwelling on it, and seeing this made her realize the time had come to leave. For the second time he let her. The quiet sound of his amusement followed her from the room and her humiliation, the idea that he might truly believe that, was punishment enough . . . Which Jonpaul knew full well.

Nichole forgot the pressing question of the Bible. Never had she felt more self-conscious. She could not guess his reason, but Jonpaul forced her to dine at the great hall and here she sat, surrounded by the people of the Alliance. No more excuses, he had told Bettrina to tell her after she declined again for reasons of health. True, 'twas a lie. Not only was her leg healed, but it had been over two weeks now since the stitches were removed and even the remaining scar was little to brag about, but then, she had reasoned, most men had not the faintest grasp of a woman's cycle of health. She had been counting on Jonpaul's ignorance. "Any woman who can drop twenty feet over battlements and spend the dark dead of night prowling like a she-cat about drafty castles can also dine in proper company," he had told Bettrina to tell her.

"What can he mean by that?" Bettrina wondered.

"Nothing . . . nothing," she said hastily.

The "she-cat" made her blush every time she thought about it, which was often. She sat at his side on the dais with the lords and ladies Adline and Bruno, the blond giant Wesmullar, and the lady Marguerite. This lady was pretty, sweet and shy, the exact opposite of her husband, Nichole thought. There was also Dornach's steward, Mickeil, and the abbot of St. Michael's in Basel, Bishop Pol de Sad. This long table overlooked even two longer tables below where many familiar faces dined among others—Father Ari, Kurtus, Bettrina, and Holbien, Madeline, Kira, and a number of merchants from Basel, Sorro and his assistant, too.

Even the surgeon's assistant wore the gold spurs, she noticed.

The noise in the great hall was deafening. While everyone seemed to be talking at the same time, the musicians serenaded a balladeer who sung the ancient story of Helen of Troy. No one could possibly hear a word. What was worse, no one cared.

She knew each time Jonpaul's gaze came to her and each second it lasted, and despite the keen interest of being seated in his great hall among people of the Alliance, the hint of amusement there somehow kept her mind on his kisses, the way he baited her, secrets between them she wanted so badly to forget . . . which in turn kept her blushing like a foolish young girl of no sense. She felt hot and shaky. It seemed abundantly clear that even when she dwelt on who he was and the horrors he had committed, the chaste, sobering thoughts did not travel down where she needed them so desperately.

Last night she had been bringing up two plates of milk for the cats from the kitchen. She had made it up the stairs before running into him. They were alone and it was dark, and these two facts seemed to attack her nerves and make her tip over one of the plates, spilling it in a puddle around his boots. Convinced she needed his help, he carried the plates the rest of the way until suddenly—

"Oh no, love. I believe we have a problem."

He set the plates down. Cats manifested from the shadows; there must have been a half-dozen of her friends prowling their legs suddenly. One of the tomcats practically climbed Jonpaul's leg to get to his arms, but she could hardly watch him pick up the creature, gently stroking his head until a loud purr sounded, but no louder than her quick breaths and the sudden onslaught of her panic, this brought by the way his eyes were staring at her suddenly.

"A . . . problem?"

He dropped the cat. As if to escape his gaze, she backed up . . . and hit the wall. He was not smiling as his arm reached to the wall behind her and leaned forward on it. "Aye . . . a potentially devastating problem."

She couldn't breathe now. He reached to one of her plaits. This was brought to his face and he closed his eyes, drinking the sweet scent.

"Have I ever told you about my boyhood?"

The oblique question hardly registered. She felt suddenly certain he was going to kiss her. The idea heated up the now-familiar serums throughout her body. Her mind suddenly caught up and she managed to repeat the last, "Your . . . your boyhood?"

"Aye. Suffice to say 'twas pretty normal. Normal until the day I learned what chasing a maid Leonie led to. And, love," his fingers caressed the long rope of her hair as his eyes seemed to devour her, and just as she felt certain she would faint with the certainty he was going to kiss her, "this scent in your hair. 'Twas the very same Leonie used." Then chuckling at the oh so obvious effect he had on her senses and straightening, he said, "And, love, I have enough trouble with you at Dornach without you using that scent."

The tip of his finger brushed her nose as if she were a child of five. She felt at least that foolish as he turned away, chuckling softly all the way to his door. Only then did she realize how hard she was breathing, flushed and nervous and—

For the love of the Goddess, stop thinking about him! She tried to concentrate on the conversations around her. The men were discussing the new guest house being built, the relative advantages and disadvantages to hard wood floor or the more expensive marble. Then they turned to Bregenz and the discussion centered on whether it was contagious or no and the hope that the horse would recover.

The horse would not recover, she knew, at least not unless he received proper treatment. Horses, pulling teeth, and birthing were her areas of expertise. She recognized the disease, rare but not completely uncommon. Nanna emphasized cures for the ailments of the beasts and only because men loved their war-horses even more than their wives—and if one cured their horse, they became indebted, an indebtedness Nanna had found particularly useful . . . Not that she would offer Lord Bruno her services; she wouldn't, couldn't do that. Not when that very creature would be used to kill the men of Lucerne . . .

Interspersed among those loud voices were the softer voices of the women, discussing in lower tones the advantages of the newer Flemish cloth to the more common German. It was the women who kept staring at her, then turning to their neighbor to whisper. For all of it, there was no maliciousness, until she found herself staring at Kira. Except perhaps from Kira, she couldn't quite tell.

Nichole looked away, ignoring everything or trying to, concentrating instead on the ballad, then when that ended, the pattern made by the marble floor, the handsome tapestries hanging on the wall, and finally the conversation at the lower tables. A debate between Kurtus and Father Ari over the actual existence of Eden grew more heated—Kurtus certain it was all made up, like the horned, dark-skinned pygmies, while Father Ari swore up and down that his uncle had found Eden in the Far East, exactly where it was put on all the best maps and furthermore, "'Twas completely surrounded by an enormous wall of fire four men high, wholly impenetrable—"

Catching this last, Jonpaul asked, "How then did this ah . . . uncle of yours know it was Eden?" Then, laughing, "Perhaps Ari, considering the fire and that it was a relative of yours—"

Laughter stopped him from finishing.

As the laughter died, Bruno informed Ari, "I have the

undisputed Berber maps. Eden is north of India, surrounded by ocean on all sides—"

"Your pardon, milord." Another man rose. He looked like a wealthy merchant to Nichole, as he wore an ornate coat of scarlet and gold. "'Tis a well-known fact that the Berber maps were erroneously sketched from many others, taking many mistakes from the lesser sources. I have the great maps of Lorraine, which show that Eden actually exists in the land of China and is surrounded by mountains so high they touch the sphere of the moon—"

"Mountains that touch the sphere of the moon?" Jonpaul questioned, incredulous. "Impossible! If that were so, the mountains would cause an eclipse."

This logic was unarguable but did nothing to augment the debate. If Eden wasn't surrounded by mountains or oceans, then it must be surrounded by fire, and truly neither the Berber nor the Lorriane map was one half as good as the Boccaccio map, which put Eden in the middle of the ocean, and so on. Nichole listened in fascination as the whole large roomful of people took up the obscure debate, passionately arguing for this and that as if it actually mattered where Eden was, if it were truly anywhere. Charles would never allow such a discussion at Lucerne and simply because he would be bored by it, then taxed by any opinion that differed from his. Jonpaul, too, appeared bored, hardly listening, but he smiled when Father Ari said wryly, "Well, in any case, there could be no wall of fire nor mountain high enough nor ocean deep enough to keep Eve, the archetype of all women, happy and in her place for long—"

"Jonpaul, what say you on Eden?" Kurtus wanted to know, and apparently so did the rest of the people as their eyes came to him and they fell silent.

"Eden? Well . . ." An amused light came to his darkly green eyes, one that caught Nichole's breath and for a reason she didn't understand. "It has always been my belief that Eden is a mythical place, a landscape that exists in our collective imagination. For where could this place be that no pests or famine or disease or even the hand of death can touch—except in our imagination? How could this earthly garden of paradise exist save but in our imaginations? This place of unsurpassed beauty and enchantment, where every kind of tree and flower grows, yet never fades, a place of a thousand delicious scents, the songs of birds harmonizing with the rustling of forest leaves and the rippling of streams over jeweled rocks and sands brighter than silver." Then his eyes came to Nichole, and in a compelling lowered voice, as if no one else existed in the room, "And in this paradise a man and a woman lived and loved, and because this love, like no other before or since, existed outside the worldly sphere, untarnished by the shield of war, this love blossomed like the very flowers surrounding their feet. No," he shook his head with a weighted pause, "this, alas, could only exist in our dreams."

There was no doubt in anyone's mind for whom his poetry was meant. With lowered lashes, Nichole's cheeks grew hot as the room broke into wild applause and laughter, laced with loud, good-natured hoots. Kira's face, too, reddened in stages, but with rage. While not specifically prohibited, it was uncommon for a woman to address the hall. "Milady—" Two thin brows rose over Kira's mischievous eyes. "A moment of your attention if you will?"

Hans and Bruno were conferring over something and were not listening, though Jonpaul saw the mischief there and he braced, somehow knowing before a word was said. Nichole herself did not know she was being addressed until she looked up to see the same.

"We were wondering, milady. The ladies here . . . Well, 'tis said about your brother, Charles, that his hand is so terribly grotesque and deformed that he must always wear a glove over it? That no one has ever actually seen this hand . . . and lived? Is that true?"

No response registered on Nichole's face, except the probe of her eyes as if to ascertain the reality of what she had just heard. Jonpaul reached a hand to her instinctively as he rose to silence the girl, but too late—

"What we really want to know, is it true that once a woman removed the glove and in the morning she was found dead with her hand severed?"

The room fell into a shocked silence. A great deafening roar sounded in Nichole's mind, and for several minutes she had no idea of what was happening. Kira in turn waited for the people to rally against the lady as they would her brother. She fully expected the hall to enjoy the lady's humiliating struggle to answer the question. With growing horror she saw this was not happening. Lady Adline, ever quick with her temper, rose first and only because Jonpaul was not a man who lost his temper often and simply because those few times he did, the consequences were so devastating as to naturally teach him the wisdom of control. Yet Jonpaul's look, her husband's hand on her arm, stopped her and told her 'twas his place as Jonpaul, too, rose.

"That comment was a breach of your station, to say nothing of a simpleton's sense of decency. You are a shame to Dornach, one I will not endure. You will leave now, banished from the eyes of all who sit in my court, banished until you can find an apology that the lady Nichole can accept, if such an apology even exists. Now."

With a lift of her skirts, in terrible shame, Kira rushed from the room.

The silence remained, broken at last by the lady Adline's apology to Nichole, taken up by Marguerite, with the rest of the women quietly aye-aying these sentiments. Nichole still could hardly listen as her fury completely consumed her thoughts. The men were far less charitable.

"For God's sakes, the girl is in dire need of a husband's backhand," Bruno said. "Why isn't she married yet?"

"No man would have her now," one of the merchants observed. "The good pope himself does not dispense with as many favors as that girl."

"Aye. Well, I would not force her ill temper on a dog so much as any of my men—"

"Stop," Nichole whispered, her eyes still lowered as the whisper of her voice caught the attention of the entire room. "The girl is not to blame. Such hatred is not her fault." The blue eyes shot to Jonpaul and she rose, adding the last with feeling, "for the ill-deserved hatred against my brother has been fanned by a most malicious hand, and even if all you good people pretend not to know, even if you do not actually know, I do. I will not pretend otherwise."

She started to leave, but not quick enough. Bruno's hand caught her wrist, a shockingly gentle but firm hold. "Those are bold words, milady, an even bolder accusation. I will not let you leave with it unanswered."

"Aye," Hans said with harsh authority. "You can believe Jon does not have to fan the people's animosity for your brother. He does the work himself. You are unmarried, a girl yourself, and it seems little more than the innocent pawn of your brother, kept cloistered and ignorant like a lamb marked for slaughter. You have no right to speak here."

Jonpaul might have warned them about her temper, the futility of trying to reason with her, but the sudden emergence of the emotion blazing in her eyes caught him, then held him as she told Hans. "I am not . . . I am not. I have seen with my own eyes the massacre of innocent folks wrought by your lord's sword! By his sword." She turned to Jonpaul. "I have seen it!"

Bruno swore, then asked, "You saw Jon murdering

village people? With thy own eyes you witnessed Jon at this place of carnage, doing murder with his sword?"

"You know I wasn't there," she cried softly, the attention, the hurt, and most of all the fury pushing her closer and closer to tears, tears she absolutely refused to ever let them see. "You know it! I would not be left to speak of it. Yet I saw it all the same, the village and the pile of bodies and the smoke—"

"So you did not actually see him there?" Bruno pointed out, pretending surprise. "This idea that Jonpaul's sword was raised to slay a woman, a child, this entire village of Stan, is nothing but a perverse brainstorm of your brother's. Was it not that bastard who put Jonpaul's name to the carnage?"

"He is not a bastard! He was born of my good mother—"

"The idea that you and he shared the same womb is one fact that's hard to believe," Hans commented wryly, echoing a frequent thought of Jonpaul, who leaned back now, certain the conversation was futile though letting it go as Hans added, "When will you see that the accusation is nothing but your brother's lie? 'Tis all you have, and the idea goes against the combined experience and knowledge of every living person in this room and beyond, to the entire Alliance. I tell you, you have been sadly deceived, milady."

"Yet I know 'twas him!" Desperate to make them see it, "'Tis true I did not actually see him there, but I didn't have to. Who else is famous for his murder of innocent folks? Even you, the lords of the Alliance, must remember the carnage and pillaging done after the Burgundy War as he turned his army to the forest people to reap his terrible revenge for our passivity? I know ten people who saw him, I know countless others whose loved ones were slain and farms burned and—"

Sudden chaos erupted in the raised fury of every man

present, many who jumped to their feet to speak. Nichole's eyes went frantic with indignation. Startled, scared now, she tried to bolt, but Bruno's grip on her wrist was now hard and tight.

"That is quite enough, young lady," Bruno's voice thundered. "Your ignorance is profound indeed—"

"And unworthy of being answered," Jonpaul said, his voice, too, abruptly changed by this last. "You can believe I will not condescend to answer it. And in any case, that accusation is just. I was responsible. Leave her with it, Bruno." Then, "Let her go."

The startled eyes shot to Jonpaul. He would even admit it!

Bruno hesitated still.

"Let her go."

He released her wrist. With a lift of skirts, she, too, fled the now-silent room, a silence broken at last by Kurtus as he rose. One rarely saw the man serious let alone as angry as he was at Jonpaul.

"Save it Kurtus." Jonpaul, too, rose to leave. "I'm in no mood for a speech."

"By God 'tis my right! I have earned it. As has every man who fought with you during those terrible days and 'tis a blasphemy to leave it like that, to let her go—"

Kurtus stopped upon seeing the familiar emotion in Jonpaul's eyes, an emotion all remembered from the darkness of those days. "And I repeat: the accusation is just. I was responsible for each one of those deaths and rapes, every part of the destruction of that time. And I will not have you say otherwise."

He said enough, and with his own fury, he left the hall.

The great stallion Bregenz lay on his side. The dark eyes were closed, fused together by a hard crust of mucus forming from the continuous drain at the eyes and nostrils. Each shallow breath came with a wheezing that made all those watching aware of the beast's pain. Bruno winced each time it came—his creature's agony was his own. He knelt on his knees to place a hand over the faint beat of Bregenz's heart while he whispered soft Romanesch words of goodbye into the creature's ear.

It was time.

Jonpaul, Sorro the surgeon, Hans, a roomful of grooms and squires watched in heavy silence and profound sympathy. Short of his own death, no greater tragedy could strike a knight. The war-horse was a knight's lifeline, the beast of luck and fortune whom far more than battle skill kept a knight alive. It took years to train a war-horse to its master and those years bonded man to beast so that a knight felt his creature's every mood, instinct, and the very beat of its heart as one's own. As Bruno was a great knight, Bregenz was a great war-horse. It would take years to train another to Bregenz's level of skill, and then, Bruno swore no horse in the world could ever replace this creature who had saved his life more times than he could count or even recall—and it was probably true. As Sorro had worked unsuccessfully to relieve the horse's agony for the last four hours, all Bruno did was recount tale after tale of the beats's heroics. "Remember the tournament in England? I was put against that fearsome Tansmen for the lancing, and as I charged, Bregenz suddenly veered to the right just in time to counter Tansman's sudden drop . . . Ah, he always knew when I did not . . . The Burgundy War, now that's when he really showed his colors . . ."

Now it was time. The creature would not live out the night. The surgeon could not relieve the creature's suffering and there was no point in keeping him alive to die so slowly. Jonpaul's best bowman stood waiting. It would be quick and painless, yet Bruno could not seem to leave, and with sympathy, Hans's strong hand finally came to his shoulder.

"Come my, friend."

A commotion sounded outside. "Please just do as I say . . ." No one paid the feminine voice any mind, for Bruno at last stood up. Tears blurred his eyes, but Hans guided him toward the stable doors. A number of the men followed, only to stop suddenly as they saw who stood in the doors.

Standing behind, Jonpaul looked over the shoulders of the other men to see Nichole standing there. Like a warring charge, determination sat in her eyes and she looked much changed in the plain clothes: a gown of forest-green muslin, covered neck to floor in a white apron, this tied tightly at her mercilessly small waist. A white cotton scarf wrapped around her head, too, keeping her long, unbound hair in a trail down her back.

She approached Bruno directly. The better part of the evening had passed in search of various herbs, medicines, and tools. These items filled the two buckets and one basket she managed to carry. Kurtus was off getting the last item.

Never one to mince words, what Nichole said to Bruno would be repeated and remembered for years.

"First I want you to know, milord," her small pointed chin lifted as she looked him square in the eyes, "I will not save your creature for you. You, sir, do not deserve the gift. I will save the horse for himself. The horse—Bregenz is his name?—came to me in a dream this afternoon as I napped and begged me to save him. You are shocked? Well, this happens to me all the time. I agreed, though reluctantly of course—you can easily grasp why. Fortunately for Bregenz, I have worked around the dilemma in this way: I need you to promise me that once I save him, if I can save him, you will never ride him against Lucerne. Now, do I have your sworn promise?"

A grin fitted on Jonpaul's face, but he was the

exception. The rest of the men were quite naturally speechless, shocked by the audacity that made her think she could save the horse when the surgeon, the very best surgeon in all of the Alliance and beyond, could not. So preposterous a number of the men laughed outright until they caught the girl's gaze. Then the exchange of glances asked the question loudly, Well who did she think she was?

Jonpaul joined the group from behind just as Sorro lost his temper. "How dare you, young lady!"

Nichole remained peacefully undaunted by the attack save for a touch of impatience as the small, corpulent man pointed a finger at her. His arched gray brows and furrowed forehead made his face go cross, which she met with disdain, as she shared Jonpaul's sentiments for all men distinguished by their heavy purple fur-lined robes and gold spurs. Not a smudge on the cloth, she noticed. Like all "doctors," he was too fine to get his hands dirty. She was surprised he condescended to treat a horse in the first place, and no doubt did so only because of the status of Lord Bruno.

"Who do you think you are?" he demanded of her again. "I have done everything possible for the creature—"

"Which means, I suppose that you have given him a sulphur bath and studied his charts?"

"Indeed, and as his birth sign shows a double conjunction of Saturn and Jupiter in the fourth degree, he is doomed to die of the phlegm—"

"Aye," she quite agreed, "he is doomed unless you lance the lump under his chin. Have you done that?"

"Lump? What lump?"

"The lump that holds the bile and keeps the creature sick."

Sorro searched her face for a moment before spinning around and marching back to the stall where Bregenz lay.

The men followed. Sorro knelt down and felt under his long chin, only to feel the shock of a small but distinct lump.

Nichole came behind Bruno as he stared incredulously at where Sorro felt over the lump again and again. "Do I have your sworn promise, milord?"

Bruno turned around. A hand brushed over his beard as he studied her. Confusion arched his brows but could not touch his grief, which yanked the strings of Nichole's great wealth of compassion. It did not seem to matter that he was the enemy, the distinction utterly meaningless alongside the human sentiment.

Bruno had never heard of such a thing. Oh, rumors of Jonpaul's mother long ago, aye, but the lady Nichole was only a girl and young at that. He never heard of any other woman knowing anything about horses. Christ, most could hardly mount without fainting in fright; Swiss women were hardly known for their horsemanship, to say the least. He could not see the horse suffer more. Yet, on the other hand, she had known there was a lump when no one else did . . .

"I forbid it," Sorro said angrily. "As the practicing surgeon, I will not stand by to watch a girl abuse the horse more—"

"I believe the decision is Bruno's," Jonpaul said. "And Bruno, 'tis a magnanimous gesture," he added in a different tone. "There is nothing to lose and much to gain. Let Nichole try."

Bruno still paused a long moment before finally nodding. Nichole looked briefly at the faces of the men before she approached the horse. Jonpaul came up behind her, and she felt a brief tingling of awareness along her spine before he took the heavy buckets in hand, setting them down nearby. At the stall gate, she genuflected once, said a brief prayer to the Virgin—Nanna would say the Christian manifestation of the

Goddess—before kneeling at the beast's side. The men gathered around to watch. Fascination marked their faces. A woman horse doctor—this was a first . . .

The new scent must have alerted the horse. He seemed for a moment to struggle, nudging his head as though trying to get up. "No, no my friend," Nichole said. "Don't try to stand yet. 'Twill be better this way." Then to the side, "I will need at least two buckets of very hot water. Boiling hot."

Jonpaul motioned to Mickeil, who ran off.

The beast's hair looked unkept, dry and dead. Great shivers rippled bodily through him. He wheezed badly. She petted his head and spoke softly to him. He seemed to relax with her presence. Then, while the men watched, while especially Sorro watched each move, she got to work. As she waited for the water, she prepared a mixture of bran, mint, dried hops, tannic acid, among a number of other herbs and spices no one there recognized.

"What do you think you're doing?" Sorro demanded harshly.

"I'm preparing a potion that, with steaming water, will open his breathing passages."

"'Twill kill the creature! You can't give—"

"'Twill most certainly not kill him," Nichole said, undaunted, not even bothering to look at Sorro. She was quite used to rivalry and jealousy from traditional doctors. "'Twill bring him a relief so great, you will see a change immediately. Be patient, Doctor."

The confident, quiet reply put admiration in Jonpaul's eyes. More as he watched her work with skilled, knowing hands. She first cut two holes in a cloth, then strung a thin rope through both holes to hook over the beast's ears. Mickeil soon returned from the kitchen with two buckets of steaming hot water; these were set at her side. Nichole dipped a cloth in the water, then soothed this over his eyes. Over and over again, the mucus disappeared bit by bit until the horse opened his eyes. He seemed to recognize her. He nudged his head against her leg, wheezing still for each breath but she smiled. "Oh, my poor, poor friend . . ."

Bruno still looked confused, but a twinge of hope and awe were working into his heart. "Milady, do you truly think you can save him?"

"I have seen worse pull through. But, then, I have seen some not so bad off succumb. He wants badly to live though, and Nanna always believed that was the deciding battle right there."

After securing the hot cloth over his eyes and tying it under his chin, she smoothed another hot cloth over the lump. Then she picked up a wooden cup. Inside was a thick, sebaceous and odd-smelling ointment, which she began smoothing over the lump. The horse tried to pull away, but her soothing voice quieted him.

At last Kurtus rushed inside and quickly made his way to the stall. He held up one kind of butcher's knife with a sharp needlepoint. "Is this it, milady?"

Nichole looked up. "Aye, that is it." She took it up and cleaned it in the pail of hot water. "I need two men to hold his head. Nay, not you, milord," she said to Bruno when he jumped forward. "Your affection will make you go weak on me. Please, if you would . . ." she motioned toward Jonpaul and Kurtus.

The horse's eyes were covered, and he responded weakly to the hands coming to his head as Jonpaul and Kurtus lifted his neck and held it tight. The intensity in Jonpaul's gaze as he watched her was matched only by the intensity in hers as she focused full attention on the lump. It was a delicate operation; one must be thorough. A towel was placed under the spot. "Please, more light." Someone grabbed a torch lamp and held it over the place she knelt. All men held their breath as her skilled hands circled the spot lightly first, and she murmured a prayer before, suddenly and with surprising strength, she thrust the knife into flesh. Bregenz jerked his head back briefly, but in his weakness the men were able to hold him still as she cut a neat round circle.

Bruno took one look at the yellow bile pouring out and, for the first time in forty-five years, he blanched and felt faint. All other men groaned, diverting their gaze, save for Doctor Sorro whose eyes burned as they could not believe the miracle of it. Hardly a man there could stand the sight, including the doctor as Nichole deftly scraped the sides of the pocket so as to leave no poison inside. Once done, she wiped the wound clean before at last applying more of the salve to the spot. The cloth was folded as she murmured a prayer in Romanesch, one only Bruno understood, then it was dropped in an empty bucket.

To a Goddess, she prayed . . .

"Someone must set the poison to fire or bury it for good."

No one stepped forward to the task. Jonpaul motioned to Mickeil again, who with fear and hesitation and whispered curses, picked up the bucket and carried it outside.

Next, Nichole picked up the long canvas nose bag with straps to go over the horse's ears. This was filled with the mix she had prepared. "You must stand for this," she said. Everyone looked around until it was suddenly realized she spoke to the horse.

Surprise and amusement reached their faces, but Kurtus sighed, "Why is it I am expecting Bregenz to answer her?"

The nervous chuckles stopped as Bregenz struggled to get to his feet. Murmurs of amazement raced through the audience. Jonpaul and Kurtus overcame their shock to help the horse up, a hard job but managed at last. So sick, though, Bregenz's head nearly touched the ground and his wheezing seemed to grow louder. "Hold his head again. He will bolt."

They did, and she attached the bag to his nose, fitting it tightly around. She poured the steaming hot water into a hole on the side that she had made. The great horse jerked back in a bolt, but Jonpaul and Kurtus managed to hold him. The steamy fumes reached his nose and his lungs, and he breathed loudly. One would swear he would choke, but—

The spicy hot steam opened and cleared the breathing passages. Nichole poured more water into the bag, which was dripping over her skirts now.

"His wheezing . . . My God, can you hear that!" Jonpaul exclaimed in wonder.

Kurtus was all awe. "I cannot believe it—"

"Holy mother of Jesus," Hans suddenly laughed. "I swear I feel relief in my own chest!" Then everyone was talking at once, everyone except Bruno, who looked starstruck by the miracle, and indeed he was. It was too soon to tell for sure, he tried to remind himself, but somehow he knew Bregenz would live. "I have seen worse pull through. He wants badly to live . . ."

Nichole beamed with pride, which at these times she was famous for having such a lot of. "Wipe that satisfied smirk off your face," Nanna would scold her, to no avail. "Pride is a great sin for you Christians, you know . . ."

Perhaps, but Nichole could not help it. She was a great healer, one of the best. Such a wonderful gift to heal the wounded, cure the sick, to make living things well again, and even Nanna said she was a natural, that she could not imagine a better, more adept apprentice. Besides, with her dual heritage, modesty had never been natural to her, especially impossible to muster in the face of saving God's life on earth . . .

A fine brow rose when Jonpaul saw this. In face of this praise, he would have sworn Nichole would be all a-stutter with modesty, blushing with humility. No modesty or humility on that pretty face. Oh, no, nothing but vanity and head-swelling pride, and seeing it made him suddenly laugh, laugh with fondness and affection. For a long while he could not seem to stop laughing, until Nichole caught on, and as she poured the last hot water into the sack, she brought him up with a petulant, heart-stopping look of anger . . . Which only made it worse, and then it was all he could do not to drop her to the ground where she stood, wet skirt and dirty hands and audience and all . . .

Sorro took as much of this as he could. His face had reddened in stages, and with horror he saw only that she had bewitched them all, that none of the men had any idea of what they witnessed.

"She is a witch and we, each one of us here, have witnessed her sorcery!"

The bucket dropped from her hands. Hot water splattered across her skirts, but the stables turned dead silent. Bregenz's labored breathing, a shuffle of hooves, but that was all the sound as Nichole turned to see the angry finger pointed at her. All initiates nourished an irrational fear of being tried and burned for the accusation and she, being part Christian, was no exception. She instinctively backed up and away—and into Jonpaul, whose arms crossed protectively over her front. Without a thought of what the gesture meant, her hands came over his, too, as if to keep him there.

The accusation put anger on Bruno's face. "A witch, you say? Because she could save my creature when you could not? Why, you miserable, little—"

"But wait! Did you not see how she spoke to the horse?"

"And what man among us does not speak to his horse?"

"But what horse understands as this creature understood her? The horse is bewitched! And all her strange potions and chanting—"

"Chanting? You mean prayers, and between the two is the difference between heaven and hell. This angel is definitely heading toward heaven. And you, Sorro, would fare from taking instruction from the girl—"

The insult could not be borne. "You, too, are bewitched! All of you . . ." He waved his hand indicting the group.

"A word of advice," Jonpaul tried to intervene before the situation got out of hand. "I had better be the only man bewitched by the girl—"

The men laughed, for the idea had been long perfectly clear. The tension dissipated with the laughter. Sorro, however, was not amused and far from being appeased. "I am going to report this to the bishops, the abbot himself. We shall let a trial by impartial judges settle the matter—"

Hushed silence came over the crowd. Nichole blanched white. No other words could frighten her more, for, like the Inquisition of a century past, no one was ever found innocent once the charges were brought to a trial. All evidence of innocence was known to be Satan's duplicity, and even her status would not likely protect her should the accusation go to a trial . . .

The only thing more frightening than the accusation was Jonpaul as he replied, "I say you will not. And simply because if you ever utter Nichole's name—so much as to sing her praise—you will lose your life. And," he said, to make it clear that it was not an idle threat but rather a fact, "I swear to the deed in honor of these good men as my witnesses. Is that clear now?"

Fear and disbelief twisted Sorro's face. He barely managed to nod, already backing up, shaking his head. His servant looked as frightened as he, following at his side.

Jonpaul added the last. "Know, too, you will not be welcome in the joined lands of the Alliance, nor in any of their free cities. Be gone with you now."

Nichole's relief was heady. How strange to be defended by one's enemies! She hardly knew what to think until she abruptly realized her hands lay over Jonpaul's. She dropped them like a red-hot coal. She spun around to see his smile. "I didn't mean to—"

"Of course not."

"I mean, I was just scared . . . I—" She stopped, swallowed, unable to bear the intensity of his gaze and the thing she found there: amusement, tenderness, and fondness, hardly the appropriate emotions from one's declared enemy. 'Twas she who was bewitched! How could she keep forgetting who he was and what he had done—especially after he had admitted it! How could something of that magnitude stray from her mind every time he was near?

Dear Lord, hurry, Charles . . . She had to leave.

She announced her price to Bruno. In the whole of her experience, Bruno was the first man who did not gulp or gasp outrage. Kurtus did it for him. "What the devil could you be wantin' with such a sum?"

She looked at him with surprise. "Why, I don't believe 'tis any of your concern."

The men watched her proud, slender back as she turned to march from the stables.

"'Tis the blood of the Medici," Hans sighed. "They are all like that."

The men nodded agreement. Jonpaul was still laughing.

Chapter Eleven

A gold-eyed calico cat sat staring at the mice trapped in the gold-gilt cage. He stretched his front paws in front, rounding his back before sitting back down, his long tail curling neatly in front of him. A mouse scrambled across the cage, seeking the farthest point from the gold eyes, yet not sure where this was. The cat hit the cage with his paw, teased, then irritated. So close . . .

Kuno listened to Charles's unfolding story. He was not surprised. Not really. Something had been wrong all these years. After all, there was the woman, the severed tongue, and always the appalling permissiveness with which he had raised his sister. Well . . . so now it was a problem. A potentially threatening situation.

Charles set the letter, a letter sealed by two elk horns over crossed swords, in front of Kuno. Kuno read it quickly, gripping the chalice tighter and tighter until, as he read the contents a third time, a diamond chip cut in his palm. He wiped away the pinprick of blood before he returned his gaze to Charles as that man spoke.

Stopping his pacing and through gritted teeth, "I should have killed that old woman long ago! God, but she was living proof that the flames of the Inquisition were just. The very night my father landed the blow on my head, she appeared in my rooms. I have the proof, she said. And I shall always have the proof. It will be used to protect your young sister when she is born, then until she marries. Oh, yes, you need not worry, Lucretia carries a female child. She knew then Lucretia carried a female child, she knew it. Until then, she added, it shall protect me. Then she announced that she should not want to die before her seventy-second year, and at the time she was only in her fifty-fifth year. *I shall count on your prayers for my continued good health, milord.*

"I don't think she spoke directly to me again for the next fifteen years. As time passed, I began to feel my position was safe—"

"But why did you not attempt to discover who she entrusted the paper to?"

"Ha! I tried to once. Only once. God's teeth, but that woman had her ears in every corner of the castle. The first attempt was my last; the witch was so mad for weeks I lived in fear that it would be all over." He paused, drained his goblet of ale, and remembering, "Then two years ago she appeared in my chambers again—after she had announced to the full court that the man Nichole married would inherit my realm. My realm! Sons of Satan, but I was blind with fury, cursing and threatening, and at last in vain. All she said was much worse. Much worse. She said she would also have my promise that my sister would be allowed to pick her own husband."

"I had no choice. I had to agree. I assumed I had only to wait until the old woman died and I did, only to be duped by her. Again! She was in a coma. A goddamn coma! No one but that cursed sibyl could have recovered, and she did, just long enough to give my precious sister the letter. Who must have been badly beaten or worse to hand it over to the lord, our terrible—"

"He cannot truly have it, though!" Kuno looked truly

perplexed, confused, his face reddening. "How could he? Why would he just threaten you? If he truly had this paper would he not just use it, damning you forever more?"

"Think, my friend! Think!" Charles's clenched fists came to the rich oak table and he leaned forward, his eyes narrowing. "If he ruins me, he has nothing. Then nothing but war could gain him Lucerne. With this," a finger of his gloved hand came to the letter, and with low, mounting viciousness, "He has my goddamn groin in his hand. The bastard can use me any way he wants! Blackmail, ransom, anything: peasant and tax reforms, my goddamn treasury. Church reforms, my friend.

"Anything. He can drop me to my knees. He can make me beg. Beg! And I," he picked up the nearest thing to his hand and swung his arm with violence, shattering the ancient Greek statue of Venus against the wall, "will not have it!"

With a screech of agitation, the cat rose, paced, then rubbed against the cage. Charles pushed his fingers through his hair, trembling with violence, pacing furiously back and forth before Kuno.

Thinking, Kuno picked up a knife and one of four oranges in a nearby bowl and began slicing the rare fruit—a particular treasure in Switzerland as it was imported all the way from lower Italy, rarer still, if one considered the season. It was amazing to think of what gold could get a person. Gold, a relatively useless metal, except for the fact that every living human being coveted it. Like power. One got the other, and the only difference was that unlike gold, power was not a fixed quantity but rather flexible. It grew or diminished with the simplest kind of manipulation . . .

"Of course," Kuno finally said, "the situation is intolerable."

"If the bastard wins his game, the reverberations will

rock Switzerland. And if I go, Kuno, you can be sure to follow."

"As I said," he smiled, "the situation is intolerable. It seems fairly clear that simply eliminating the lord Jonpaul from the face of the earth would not completely eliminate this threat. Not at first. This weapon amounts only to a merciless, thin piece of paper. It is this paper that must be destroyed, is it not?"

"Don't be so thick-skulled, Kuno! If there was any way—"

"Ah, my friend, but there *is* a way." Kuno's dark gaze filled with unnatural excitement as he swallowed a piece of the succulent fruit. "Of course the price is high, but then ultimately so is the reward: to gain the Basel trade routes, Dornach and its townships, Elkhorn, too, and all without a war, without losing a single life to battle."

Charles's alarmed gaze riveted to Kuno.

"Listen, my friend: the lord Jonpaul owns this paper that would lose you your inheritance and he threatens to present it. You cannot get the paper away from him. You cannot stop him from presenting it, even with his death. There is only one way out then. We must cast the good lord Jonpaul's motives in suspicion. Paint his motives bloodred so not a living soul will believe in the authenticity of this . . . ah, damning paper."

"Aye." Charles's gaze narrowed. "I am listening, Kuno . . ."

"Well, 'tis rather remarkably simple, Charles. If, for instance, Jonpaul would gain Lucerne if you were to lose it, who, what governing body in all of Christendom, would not put the paper in the highest suspicions? And the man trying to pass it off in contempt? Throw in a few bodies willing to swear to a conspiracy and his falsification and this paper will be virtually meaningless, would it not?"

Charles's pale gaze searched Kuno's face over and over

as his thoughts raced over these words. Words that changed everything. Words that gave him the wings of a hawk swooping down on his enemy as if he were indeed no more fearsome than a mouse. "Oh, God . . . Oh, God . . . 'Tis too simple . . . 'tis too simple—"

"Oh, but there's more."

Charles's gaze froze on him.

Kuno smiled as the pieces fell neatly into place. "Nichole's marriage would put you, her closest male relative, next in line for inheritance should some . . . ah, unforseen tragedy befall the lord."

The pale-blue eyes searched his friend's face. "Nay, there is a relation . . . there is a boy from his first marriage, is there not?"

"Indeed, but this boy is sadly deaf and dumb and"—he chuckled, "and so his inheritance would be easily contested."

The tall man just stared. "To get Dornach and the Basel trade routes without war . . . Oh, God," and with a rarely felt excitement, Charles started laughing. "'Tis too bloody easy . . ."

"Is it not?" Kuno started laughing, too, and laughing, a great, glorious laugh that promised a rich future. "And it's all so very easy to arrange. The one thing, the only thing the Church is very clear about, is a virgin's matrimonial rights."

The cat curled in and out of Charles's legs, sensing the man's excitement, and with a low, cruel chuckle, Charles reached into the cage and pulled out the terrified mouse. The cat watched with hair-raising interest. The tiny creature dropped directly before him and he immediately pounced, caught it, and sunk teeth into the neck before carrying the treat quickly away.

A smile curled on Charles's lips as his gloved hand stroked his mustache. "Unlike us, animals are so very merciful about their killing . . ."

Kuno only chuckled.

A crowd of a dozen men and a half-dozen ladies gathered to watch Nichole's performance. After she had saved Bruno's prized horse, she had been questioned extensively about her abilities. Bruno had arranged this demonstration. As she approached, she saw that Jonpaul was not there. Relief swept through her, as if she were a caged bird and the door just opened to let her free.

She was smiling and her heart pounded with this happiness. When he was gone, she was in control. She bowed slightly to her audience as she surveyed the crowded room until she found him. The merchant, Folchart, sat nervously in a chair, obviously but unnecessarily frightened.

The roomful of people fell silent. Kurtus set her trunk down on the table, unusually quiet, too. Nothing upset him more than this. He had witnessed the miracle she performed on Bregenz, but this was another story. A woman, too! No woman, not even Hera herself, could or should perform the operation . . .

"Well," Nichole smiled broadly, greeting his fear with cheerfulness, "I suppose you're ready?"

Folchart's nod came on the heels of a long pause.

"Very well." With a wide-eyed Gavin at her side watching every move, Nichole opened the small trunk and removed one of the wood cans. "Open up. Very good. Now, I am going to smear this ointment around the side of your mouth. It will burn."

The man's eyes grew wide, then closed altogether as he opened his mouth again. Nichole proceeded. After smearing the ointment and waiting for it to take effect, she removed the two instruments—a small, specialized hammer and a miniature chisel. "Do you feel the burning? Yes? Good. It is poison, sir, so please do not swallow."

The crowd took a collective breath. The man's brows drew together as he felt a not-unpleasant burning sensation.

Lord Bruno looked at Kurtus, then to Nichole. It normally took four men to hold one down. "Shouldn't we hold him down, milady?"

"No . . . shouldn't be necessary." She took up her instruments, positioned them. "Open wide . . ." Braced, gripping the side of the chair, he did. Nichole aimed, hit the tooth once, and cracked it clean. Folchart had no sensation. Pleased, she took up the dreaded pincers and, with all her strength, she pulled one side and dropped the tooth into a jar, then went for the other half. The crowd gasped with amazement, then everyone murmured at once. Kurtus was not quite sure what he had witnessed until Nichole had placed the tooth in a glass jar, told Folchart to rinse and spit, and announced it was done. Folchart did not believe it until he felt in his mouth to the hole. The crowd broke into applause . . .

Until Nichole asked for her fee.

The room gasped, then laughed. "My God, that's robbery!" Folchart cried, rubbing his jaw where he was beginning to feel pain.

"Robbery? But, my dear man, you just said it was a miracle, and miracles are expensive," she explained, having been through this conversation many times before. The more someone paid, the more they valued the service, Nanna always said, and goodness, Nichole saw the truth of that time and time again. Especially for all the potions that worked on faith alone, it was essential for the treatment to charge exorbitant fees. The more a person paid, the better the potion worked.

Despite her price, two of the people watching, Jonpaul's steward, Mickeil, and one of the guards were so impressed, they submitted to the painful operation. As she worked on the men, a young girl from the kitchen gathered the courage to ask if she had a potion or anything that might relieve the unsightly acne on her face. Nichole promised a potion on the morrow—she knew a good one, though nothing worked on that problem for a girl quite as well as marriage and pregnancy. Another lady asked if she might have a remedy for her mother's chronic fatigue and irritability. Nichole promised that potion on the morrow, too, and quite unexpectedly, she saw she was in business once again.

The chilly morning air made Nichole move quickly. She threw back the covers, and putting bare feet to the cold stone floor, she tiptoed to the dressing water. No time for a fire. She splashed cool water over her chilled skin and, careful not to wake Madeline, she remembered to speak to Jonpaul about the necessity of making Madeline sleep with her. She hurried into her dress, a warm blue winter dress that laced over a thick cotton blouse. She brushed out her plaits and, not wanting to dress them, she simply tied them tightly back with a band.

Grabbing her purse, full now, and a shawl, she quietly opened the door. Kurtus was on guard. He normally did not arrive to watch her until much later, as it seemed to be his habit to retire just as she was rising. Oh, if she could just slip past him . . .

Kurtus waited until she reached his boots before dropping his sword in her path. A startled scream came as his reward for waking. "Off somewhere, are we?"

She glared, not bothering to respond. Pulling her shawl tight about her shoulders, she hurried on. Kurtus followed reluctantly and with a yawn. Only Jonpaul rose so early, as unnatural a habit as piety.

Nichole made her way down the two flights of stairs into the entrance hall. The great doors opening to the outside were closed. She pushed with all her strength. Too heavy to budge. She swung around to face an amused Kurtus, who watched passively.

"Would you make me beg your help?"

"Worse. A bargain. I'll open the doors if you promise to stop at the kitchen before . . . before . . . Just where are we going?"

"I am going about business. Business that doesn't involve the kitchen—" Well, she could surely find scraps in the kitchen. Every castle, especially one this large, had scraps. 'Twas no doubt necessary, too, for Dornach probably had legions of waiting hungry. "Oh, very well."

Kurtus opened the doors rather effortlessly though Nichole pretended not to notice as she stepped into the cool morning mist. It was still dark outside and quiet. The castle appeared deserted, a long time left to the weather. Nanna thought 'twas a good idea to plant herbs in the fall even though the seeds would not grow until spring. The seeds draw nourishment from the earth all winter long that way, and Nichole was thinking of this as she passed the abandoned herb garden, alongside well-tended vegetable and fruit trees. Herbs were the ladies' work and, true, Gavin's mother had died some time ago, but one would think someone would have thought to take up the task.

She stopped a sudden. "Oh, the dovecotes, too, are abandoned."

"Aye. The birds left the day Lisollette died. How she loved the birds, she did. She had a way with them. They were wild, but like pets to her. Jon says they left because of the hard winters of these last years, but I don't know . . ."

Nichole reached a hand into a nest and removed a handful of debris, dried straw and leaves. A long white feather came, too. "Were they the white doves, Kurtus?"

"Aye, only the white ones."

The Goddess's favorite . . .

"What was she like, Gavin's mother?"

"Lisollette? A gentle woman. Kind and good, as fair as a summer's day is warm." He did not add too gentle, at least for the woman who was Jon's wife. As fragile and delicate as her birds. Too fragile, Jon would say, and while he had loved and cared for her, there was never any passion . . .

Nichole nodded. 'Twould be so of the mother of young Gavin. There was something sad about the abandoned dovecotes and Gavin's loss, and not wanting to dwell on it, they turned away.

The chilly morning air contrasted sharply with the warmth and heat of the kitchen. A busy place, she knew from experience, and as they stepped inside, she counted ten, eleven people bustling about. Heavenly scents filled the enormous space, too: ham, sausage, and pork strips sizzled on the stove, egg and wheat cakes and bread emerged fresh from the bread oven, and there were turkey pies and cinnamon rolls. She received the interested stares of many as Honore swept her under her arm like a mother hen, asking her how she liked the meatless dinners she had served her last night, telling her again all about Jonpaul's mother who also disdained the eating of flesh, how she was like that good woman in many other ways, too. The fresh cinnamon rolls were pressed into her hands as Nichole was led to the front of the ovens. In Honore's eagerness to please Nichole she nearly knocked over the two scullery maids leaving the kitchen with arms full of plates and mugs and hardly stopping as she proudly pointed out all their fine modern qualities. Nichole listened politely, smiling and impressed until—

"Do you have alms for the poor that I might bring out?"

Kurtus was enjoying a plate of bacon and a mug of sweet cider as he flirted with the pretty dairy maid, but he stopped and turned. "Alms? Who for?"

"The poor people. Surely Dornach can afford to feed the poor?"

A number of people who overheard this smiled, but Kurtus said, "Well, I suppose we could if there were any poor to feed."

Nichole's eyes searched his face, not understanding. What could he mean by that? Every castle had the poor unfortunates gathered outside their gates in the morning, for the alms that were given, leftover food, old clothes, or coins when someone had them. 'Twas where she was headed this morning. She'd pass out her coins, all but the ten percent she'd keep for some new cloth or a ribbon or two. "Surely there is charity at Dornach?"

"Not much," Kurtus said.

"Well, where do the table scraps go?"

"To the pigs."

"You mean to tell me he would have you feed the hogs before the poor?"

"Oh, heavens, you don't understand, milady," Honore hastened to explain. "There just aren't any poor people in these parts. Not everyone's rich, but I don't know a soul who can't afford to feed themselves."

The news hit her like a blow to the head, and she stiffened with alarm. "Mercy in heavens, what has he done to the poor people?"

"Mostly," Kurtus swallowed his cider and set it down,

"he gives them work. Jonpaul has as many ideas for putting men to work as the sun has of shining. If they can't do labor or work the fields, he sends them to the guilds in Basel. There's always something a man can do."

She just couldn't believe this, she didn't believe this. "What about widows and children?"

Nonchalantly, "Well, Jon made laws. Rarely enforced here," he said as he stuffed a hot pastry in his mouth. "There's not much need. All dependents go to the next nearest relative, of course, and, in turn, if the number of the man's dependents exceed his ability to feed and clothe them, he may plead for increases in pay every first Sunday in the *landsgemeinde*, and if the men decide the need is genuine, the money is given or more work for more pay is found. When there are no relatives, the women are given some kind of work here at Dornach, whereas orphaned children are adopted always into households. Same with the infirm and aged."

After a long pause in which thoughts piled one after another, she asked, *"Landsgemeinde?"*

"The people's law. All matters of jurisprudence are decided by the men of Dornach, who meet on the first Sunday of every month."

What? The people's law? She had never heard of such a thing. How could he let common folks decide such things, the fate of others? 'Twas too dangerous, too . . . too something! "Even criminal wrongs?"

"Aye."

Common men folks deciding the matters of justice? She didn't understand how that could possibly work. "But how can common folks think of . . . of justice? What does a common man know of laws or God or—"

"You would be surprised," Kurtus said with a knowing smile.

"Well then, what about the mad folks? The deranged? What about drunkards? What befalls them?"

Kurtus laughed, thinking of what Jonpaul did to that sorry lot, "Nothing that is nearly so pleasant."

He killed them! Probably by hanging them or . . . or just slaughtering them as the poor unfortunates slept! A man like Jonpaul would show no mercy for that kind of human failing and suffering. He might let men partake in local justice, probably because he did not care, and he might take care of women and children, but he'd show no mercy for the rest. At least her brother left them alone to their misery.

The thought made her shudder, and she resisted the impulse to press Kurtus for the gory details. She did not really want to know, after all . . .

Nichole still dwelt on these things later, in the stables. She just didn't understand, didn't understand anything; 'twas becoming a confused rush of contradicting ideas in her mind. Maybe some men could be like that, murderous beasts, raping and killing indiscriminately, then have the elevated lift of mind to introduce this strange notion of *landsgemeinde* where common people dictated important affairs and trade schools where common people were given a chance to enter the lofty ranks of merchants, or make a law that said no child shall be homeless. Maybe this same man's darkly green eyes could fill with heart-warming tenderness as he watched his son fall asleep in his arms or with kindness as he helped an old woman to the gate with a heavy bundle. Maybe this same man's voice could lift with laughter and song daily. Maybe this same man eould change the pace of her heart with a look or own a touch so gentle, compelling, she welcomed the caress as a flower opens the sun—

Heavens don't start on that . . .

Yet how could he be so kind to people? As if the great war of good and evil took place in his very own soul. As if he were a mad, insane jumble of these competing forces and impulses. Aye, a terrifying manifestation of insanity.

A picture of this grand and happy place, Dornach Castle, rose in her mind, changing, changing more as each drop of sunlight left the earth, becoming a castle of horrors where what he did to the poor, mad people was just the beginning . . .

Abruptly she saw she had stopped brushing Bregenz and, with a sigh, she resumed with vigor. She had to be rescued soon or go mad—there it was, a fact. Dear Lord, the price paid for breaking the marriage plans to the duke! Like making a poacher pay with not just his life but the life of his family, too. Still, if she could not escape . . . and so far this seemed the case, the way the gates and battlement were guarded and Kurtus and Ari, all the women and even Gavin watched her every move amongst all these smiling guards everywhere . . . "Milady, surely you wouldn't be goin' there? Not that way, milady!" and so on, and Lord, she was never alone . . .

So escape seemed out. The place might be a good deal happier than St. Gallen, but 'twas also a far tighter prison. If only Charles would hurry! He was planning something, she knew it. Paper or no, threat or no, somehow he would find a way to get her back home—hopefully through the peaceful means of the Church. Not just because he needed her but, despite everything, he loved her too much to sacrifice her like this . . .

Dear Charles, forgive me . . .

Home . . . She paused, and the brush on Bregenz's back stopped again as she conjured the Castle of the Lower Lake. Home—where everything made perfect plain sense, where her people were, her women and friends, where her quiet chamber overlooked the view of the lake . . . though already the people here were becoming dear, too . . .

She sighed and took up the brush again, obsessively returning to the puzzle of Jonpaul. How his people loved him, too! The men worshipped him, his every word and move, while the women—

Well, the women! Every female between four and eighty drew in enough air to float every time he walked into a room, the mad boom of their hearts like the beat of drum rolls announcing his presence. A wink could drop them into a faint! Not that she didn't understand all too well the phenomena. One look into those darkly green eyes and she forgot to breathe, falling headfirst into the depths, suddenly only able to think of how it felt to be kissed by him—

"Lady . . ."

Nichole jumped a foot, lost balance, and tumbled over a bucket at her feet to land, at last, on her bottom. A tiny, startled gasp came from behind her. Bregenz neighed, danced a bit as if to say Goodness get a hold of yourself! Still startled, torn between laughter and tears, Nichole gathered her wits to turn and confront the owner of that voice.

A little girl stood several paces away, staring in surprise. Not just any little girl but the most beautiful child she had ever seen. An angel she was, a little girl of about four years, with round, chubby cheeks, painted red and smeared with dirt, and large green eyes. Eyes much like the ones she was trying to forget, but so much prettier, with the tangle of unruly curls that fell over plain rag cloth—

Rag cloth, Nanna always called the potato-sack children, those whose parents were too poor to afford real cloth and used the discarded potato-sack instead. These clothes were surprisingly clean as if great care had been given to what little they had.

The little girl held a newborn lamb on a short lead.

"I must look as silly as a festival mask, do I not?"

The little girl almost smiled, but the "almost" made Nichole abruptly realize the child's distress, the rapid quick breaths, and those precious moments before tears in a child's eyes.

"You wouldn't be laughing at me, would you?"

The little girl shook her head adamantly.

Nichole stood up and approached. "What's your name?"

"Mary" came in a whisper.

"Mary! The name of princesses." Nichole knelt before the little girl, glancing behind her. "So, Mary, where's your mother?"

"In heaven."

"Oh, I see. Is this your friend?" she asked as she petted the lamb's head.

"Oh, yes. Her name is Hanna."

Nichole smiled. "A fine name, too. Well, Mary, I know you don't live here at Dornach, so where did you come from?"

Mary pointed behind her without looking, still staring intently at Nichole.

"In the village?"

Mary shook her head.

"On the hillside?" The little girl nodded. "Did you come all the way yourself?" Mary nodded again and Nichole asked, "Is there a reason for your visit to Dornach?"

"Hanna hurt her foot."

"Oh, my."

"Thc lady in the castle fixes things. Are you the lady?"

"Aye. My name is Nichole." She smiled, reaching out to brush the little girl's cheek. How unusually articulate for her age! "Well, let me have a look. Walk Hanna about."

The little girl walked the lamb in a circle. Nichole motioned for her to come back. Then, gently lifting the lamb's hoof, she spotted and pulled the thorn out. "Naught but a thorn . . . Oh?" Nichole gasped. "Did you hear that?"

Looking confused, Mary shook her head.

"Hanna says thank you, Mary, for bringing me to Nichole to fix my foot, that now she vows to be your fine friend forever."

With a child's belief in these things, Mary studied her lamb before she hugged and kissed her. Nichole didn't understand the tears still lingering and was about to assure her the lamb was fine when the little girl said, "But Hanna is going to heaven soon, too."

"Oh? Who told you that, Mary?"

"Grandma. Grandma says we have to send her to heaven to get food. Grandma can't go down the hill to get bread anymore."

"Oh, I see. Why can't she get bread anymore?"

"She has a cough."

Nichole paused for a moment, her thoughts racing over this, and just as she was about to ascertain if there was not anyone else to go for bread, a tear slipped down the chubby cheek and Mary told her, "But I'm not hungry at all."

The convincing assurance that she would hide her hunger before losing her pet broke Nichole's heart, and she took the little girl in her arms, holding the small, warm body against her breast as Mary cried. She promised the child Hanna would not have to go to heaven, that she would help Mary save her, and as she held the child the miracle happened, the thing Nanna promised would happen one day, and Nichole knew, she knew even before she woke Kurtus and told him where she was going. She knew before she met Mary's grandmother.

Nichole held Hanna on the rope as Kurtus held Mary on his shoulders, his goodly strong voice raised in one of the silliest songs Nichole had ever heard . . . or Mary, by the sound of the child's laughter. Nichole might have been laughing with the little girl but for the race of her thoughts over the problems the child presented. Seemed the very worst time. 'Twas impossible, for at present she had precious little control over her own destiny let alone—

"The Goddess makes no mistakes," Nanna always said, and Nichole wanted to believe that, knew she ought to believe that as she lifted her eyes to search and see the miracle of life everywhere in the changing air of this fall afternoon: the winter geese flying in a perfect triangle beneath a sky made of fall blue and swelling white clouds, the brush of a fresh, cool wind and the rain-washed green grass of the hillside where dozens of brown tree squirrels looked for food, the familiar wood warbler song came from the gold-laden branches of a tree, and—

"Look," Nichole whispered.

"Ah, the fallow deer. A doe and her fawn enjoying the protection of the strictest laws on the Continent."

No deer or elk poaching on Jonpaul's lands. She had heard of these laws and indeed the mother looked up to see them, and as if she knew no harm would come to her offspring, she returned to eating the grass.

"Deers are my friends," Mary told them, just as she had told Nichole that the only others who lived with her grandma were the forest animals that they loved. Halfway down the hillside Mary pointed to a narrow path that led into the pine forest. Needles crunched beneath their feet as they made their way through the towering pines. Mary's house appeared in a small clearing surrounded by pines. A shepherd's modest house, but Mary said she had no father . . .

Kurtus swung Mary from his shoulders, and took Nichole's hand to lead her to the door. He still did not quite understand why Nichole would not send the pretty child back with a servant . . .

The door was shut tight, Mary could not open it. Nichole knocked and knocked. Mary called out anxiously, not understanding this at all. They waited, then waited some more. "Would your Grandma go out now?"

"She is too sick. She is too tired to get our bread. Grandmama! Grandmama! Oh, why does Grandma not answer?"

Nichole turned to Kurtus for help, but she stopped, hearing the old woman's cough. In that same minute she found herself staring at an old mortar and pestle abandoned in the yard near the place where Hanna grazed.

As Kurtus took a turn at the door, Nichole knelt down and picked up the wood bucket and instrument. Tools of an initiate. Of course, she might have guessed . . .

"Wait, Kurtus." She turned to the little girl, who still stared in wild confusion at the closed door. "Mary, who told you to bring Hanna to the lady at the castle?"

"Grandmama . . . she said the lady is the one."

Nichole looked from the little girl's face, and with sudden understanding, she called out through the door, "The trust is sacred. Just as my chosen never abnegated it, I will not abnegate it, either. Lay aside your fears, old woman. Please open the door. You must say goodbye! You owe her this."

A long moment of quiet followed the plea. Confusion rose on Kurtus's face as he realized he had missed a crucial scene in some secret drama . . . but the door was opening. There stood an old woman. Not the child's grandma but surely her great grandmama, frail and weathered and ill now, too, a bloodied cloth pressed over her mouth to stop a cough and her figure crushed by the weight of many, many years. Mary grabbed the old woman's legs, hugging tightly, bursting with the happy news that Nichole would save Hanna so Hanna didn't have to go away after all and wondering why she would not open the door, and on and on, the child's chatter the backdrop for the meeting of two gazes, locked, the key tossed away.

Grief sat in the wise old eyes and there was gratitude, too, though there needn't have been, for it was, after all, her right. Kurtus watched this scene with bewilderment, not understanding at all, less when Nichole knelt down to face Mary. Gently, quietly, "Mary, your grandmama must leave you now . . ."

Soft green eyes shot up to the old woman, who could only nod. "Oh, but where, Grandmama . . . where will you go?" The old woman bent, too, facing the girl, but the swell of her grief stole her breath, her very voice. Desperately the old hand gently smoothed the unruly long curls.

"She must go far away, Mary. Where your mother is—"

The eyes went frantic. "Oh, but I'll go, too—"

"No . . . no, my darling. She must go alone. I will take care of you. You must say goodbye, now."

The little girl threw herself against the old woman, who shut her eyes tight and, using all her last strength, held the small body tightly. Nichole let the time last as long as she could before finally prying the small arms from the old woman, then lifting the girl as she stood. Mary clung tightly to Nichole, the transference quick, complete, as it should be.

"You have chosen well indeed. Your duty is done," Nichole whispered the last words. "May she call softly for you."

The Goddess who never does make a mistake.

The men entered the entrance hall amidst the clamor of muddied boots and noisy mail, rancorous shouts and laughter. Jonpaul slapped Mickeil on the back, laughing with the success of the negotiations to open a new trade route directly from the Venetian textile port through

Basel into the northern German Austrian states. "You will be too rich to be my steward—"

He stopped upon seeing Nichole there. The men all stopped, too, took in the girl, and with knowing smiles, they hurriedly submitted to their servants' help in removing their garb and boots before disappearing up the stairs. Williams removed Jonpaul's mail in record time, gathered his weapons, and disappeared as well.

"You look worried," he first said and cautiously, too, taking in the apprehension marking the lovely face. Her hair was lifted in a tight-woven crown on top, and though she wore an embroidered apron over a plain work dress of blue, he had long since realized the girl could be garbed in leaves and mud, rags or silks, it mattered not at all. Ari believed her beauty radiated from her soul, and while that was no doubt true, the outward shell was as comely as the first spring roses . . .

"There is something I must ask of you."

"Ah . . ." He nodded as if that explained it, a familiar teasing light in his eyes. "What would you have of me, love? Shall I catch the wind at the meeting place of the four corners of the world? Harness the power of the tides? Fetch you a star? What?"

His reward came in a pretty blush, a stammer, and even more uncertainty. She never knew quite what to think of his teasing, past the absolute certainty a tongue-lashing or beating would be far easier to understand, if not to handle. "You seem . . . happy with your success?"

The sudden shift of tactics only told him something of import sat here. He had never seen her tongue-tied before. It also told him it might take some time before she got to the point. "Aye—"

Williams appeared, "Milord, the bath has already been drawn."

Bathing was a shared event in Switzerland, and while Jonpaul could make people wait, hot water would not.

"Look, love, I am hungry and cold. Perhaps you can save your question for after I've bathed and changed?"

"Oh, yes. Of course. How stupid of me." She nodded, relieved to put it off, still nodding even as he disappeared. She stood there dwelling on Kurtus's warning, his certainty that Jonpaul would not permit it, that, aye, "The man is generous to a fault, but he cannot be taking all the little orphans of Dornach! And you, milady! What about you? You are not even married, and well, for God's sake, your . . . ah, situation hardly makes for nestin' the little ones now, does it? I know the darlin's special. One look in those eyes says that—"

He had stopped suddenly, as if a troubling thought crossed his mind before he seemed to shake it from his head, resuming, "I know Jon. He will insist the child be placed in a proper home. I'm just trying to spare you the disappointment."

Nichole leaned against the cold stone wall and closed her eyes. He just didn't understand. Mary belonged to her, belonged to her as if she had been made with her own flesh, more, as Nanna was more. They were chosen. She could no more turn Mary over to a "proper family" than she could slit her wrist.

Without knocking, Nichole burst through his door, stopping Williams midsentence. The young man was quick. "If that is all, milord?" And without waiting for the answer, he disappeared out the still-opened door.

Jonpaul sat on his bed, shirtless, pulling on his fur-lined suede boots. The curly hair was wet and combed back, accenting the handsome, sun-touched features. He was smiling as he finished with the boots and pulled a brigandine over his head, then the muscled, scar-marked chest.

"Please don't say no. I will do anything."

"Indeed . . ." He smiled at the thought. "Well, before I let my mind wonder, love . . . what is it you want?"

"There is a little girl. Mary. She came to me today . . ." The story poured out, though she did not dare explain the meaning, only the facts about the grandmother—dead now, she had already sent two men after the news—then, "I know it seems not right. I am not married. I am even a prisoner of yours, with an uncertain fate waiting for me. I know . . . I know . . ." she wrung her hands, "I am in no position to accept a dependent. I have never even had a dependent before. Yet I know not how to explain how the child affects me—"

She stopped, not understanding the way he studied her as he stepped to where she leaned against the door. His nearness did not help her speech and she struggled to rally her senses above the lure of his beckoning warmth, the fresh, manly scent, the magnetism of those eyes as he studied her.

"Kurtus said—"

"That I'd deny you this?"

When she nodded, he said simply, "He is wrong. Love, if you said, "Milord, I want to house and care for all the lost children of the world, I would start building it for you." With a tender smile he watched those eyes search his for understanding. "And, love, do not doubt that I know the content behind this emotion so plain. You were chosen for the girl, am I right?"

He knew . . . he understood. She searched his face still as the words made sudden emotions swell in her heart, emotions triggered by his tenderness, wrapping around her like a warm cloak, while his sentiments, somehow so masculine, were a magic that would grant her every wish. He never considered denying her . . .

"I remember when my mother was chosen," he went on. "Melody was her name and, Lord, my mother loved the girl as she loved me, more I think."

She saw his sadness. "What . . . happened?"

"Ah, your intuition again . . . She died in the last

outbreak of the black death, thankfully, after my mother. No, your sympathy is not necessary, for, while I cared a good deal for her, 'twas some many years past now." Curious, he asked, "I remember my mother said until Melody she always thought 'twould be her own daughter. Was it so for you, Nichole?"

"Aye . . ." She seemed to drift off with this idea, still so new to her. "Most often a daughter is chosen, but . . . but perhaps I will not have my own children, though Nanna always did say I would have many sons—" Sons, Nanna always said, never children and why, how strange she never thought about this before. Though certain couplings do seem to result only in one sex—

She looked up suddenly, drawing a sharp breath upon meeting the strange look in his eyes. "Why . . . why are you looking at me like that?"

"Like what, love?"

"Like . . . like," *you're about to kiss me.* She forced her eyes away, abruptly panicked until she heard the soft sound of his chuckle.

"Come, love, show me this young Mary who has so obviously captured your heart."

Dear Lord, how he affected her! Nichole nodded quickly, relief piling on top of relief as she stepped aside and opened the door. Mary waited outside with Bettrina, in the center of an assortment of dogs and cats that always followed Nichole about, including now a lamb. "Mary, darling," she smiled. "Please come to meet the lord of Dornach Castle."

With her back straight as Nichole showed her, and a very pleased smile, Mary marched proudly into Jonpaul's chambers. Her cheeks still held the rosy glow of her bath and her hair was dried and plaited with two pink ribbons that matched perfectly the little pink-and-white muslin dress, the tiny slippers Honore had donated to the project of getting Mary ready for Jonpaul's inspection.

"Milord," Nichole said with mock formality, "may I present young Mary."

Mary demonstrated a perfect, deep curtsy and Nichole was pleased, smiling, more as Mary looked up at Jonpaul and burst into giggles, as if expecting him to see the great fun of her masquerade and he did. Jonpaul knelt down but only to pick the little girl up in his arms. "Mary . . . you are the prettiest princess Dornach ever had."

"Oh, but I'm not a princess," she told him, shaking her head. "But Nichole says my name sounds like a princess."

"You also look like a princess in this pretty dress. And I happen to know Dornach needs a princess. Wouldn't you be our princess, Mary?"

Wide eyes shot to Nichole to see if she would let her. Marveling at his charm, Nichole suddenly froze, staring, staring incredulously at the picture of Jonpaul holding the little girl. She stepped closer, not understanding. "Milord . . . Mary's eyes . . . why, they seem so similar, and she looks, she looks—"

"Why, she does look a bit like Gavin, does she not?" He was smiling as he stared, not realizing at first. "The same color hair and the same eyes, except Gavin's are blue and Mary's are green—"

He suddenly realized what he was saying. He set the little girl down, then knelt at her side, and searching the pretty face, he asked, "Mary, Nichole told me your mother went to heaven?"

"Yes and now Grandmama, too. Nichole says she is gone now. Nichole says her love will always be here—" She put a little hand to her heart and Jonpaul smiled.

"Aye, her love will always be in your heart, but still, 'tis a sad thing to lose a person you love." The little girl nodded, her eyes holding the very sadness, and he asked quietly, "Mary, do you remember your mother's name?"

"Grandmama said 'twas Susanne."

Nichole watched the effect of the name on Jonpaul's face and nervous, alarmed, she spoke quickly. "Mary, say goodbye now. Bettrina is waiting to get you your supper." Mary waved goodbye as Nichole ushered her out of the room. She quietly shut the door behind her and watched as Jonpaul moved to the open window and cast his gaze down to the darkening courtyard.

"She is yours."

"Aye."

"But how . . . how could you not have known?"

"A man doesn't always know the products of his couplings, love. 'Twas shortly after my wife died. I was crazed with grief. I used to run through the forests. I'd run and run and for no reason save—" He stopped, pausing as he remembered the pain of those days. "One day I came across a comely young wench bathing in a stream. Susanne. I saw her fairly regularly for a spell, a short spell before I left to oversee the building of Elkhorn Castle on the southwest end of my lands. I returned by the end of winter but not for long. I don't think I thought of her again for over a year. Then one day she appeared in my mind and . . . when I returned to the small shepherd's house where she lived with her grandmother, the old woman, kindly I remember, a long-ago friend of my mother, she told me Susanne had been recently buried. I asked if there was not anything she needed and she said no. That was that."

He turned back to Nichole, only to see her fear. He came to where she stood. "Love . . . love . . ." He gently touched her face, raising her chin to see the fear there. "Though Mary is surely mine and I would naturally extend my protection with my name, I would not place my claim over yours."

She wanted desperately to believe this. "No matter what happens?"

"No matter what." With feeling, "I am only too glad you were chosen for her."

She felt the powerful warmth and tenderness in force again, and as she wondered at the trick, if it could possibly be a trick, the questions confused her, made her dizzy with confusion. She nodded quickly before leaving, trying to find comfort by the thought the Goddess never did make mistakes . . .

The two elderly men, prelates and representatives of the Holy Roman Church, made the announcement formally, accented with exaggerated fanfare and flattery. Thinking it was welcome news and knowing well how to honor His Holiness's richest tax-payers, they at last fell silent, waiting for the good Lord's response with crescent-moonlike smiles . . . which began to wane as the lord Jonpaul stretched the silence, finally disappearing altogether as they suddenly felt the explicit threat of the lord's inexplicable antipathy.

The entire hall fell quiet, too, as all gazes watched Jonpaul, waiting for his response. He leaned forward with his hands on the table, his scrutiny of the two visiting prelates intense and frankly suspicious. The two men shifted nervously as Jonpaul began to look . . . well, dangerous, as menacing as Tamerlane—who left no victims alive. The idea was hardly helped by the fencing gear he still wore: a plain brigandine and thick black belt and boots. Enormous iron bars wrapped around his forearms, from his elbow to wrists, with black leather gloves on his hands, minus the fingers, a black headband. The long blondish hair circled his handsome face like a crown or even a halo, curling at the broad width of his shoulders but doing nothing to offset the harsh scrutiny setting the two men to a nervous dance. "And what is the purpose of this proposed visit?"

The two elderly men exchanged shocked, uncertain glances. The harshness of the lord's tone even more than the inhospitable words gave them pause. "Milord, the bishops, as representatives of his Holy Eminence, need no reason to commune with his faithful subjects, no?"

Jonpaul's smile was not kind. "Do not play games with me. Not since Pope Innocent the Good has the Holy Church done anything without a political motive. I know not the Prince Abbot of Toulon, but I assure you his companions Charles of Lucerne and Kuno of Stoffeln have never known a 'benign motive'."

The man's face reddened, and his mouth hardened to a straight line. "Lord Charles would use the occasion to ascertain the well-being of his sister, over whom naturally there is much concern. He would also use the occasion to discuss the lady Nichole's future."

"You may ascertain and report on the lady Nichole's well-being. Just as you can tell Charles that the lady's future is not open to discussion—"

With a frown and concern, Kurtus leaned over and stopped Jonpaul midsentence. "Jon," he deplored in a whisper, "since when can't you listen to words? Let the man come—there can be no harm in hearing him, can there? Besides, by law you cannot refuse a night of shelter."

Jonpaul stiffened, paused, then took a deep breath. Of course Kurtus was right. Entertaining Charles for a night did not translate to letting Nichole go home. If anything, he would make it clear at the meeting that this, at least, was not negotiable.

When he looked back up, it was with resignation. "Very well," he said. "By law I am required to offer shelter for a night. So be it. You may report that I am willing to open Dornach's gate for this one night." He turned to Kurtus, thinking. Lords Bruno and Hans had recently departed in hopes of reaching their homes before the first snows. A fast messenger could catch them in time, considering their entourage of family, servants, knights and guards. "Kurtus, send Gaylord and . . . ah Gregory to tell Bruno and Hans—I'll leave it to their discretion as to whether to return or not."

Madeline burst into the room and told the news. Nichole rose from where she helped Gavin and Mary finish a puzzle, scattering pieces as she did. Searching her friend's face, she grabbed the stout woman's arms. "Is . . . is this true? Charles is coming for me?"

She never waited for an answer. With a lift of her skirts she fled from the room. The guard rose with shouts and cards flew as he scrambled up to give chase, but as Jonpaul had already learned, for a girl in skirts, she was quick . . .

Nichole flew down the two flights of stairs to the main entrance and out the door. Clouds covered the sky and it was cold. She took no notice as she raced across the yard, scattering chickens and pigs as she flew. Posted at the gate, the two guards watched the ballgame down the hill in the clearing of the forest. All they saw was a streak of blue followed by two long ropes of black hair and a ball flying in the air.

Already running, Jonpaul caught the ball with a hard smack. The chase was on to the finish line. The men were all half naked and covered with mud, wearing only breeches despite the chilly air and cursing and yelling like heathens. Pursued by five opposing team members, including the faster Kurtus and Franz, he darted full speed to the right. Washed by recent rains, a mudpool lay in his path. Feet behind him, Kurtus took a daring leap, landing hard on Jonpaul's neck. This alone might not have brought Jonpaul down, but his bare feet seemed to suddenly sink right through the earth, stealing his balance. Five men, then four more piled in and on each other.

There came yells and grunts and cursing and laughter as one by one the men pulled themselves from the pile. With fascination and considerable anxiousness, Nichole watched as Jonpaul emerged at last from the bottom of the pile. Laughing and cursing louder than the rest, he struggled to his feet in the slippery pool of mud. Kurtus rushed to offer a hand and Jonpaul grabbed it, but just as he got one foot up and rose, Kurtus let go, sending his friend backside to the mud again. The men went wild with their laughter, Jonpaul especially, until, seeking revenge, he lunged in the air and knocked Kurtus smack on his back. Five men immediately flew back into the pile and a fight was on.

Nichole stared in wonder, bothered by his laughter, this glimpse of boyish abandon—so unexpected when paired against the deadly warrior she remembered so well. Indeed, he was laughing so hard as he wrestled his men, as without even seeming to move, he almost carelessly, fended off the assailing blows, laughing, taunting, playing just as he did with Gavin and now Mary, as if it weren't a ruse for the children. The laughter finally put him down. Acting as one, the men took advantage of his breathlessness and managed to knock him backside to the mud and pin him there, demanding a concession to defeat—which he could not do, mainly because he was still laughing too hard. Suddenly he swung his legs up, knocking back two of the men and then throwing off the rest as he came to his feet . . .

Yet his laughter stopped the moment his eyes found her. She stood there beneath the gray clouds in that blue dress, the front-laced white bodice clinging to the high, full curves of her breasts, tight at her small waist. *Oh God, not that dress. Not now, Nichole.* He felt suddenly dizzy, and wiped at his mouth with the back of his hand as he approached where she stood, not even seeing her emotions with the sudden sharp stab of raw desire . . .

Worse than last night when he had found her sound asleep on the pillows around the fire in his study, Gavin sleeping on one side and Mary on the other, a picture book of exotic treats open on her lap, four cats and his dog sleeping in a circle around her. She was the last one he had carried off to bed and she had not wakened, not even for the nearly half hour he stood between his chambers and hers, trying desperately to remember every reason why he shouldn't turn one way. Yes, worse than last night.

"What?"

The single word sounded harsh, though he never realized, wouldn't have cared if it had. He was staring at the upturned face, its delicate lines, and those eyes, drawn nightly in his dreams when he covered them with kisses, as her small, hot body clung to his. Yet she dropped her skirts and grabbed his muddied arms to ask, "Is it true? Is it true?"

To his disbelief, he saw that after all she had been through, after all he had put her through, this could at last make her cry. The tears hung like mist in her eyes. "Aye, it is true."

She could not hide her desperateness, she did not try. "He's coming to take me home?"

She waited for a nod that would set her free and change her fate. Yet the silence grew strangely, then loudly as if the whole world stopped and waited with her. Something cold and awful came to his gaze, striking her like a knife to her heart. The massacre at Stan flashed through her mind and in the moment she knew those eyes had committed the atrocity. Those same eyes prepared her for the inevitable words.

"You won't even see him."

For a moment he didn't think she heard. He was not

braced for the clenched fist that landed hard against his face, swung with the power of her rage. She split his lip and watched it bleed in a fast, thin, trickle down his chin.

She had not a thought of where she was going, only that she could not run fast enough down the grassy slope, her small black boots sinking into the moist ground with each leap. To the side the grazing cows looked up from the grass to watch curiously, but then the girl was gone, flying over the berry thicket on the edge of the forest. Her skirt caught and with a sob she yanked it free, ripping the cloth at the waist. She was flying again, maneuvering through the thick maze of towering pines, flushed, gasping, crying, crushing needles with each step.

The first sound she heard was the close gasp of breath, so close, too close, and she turned to see him barely a pace away. Startled, she stumbled and tripped, flying into a free fall through space—a split second of a wild, frantic panic, braked by long arms snaking around her waist. She half cried, half screamed as he lifted her clear off the ground. Instinctively, nails dug hard into his arm. He dropped her. She swung around, suddenly crazed, panting and feverish and furious, her arms and legs pummeling like a windmill. With a vicious curse, he managed to grab her wrists, then her waist, and bracing her back with his arm, he threw her to the ground, pinned her arms and came on top of her.

A curious triumph. Not a word was said, could possibly be said with the jolt brought by the press of their bodies. Raw, hot sensations washed over them, so many, many millennia removed from Dornach and Lucerne and all that meant, and she stared up in a trance of astonishment as if he would now provide a lengthy explanation. Excitement was a potent fuel rushing through her veins, pumped by her pounding pulse. Confused by it, she struggled to get enough air, then got too much, each breath riveting her consciousness to the naked muscle and heat against her, the press of her breasts against his naked chest, his hard shaft against her side, his thigh pressed between hers.

His each breath came hard and fast, too, and not from running. His hair fell in a riot of curls around his handsome face. Mud smeared across a cheek. For a moment she thought he struggled through the same astonishment, but no, his pause was a desperate measure to catch the wild race of his desire—which was as impossible as harnessing the tides as he drank the bewitching sight of her inky-black hair spread around the grass, the lovely, bewildered eyes, the beckoning rosiness of her parted lips, the thrust of her breasts against his chest, and the flood of sensation as she struggled beneath his weight . . .

Struggled but briefly. The movement shot hot liquid heat through her chest and loins. Enlightenment came in a gasp. She was helpless to stop it . . . him . . . His will reigned dominant, all obliterating, though still she tried, she had to try. She shook her head, her eyes blazing with blue fire. "No . . . no, I hate you! I—"

The hollow words disappeared as they were uttered, falling like a silent echo beneath this wild sweep of sensations, all of them: the steady beat of his pulse pounding against her wrists, the tingling rush along the nerves of her arms and tightening of the tips of her breasts, the terrible ache building deep inside that made her twist and writhe beneath his hard shaft, inciting this yearning until, at last, even her warring emotions were rendered meaningless . . .

Which he knew. "Say it again, Nichole. Say it again and mean it or here and now beneath these trees and a darkening sky, I will have you."

She closed her eyes and tried to shake her head, but instead she heard his name, the whisper of his name on her lips, paired, it seemed, with strange urgency as if only he could save her. And the idea, the knowledge that it was true brought a panic, a panic that exploded in a fiery burst as he brought his mouth to hers. So totally incoherent with the race of her emotions and the force he used, the kiss molded her mouth to his, made her blood pound through her head until it burst into a simmering sea of colors in the deepest part of herself. The shocking hunger of his passion swept through her veins, more real, immediate than her blood . . . then even more as his insistent, demanding tongue slid into her moist recess, forcing her to drink from his mouth as if her very life depended on it.

His hand reached for and pulled apart the lace binding her bodice, pulling the strings until it came apart. Cool air grazed her skin before his hand slid with unconcealed impatience over her shoulder and side to cup the soft mound, massaging erotically while catching her feather-soft cries in his lips as he kissed her still. She felt a hot congestion, a tightening constriction in her throat and chest and loins that made her arch her back and pull her mouth from his with another soft, anguished cry.

She clung to him as his lips came to her bare breasts, laving the swell until he reached the tip, circling with a heat-building swirl of wetness. He drew softly, then more urgently. Shivers exploded into hot rushes between her legs. His own flesh trembled with the feel of her small body yielding, then tense, then yielding again, not even her own rhythm but his, finally theirs as he answered her soft cries with the equally anguished sound of her name.

Then with a cool shaft of air, his muddied chest was against her breast and his mouth was on hers as his hand lifted her skirts. Her undergarments were twisted and torn, finally ripped from her, his hands sliding under her buttocks, lifting her for his entrance. Tingling anticipation rose in shivers, falling then rising again as his smooth hot sex slid over hers again and again. Warmth gushed out in waves and she didn't know she was crying out, clutching at him as he slowly entered her, stopping, remembering only too well how small she was, not wanting to hurt her . . . but the feel of her sent the hard drive of his passion soaring, controlled, but only long enough to take her with him . . .

A chill woke her and she opened her eyes to find herself in his arms, yet surrounded by darkness. Even the warmth of being held against his naked chest could not offset the night's cold wind and she shivered, struggling up through the layers of hazy consciousness. He was making his way up the grassy incline to Dornach's gates, no easy task in the darkness. A pitch-black night, she could not so much as see his face. The only light came from the turrets in the distance.

"I can walk myself."

Her voice sounded curiously weak, distant; as if it belonged to someone else. She felt suddenly shaky as emotions tumbled to the surface. Hot . . . swelling—

No, not now. She would not cry—

"Love, your dress . . . it's in shreds. You're so cold, too. God, but if you caught a fever . . ."

The reply of a parent who was lost to troubled thoughts, abruptly interrupted by an innocent child asking for a treat. Restrained, offhand, distant, "Not now . . ." She shivered, trying to see him in the darkness, making out only an outline of his face. He, too, was deeply disturbed by something. The idea that he might feel guilt, remorse over his raping seemed patently implausible, but the thought, the memory brought uncontrolled anguish that demanded revenge, to hurt him back.

"At least, my lord, a fever would save me the trouble of ridding my womb of your seed."

She felt his body tense, could almost feel the sudden, sharp focus of his gaze as he dropped her legs but held her tight against himself. "You wouldn't."

"I would! I hate you! I'd never carry your bastard . . . never!"

He grabbed her hands and held them tight, his face torn between sudden anger and an innocent shock, a shock she could hardly believe was real. "My bastard would be a boy . . . Like Gavin, a joy—"

"A joy?" she cried, emotions suddenly ripped from her, spilling out. "A joy? How do you think I would feel carrying your bastard? *Yours?* I would rather die! Die—" and she pulled from his grasp and ran. She never knew what tripped her, her torn dress, a stick or log, but she hit the ground stomachfirst and hard, her consciousness vanishing with the impact.

It took the women nearly a half hour to convince Jonpaul that Nichole was unhurt, almost as long as little Mary. She had even woken in the bath, not a bruise on her, let alone a broken bone. "She is fine . . . fine, sound asleep now." Still, he had to see her lying beneath the huge down quilt, her skin scrubbed clean, pale now. He gently laid his finger across her mouth, and as he felt her soft, warm breath, he drew *his* first easy breath.

That night Jonpaul told Mary and Gavin the story of a beautiful princess who could not see. She was blind, he said, blind to the evil of her guardian, but at last a prince abducted her. "To save her," he said with the knowledge of foresight. Yet, he continued, because the princess could not see, she thought her prince was a monster in the form of a man. 'Twas only after her sight was restored that she knew the prince for who he was. He ended with a conspiracy, one that began, "Now, Nichole is like that princess . . ."

Chapter Twelve

The need grew by the minute, the hour, the day, gathering force like the winter storm outside, accumulating to a shrill feverish pitch in her mind that might well be madness. The need to tell the girl, this ferocious monster growing inside, becoming desperate for the vent denied by her severed tongue, it started to feed off her sanity. Katrina lived with the knowledge she was going mad, a certainty far more absolute than God ever was, and though in this desperation she did try, praying brought no solace. Praying never had and never would, and without the hope of prayers, there was nothing but this hellish silence.

The silence filled two hours and there was another left to endure. Katrina's gaze lifted, sweeping across the landscape that was as barren as the silence itself. Not a complete silence, she realized, hearing the steady pour of rainfall outside the church where the sisters gathered to pray. Cloth bound their knees to ease the strain of these endless hours of kneeling in prayer. Stacked in neat rows of somber black, the others knelt motionless, their eyes closed in concentration and so still, she often, like now, stared endlessly at their sexless chests, looking in vain for a rise or fall, however small, that would tell her she was still among the living.

The feverish pitch in her mind sometimes stopped. For no rhyme or reason, it stopped and then she felt certain she was dead, lost in the endless cycles of the eternity of purgatory; she began to think that this need, this hunger to speak and be heard, if only to know her anguish was real, was the absence of God. The sound of the lost soul's desperation to find Him again. The mounting madness of these thoughts created the wild urge to suddenly jump up screaming and lash out at something, anything . . . these fellow creatures, lash out at the blur of nameless faces, if only to see their bruises as the evidence of life. Only the thought of the severity of the consequences stopped her, and then probably not for long. She felt certain that soon she would welcome the rack or whip or any of the hellish methods used to exorcise demons from the flesh . . .

A bell mercifully interrupted the feverish pitch, and the sisters genuflected, rising in silence before leaving the church single file. Once outdoors, rain carried in a bitter wind hit Katrina's face, and yet the sensation felt liberating. A moment of sensation against the backdrop of nothing. With her head down like the others, they made their way across the yard. She watched her worn boots sink into the mud as she perversely took care to make her own tracks instead of using the others. Yet she stopped abruptly. The sister behind her stepped into her, and then as if she was no more than a tree stump or fence pole, the woman hurried around her. The other followed unquestioningly, and it was just such invisibility that was driving her mad. But the small feather she saw consumed this mad pitch of her thoughts. A muddied feather pushed out from beneath her boots. Aye, 'twould take a year or more and then might never come. She had this time, though, the only coin she had to spend. Somehow, somewhere, through the feverish pitch in her mind she would find the rest. With this once-fine white feather came these fragments of an idea, and ideas were always the vehicle of hope.

Fingers trembled as she bent down, grasped the feather, and quickly hid it beneath her habit.

The trumpet sounded. Bettrina stopped, froze, with her hands on Nichole's hair as she finished fitting the rich maroon-and-black embroidered cap over her lady's dressed hair. Alarm lifted on her face. Nichole, too, gripped the dressing table, her face draining of color. "'Tis him! He is here at last! Hurry!" With a rush of movements Bettrina turned and swept up the maroon cape, placing it over Nichole's shoulders, even as she swept across the room and through the door.

A light, cold drizzle fell from the gray sky where a large crowd already watched the arriving retinue from the battlements. More people arrived to see the visitors by the minute, called, like Nichole, by the trumpet. Yet Nichole did not join the crowd. She stood noticeably off to the side. The visitors were her people, but welcomed here at Dornach with hostile, suspicious eyes, so she felt her emotions, indeed her whole being, rally protectively and defensively around her brother.

The first banner flew with the colors of St. Gallen: the familiar gold cross and shield on velvet orange, this carried between two horses in the distance. The bishop followed, clad in a rich ermine cloak that spread completely over his mount. Four knights followed him on horses, then twelve foot soldiers, two archers, all of these men wearing the gold and orange colors. With an accusatory lift of brow, she thought only the bishop could afford the finest velvet livery not just for his retainers but for their beasts as well. If the Church were only half as concerned with the dispensing of wealth as they were with the accumulation, how better the Christian kingdom would be! Next came the Prince Abbott of Toulon, Richelieu, a particularly wealthy benefice showing in his equally impressive retinue, his men as well donned as the bishop, though at least in the more somber black.

Nichole held her breath. The Lucerne colors emerged in the distance, the beloved banner, maroon and black, with the two crossed swords over the tower. Sentiment filled her like a potion, more when next she saw Charles riding his stallion. Oh, how regal and princely! As regal as England's very own Richard once appeared!

Pride swelled in her chest at the sight of the proud, straight back, the aristocratic lift of his head, even the fine prance of his prized stallion. The good people of Dornach would see what manner of man he was!

Nichole bit her lip and suddenly gripped the icy cold of the high stone ledge, feeling a sharp pang of remorse and regret like a knife carving out her heart. The secret, whatever it was, was deadly. She had had no right using it as a weapon against him. May God above forgive her!

She closed her eyes, with her hands still braced on the icy cold stone. Her arms, her whole body tensed as she assured herself he must have found a way to get her back. It had to be . . . it had to! All her many transgressions against him—refusing his choice of her husband and threatening him with the revelation of the paper—all seemed trivial to the circumstances imprisoning her now. Trivail and, God knows, she could not regret them more. Charles forgave her—after all, she could not have been more severely punished, she felt certain, had she spent this time in hell—and now he came to exercise his right, his power, justice over the lord Jonpaul.

My fate, dear Charles, as it always should have, rests in your forgiving hands!

She opened her eyes, and as she stood watching him, shivering against the cold winter wind and filled with terrible regret and remorse, two guards, also dressed in ceremonial garb, came to her side. "Milady, 'tis time to retreat to your chambers."

She turned to face them, about to send them away when she stopped. The look on their stone-cold faces said all. This was not a request. This was an order. Until this moment she hadn't really believed Jonpaul when he said he would not even let her speak to Charles, and for a long, shocked moment she stared, aghast . . .

Yet, hands came to her arms to lead her away, and she knew it was true. He would not let her speak to her dear brother. What she didn't know was that on this Jonpaul had no choice—it was a matter of life and death.

The great hall fell suddenly dead silent. Jonpaul carefully set down the brass goblet and rising, slowly, he met the distinguished bishop's gaze, a man he might normally hold in respect and said, simply, "What? You would have the lady answer what?"

Charles remained impassive, his hands clasped in front of him. He looked thoughtful and concerned, though of course this was a deception. He was actually elated. Dornach was splendid, far more so than he would have guessed, far more than even rumors had supposed. A king's ransom, more than a fair price for his little sister, indeed, a great deal better than the sorry excuse of that duke.

"My dear lord," the good bishop said evenly, "you must see the issue is of . . . ah, no small consequence. The natural laws of man and God, as well as those of the state, are very clear on this matter: The lady Nichole is a highborn lady. Her birth, marriage, and death are matters of state, to be arbitrated by the Church . . . and God," the last he made a point to remind the lord. "The question then, I believe, is not unreasonable."

Jonpaul searched Richelieu's kind face, as if for meaning. Were they after some form of monetary compensation? Huh! Over his dead body!

Jonpaul's angry gaze fell on Kuno, who looked oddly impassive as he motioned to the page to refill his goblet—his jeweled fingers catching and reflecting the late fall sun streaming through the tall windows. And Charles, stroking his mustache but otherwise looking unconcerned, even bored, as if he had nothing to do with this.

On the edge of his seat, Lord Bruno waited for Jonpaul's enlightenment—which was curiously long in coming. Kurtus and Father Ari, too, looked just as confused. Dear God, had they gone daft? It was so obvious!

"Ah, gentleman," Bruno's forged smile disappeared a bit too quickly, "it seems Jonpaul has forgotten . . . ah, how did you put it, my good bishop? Ah yes, the natural law that might follow the question. Jonpaul . . ." his tone changed. "If you set your mind in a different direction, you might grasp the point, the reason, I might guess, that we are gathered here?"

"Indeed . . ." Charles drew Jonpaul's harsh gaze. "Perhaps if you put yourself in my position: of having an unmarried and innocent dependent of some considerable consequence to the state, who has been abducted from my protection by a neighboring lord, then left in his dubious mercy for . . . how many nights alone? Would not, you, too, demand justice?"

"Huh! Demanding and getting are two different things. This is a waste of time—" Jonpaul stopped, just as he was about to tell the snake to go back to Hades, when the words, "the point," were abruptly comprehended. He looked at Charles, then the bishop, then Lord Bruno.

"That, my friend, is the slowest I've ever seen your mind work," Bruno managed to say before he started laughing. Not a little chuckle but a great roar of a laugh, joined by Kurtus and Father Ari and finally, as he let it all sink in, Jonpaul himself.

Of all the possible reactions Kuno and Charles anticipated, laughter was not one of them. They exchanged alarmed glances, confused until Jonpaul surprised them again. "My dear lord . . ." He raised his goblet to Charles with congratulations. "'Tis a move that does honor to thy name—no bolder one have I ever heard." Bruno ayed the sentiment and Jonpaul chuckled again. "And it might indeed save you much. Kurtus, fetch the lady Nichole. It seems she has a question to answer."

Nichole paced the room in a state of extreme agitation. Where was Bettrina? It was nearly two hours since she last took Mary off to play with Adline's youngest girl, Sharon, and nearly an hour since she last reported on the proceedings in the great hall, where she listened with others behind closed doors. Bettrina said the lord Jonpaul had made Charles and the bishops wait over two hours. This she reported four times, then, how when at last he arrived he brought a "great frosty chill" with him. Bettrina told her how they inquired after her health and well-being and Jonpaul replied as if they were discussing a pleasantry . . .

So now what was happening?

Nichole swung onto a bench and clenched her fist, imagining Charles standing up and shouting across the hall, "Immediately! In the name of God, I say immediately!" The bishops then would threaten excommunication if Jonpaul did not agree, far too heavy a price to keep her worthless personage prisoner. What could he want with her now? A vent for his great lust? Well, Jonpaul of all men, seemed to find that everywhere. Worthless was right, for what good was she now to him? She had long since given him everything, he had little reason to keep her now—

Aye! She jumped up, suddenly certain this must be happening. Why else bring the bishops? What power had they? Only the threat of excommunication, the worst punishment in all Christendom. To be shunned by all Christians for as long as one lives, then condemned to everlasting hell. Even Jonpaul would scramble to avoid that most terrible punishment!

So she would be going home with Charles tomorrow. What would he do? Would he just be so glad to have her back that he forgave her? Would he still want to force her to marry the duke? And would she? Had she repented that much? How could she fight him anew? And what if Jonpaul did have the Bible, the paper? She felt fairly certain he was bluffing, but—

Dear Lord, more trouble could not be found in Pandora's box.

Trying to confront her uncertain future, Nichole's thoughts raced in these circles. A knock came to the door and she rushed to open it as Kurtus called to her. "Yes?"

"Milady, I am to escort you to the hall."

She grabbed his arm. "Am I to be allowed to go home?"

"'Tis hardly my place to discuss your fate. However, I am instructed to warn you," Kurtus's voice held an unnatural sternness to it, "you may only speak when answering the questions put to you. Not a word more. I am to have your foresworn promise?"

She stared for a moment, not with anger but with sudden irritation. "What is he so afraid I might say? That you beat me? That I've been tortured here and fear for my life?"

Disbelief crossed his face, and he cocked his head. "You really don't know?"

Nichole felt a hairsbreadth from screaming. "I don't know *anything* anymore."

"Well, know this: Jon has his reason for minding your words with your brother and a damn good one it is. Come now, a roomful of people are waiting."

With Kurtus at her side, Nichole, wide-eyed, expectant, emerged into the room. Silence descended like an iron gavel as the roomful took in the dark-haired beauty draped in a heavy maroon velvet. The gown was remarkably simple. The low-cut bodice opened to a vee at the middle, temptingly revealing a white silk blouse laced to her small waist and long, loose sleeves that gathered tightly at her wrists. Folds of rich fabric dropped to the floor. She lifted her skirts, as if to run, revealing a pink silk petticoat beneath, and with the expectancy on her face, she searched and found the one man who mattered to her now.

Bishop Richelieu's brow rose, and with a curious smile. Well, little wonder the lord did not seem upset—who would be with this treasure of beauty?

"Charles!" She rushed toward her brother.

Jonpaul was quicker. With one hand on the table, he leaped over. Nichole fell into his chest with a startled gasp as he took her arms, a gentle hold. He wore the green velvet doublet, trimmed in gold with a gold sash and black leather breeches, tall black boots. She looked up with unmasked fury. He shook his head, his blond curls brushing the broad width of his shoulders. "I cannot let you."

Breathing hard, with her color rising, she looked at Charles, her look a plea for his intervention. Charles met her gaze squarely with a slight nod, telling her to do as Jonpaul bid. A small stab of pain, then a question flashed into her eyes. That hurt, and with transparent distress, she stared, searching the familiar face for a sign of his forgiveness, a familiar wink or smile, or even some gesture of his concern. Yet there was nothing, neither forgiveness nor condemnation.

Jonpaul led her to a chair at the table. Then she felt the tension in the hall—as thick as cheese, Nanna would say.

She searched the room for its source, but found Lady Adline instead, the only other woman in the hall. The kind lady nodded encouragement, which brought surprising comfort, reminding her that Nanna also had said: "Whatever ye do, don't look to men to provide comfort. That is mostly found with yer own sex."

Bishop Richelieu approached the young lady. His hands were folded in front of himself. Kurtus provided the introductions. Nichole rose to drop a curtsey and formally kiss the bishop's ring before sitting again. The good bishop circled her chair as if deep in thought. "Milady Nichole, we are told that you are well."

"Perhaps in body, milord, but not in spirit."

The bishop rarely found a woman's spiritual discomfort a cause of much alarm. Since Eve, woman had never known a moment's peace, and in any case he knew well the source of her trouble. It was his purpose in being here. "No doubt. Well, my dear, you have been through much. We have come to try to right this situation for all parties concerned—which we suspect means forcing the lord Jonpaul to rectify before the eyes of God and His world the crime he committed against you."

So she was going to go home! Hope changed her face as she waited eagerly his next words.

"So we need you to answer the question: Was there an injustice committed against you, my dear?"

The question struck her as absurd and she opened her mouth to speak, then shut it. What? "Indeed! My very presence here is proof, is it not?"

"I am speaking in biblical terms, my dear."

Nichole did not grasp his meaning. "I'm not sure I understand. Surely I do not have to tell God's own respected authority that the Good Book does not condone abduction, the holding an innocent woman against the will of her family and country?"

The eloquence of her speech brought a lift of brow.

"No, of course not, though these are not issues we feel are within the domain of the church . . ." He paused, struggling with the choice of words. "I see I must speak bluntly. My lady, in the nights that the lord Jonpaul held you alone, with neither chaperone nor company, did the lord Jonpaul . . . force you to lie with him?"

The shock registered visibly. She paled and her eyes shot to Jonpaul, questioning, searching his for an answer he would not give. "I will not answer that question!"

"You must and before God, you must swear to tell the truth."

She didn't understand. "Why? Why must I!"

In a sterner voice, the bishop demanded, "Answer the question, my dear."

"I can't . . . I can't . . ."

Lady Adline rushed to Nichole's chair and took her hand. Nichole clasped it tightly as the lady begged in a whisper, "Quickly, Nichole, and 'twill be done."

The question scared her senseless. She could not guess why they would ask her such a thing, but she instinctively knew it bode ill. There was only one thing to do—render the question meaningless and moot. "Very well. I shall answer the question." She looked up courageously. "No. He did not."

Charles straightened, alarmed.

Kuno shot him an irritated glance. It was obvious to everyone she was lying. Women were so easily intimidated—which he himself was happy to do, and rising now, he said, "If so, then you shall submit to an examination. That is, if you swear before God that you are telling the truth."

An examination . . . Thoughts rushed dizzily. An examination would prove she was lying, since she was, in fact, more than one coupling seperated from her maidenhead. She'd have to name a person and whoever she named would be punished. Oh, God, what were they doing?

"Nichole . . ." Jonpaul's voice answered her fear. "Answer the question again. Truthfully, without concern for my condemnation. I am willing to bear the consequences of your answer."

She met his gaze for a long moment before her eyes lowered, and in a whisper she said the fateful words. "Yes. The answer, then, is yes."

Charles jumped to his feet and in a pretense of outrage, he slammed a clenched hand to the table. "Then as her guardian and brother, I demand retribution!"

Jonpaul's brow rose. "And I believe I said I was willing to accept the consequences of the lady's answer."

The bishop was so pleased, for the business went far easier than anyone anticipated. "So then, you, the lord Jonpaul Van de Birs agree to marry the lady Nichole?"

The words spun around her like a whirlwind, then a tornado that lifted her to her feet. She could hardly breathe. For the first time in her life she thought she might faint of shock alone . . . then she was certain of it and she would, she truly would if she did have to get the outrageous idea out of his mind. Her gaze found Jonpaul, expecting to hear his familiar laughter as he said, "A jest, Nichole, only a jest."

Instead she heard these terrible words as he studied her. "I would also have it publicly known to one and all that I agree willingly."

"No . . . no!" She was shaking her head, fearing the worst. "But I won't! I won't . . . Charles! Dear God, Charles . . ." She was a hairbreadth from hysteria, and before anyone could stop her, she ran to her brother and fell on her knees before him. "Charles . . ." She grabbed the cloth of his maroon velvet doublet in a deathlike grip. "Tell him! Tell him you would never consent! You would never let me marry our forsworn enemy! Never!"

He took her hands in his, stopping himself from shaking her senseless for this melodramatic show, and she saw his anger. It frightened her, she just didn't understand . . . less when he said under his breath, "My motives are many. You would not be capable of grasping them—"

"Surely," the good bishop tried to intervene, somewhat shocked by the extent of the young lady's distress, "my lady Nichole can understand how far the proposed marriage will go to align Lucerne with Basel and the Alliance. It would not be the first union God made to prevent war and, dear God, but He," the bishop pointed upward, "blesses all such unions—"

"Curse His blessing," she swore, "if he would have me suffer so for it!"

The priests in the hall immediately genuflected. Shock made the bishop gasp. He shot a glance to Jonpaul, afraid that good man would change his mind seeing this wild, rebellious side to the girl, so obviously . . . ah, upset at the idea of marrying him. The lord watched warily indeed, obviously displeased, but not with the girl. No, 'twas Lord Charles who owned his displeasure. With one booted foot on the bench, resting his weight on that bended knee, the lord Jonpaul measured the lord Charles's response to the girl, rather than the other way around, and measured it carefully.

"You cannot want it, Charles!" she whispered, but loud enough for all to hear. "I don't believe you want this! Are you trying to punish me? If that is so and I think it must be, would it not be easier to slit my throat than to bury me inch by inch over the long years? Charles, I beg you . . . I beg—"

"Enough!"

The command thundered above her, scaring her, more when she saw the cold emotion in his pale eyes. A deadly quiet fell over the room, a collective shock. She didn't understand what was happening and she shook her head as the room suddenly blurred and the word no . . . no echoed futilely in her mind, over and over . . .

With a wave of his arm, Jonpaul dismissed everyone in the room. They filed out silently. Charles dismissed his sister with an irritated glance before rising, a glance that challenged every ounce of Jonpaul's control . . . which he managed, and only with thoughts of what a confrontation would cost Nichole now.

The pain was deep and swift and strong. The brother she loved and cherished all her seventeen years had abandoned her to their enemy like . . . like Bruno had said, a lamb to slaughter. Seventeen years of her brother's love ripped from her as her lifeblood from an open wound. His boots sounded quietly on the marble floor, echoing like the "no" in her mind, and she looked up as he knelt in front of her.

He reached to her, but she retreated. "No . . . no . . . please, I—"

Yet his hand came to her chin and she closed her eyes as she felt the gentle trace of his hand to her wet cheeks. When he felt her tremble, he cursed, and ignoring her plea, he lifted her onto his lap in one fluid motion. Pain made her weak, so weak, far too overwhelmed to fight him, and though she went rigid with the contact, the very next wave made her suddenly bury her face in his chest as she cried. She did not know how long they sat there, and she was only vaguely aware of his hands brushing smooth her hair over and over as he waited for the first shock to subside.

"You know, love, this is an intractable blow to my feelings. Come, Nichole, you've hurt me enough."

With a wipe of her eyes, she looked up with the penetrating gaze of a child passing judgment. And she was. He meant it as a comforting tease. Images filled her mind: the warrior who fought the men of St. Gallen, flashes of the horrific carnage of the village Stan and, aye, even his unholy passion as he laid her to the forest floor—all of these juxtaposed against moments, like now, of his tenderness. The two sides that could not be reconciled.

She remembered last week when she, Gavin, Mary, and two of Gavin's friends were climbing the stairs with the runt of a pig's litter. It was the rare late litter and the common practice was to kill the runt, a sacrifice in winter months to make the others stronger. She and the children had begged the piggery man, Stefano, to let them keep the piglet instead. They were carrying the poor little thing up to her rooms where she was going to show the boys how to feed and care for the little fellow when they ran into Jonpaul and Kurtus. She was certain he would forbid it. It wasn't just the pig, either, but the whole entourage: the children and Hanna, too, the three cats who always followed her now, Hercules, his dog, and now the poor little pig.

With laughter, Jonpaul said, "I best have the girl housed in the stables before she has the stables housed in my solar."

"'Tis too late by far by, lord," Kurtus laughed. "The other day I came across the lady and the dozen children that follow her about, all with boxes of baby chicks—to keep them warm through the night's frost."

"If only I could be so lucky," Jonpaul laughed as they left, apparently not caring at all about the animals.

"Ah, 'tis a sad day when a man is envious of a goddamn chick . . ."

She had to sit down after that, right there on the steps. Times like that—and God knew, that was not the only incident—she found it nearly impossible to keep in mind his duplicity, or the other side to his nature. She had to remind herself of the worst of the stories of Jonpaul the Terrible, his rage and pillaging of the countryside after his victory in the Burgundy War. She had to conjure the terrible nightmarish vision of the village of Stan—of a mother lying slain with her baby.

Those very thoughts made her desperate. She had to get out of this, and she withdrew from his lap, yet the pain felt like an iron weight on her heart, and she almost could not stand. "I still just can't believe he did this to me . . . I—"

"He had to, love. If I had only thought of it myself, I would have foreseen it."

Shock and confusion vied equally in her eyes. She was afraid he would tell her, then she was afraid he would not. "Why? Why did he have to?"

"As your husband, I would stand to inherit Lucerne. It would cast considerable doubt on any . . . ah, paper I might present that questions your brother's inheritance."

She stared for a long moment, then suddenly sat down again, her hands braced on the side of the bench. "Oh, God. I never . . . I never thought." It changed everything. She might never forgive Charles, but at least now she understood. He did so not to punish her but to save himself. She was indeed the sacrificial lamb.

Those blue eyes suddenly found him. "Do you have the paper?"

"I won't answer that."

"I don't believe you do! You are lying about it! If only I could prove—"

"Yet you can't."

She stared for a moment before turning, presenting him with her back. Silence passed with the swift beat of his heart as he waited for what would come next. He thought he was prepared.

"You know, before I was called down to the hall, I was thinking, I was certain, in fact, that 'twould be you who was threatened with excommunication today. Jonpaul . . . would they?"

His words followed on the heels of a long pause. "Your brother, Nichole . . . would stop at nothing."

She swung around to face him. "Then, dear God, refuse for me! You cannot want to be married to someone who has nothing but . . . hate—"

In the next moment he had her by the arms, his height towering over her, his gaze locked to hers. "Hate, love? I think not. What you hate is a lie, a falsehood—"

"Your lies, your falsehood!"

"Nay, love. Answer me true, girl: would you refuse the marriage if you knew for a fact that I never so much as saw the village of Stan?"

"But I don't—"

"But if you did? If you knew I was a just man? Answer me!"

"I don't know," she cried. "I don't know anything but that if you were this just man, if you were not a pretender, you would not want to take a bride who harbors the most vile suspicions, suspicions that would put her in a constant state of fear and worry, suspicions that would make her recoil from your every touch and word. Please, I beg you, milord, for both of us, refuse!"

Chapter Thirteen

Jonpaul studied her upturned face for a long time. As beautiful as she was naive, the plea sat in the bluc eyes, shaded with her desperation and washed with waiting tears. There was nothing within his power he would not give her, nothing but the answer she wanted. This was no more possible than stopping the winter snows or, as hc remembered, harnessing the tides.

"I can't, love. I won't."

The battle was lost and with it the war. Despair was a knife put neatly through her rib cage, and she collapsed with her wound, toppling like a tower of child's blocks.

Katrina cursed the slight tremble in her hands as she held out her plain wood bowl for the soup. Yet no one noticed or cared. Invisible, she was invisible. A sister wordlessly poured a ladle of the almost-clear broth. Made from bones and potatoes, no meat ever went into this broth. Yet even if it were like the thick, hot stews she remembered at the Castle of the Lower Lake, she would gladly give it up for this glimmer of hope. 'Twas only the danger that made her tremble.

She stepped aside.

A gruff-looking man wielded a sharp knife, neatly slicing the still-hot bread. He waited for Katrina to pick her piece and move along for the next in line. His gaze came up when this did not happen. For one terrible moment she lost her nerve, then, closing her eyes, she conjured the vision of Charles riding past her. The pained cry rose from her heart, unfeigned, sounding mute and strangled as she threw her head back and tossed the bowl of soup up in the air.

Boiling hot soup spilled over the man's arms and apron front. He let out a howl as the knife dropped from his hands to wipe frantically at the burning liquid on his arms. All gazes turned to the commotion. Katrina pretended to collapse on the table in a fit. The knife disappeared under her habit seconds before hands came to her person, lifting her up.

Kira pressed against the wall in the crowded chapel. Breathing hard, her gaze, wild with emotion, focused on Jonpaul standing with Lord Bruno before Bishop Richelieu and six dark-clad priests. She couldn't believe this was happening. He was to marry her . . . marry her! Curse to hell that starry-eyed witch!

"I forgive you, Kira," Nichole had said to her the very next day, staring at her with those strange, piercing eyes, as if she could measure and assess her very soul. She had born it trembling with an impotent fury, nodding quickly and looking away, unable to say a word.

What a fool Jonpaul was! Blind to the lady's ploy, the way she used this pretense of hate like a lure, arousing, nay, inciting his fooish masculine interest, until now . . . now he was caught. Snared like a cod in a net. Dear God, the girl bewitched all of them, only they were too stupid to see it. All her airs of superiority, then her potions, and, of course, how could she forget the way she saved Lord

Bruno's horse—that had worked better than an outright seduction.

Oh, she was a clever one, she'd give her that.

What to do? What to do?

Kira was not the only person unhappy with the marriage. Surprisingly few, if any, of Dornach's people were actually glad for it, though, unlike Kira, nearly everyone was overjoyed their lord would take the lady Nichole Lucretia for his wife, as her medicinal skills were God's very own blessing to Dornach. "What did Kily say the dowry was?" Kira turned to see the speaker, sitting in the pew at her side.

"A treasure, he said, a fat, large treasure."

"Still, 'tis a shame!"

"Aye. Why couldn't they wait? Why? Imagine our lord's very own weddin' on the day the betrothal was announced! No feasts to speak of, no parties, the great dances, theater, hunts and games, the whole wonderful three days needed to properly celebrate a marriage! Gone . . . vanished. 'Tisn't right, I say—"

"Aye, in all my days, I've not heard of anything like it. Not a soul from Basel is even here—I mean to go visit my sister tomorrow just to tell her. 'Twill be the first she hears about it, too, I wager."

"Aye, the messengers won't be dispatched till tomorrow. Lord, 'tis a shame—"

The doors opened again and Lord Charles and the Bishop Kuno's names were announced. With the rest of the crowd, Kira craned her neck to see this ill-famed man. Her gaze riveted the tall, darkly handsome man. She drew a sharp breath and she was not the only one. The packed chapel fell suddenly quiet with the collective impressions before whispers rushed up and down the aisles. Everything about him—the famous velvet colors and pale, jeweled eyes, that mustache and goatee, the taxed, bored air about him as he moved to his seat—no, not bored but amused, as if this were a child's carnival he was forced to endure—everything about him accented his uncommon stature, a certain tension or danger about him. Danger! The thought made her search and find his black glove. Her heart was suddenly hammering. She had to get closer.

"We must get her dressed," Madeline whispered to Bettrina as if it was a secret. There was urgency in her voice, as the wedding would take place in less than a half hour. They would be called any minute, which Bettrina understood only too well. She twisted a handkerchief as another might wring their hands, staring at the young lady's back where she knelt at the altar of the Virgin, deep in prayer. As soon as the lord had sent her in her room, she had discarded the stunning velvet maroon dress for a plain yellow day dress. Then the lady had not moved for the next three hours, though every once in a while a hand would reach to her face to wipe the tears.

Why would any woman cry when she was to be married to the lord Jonpaul? Even if they were once enemies?

"Milady . . . the time . . . You must be getting dressed."

Nichole did not at first move. Then after genuflecting, she turned. "Yes . . . I should be dressed." She pulled the pins so that the maroon hairpiece came off, bringing this to her trunk. She shifted through her hair ribbons till she found yellow and black ones. These she simply tied around her lifted hair.

Bettrina stepped behind her to undo the buttons on her back. Nichole swung around, "No, I must wear this dress." Madeline gasped as Bettrina exclaimed, "But the pearl-and-pink silk!" She pointed. "'Twas his own mother's wedding dress, the most beautiful! And with your maroon cloak—"

"I will wear this dress. I must wear yellow on this day,

and this is the only yellow in my trunk."

"But what will people say!" Madeline wanted to know. Even more to the point, "What will he say?"

She shrugged, not caring at all what anyone thought, much less him. Madeline started to protest, but Nichole stopped her, "No, please. I will hear no more about it."

Madeline and Bettrina exchanged worried glances. Their lady was not well, that was clear. Her eyes were red and swollen, her skin unnaturally pale, translucent against the yellow color, and her voice was weak from emotion. They had tried to ease her trouble, knowing of course she held Jonpaul responsible for her abduction and . . . well, everything else, that until today Lucerne and the Alliance were not on the friendliest terms . . . but was he not changing all that by marrying her? What more could she possibly want as restitution?

"Milady," Bettrina reached out to her, desperate to help, "are ye sure? The people will not understand you wearing that dress—"

Yet the knock sounded at the door and it was time.

Nichole appeared in the entrance. Over two hundred people, waiting in the chapel, turned to see her standing there. She saw none of them, as her eyes were downcast, though she heard the rushed, shocked whispers that followed the stunned silence. She didn't care. She didn't care about anything . . .

Until the moment Jonpaul's gaze came to her. She felt the exact moment. Silence came over the entire room again. She didn't understand what was happening now. Kurtus was supposed to escort her to the altar . . . but he was making no move toward her . . .

Jonpaul set Mary to her feet. Gavin took the little girl's hand, his blue eyes wide and round as he wondered with part awe, part horror how a woman—even Nichole!—

could dare to provoke his father like that. With shock, the roomful of people wondered the same as they pressed back to make room for his way. Charles himself cursed viciously under his breath, irritated with the delay this would cause but admittedly amused by her theatrics and only because now another man had to deal with it. A relief all around, this was.

Before Nichole guessed what was happening, his boots appeared before her on the crushed petals of flowers thrown against the chapel's wood floor. "A dress of mourning on my wedding day?"

The question surprised her. She kept forgetting his mother, his mother who would have had a yellow mourning dress as well. She held perfectly still, trying to stifle her natural response to his anger, which was felt, if not heard by the entire room, more when he whispered, "You push too far, love. I will have you change—"

"Nay." She looked up, a whispered cry. "I will not—"

He silenced her with the gentle press of his hand, unlike his words. "You don the gown I selected or I will publicly strip this rag from you and dress you myself."

Nichole didn't move; for a long moment, she couldn't move.

"Quickly now, I've been kept waiting long enough."

She caught her trembling lip, then suddenly turned and fled. She hardly remembered the rest of that day. Bettrina and Madeline were with her and wordlessly, they helped her into the other gown. She could not stop trembling, even as with more sympathy than she knew, Bettrina finished her hair, a thin braid wrapped loosely around her unbound hair, crowned with a delicate wreath of pale roses, her wedding gift from Gavin.

Gavin. The only hope for the future. Someday young Gavin would inherit. The wealth of her intuition spoke loudly about the special boy. He was not just good and kind, but one day he would be great. She would use all her influence to enhance the good in him . . .

Madeline placed the cloak on her shoulders and then gave her over to the waiting arm of Kurtus.

Nichole appeared again in the chapel, though the response she elicited was quite different this time. Murmured awe raced through the crowd. The gown was simply beautiful and she in it: smooth long folds of pearl silk, gathered loosely at the low-cut bodice and trimmed with delicate lines of pale rose, this decorated with hundreds of tiny pearls. The sleeves were long and tight, old-fashioned in the way they draped over her hand, while the gown and cloak trailed two feet behind her.

The blue eyes never once were seen, for she never dared to look up. Kurtus led her to the altar, where she knelt at Jonpaul's side as he took her hand before the bishop. The touch of his large hand made her aware of how terribly cold hers was, of its slight tremble, orchestrated, it seemed, by the irregular beat of her heart. Kurtus gently removed her cloak, watching like the rest as the long dark hair cascaded over the pearl silk.

Even as she listened to the bishop's litany of Latin, she waited for something to happen—a sudden storm, or hurricane or fire, an act of God to demonstrate the extreme injustice of what was happening to her. As if this were no more than one of hundreds of childhood disasters she always managed to escape! Nothing happened. The litany of the Latin was taken in chorus by the other priests, then Jonpaul was repeating his vows and then, fatally, she heard the whisper of her own voice repeat hers.

A ring was placed on her finger. A delicate band of platinum sprinkled with tiny diamonds, the simplicity of it more beautiful somehow than the combined gems of France and England both. He leaned over to kiss her, taking her chin in his hand as he lowered his mouth. Grief had so numbed her heart, mind, and body, she could not even say for sure how long the kiss lasted or even when it was over except that, as the audience cheered, throwing flowers over them, she became aware of the scrutiny of his gaze. As if the kiss made him understand the depth of her feelings for the first time. But then it was over and, too late, she was his wife.

A single torch threw shadows against the stone walls of the hall, and the distant sounds of the drunken feasting below drifted through the corridor like a cool draft of wind where Jonpaul leaned against the wall opposite the courtyard window, waiting impatiently. Where was he? God knows, this was the last night he felt like waiting.

He smelled the ale before he heard the scuffed footsteps climbing the stairs. Father Ari, in his dress robes, appeared like a ghost, a very drunk ghost, this giant, dark shadow floating unsteadily down the corridor. Jonpaul stepped from the shadows at the last minute, purposely startling the man. Father Ari gasped like a scream. The brass goblet in his hand dropped with a loud clamor to the floor. The wine spilled, and Ari, clasping his heart dramatically, accused, "Dear Lord, you'll give a man a heart seizure!"

"Much deserved. You are drunk."

"And why not? For God's sake, 'tis yer wedding day!"

Irritated, Jonpaul got right to the point. "Where is he?"

"Being neither adept at nor overly enthusiastic about spying upon others, I cannot say for sure, but I believe he is easing his weight on a well-used piece of Dornach's property—trespassing where many have trespassed before—"

Jonpaul stopped him with a chuckle, one without humor. The more drunk Ari got, the more maddeningly verbose. He had managed to slip Nichole from the wedding feast without anyone noticing, sparing her from the obscene, drunken and wild cheers of the crowd, and now she waited in his chambers. "My dear friend," his tone was warning enough, "you can believe I am not interested in your drunken revelry tonight. Get to the point, man."

"The girl, Kira. In his room."

A brow rose. "Now there's a piece of trouble."

"Only if the man is as drunk as I, which as far as I could tell by the perspicacity of his conversation, however mundane the subject matter, he is not—yet."

"Ari, I want you to listen to them—"

"Listen? Oh for God's sake—"

"Then find someone to do it for you. I want to know what the man has planned. You can believe it has naught to do with either my health or the well-being of the Alliance."

"I doubt that he'll be discussing strategies while straddling—"

"In the event that he does . . . Something about him—"

"Suggests the terrible or terribly perverse, I know. Very well." He peered around Jonpaul as if fearful of being overheard, "What of the lady? Is she faring better?" Nichole was silent and despondent throughout the feast, neither eating nor drinking. Once he thought he saw a tear, but—

"Nay, I think not. Which reminds me . . . You did get them, did you not?"

For a moment Father Ari couldn't guess what Jonpaul meant. "Oh, aye! Well, not me exactly. 'Twas Bettrina and 'twasn't easily got, either. None left in all of Dornach. But we did get two from Basel and they are in your chambers—"

"Good—" Father Ari started to interrupt, but Jonpaul held up his hand, dismissing him. "That's all. Good night now."

"But," Father Ari held up his finger, but Jonpaul turned down the hall, disappearing into the darkness. Father Ari thought of what Bettrina just told him and then what was going to happen when he tried the old trick on Nichole. He didn't want to laugh, but the idea of Jonpaul, the smoothest of smooth-talking rakes, trying to explain it to the lovely Nichole, made him laugh, a great roar of laughter . . . until he remembered who Jonpaul would blame. He sobered up quickly and left to find the poor Tom who would land the unpleasant job of listening tonight.

Jonpaul passed through the door of his chamber, shutting it quietly behind him. With two gold-plated goblets in hand and a bottle of the sweetest wine to be found in three countries, he leaned against the door. Only firelight lit the room, but it was enough, for Nichole sat on a small wood stool before the hearth, to keep the chill at bay. She did not look up; her eyes were lowered. She kept her back perfectly straight and shoulders squared, her hands neatly placed on her lap. She held perfectly still, save for the nervous turn of the wedding ring on her finger. Bathed in firelight and circled in the pearl silk, she looked ethereal, otherworldly and, dear Lord, so beautiful.

"Nichole."

Those eyes lifted, but briefly before lowering again long enough to reveal her fear. He set the glasses and wine on the ledge of the hearth before kneeling before her and taking her cold hands in his, willing his warmth to chase her chill and the tremble there. "Love . . . love, this fear? You know I would not hurt you?"

Not willing to move, especially unwilling to meet his gaze, she held still, but he felt the shudder go through her. He could almost feel how much she was trying to stop it, control it, but why? She must know at least that much by now, did she not?

She looked up again to speak but stopped. What could she say? The present night so pressed on her mind that the unpleasant future was pushed far, far away, and all her fears, its darkness for Lucerne, for all of Switzerland vanished beneath the weight of these next hours. She tried not to think of it, the heat of his kisses and the caress of his hands, the way he forced her surrender, bit by bit, demanding all of her, mind, body, and soul, everything, rewarding her with the heavenly pleasure until . . . until it was over and her senses returned and she saw it was him . . . him.

If only she were a virgin, then in ignorance she would find her courage. But she wasn't. Just the memory of her vulnerability, of being shaken to the depth of her soul was enough to make her bolt. The vivid memory of his possession pressed on her mind, always, so that night after night, even before the coupling in the forest, she lay sleepless in her dark room remembering, crazed, mad with confusion over how he could do that to her and then, when she imagined having to endure his love-making nightly, she thought it would be easier to die . . . it would . . .

She would not cry, not now—

A gentle hand reached to her chin, lifting her face to view the tears lingering there like mist on a lake. The effect of her emotions caused a sharp breath as he searched this luminosity in her eyes, understanding only too well. "Nichole . . . love, I will have our marriage consummated. Tonight."

She drew a deep, uneven breath, closing her eyes again, as if to the fate itself. A gentle hand brushed a loose wisp of hair from her face, and so gentle, he leaned over and kissed her mouth where it trembled slightly. She shivered beneath the warmth of his breath, which carried the sweetest hint of the wine. He pulled back a bit, measuring her response, the quick rise in the beat of her heart, the pink flush rising on her cheeks.

"Yet I have always had your passion, haven't I?"

Pride shot her eyes up and she started to deny it, but in the next breath he leaned over again, so close his lips almost touched hers. She held perfectly still, maddeningly aware of the heat from his body, that clean masculine scent of his, like a warm, fresh breeze across the lake. She felt her senses reeling, heightening with his closeness, and while her eyes were closed and she did not see his humor, she heard it in his voice as he said, "You little fool. Should I prove that to you?"

No was an answer but also a confession . . . Yet he was interested in the proof, one got as he covered her mouth with his. Her lips were maddeningly soft and compelling, and with a previously unknown gentleness, he pried them open to his pleasure, a pleasure impossible to resist and she did not try to. The kiss, so slow and tantalizing, felt like a hot wind blowing into her body, a wave of sweet desire, rising, rising, like her hands. Helplessly her small, clenched hands rose as if to circle the velvet of his brigantine, then dropped with the will of her resistance. Then, as the kiss deepened ever so slightly and her head swam, she felt his hands beneath her hair toying with the buttons of her dress. Her heart started hammering even harder beneath the sweet onslaught of his seduction, and it was with a bittersweet mix of relief and agony that she imagined it began. What begins ends, and she tried to hold the thought . . .

Not when his hands brushed over the sensitive skin of her back with shivers and shudders, drawing the gown from her, smoothing it over her hips where she sat, and still kissing her deeply, he brought her up so that her wedding gown slid to a heap at her feet. He broke the kiss, but their gazes were locked until the intimacy brought hers down. Her whole body was alight with the promise of his kiss, and the knowledge was shared. She was breathing irregular, short quick breaths that could not keep pace with the race of her heart. She was blushing, too, less because of the lost gown, for she wore a silk chemise beneath, but all because of the heat of his scrutiny, which made her feel as if she had been sitting too close to the fire for too long.

Even when he stood up to pour the wine, handing her the gold goblet, the scrutiny of his gaze proved too much. "Drink it, love."

She did. The smooth, sweet liquid filled her with warmth. This pause still stretched as he stared at her, his eyes dark in this light, and yet she could feel his desire reach across the distance, claiming her with no more than his look. The moment continued, stretched taut like the high string across a harp. She felt the rising temperature of her blood, tingling from her toes to the top of her hair, ending in a sudden explosion of shivers. She grabbed the goblet with both hands. He was going to kiss her now, and dear Lord, if you could just be quick about it—

A warm chuckle brought her eyes up quickly. A hot wave of embarrassment washed over her . . . more as he knelt down again and she watched, confused by the humor and warmth in his eyes as he placed his hand over her breast where her heart raced wildly. Then he reached a hand to remove the crown of roses in her hair, pulling this over the long length of her unbound hair. He examined it with interest. "Roses . . . Nichole, I wonder . . ." His eyes were laughing even if he was not. "Love, tell me . . . did your mother ever share the tale of the two lovers who held the red rose in the blue flame of the fire, while the sound of their names kept the rose intact from this, the hottest part of the fire?"

Surprise lifted in her eyes as she searched his face. "Not my mother but, but Nanna . . . Nanna told me that story. She said it's a test of the truest love, the love that survives all elements, even time and history, the love of the blue flame. But—"

Jonpaul retrieved a red rose from the mantel and held it up. She greeted it with confusion, more as his hand brushed gently through her hair, a gentle tease as his voice lowered to a compelling whisper. "From the first moment I saw you, I've wanted you and with a desire that seems to rage ever more with each day's passing. Aye, I have your passion but I want your love. I don't think I've ever wanted anything more."

She was shaking her head ever so slightly and he paused, with the barest hint of a smile touching his lips, as he reached his eyes and continued. "Sometimes I think I have it, that the treasure is mine . . . only it's buried beneath the lie you cling to—"

"No," she cried in a whisper as she stood up to tell him, wanting him to know, needing him to know. "You don't have my love. It cannot come with your kisses or our marriage or even your displays of tenderness or kindness. I don't love you. I don't—"

"Prove it."

He was unnervingly calm as he held out the rose. She stared at it but hesitated. She had dreamed of this, yet nothing could survive the blue flame. The blue flame was the hottest part of a fire, from which evil draws its power, devouring and consuming all life. Even if she had love to protect it, and she did not, the blue flame would devour the fragile petals of a rose, and, and—

She did not love him!

At last she took the stem in hand. The velvet petals were soft to the touch and the fragrance was fresh and sweet. The idea of holding up the burnt ashes of the blossom to his gaze made her look into the fire. The blue flame burned beneath the licks and leap of the orange fire. Holding the long stem, her heart pounded curiously and she held her breath as she slowly brought the rose and held it in the light of the blue flame.

"My name, love!"

"Jonpaul . . ."

The blue flame surrounded the rose. Against the crackle of the flames, long, precious seconds sang loud in the silence when finally, with a trembling hand, she withdrew the rose from the engulfing flames. Her eyes grew wide as she stared at its perfect, untouched petals.

Nichole's eyes shot to him with a small, startled breath, only to see he held another single red rose in his hand. Without taking his eyes from her, he brought the blossom to the blue flame and said her name as if it were a sacred sound, a promise, a caress. She swallowed, staring as he withdrew the untouched petals of the flower.

Both flowers dropped silently to the floor as he stepped close to take her into his arms. She didn't know she was shaking her head until his hand came to her mouth, and in a compelling whisper of a voice, "For tonight, Nichole. 'Tis all I ask, to believe it for tonight, the love and passion of the blue flame. For tonight."

Magic was made of the elements; she believed in it, she had always believed in it. There was no other thought as she stared up at him. "Jonpaul . . . I—"

"Love, let me show you."

A nod came on the heels of a long pause as if entranced, and she was, a small part of her consciousness aware of it, less as the compelling warmth of his body on her almost-bare flesh was a caress. He touched his fingertips to the rise of her cheeks, feeling her flesh heat under his skin. Her pulse skipped a pair of beats and the constriction in her throat spread to her breasts. She swallowed as his fingers slipped light caresses along her throat. The warmth of his body continued to alight her senses. His hips aligned against her, until his knee slid up to the stool, bracing his leg, the slight motion cradling her against his thighs. He shifted, her body pressed closer to him, her breasts a soft caress against him.

He reached to the mantel. "Drink," he whispered as he brought a goblet to her lips. His other hand still cupped her throat, gently touching as she drank. Taking the goblet in hand, the coax of his fingertips made her head tilt and he bent, bringing his mouth down on hers. "Wine has never tasted sweeter," he managed, and encouraged by the telling light in her eyes, he took some of the sweet liquid on his fingertips and trailed a slow path along the wet silk of her lips, then followed it with his tongue. Her eyes shut and, already carried so far from the maddening hum of her thoughts and worries, she abandoned herself to the sweet hunger of his kiss . . .

She was hardly aware of his arms coming under her to carry her to the bed, where he gently laid her to the soft cushion and parted to remove his own clothes. She clutched the velvet quilt in her arms and turned on one side, shivering with the loss of his warmth. When she opened her eyes again it was with a question and to find him sitting on the edge of the bed, staring at her, his gaze as compelling as his touch. A maiden's modesty would not let her take in the full scope of his nakedness; she had hardly more than a glimpse of the strong musculature of his arms and chest before her eyes lowered and her cheeks flushed.

"Jonpaul," she began, her voice trembling with uncertainty and yet so changed by his kisses. "You are my husband now. By rights, I cannot refuse you the wedding bed—"

"To hell with my rights, love," he interrupted, his voice husky, passionate, as he leaned over, his hand catching her hair. "Would you?"

Desperately, she wanted so bad to know, "Was it a trick?"

"Nichole . . . Nichole," he whispered, coming full onto the bed, drawing her shivering body against his warmth and slowly letting her senses absorb the hard readiness of his body. He used all control as he felt the flush of her shivers, the instinctive arch of her back against him. "You have the answer . . . you've always had the answer . . ." His fingertip traced a line over the curve of her shoulder, drawing the thin silk down the smooth, trembling flesh of her arms. The silk, gathered at her hip, seemed to shimmer in the firelight as he brought his hand back to stroke the long length of her hair. "You feel it when I stand close, when I touch you . . . when I kiss you . . ." And to reassure her with the proof, he brought his mouth back to her lips where he gently rocked them until her breath came in small delicious flutters, and he parted them to kiss her again.

The pressure grew within her body and she lost herself to it . . . him . . . as his hands sank downward to lift and caress her breasts. Her breath caught and his lips left hers as one hand reached to the side, where he dipped his fingers in the wine again, then traced these behind her ear, to her temples, to the wildly beating pulse of her throat. His mouth, his warm breath and tongue followed the pattern, and through drugged, heated lips he whispered, "For you, love. This time is for you. I want your passion with your heart. I want your soul."

The erotic, feverish play left her breathless and trembling, needing to cling to him until the press of his body would bring the rising tide of desire to ease. Fulfillment came as her untried hands followed the same pattern over the handsome features of his face, then down his neck and the smooth muscles of his back, and she heard his sharp intake of breath, felt his own escalating tension. Her head swam with the intoxicating scent of his skin on hers, the melody of whispered love words. She felt the heated wine nectar circle her breasts, her body tense, then shivering as the moisture aided his mouth's exploration there.

Damp tendrils of hair licked her forehead. He felt the restless movement of her body beneath him, watching her eyes darkening with passion. His need for her ran through his body and her fragrance, of scented soap and passions awakening, possessed his whirling senses and made him fight for some small control. He tenderly nestled his face in the warm cloud of her softness—her breasts, hair and arms—before his mouth returned to hers and his hand glided gently over her legs, lightly kneading the soft, slight curve below her navel, the silky curls there, before finally slipping into her moist softness.

Hard shivers rocked her and she was in a restless delirium of pleasure until, just as she reached a peak of release, he withdrew, and only to tell her, "It can be even better, love . . ." His lips rocked gently over hers and his eyes were warm and moist. "Higher . . . Let me show you . . . yes," but it was she who showed him, for this time when he kissed her, she met him with a burning passion that exploded through his soul . . .

Father Ari nearly passed out with relief when the good Prince Abbott Richelieu finally bid him a good night and left happily more drunk than he. Why is it a certain type of man, Richelieu, for instance, a man who's fascinated with the question of whether failing to genuflect correctly was a venal or mortal sin, a humorless man who spent the last hour debating the question with himself, a man who didn't understand when he dryly proposed, "If an error is a sin, then is all sin simply error" . . . why was it that type of man always relished his company? Why at every gathering did this mold of men seek him out?

Father Ari sighed. Curse the good man's hide to heaven, he now felt as sober as the night was long. At least the bastards Charles and Kuno didn't tax the hospitality of the good people of Dornach by staying long for the feast. There were still two hours left of the night and a serious game to play, he saw as his gaze settled on the group of men gathered in the corner, Kurtus among them. Laughter erupted from the gay group and he smiled. They'd be knocked down drunk by this hour and easy prey.

So all was not lost. Sobriety had a purpose after all. He'd manage to steal them blind, and before his own goblet hazed his wits, he's have half the fortune on the table. A tidy prize to send him in to blissful sleep! Oh, better first check on his Tom and make sure the poor man had scrolled the bastard's every sordid word before falling asleep.

"Gentlemen, deal your poor friend in with the next hand," Ari shouted to the table as he rose. "I'll come in a twinkling."

"So the wenches keep complaining."

The men chuckled at Kurtus's acknowledgment and Father Ari smiled, a passing slight Kurtus would pay for in coin. The older man rubbed his hands together in anticipation and hurried through the doors, into the entrance hall, and then up the poorly lit steps.

Dornach was built half a century before by Jonpaul's maternal great-uncle during the time well before the Alliance when the entire country was divided into smaller factions. There were four guest chambers housed on the second landing, and three of these had small side chambers that were aligned at a place where a tapestry hung. A rather large hole joined each of these small chambers with the larger room, built to enable one to hear the voices in the other rooms. Though many people knew about them, as far as Ari knew they had not been put to use in all of Jonpaul's time . . . until tonight.

Bruno and his family resided in the west wing, Richelieu in the chamber alongside. Father Ari passed Bruno's sleeping pages, careful not to disturb them. Half a field down the hall sat another page, a young prelate, half awake outside the prince abbot's doors. "God's peace, my son," Ari nodded slightly as he passed. That man, too, would be asleep inside the hour. Now the tricky part . . .

He quietly rounded the corner. Lord Charles's two guards dozed, one actually leaning precariously on his sword handle. The small wood door to the spy chamber appeared as a servant's door, no more than a cubbyhole really, and this he quietly opened and slipped inside. He pushed his bulk down the narrow, dimly lit hall to the faint glow of the Tom's candle at the end. He should have remembered to bring his own.

Ari strained to search the cold, dark ground, though God knew Dornach had precious few rats—present guests excepted—for Jonpaul had a fondness for cats, and he let them breed indiscriminately.

Ari took in the scene in the tiny room with a low curse. His Tom—what was the man's real name? Ah, Skye . . . was sound asleep, his head resting on his arms on the table. The feather lay across the small table, an ink smear alongside the discarded listening cup. His soft snores sounded loud in the airless space.

Ari's hand grasped his beardless chin and he scowled. He had picked Skye because he was one of the few scribes available for hire. "Well, my man," he whispered, "you shall see your master in the barony court for this."

Skye did not wake. Ari picked up the scroll and read the half-dozen words the man had got before falling asleep.

Coupling sounds . . . endless . . . shocking, vicious . . .

Predictable so far. He had told the man it was certainly not necessary to provide detail of that, only conversations but then Skye wrote:

Sounds like the lady collapsed in pain or release? Bishop Kuno and LC . . . a map of Dornach . . . and mass and productively . . . Marvel of defensibility . . . Height of machicolated towers and gatehouse . . . The Church . . . the pope . . . View of the Italian nation states . . . Likely successions . . .

That was all. Confused brows drew over Ari's widely spaced eyes as he contemplated this. It made little sense. Sounded like they were discussing Dornach's defense posture, but by God, even these nefarious bastards had the wits to know they could not in all eternity take Dornach?

Before Father Ari woke the man, he picked up the listening cup and put it to the wall, only to be surprised by the male laughter.

"Well, my dear friend, a last toast before dawn on this auspicious day," Kuno said as cups were raised. "To your precious little sister and the prize she landed us—"

"Aye, to Nichole."

"Well, the paper is as good as burned and the world," he laughed, "is as good as ours. All in a fair day's work. May God grace us with the wealth of his earthly rewards."

"Indeed, indeed."

There came a shuffling, fare-thee-wells, and a door opened and shut. Sweat laced Father Ari's brow, his thoughts were racing. Oh, God, he should have been here . . . It was terrible, worse than even Jonpaul supposed . . .

"Oh you're . . . alone now?"

"And does that please you, Kira?" Charles asked indifferently as he moved to a chair. "Say it."

"Yes."

"Throw back the coverlet. Now. You are extremely beautiful. Take off the chemise . . . slowly. Yes, too beautiful, I think, to be trusted—"

"No . . . no, Charles, I swear, you can trust me."

"Can I, Kira? Hmm. Lay back and close your eyes. Let me watch as you pleasure yourself."

"Charles, I—"

"I need a little inspiration, my angel. You do know how to pleasure yourself? Yes, that's it . . ."

Father Ari blushed hot with the sounds that started coming from the room. He set the horn to rest as he drew deep unsteady breaths. Skye still slept soundly, the indolent leech. Was it necessary to listen anymore? The idea of too much already missed decided the unpleasant issue, and after what seemed like several long minutes, he returned the horn back to the listening hole.

"Are you ready?"

"Yes . . . please—"

"And I say nay . . ."

Men waited at the door. Jonpaul leaned over the bed where she slept. The aftermath of their love surrounded her with a flush and a glow. She looked more beautiful than ever. "Nichole . . . love."

The whispered voice came to her in a dream, where she surrendered once more to his passion and, drugged with sleep, she opened her eyes. Jonpaul's dark shape leaned over the bed. Her hand reached to his wrist and her touch was a caress, a question.

"Something has happened. I must go. I'll be back in an hour, maybe two." His hand came to her forehead as he brushed back an errant hair, the finger lingering over her mouth. He leaned over to kiss her again. Her mouth was soft, so pliant, unknowingly beckoning with the love so recently awakened, this night that had changed her forever. The kiss lingered, his desire strong and growing stronger, but a situation not likely to change in this lifetime. He could only leave with the knowledge she would be there when he came back and each night hereafter.

"They struck in Dornach?" he asked as he came through the door.

"Aye. Three dead. As if the bastards knew all but a few of the guards would be dead drunk . . ."

The door shut.

Nichole came fully awake to take in her changed circumstances. Changed they were, too, for part of her consciousness seemed as intertwined with him as her body had been. A strange panic gripped her, her heart kicked in. She sat up, her mind abruptly racing. Her husband and his wife, passion and love, the love of the blue flame—

Her gaze flew to the hooded hearth where the orange embers cast an eerie light over the two fallen roses. She slipped from the covers and out of bed, naked, holding herself tightly against the night chill in the room. She had no clothes here and, feeling vulnerable, shaky suddenly, she picked up his discarded brigandine and slipped it over her head. The velvet cloth dropped to her knees and covered her hands as she pulled her long hair from beneath. Her body felt strange to her; every familiar and unfamiliar fiber had been worked, exercised, strained. Her inner thighs were chafed and sore and she had numerous small marks where his kisses had lingered, but for all of this, these sensations were nothing compared to the profound, indescribable satiation.

She quietly approached the hearth, bending to retrieve

the fallen rose. Bringing it to her face, she closed her eyes, breathing the sweet scent. The love of the blue flame—a love that survives history and time, the physical worldliness of evil . . . the most enduring true love of all.

Yet even more than the test of the red rose in the blue flame was his lovemaking—the way he had possessed her, sending her spirit scattered in heaven, shimmering mistlike in a pleasure too great to be worldly, then collected and made anew, even more wondrous by his love . . .

The whirl of hazy thoughts left her confused, frightened because of it. The world was askew, circumstances were amiss, and her intuition sang in alarm. She had to force her way through the dangerous maze. There was her brother and Lucerne and inheritances. There was Jonpaul and Gavin. There was the lingering accusation of Stan, of unspeakable atrocities that were committed, that had happened just as surely as she had watched the untouched rose licked by the blue flame . . . Her eyes flew wildly around the room, as if the clue lay hidden in the dark shadows of the room. She had to find out. She knew what Jonpaul would say, but this would not be enough now.

She picked up both roses. Men were notoriously unsentimental about these things and she was afraid he would discard or lose his. She would treasure the blossoms till the day she died, and with both in hand, she crept silently from the room and into the dark hall.

The dark hour before dawn sang quietly at Dornach, that had not changed. Even the crows were silent, still roosting in their nests. The whisper of a breeze blew down the darkened hall, rousing the torchlight. Fur brushed her legs and she jumped, only to realize it was one of the cats. He meowed, distressed, and she stooped down to sweep him in her arms, rubbing his ears with her free hand as she made her way down the stairs. A cat's purr was both a comfort and lucky, and she needed both.

He would be in one of the guest chambers on the second floor. She would know by the guard outside the door, who now dozed, one leaning on his sword. Holding the cat and roses, she quietly pressed the latch and stepped inside. "I will reward you richly . . ." Charles whispered, his voice heated and low.

Standing in the doorway, Nichole did not hear the reply past a murmur of affirmation. There was no surprise that a woman was in his bed. There was always some woman in his bed. He always had a long string of mistresses, was the kind of man who openly dismissed monogamy as a woman's idea.

"Charles . . ."

"Nichole?"

Charles pressed his fingers to Kira's mouth, "Shh," even as he pulled on his leggings and then threw on his shirt. He parted the drapes to rise from the bed, letting them fall back. A candelabra cast a dim light over the chambers, throwing his enormous shadow over the drapes and onto the ceiling, highlighting his sardonic expression as he considered his sister.

He walked slowly to her, his shadow seemed to stretch and grow, as if it had a life of its own.

The cat leaped from her arms.

Emotions trembled through her, blinding her, as the familiar sight triggered a montage of images drawn from the last long terrible months since Nanna's death. She'd traveled through this dark passage so long, this tunnel that had no way out . . . Until now. Until seeing him, Charles, the one person still alive she had known and loved forever. She closed her eyes, remembering, feeling the treasure that had always been his love and admiration, as if everything she did and was had been for him—his smile, laughter, pride. "Charles . . ." she said again, the whisper of his name carried on the hazy cloud of emotions.

A familiar spirit hovered nearby, deploring her to take care, that these emotions were indeed sacred but belonged to the man who had just awakened them, that this was a mistake . . .

Nichole saw only her brother.

"Say it and be done, sister mine," he said with his own emotion. "You hate me now and will never forgive me."

"No," she whispered, shaking her head. "He told me why."

Clenched fists rested on his hips, his brow creased with concern. "Yes?"

"That it was a means to protect yourself against the threat posed by the paper. That should he ever present it, my marriage, the laws of inheritance, would cast his motives, the very thing itself in suspicion. Only . . ." She swallowed the pain, struggling. Secrets, deception, the vicious cycles of intrigue were wrong, she knew that now. She'd have no more invisible ghosts, these secret webs of malice. "Only, Charles . . . Charles, I don't believe he has it. I never did, you know . . ." She watched his reaction, the expected surprise, this edged with mistrust. "Nanna," she explained at last, "died before she could tell me where it was, but he . . . the council of the Alliance, forced me to disclose this . . . I don't know . . . I think he saw to use it like I did, not as a real weapon but only the threat. I don't believe he really has it, either."

His expression changed as she spoke, shifting like a sudden cloud over the moon, and he suddenly gripped her thin shoulders in a painful grasp. "No . . . no!" The denial was whispered in fierce emotion. "God in heaven, Nichole, tell me 'tisn't so! I didn't lose you to him for nothing . . . you who I treasure most in the world, above my own breath. So help me God, say it can't be true!"

As she watched the whole horrible truth dawn on him, she threw herself in his arms until they came around her, holding her tightly against his strength. "Charles," she cried, looking up at his face, "what is this paper? What has made this happen?"

He pulled from her, staring down at her upturned face before, with a nod toward the bed, he pulled her toward the farthest corner. In a whisper barely above a mouthing of the words, "I cannot in truth say. I've never known exactly myself. I believe or I have reason to believe 'tis a document, nearly a century old, that throws doubts on our inheritance. I'm not even sure it's real let alone legal but Lucerne, my first mistress, is a treasure, our treasure and I know you of all people understand when I say I could not as I live dare risk her—not even for you."

She searched his face, her thoughts spinning like a child's top over the revelation. "But if you don't even know—"

"Hush now . . . we don't have time. I'll move, I'll try to get an annulment—"

She shook her head. "The marriage has been consummated, there are no grounds. 'Tis too late." She spoke the words as her eyes fell on the roses in her hand still, one crushed by her brother's embrace. His eyes followed, too, seeing the roses suddenly against her disheveled appearance.

"These roses . . ." His tone abruptly changed. "Christ Almighty, he didn't pull that tired trick, did he?"

Her eyes shot up with alarm.

"You little fool. I swear to Satan that old woman wrecked her senses with all her old wives' tales of magic and miracles." With exasperation, irritation, "Dipped in a waxy mixture that burns before the blossom. I've used it myself on occasion. Nichole, Nichole," his eyes shone with sudden conviction and alarm as he grabbed her shoulders again. "for God's sake, do not be fooled! The man is our enemy . . . as dangerous as the devil incarnate—"

"No . . . no, I don't believe it anymore."

With hatred, feeling, he demanded, "Dare you forget the village Stan?"

"He says he didn't . . . he never . . ."

"Don't be dense, girl! For God's sake, of course he would deny it to you!"

Horror made her eyes wide. "But . . . his people . . . I . . . he—"

"His people are sheep that he lets graze, that he uses for cloth or slaughter as his need dictates. I will not have you live with his deception, too—not my sister!"

"No . . . no . . ." She could hardly speak, the fear that it might be true too terrible. She didn't believe it now. She couldn't. He could not have loved her like that . . . Her intuition . . . his people, their goodness—

"Listen to me. You are young, too young and 'tis your sex as well. Men have only to lay with a woman to own her emotions, if not her will. I won't let him deceive you."

He watched as her eyes filled with tears. He could not tell if she was confused or still uncertain. With vicious hatred, real and potent, he said in a low voice of conviction, "Do you know he recently had a dozen men from St. Gallen and Lucerne hung as a warning to me—A most hellish hanging, by the poor bastards' testicles!"

"No . . . nooo!" Nichole fell against the door, her eyes blinded by a vivid vision of this horror as she cried, "Dear God, say it isn't true! Charles . . . Charles, it can't be! I am wed to him! He is my husband until death do us part—"

A hard, frantic knock sounded at the door. Charles pulled her to her feet. "Remember the last . . . till death do you part, and know, know, my love, I will not forsake you to him for long."

The knock came louder, more insistent, guards shouting outside. "Open up! In the name of—"

Charles opened the door, straightening to demand, "What the devil is the meaning of this?"

One guard stepped forward, his gaze searching the room until he found Nichole. "The lady is not permitted here."

With her hands clasped over her mouth, she watched Charles's two guards step behind Jonpaul's, their swords drawn. "How dare you speak to me—"

"No . . . No, please . . . I'll have no blood-letting over my actions." She stepped forward, taking a long look back at her brother, her emotions spinning dizzily with his last promise, his last words: "Remember, sister mine."

Chapter Fourteen

A tallowed candle lit the small dark confessional booth where Katrina knelt. The extreme quiet of the church at the midnight hour cautioned her to be quick, to hurry, lest someone discover her missing from bed. From the folds of her habit, she spread out the torn potato sack she had managed to steal that morning. With extreme care she smoothed the wrinkles and sides so that the small piece of cloth lay flat and neat in the dim light. She carefully placed the sharpened quill of the feather alongside.

Next she removed the knife . . .

She picked it up and raised her wrist over the light. The sharp point gently touched a vein where her pulse fluttered. Closing her eyes, she cut. Bright red blood poured from the cut, quickly creating a small pool on the confessional ledge. The quill dipped into the pool, and with extreme caution, Katrina began to paint the first picture on the smooth cloth, the first of a series of pictures that would catch the lady Nichole's attention.

"Nichole would not believe that—"

"*I* almost believed it!" Father Ari's normally level

voice rose to emphasize this to Jonpaul. "She was so distraught and confused and I stood there practically shouting through the goddamn hole 'Tis a lie, 'tis a lie, but Jeezus, when he said that bit about the hanging—his pretense so real, as if he had rehearsed it a hundred times! Oh, 'twas terrible."

It had been a terrible scene. Jonpaul, Kurtus, and Bruno had returned at dawn to Dornach Castle from the township where three men lay dead and a fortune in spices, teas, and jewels had been stolen. Charles had something to do with these thieves, Jonpaul felt certain of it. Then as Ari had presented the words spoken to Nichole, Jonpaul had lost his temper. Roused by knights at dawn and shattering the illusion of diplomacy, Kuno and Charles were fortunate to leave Dornach unharmed. He made Charles watch Kira's punishment, so Charles was there as Kira was dragged out to the courtyard and her head shorn, brandished both whore and traitor and set on the drunk cart that routinely rounded up the drunkards and mad folks and carted them off to France, dispersed like so many rats in various townships. The men had not known what angered them more, the woman who promised to spy for Charles or Charles's amused indifference as Kira begged and pleaded with the bastard to stand for her, until Kuno said, "Do silence the wench before I am sick." So Charles rode over to her and seemed about to kick a boot into her face until, alarmed, Kurtus drew his sword. Charles only laughed as Jonpaul told him to leave before he did so in pieces.

A rain fell steadily against the windows, and the winter fire crackled in the great hearth at their side in the hall. Few servants were about, as most still slept, and even the soft snores of Hercules, sleeping near the fire sounded loud as Bruno, Kurtus, and Jonpaul considered the situation.

"What in hell are the devils planning?" Bruno asked

as he stroked his dark beard, as his amber eyes filled with the outrage. "I just cannot fathom how Charles and Kuno could reason Dornach could ever fall to their hands! The fools may be stupid, but they'd have to be witless to think they could win a war with the Alliance—by God, not even if they got the House of Hapsburg to join them again, or even the French dogs—"

"The Hapsburgs and the French!" Kurtus spat with scorn, "Hell, their dignitaries appear weekly to lick Jon's boots, all but begging for our aid, our help, our men, with their infernal bickering and wars. Jon has the favor of the goddamn throne in both houses now. After Burgundy they'd never dream of war with us again."

This was true. Dignitaries from around the Continent courted Jonpaul with a neverending stream of requests for Swiss mercenaries to fight their wars for profit, including both France and the House of Hapsburg.

"'Tis true," Father Ari agreed. "Obviously, without help, the combined forces of Lucerne and St. Gallen amounts to nothing against the Alliance. 'Twas what I kept saying as I listened; 'tis madness in his mind!"

"We are on the wrong road," Jonpaul abruptly realized. "We must assume they have enough wits to grasp what any milking maid can, that a war cannot be won. So how is it they could think of Dornach as a prize they shall soon win?" He met each of his friends' gazes, "'Tis through my death—"

"Your death?" Kurtus interrupted. "But young Gavin will inherit Dornach!"

"Will he?" Jonpaul asked the painful question, one he had dwelt on more than once these last years. "His deafness would present a dispute. One that could not be answered in any *landsgemeinde* of our land. 'Twould go to the Holy Church for arbitration, and with the combined leverage of Kuno, Bishop Richelieu, and God knows who else Charles could bribe, it seems to me the case for my new wife's next male relation would be strong."

The silence was broken by Bruno's curse. "Oh, my God."

Kurtus felt the blood rushing to his ears, his fists clenching as he slammed one against the table, and said with passionate intensity, "It cannot be—" But he stopped, for even as he said it, he realized, they all did, that this must in fact be their plan.

Bruno said, "A new heir—"

"Nay," Jonpaul shook his head. "Even if Nichole carried a boy child now, as we speak, 'twould be too late. Besides, upon my death, Charles would be the child's guardian, and no doubt, eventually, the child's murderer as well."

Bruno stood, drawing Kurtus up, as well, as he said with soft viciousness, "Then, by God, we shall murder him first!"

"And I say we won't," Jonpaul answered, his tone and manner calm but firm. "Think, my friends. How would a lord be tried for the high murder of his equal. Aye . . ." He watched the consequences dawn on his friends' faces. "Trial by the ecclesiastic court. And, God knows, the Holy Roman Church would like nothing better than to rid themselves of me, our Alliance and reforms, this threat posed by a united Switzerland."

Bruno fell back into the chair. "You are right."

"But if we refused to acknowledge the authority of such a court—"

"'Twould mean immediate excommunication, and while that might not bother all of us," Father Ari shook his head, "more people are willing to die for the promise of heaven than any other cause. Like England before us—"

"It would cause a bloodbath of civil strife," Jonpaul finished the thought. "Besides, I do not send assassins creeping about in the dark dead of night to do a coward's deed. I do not! I might be only too happy to meet the bastard on the battlefield, but that is a far cry from paying a killer to slit his throat as he sleeps. I have worked my whole life to build our land into a nation of laws and, by God, I will not let this tyrant, however terrible or threatening, forsake the noble, the good, the just—"

"Oh, for Christ sake, Jonpaul!" Kurtus said with vehemence, a dismissing wave of his arm. "This talk might be fine for speeches, for common folks and merchants and clerics, but the man, I remind you, is trying to kill you! He will care nothing for these ideas—"

"Convenient ideas, too, I say." Bruno's gaze narrowed as he, also, took up the attack. "Ideas you seem to forget when it suits you, like . . . ah, those days you feel like abducting beautiful young ladies? Those days you—"

"Enough," Jonpaul said, knowing just how long the list of his indiscretions could get, and it was long. "Jeezus, I must be failing if my closest friends refuse to humor my pretenses."

"We just can't sit and do nothing, waiting for your murderer to show up! We must find a way that rids the land of his plague, without drawing the Church—"

"Aye," Bruno agreed.

"Even if we found it," Jonpaul pressed the point, "there is still another reason I cannot murder him now. She sits upstairs in a state of terror that no words can ease as she imagines her husband is not just bad but evil incarnate. So far I have not given her much reason to doubt. Needless to say, murdering the brother she loves will not go far in easing her doubts or terror."

The silence made the crackling of the fire, the steady pounding of the rain, and the sleep of the dog loud, familiar tranquil sounds, each at odds with the emotions at the table. For several moments no one spoke, though they each had the same thoughts, thoughts finally voiced quietly by Bruno: "To be sure, Jonpaul, Nichole is like no other. From the very first night she stood before us, such a pairing of courage and spirit and beauty, not even knowing then the far more valuable treasure of her other gifts . . . from that first night, I knew she was fated to you. She had to be. And indeed the girl has captured so much of you, Jonpaul . . . much of all of us." Bruno's gaze swept over the others, who nodded in silent concurrence before he returned to Jonpaul. "Yet, Jonpaul, no woman is worth Dornach, the seat of the Alliance and everything we have fought these many years for. Not even Nichole."

Jonpaul watched the hot light of the blue flame wrap circles around the log, sending bright leaps of orange fire up into the air as he remembered the passion and joy of last night. "But I say she is."

Jonpaul said his name as he knocked on the door to her chambers. Footsteps sounded, stopped by her plea, "No, please . . . Tell him I'm ill or sleeping, I—" The plea did not surprise him, but the emotion in her voice did, emotion he'd not have.

"Enough. Open the door. Now."

Bettrina opened the door, hurriedly passing through it before Jonpaul told her to take leave, shutting the door after her. No emotion showed in his face as he took in the harsh scene. Never had he seen her like this, not even her first night at Dornach when she appeared before the Council exhausted and starved and bleeding, more frightened than a man could know. She sat at the window, bathed in the diffuse light of the gray day, all the naked anguish of her heart plain. She looked pale and drawn and frightened. Red circles underlined her lowered eyes as she nervously clasped a lace kerchief in her hands. She wore a common cloth robe dyed a dark blue, and as he stared at her and the silence stretched, a small hand reached to clasp the folds tightly about her neck.

"Can you be this frightened of me after what passed between us last night?"

Especially after last night. Especially. After his will brought her to the quivering, exalted peak where she said his name, branding it to her heart as he sent her spinning into heaven. Especially after last night. After he owned her will, her heart, her soul.

Though she made no reply, the anguished silence conveyed her thoughts. "I see." He stepped toward the window. She watched with alarm, like a caged distraught creature, fearing the worst, and the very worst would be his touch. "Nichole," he said as he reached a hand to her face. More than her withdrawal, the fear pronounced in her eyes brought a hard light to his eyes.

He had enough. Kneeling before her, one knee raised and bent, and looking suddenly like the very devil Charles had painted for her, he ignored her gasp and took her small hand in his. With his green eyes lively and menacing both, he brought her hand to his mouth. She tried to pull back, restrained by his gentle force as he lightly brushed the tips of each finger to his lips, sending a rush of shivers up her arm. "What is it you're afraid of when I touch you, Nichole?" he asked in a compelling whisper, watching color rush to her cheeks, that effort she put to stopping the impossible.

"No . . . Please, I—" She tried to pull her hand away, but he'd not let her now.

"Why is it I'm certain it has nothing to do with me and everything to do with you?" He brought the palm of her hand over, opening to him as he pressed light kisses to the velvet softness, that was all. She bit her lip to stop a gasp and closed her eyes as his lips reached her wrist. "Is it not so, love, that my touch, my slightest touch, makes you doubt not me but him and his lies?"

She started to shake her head, but his free hand traced a sensitive line over her ear with another slash of shivers, then across her cheeks to lightly circle her lips. "I have only to touch you, love . . ."

Her eyes flew open. "No . . . No—"

He rose up, forcing her back against the wall with alarm and, leaning forward, he brought his mouth dangerously close to hers. She held her breath and closed her eyes, certain, terrified, he was going to kiss her. Yet nothing happened past the rally of her senses to his nearness. She felt the heat of his steady gaze, the warmth of his skin and breath, that maddening scent his nearness brought, all of it triggering the dizzy memories of his possession of her last night.

"You little fool, Nichole. He was deceiving you."

She opened her eyes to his, staring too close, as if to see the truth there. "And he said 'tis you who is deceiving me!"

He stood up, withdrawing physically but, it seemed, only to better consider her. "Oh, aye. He said a number of things, I know."

She looked confused for a moment. "What do you mean you know? You didn't . . . you wouldn't listen?"

"Jeezus," he swore as he watched her reaction to this, his tone suddenly irritated. "Your sex is as consistently inconsistent as the cycles of the moon. You would now pretend to be shocked that a man who hangs his enemies by the flesh of their . . . ah, manhoods, was it? would stoop to spying?"

Thoughts clamored for her attention, not about being spied upon but about the disgust and mockery as he greeted the horror with which Charles had accused him. "Do you deny it?"

There was a desperateness to her soft voice, edged with the fear that it was true, and it angered him. He couldn't even pretend to humor her. "Oh, aye, Nichole," he said with masculine scorn, "I regularly see men hang from various unlikely portions of their anatomy. Huh! And if you think that's barbaric, you should see what I do when hanging by . . . ah, staffs takes too long. Why, then I—"

"Stop it . . . Stop it!" She covered her ears like a tormented child, coming to her feet.

Jonpaul seized this, and like a cat seeing a sudden weakness, he pulled her hands from her ears and held her. "Aye, if it weren't so sick 'twould be absurd, love. Now," his voice lowered, "who is it who's deceiving you?"

She tried to meet his gaze but couldn't, as if she knew how dangerous that would be as her thoughts spun with confusion. The horror with which Charles spoke of it last night came back to her, warning her, and this was placed against the slaughter at Stan, the fact, absolute fact, of the equally terrible deeds Jonpaul's army did after the Burgundy War on its way to Lucerne, of what she knew of men and the way they treated women, of how terribly clever Jonpaul was—smarter than any man she had ever known—and how if he wanted her to believe otherwise, and he had done all these terrible deeds, if he was this evil person, he would present the case exactly so, as if the very idea was absurd.

Yet there came the whispers of her intuition . . .

"I don't know . . . I don't know . . ." Thoughts spun with a vicious incoherency. She felt suddenly weak with exhaustion, dizzy, not having eaten or slept now for . . . for too long. Gathering all her strength, she returned to him to say, "If you were this person, would you not say these very things to me? And why, tell me why, my brother, who loves and cherishes me, why would he lie to me?"

"Loves you? Cherishes you? So he gives you to a sadistic barbarian to wed? Till death do you part—"

"He thought he had to for the paper!"

"Aye, sacrificed you to save his unworthy hide. If only that were his motive. The real reason, love, is your brother covets Dornach, and he means to get my lands through our marriage by having me murdered—"

"No!" She shook her head, certain at last of this. "He'd never do that, never! It doesn't even make sense. Young Gavin will inherit before me."

"My son is deaf. Gavin's rightful inheritance would be easily contested upon my death. Dornach, all my lands, would fall to you, which means your closest male relative."

Wide blue eyes met his, searching, incredulous. "No" sang so loud in her mind, she might have said it. She thought of the roses, a smaller deception alongside much greater deceptions. She knew who was lying to her. "No, 'tisn't true . . . I know that isn't true—"

"It's been said before to you, I will say it again: Your belief in the truth doesn't alter its light—"

She started to protest with another accusation, but he was weary of these endless cycles of her doubt. "Enough now," he stopped her. "I'll be damned if I'll waste any more time defending myself against his malicious intrigues. In time you will come to know the truth."

He released her then, but weakened with sleeplessness and hunger, weakened most of all by the terrifying circles of her thoughts, her knees gave way the second his support left her arms. She started to fall and, though startled by this, he was quick, managing to catch her up in his arms before she fell.

A profound dizziness, like a drug, swept through her, and the room seemed to suddenly swim, then turn a menacing gray color like his words coming from somewhere far away. "Christ Almighty, do I have to give you a nursemaid or what, love? A gnat has the sense to eat and sleep with regularity, at least enough to keep from falling faint every time I . . ."

It seemed to go on and on, this tirade, but her dizzy thoughts seized a word, changed it to find a sudden comfort that she echoed back in a weak whisper. "Nanna . . . Nanna . . . Nanna . . ."

As he carried her to his chambers, he recognized the name as a plea for help, help he would more than welcome, for though he had complete faith in his young wife's ability to eventually discern the truth, he feared it would not be in time.

Nichole woke in the dark middle of the night. She sat up, rubbing her eyes, then staring across the room. She was in his chambers. Alone, oh thank the Goddess. Mary would be asleep in hers. But where was he? A candle burned on the night table, where she saw a glass of milk, some cheese and bread alongside a fruit bowl that had two apples in it.

Hunger won out over confusion. She reached for the milk, drank it down, then began eating a piece of cheese with the apple. She looked to the window as if it would tell her the hour. Nothing but the light of a moonless night. It could be anywhere between midnight and dawn . . .

Her gaze finally fell on her trunks. Someone had brought them here. She froze with the idea of sleeping with him, every night, for the rest of her life. No. She just couldn't. She imagined the utter horror when he touched her, and her mind produced the stream of deceptions, images drawn from who she felt certain he was. She would die in repulsion, that was all, just die. She swallowed with effort as she felt a sudden sick dread.

She must save herself. The covers flew back and her bare feet touched the cold floor. Frantically she searched for her robe, spotting it laid across her trunk. She put it on and, regretting that she couldn't lift her trunks, too, she hurried out the door.

A torch lit the darkened hall. A cat meowed upon seeing her, another leapt down from a bench to curl around her feet. Without thinking, a habit at this point in her life, she picked him up, dropping her friend, though, when she came to the *garde-robe.*

She picked the waiting cat up again as she emerged and, because she turned him upside down in her arms like a babe, stroking his whiskers and wondering why her panic wasn't agitating him, she almost ran into him. With a gasp, her eyes flew up to his face, only to see a strange amusement, as if scaring her had been a singular pleasure.

"Did you just wake, love?"

She nodded wordlessly, swallowing what she felt certain, what she prayed, was an irrational fear. With his gaze locked to hers, he took the cat from her arms to his. The cats loved him. She numbly watched as he stroked the cat's head until the capricious little fellow's purr sounded as loud as the hard, slow thunder of her pounding heart. Tension immobilized her as she thought, as she imagined, if he forced her—

"Did you have something to eat?"

Again she nodded.

"Do you feel better now . . . ? Yes? Then why are you going in the wrong direction?"

She started to speak but stopped. There was something about him, a disarming recklessness and mischief, the amused look in his eyes as he considered her, as if her worries and concerns, the very magnitude of her fears were now inconsequential. She nervously brushed her loose hair from her face. "You know . . . I know you know."

"Indeed?"

He would make her say it, she saw. "I don't want to sleep with you."

"Which wouldn't be a problem if I did not want to sleep with you."

So conscious was she of his gaze, his height and strength, a threat she felt from him, that it took her mind a full minute to catch up with his words. "Why, you wouldn't . . . you couldn't want me if—"

"Wrong," he said, and he thought of just how wrong she was. Since the first day he saw her he had wanted her, wanted her with a desire that never diminished but only grew and grew, like the gathering force of some great, terrible storm. The magnitude of this storm reached proportions startling to him, often waking him two or three times a night, sometimes stopping him in the stark middle of the day, for no reason at all past a sudden unexpected memory of her scent, his hands in her hair, his mouth on hers, the sound of her pleasure as he brought the miracle of the flesh trembling through her . . .

The cat leapt from his arms as he backed her against the cold stone wall, trapping her with his long arms braced on either side of her head. A kind of wild emotion lit her eyes as his gaze fell to the rise and fall of her breasts beneath the robe, her breaths coming fast and deep. "I can honestly say I cannot think of a circumstance where I would not want you."

"No . . ." She shook her head, whispering in a rush of panic, "You cannot want to force me . . . I need—" She had been about to say "time" when she stopped.

Something cold and dangerous came to his eyes as he searched her face, first with surprise and then with a hint of anger, anger mixing but hardly overcoming the desire there as he said, "You are my wife, Nichole. There can be no question of force. And while you may think it wildly improbable that I might want to lay with my wife, you may as well know now, it is only one of the many things I will demand from you. If I cannot have your heart, I will have your will. Which means your obedience, love."

The blue eyes flew to his. He was referring to last night when she had left him to seek her brother, the one thing, the only thing, he had ever explicitly forbidden her, which she understood only too well now. He had been afraid Charles would fill her mind with Jonpaul's deceit, the fateful idea that her intuition was failing her, that it sent her off to hell with the happy ignorance of a simpleton.

Her eyes faltered beneath the challenge in his, and she cursed the only living soul who could do that to her. She caught her breath, though, pressing harder against the wall as he leaned closer still, a finger tracing a line around her ear as he whispered there, "And there's more to love. Much more . . ."

The question appeared in her eyes, her gaze suddenly caught in his, unable to look away as the errant finger fell to her neck, shooting a hot rush of shivers through her. She shook her head with a sudden avalanche of confusion, not knowing what he was saying, what more he could want of her, but she couldn't think, not as his fingers came to the edge of her robe, back and forth, and his warm lips caressed a spot beneath her neck. Please to God, she had to stop this. It would be all over if he possessed her again when she thought . . . when she was certain . . .

"My children, love . . . I want you to give me my children."

"Oh, no . . ."

"Oh, but yes."

The words were the whisper of a promise to her as he started to part her robe. With a gasp, she caught his hand, hers curling around his index finger as if that would stop him. It didn't. He brought her hand behind her back, and with the gentlest of pressures, he made her arch against him. His other hand slipped inside her robe. Fire shot through her limbs. The warmth of his hand swept along the curve of her waist, stopping beneath her breast as his mouth hovered over hers, waiting for the next breath before he kissed her. Warm and firm lips came to hers. The pressure of his mouth brought her head back, and her lips parted as her warring emotions soared, rising with the wild surge of desire brought by this kiss.

His arms crossed over her slender back until his hands cupped her buttocks. He lifted her up over his length. Her small, clenched fists came to his shoulders with a frantic idea of pushing him away, an idea that disappeared as he was suddenly holding her with one hand while his other took a handful of hair, tugging gently to tilt her neck more. Then his lips grazed her bare, arched neck as he lifted her higher until his breathing changed and his mouth found the tip of her breast to draw first softly, then hard . . .

"Tell me you don't feel this, Nichole. Tell me you don't want my love . . ." he said as he lowered her to take her mouth again and, she knew, she knew she had to stop it now.

"No, don't . . . Please, Jonpaul, don't do this to me . . ."

He stopped suddenly. His hand came under her chin to lift her face. "Look at me." She opened her eyes. Tears hung like a clear veil over the emotion, so plain there, her confusion and fear mixing with the desire.

"I need . . . I need time. I'm just so confused and scared. I—" Her voice faltered. A cold shiver shook her and, with a trembling sigh, she collapsed, as if the whole thing had overwhelmed her and it had, it had. His hands came to her arms. "I don't know what's happening to me. I only know if you make me love you, I'll . . . I—"

The startling honesty of her plea made him tap some previously unknown strength to harness the race of his desire. Still, it was not easy to do so, harder with the clamor of his reservations, voiced when he said, "Time . . ." A single finger caught a strand of her loosened hair, twirling it as he considered this. "How much time, love?"

She shook her head, "I don't know." She could no longer look at him; her eyes were lowered and her hands clutched the robe tight about her neck. The magnitude of her struggle came to him as he watched her trembling, and this was a shock.

"For now, love. Know, though . . ." he leaned over, lightly kissing her mouth, lingering when he tasted her tears, "there's only so much time I'm willing to give."

She nodded numbly. He abruptly turned away. A cold chill replaced his warmth.

Kneeling on the frost-covered ground, Nichole looked up. As her hands were muddied, she wiped the loose hairs from her face with her forearm and drew a deep breath, released in a cloud of fog. Her gloves were soaked through and her tired fingers burned with the cold, which was a good deal better than her toes, which she could hardly feel any more.

The laughter and shouts of the children who had joined her sounded distant but louder than the wind. Playing fast and furious, Mary and Gavin were scattered among them throughout the forest in a game. The children's fun kept them a good deal warmer, but they would be feeling the cold soon, too. Still, she would not gather them to return, not yet. She had to find the verdigris today. The wind and cold had brought dark clouds billowing across the sky, all promising the first snowfall tonight, and by tomorrow the land would be covered in white—snow that would keep the rotting bark hidden until spring . . .

Spring would be too late.

A smile came to her eyes as she thought on Mary and Gavin. The only person Mary loved more than Jonpaul was his son. Young Gavin first looked on the little girl with masculine indifference, but the girl's wide-eyed worship and obvious crush worked quickly to melt this, and aided by his father's words, "Mary's a bit too young to be among the other children so 'tis your job to watch over her and see that she is safe," Gavin thought of Mary as a new pet—forty or so pounds of life, laughter, love that was his responsibility.

It just wasn't here . . . Nichole stood up, gathered her basket, and headed for another berry patch, where the bushes often grew. "Milady! Milady!" She turned to see young Johannes running toward her, arms raised and waving, followed by all the children. "Look, look, I found it!"

"Oh, please, please," she murmured as the children quickly gathered around her. Gavin reached to her hand, taking her basket for her. Nichole took the dark bark from Johannes's hand to examine it. Expectant looks marked the children's faces as they waited, rose-cheeked and wide-eyed, sensing the import. A smile changed her face and she cried out for happiness. A cheer went up as she bent to kiss the older boy's forehead. "Oh, my hero!" she laughed. "You did find it!"

Gavin was not the only boy with a crush and Johannes's blush, made of equal parts embarrassment, pride, and pleasure, warmed his cheeks as for once he beat Gavin to Nichole's praise. "There's plenty more, too, right where you said 'twould be, near the berry brambles yonder!"

"This is enough, this is enough!"

Men and horses crashed into the small clearing, reining the mounts to a quick halt upon greeting the unexpected scene. Hands wrapped in hands, Nichole led a long rope of ecstatic children, their voices raised in all children's favorite celebratory song, "The First Snowfall." They stopped at the sound and, with happy cries, two of the children ran to their fathers, who had accompanied Jonpaul to fetch them. Gavin followed the looks on his friends' faces and he, too, ran to greet the unexpected company.

The first snowflakes mixed with a heavy rain before turning to a soft flurry of whiteness. Mothers had rushed to find the men to go out and to fetch Nichole and the children, hopefully before their garments were soaked. Alas, too late for that.

Gavin's pony and two extras were in tow to bring the troops home. With a smile, Nichole watched the excited children clamor onto the mounts amidst shouts of glee. "'Tis snowing, Father, 'tis snowing!" Stefan and Marie mounted alongside their fathers, the other children doubling up on the ponies. Mary rushed to Jonpaul as Gavin rushed back to return her basket before hopping gaily on Zur's back. Jonpaul kissed the little girl before swinging her up in front of Gavin on his pony. "No jumping with Mary," he warned Gavin, who nodded and, filled with the pride of this responsibility, he turned the pony home. The others followed.

Jonpaul did not have to push Zermatt to the place where she stood, looking suddenly so small among the swirls of snow and the towering pines; his horse anticipated his desire. His nearness brought her acute self-consciousness descending like a curtain of ineptitude she knew from experience. She tried to ignore the rush of her blood and the escalating beat of her heart as he stopped Zermatt in front of her, tried instead to focus the whole of her consciousness on Zermatt. But she found this impossible, for she could feel the warmth of his gaze, the maddening humor he had stopped bothering to hide when he encountered his oh so obvious effect on her senses.

Just last night as she was to retire from the hall, he had

gently tilted her head until she met the bright light in his gaze. She had first frozen with the surprise of his kiss, but so gently and tenderly did his lips take hers, sweeping her with that warm summer breeze. Her body went soft, pliant as the tingling warmth spread, changing the beat of her heart. Just as gently he stopped the kiss. "My desire makes time my enemy." Then with a lingering look at how he had changed the color of her eyes, he watched her rush from the room.

She was remembering this kiss as she reached up a hand to stroke Zermatt's proud head. The beast nuzzled her hand, searching for the treat that was usually there. "Oh, you greedy beast," she said as she reached in her basket and withdrew one of the small green apples he loved. She forced her blue eyes up to Jonpaul's at last. He always looked even taller atop his horse, and especially fearsome in the sheepskin vest over common work clothes, and the way he was staring—

Blushing for no reason at all, praying it didn't show, she quickly turned her gaze to Zermatt as he chomped the treat and tossed up his pretty head with an impatient snort.

"Come, love," he beckoned as he leaned over to lift her to the saddle.

"Oh no, I'll walk back—"

"Like hell you will."

His tone shot her eyes back to him. She was not used to being talked to like that and it brought the memory of that night back to her. "If I can't have your heart, I demand your will, which means your obedience, love." She had been surprised that he understood this: how a woman's devotion followed her heart, but, without this, a man must demand obedience, and this was particularly necessary when his wife's loyalties lay with his enemies.

As she stood there stupidly searching for a convincing argument, his hands snaked around her waist and he lifted her swiftly to the saddle in front of him. She tensed but only for a minute as the incredible blanket of his heat seemed to spiral over her. Apparently 'twas not enough for him. He took her frozen hands in one of his and, with a curse, he placed her basket over the saddle horn before pulling off her wet gloves. "I suppose I should be thankful that at least you're eating and sleeping regularly now."

Sleeping regularly? If he only knew about the dreams! Dreams of his kisses, the caress of his hands on her form, of his hard, warm body coming over hers, dreams that woke her two or three times a night with her heart pounding and her breath racing and a familiar ache she did not know how to ease without him.

He removed his own gloves to place on her hands.

"Please, I'm fine," she said. "I'm not that cold."

"And I say you are as cold as an icefall. What are you doing out here?"

The question was asked as he brought the too-large gloves over her numb hands, gloves that were lined with sheepskin and warmed from his hands. She started to tell him but stopped with a gasp as his hands suddenly came to the top buttons of her coat. "Jonpaul, I . . . You wouldn't—"

His hands came over her breasts to undo the buttons there, almost resting on the curve there. She drew a sharp breath, as through the layers of coat, dress, and chemise she felt the tips of her breasts greet the contact with embarrassing eagerness.

"Wouldn't what, love?"

The question sounded as a whisper as one by one the buttons came undone, before his hand slid over first one arm, then the other to remove the wet coat. She could not see the wild amusement in his eyes. All she could think was that he couldn't, wouldn't do that in the snow! On Zermatt! That, besides, he promised and—

"Wouldn't dream of removing your clothes in the snow? Ah," he chuckled, "I might dream about it, but even I, lusty bastard that I am, would try to resist that temptation. Hard as it is. I only mean to remove the wet coat before you're chilled. I have a fur here." He reached behind him to present the ermine fur. The thick coat came over her and he tucked it in on the sides before settling her back against his chest.

Just how foolish could he make her, she wondered, drawing her first easy breath, only to realize how the idea, the mere thought, had warmed her, and from the inside out. Toasty warm. Even her toes tingled as new life chased away the cold.

Zermatt started forward as she felt his hands upon her hair, brushing off snowflakes. Several seconds passed in a trance of memories of his kisses: the feel of his lips on hers, the wild pleasure of it, and the way that night, their wedding night, she had felt as if his kisses would never stop and how glad she was of it, as if she could happily spend the rest of her life being kissed by him—

She closed her starry eyes and banished the thoughts. Not now. Perhaps not ever. She had already confronted the idea that however horrible the passion he gave her, it was nonetheless a fact. Instinctively she knew no one else would, or even could, make her feel this way, and this from a man who . . . who—

"So, love, what were you doing out here?"

She focused her thoughts. "Looking for this," she said as she reached in her basket, found the precious bark, and held it up to his inspection.

"A piece of bark?"

"Aye, verdigris. 'Tis a small bush that usually grows near berry brambles. It has to be aged in the earth or 'tis no good. I've searched for four days now . . . lucklessly, until young Johannes spotted this."

The Goddess had answered her prayers at last . . .

A slight tension alerted him. "What is it for, love?"

"A potion."

"Yes? What for?"

Nichole looked across a cleared field turning white now with this first snow. The steady pick of Zermatt's hooves interrupted the harmony of a snowfall's silence, and still she heard in the whisper of the words the Goddess would prove wrong: ". . . his inheritance would be easily contested . . ." Somehow she knew that by proving Jonpaul wrong she would come closer to the truth.

"I can't tell you. 'Tis a secret."

"A potion to . . . ah, dampen my ardor?"

To his utter surprise she laughed. He had never heard a gladder sound, and it passed through him like a hot, sweet tonic.

"Milord, do you think that would work?"

"Only through my death," he replied, and with humor so she could take it as teasing and she did, the idea apparently preposterous to her.

She knew to change the subject. "Yesterday that merchant came. Did you buy anything?"

"Aye." He suddenly wondered if she had wanted something.

"He was a Jew?"

"Aye. Abrams, a good fellow from Basel."

"I heard Stefano and Gallman talking in the stables about the Jews in Basel. Stefano was telling about the last outbreak of the black death here, some many years past now. He said that the people of Basel got it in their minds that the Jews had poisoned the wells with the black death and they gathered to avenge the deed."

"Aye. 'Twas a terrible day, that."

She nodded silently, Nanna's wisdom sounding in her mind as it always did: "Oh, I've heard it, the Christ killers, these people say, forgetting that Mary and her child were Jews! Forgetting that God made all people everywhere! Some of the sorry souls that blame these wicked things on the Jews have the thief of ignornace for an excuse but not many. For by far and away most of these 'holy' Christians do it to feed their greed. The Jews, like us, do very well in the world—thank the Goddess that—and these people covet their hard-earned possessions. 'Tis the very same reason we, too, are persecuted by the Church . . ."

"Stefano said you gathered men to save them when the city guard would not? He said you arrived—"

"Aye, too late. The mob had already killed eleven by a burning of four houses."

"Yet you saved a hundred more?"

"Who knows how far their greed and small-minded hatred would have led them? Mobs . . ." He shook his head. "No more dangerous animal exists, and for some ungodly reason, this animal is most vicious when turned against the poor Jews . . ." And then Nichole heard him express almost word for word the things Nanna has always said, and her thoughts were spinning, madly spinning round and round the puzzle of Jonpaul.

Zermatt pranced through Dornach's gates. "Oh, I almost forgot," he lied. "Before Bruno left, he sent a present. For you."

Jonpaul swung the reins over Zermatt's head, then dismounted. He reached up to lift her weight to the ground. "Oh?" she questioned, and the look on her face made him laugh.

"At least when it comes to gifts, love, you are true to your sex." He waved the groom away, then told Williams to order a hot bath for the lady as he took her small hand. "Come. Help me put Zermatt to stall."

Holding her hand and Zermatt's reins he led the way to the stables. Two grooms ran ahead smiling. The stables were warmer by far and filled with the happy sound of children laughing. Up in the hayloft, a boisterous wrestling match ensued as the children's fathers were putting the mounts to stall. One by one they fell silent as Jonpaul and Nichole appeared. Heads peeped over the ledge, each with a waiting smile, too. "There she is . . . Here she comes," they all said excitedly, knowing the surprise in store. Gavin scrambled quickly down, unmindful of Mary's call to wait.

Jonpaul led Nichole to the stall where a magnificent young dark mare stood waiting. She was quite simply the most beautiful horse Nichole had ever seen. Tall and leggy, and muscular and strong, she had those rare, perfect proportions of the exceptional horse. Save for her sex, she was in the class of the very best war-horses. A shame, for only knights rode stallions.

Entranced, Nichole dropped the gloves she held to the ground, knowing but not as the dark head lifted over the gate to greet Nichole's touch. A beautiful head with dark-brown eyes that shined with an untamed spirit. "Oh, she's beautiful . . ."

The whispered awe made him smile. "Bruno couldn't decide whose gift she is. Bregenz's or his. For this, love, is Maseen, Bregenz's finest daughter."

"For me?"

The cry made him laugh and his laughter answered the question. Jonpaul had already been through these same battles with Gavin the day the boy had received his pony and so he knew to keep a firm hand. She might not be sleeping in his chambers, but he would be damned if she'd be sleeping in the stables, either.

"A year, maybe two, and then—"

"A year!" Charles almost laughed. His stallion danced and snorted, puffs of fog rising from the beast's spread nostrils. He tightened the bit, and stated the fact, "I will not wait a year."

They sat mounted on horses at the crossroads between St. Gallen and Lucerne. The last detail of the plan had never been discussed. Kuno had simply assumed Charles would be smart about it, but he saw how he was wrong. "If you send an assassin now, the whole world will guess the source, then know the motive, our motives! The world will condemn you!"

"World condemnation amounts to little more than an old woman's clucking, and I care as much." There was scorn in his raised voice but also excitement, the excitement of a hunter going in for the kill. "Without proof there will be no consequences. None past the lordship of Dornach, which," he smiled, "I so badly want."

Kuno stared, just stared, seeing that Charles thought the murder of the lord Jonpaul little more than the last small obstacle to scale on the grand way to Dornach. He was afraid to ask, "I suppose you have the way all figured out?"

Charles laughed. "Not just the way but the means as well." He rallied his mount to Kuno's side, grabbed his friend's reins to subdue the other horse's nervous dance, and in a lowered voice filled with the same excitement, "As we speak, two assassins wait on the Kotkin Pass just past the township."

"The Kotkin Pass? Between Dornach and Elkhorn?"

"Aye, the only one that's open during the winter snows. They will be informed when the lord is traveling. He is said to travel there and back two or three times a winter. So then it's only a matter then of months. Maybe less." Charles laughed softly, as if he had just shared a secret with a lover, then harder as Kuno's small eyes filled with anger.

"You fool, Charles! And what if they are caught and your name is given as purse payer?"

"Tsk, tsk," he scolded, mocking the smaller man as his pale eyes filled with an unnatural light. "Kuno, you must start trusting me. There is no 'if' to my equation, because, you see, money is not always the very best motive. These two Frenchmen both lost brothers and cousins in the Burgundy War, and by the fall of the lord's sword. And neither, I assure you, can trace their benefactor to me."

As Kuno's face registered surprise and as his gaze fixed deeply on his, Charles laughed again, thinking, Not I, Kuno, but the benefactor named will be you.

"Three days? At the very least? Oh, no," Father Ari shook his head, "Jon does not give Gavin any holidays but the high ones . . . you know, Michaelmas, Lent—"

"Milord cannot know about it."

Alarm gradually replaced Father Ari's surprise as he stared at the young lady. There was something strange about her, a thing that surpassed the sadness and worry he understood only too well. It was as if a part of her had withdrawn, then been replaced by an unnatural calm. Somehow, someway, he knew this calmness acted as the emollient for a great determination. Determination to do what, though? "What for, milady?"

"Please," she said softly, her eyes seeming to be focused on him but in truth, looking straight through. A wet, smoking log had been mistakenly put to the fire and the smoke had made Ari open the window to the cold. A chilly breeze blew through the open, frost-covered window. "I cannot say."

"My dear girl," he began. "You cannot ask me to deceive Milord, perhaps even lie to his face without telling me the reason? I mean, you must see—"

"I need your help." She stated the simple fact without emotion, save for that which shone strangely from the lovely eyes. "You will not have to lie. With the winter work, he rides out before dawn each morning and rarely returns before dark. He will never even know."

"Then why can't you even tell me what you want with the boy?"

The blue eyes took on a radiant, ethereal light, and she said simply, "One receives the Goddess's blessing through silence."

The kindly man stood for several seconds, staring as his thoughts rushed where she led them. The Goddess, potions, magic, and Gavin—Gavin's failing that could cost Jonpaul his life. Silence because the hope, if lost, would be painful indeed. Oh, but still—

He first heard the flutter behind him, a gentle flap of wings and, startled, he turned to see a large white dove fly in through the window. "My God!" The doves Lisollette loved and fed, the lovely creatures he had not seen at Dornach since her death! But how incredible!

The creature flew to Nichole, making circles around her. The girl, bewitched for sure, closed her eyes and lifted her hand. The white dove settled on her fingers with a flap of wings and she smiled, for, as Nanna always said, the creatures might have been made by God but they shall always belong to the Goddess . . .

With a soft coo, the bird took flight, circling the bewitched girl once again before finding its way out the window. Only then did Father Ari realize he had forgotten to breathe. Lisollette's doves, as if that good woman herself had sent Nichole a gracious blessing for her child!

"Will you, my dear friend?" Nichole asked.

"Aye," he managed to say, and with a genuflection, the first sincere genuflection in many, many years.

The fields had to be covered and the grain had to be

collected and stored, an arduous task in and of itself, and one demanding every available man. The first weeks of snow were as hard as any week in spring, and though normally Jonpaul savored the physical exhaustion that came from the many hours of labor, he felt these last days a maddening agitation hardly touched by the back-breaking work. He knew the source, indeed he could not escape it. He was afraid. Fear was hardly unknown to him. It appeared regularly before any battle or fight, but always then it could be used in the force of the halbert, lance, or sword. Yet this fear was different, this fear had no name.

On his return from the last field, he stopped Zermatt for a moment and sat staring at the darkening landscape. Two feet of snow covered the land, shading trees and burying the bushes, all hauntingly beautiful beneath the darkening colors of twilight. Still, the shadows put his thoughts on a waiting treachery. Nichole . . . Nichole . . . Her name appeared again, and he knew he faced the vague sense that his fear belonged to her. Charles might be bent on his murder, but he would not hurt his sister, would he? Yet who else could pose a threat to her? Besides, how could she be harmed at Dornach?

The questions brought no assurance. If Charles's plans were known, he would receive word soon. Perhaps then he could name the fear at least well enough to fight it. And, God forbid, it did have something to do with Nichole!

With an impatient snort from Zermatt, Jonpaul gave the beast rein. There was something else strange, too. He had not seen Nichole for three days now, leaving before she woke and returning after she retired, an absolutely necessary condition if he were to wait for her. He wanted badly to give her this, sensing the danger of forcing her passion when he did not own her trust . . . but what a battle when he found her presence more tempting than a feast after famine, and this more maddening each day it lasted . . .

What was strange, though, were the queerest of replies of late to his inquiries after her.

"Oh, aye, she's fine . . . fine. Yes, the girl is quite fine. A virtual picture of fineness, yes indeed. Excellent really—"

"Excellent?" he had laughed at Ari. "What do you mean by that?"

"Oh . . . oh, nothing, I assure you."

Then Madeline last night: "Milady? Oh, she is fine, just fine. How is she spending her time? Oh . . . oh, well! That horse of hers and, and she reads, yes, that's what she does all day . . . well, not all day, but much of it, indeed more than anyone, even young Gavin. Gasp, did I say Gavin? Oh, dear, is that Martha calling me?" and off the woman ran like a chicken with its head cut off.

Even Kurtus acted strange to the inquiries. Probably something to do with that potion. He had searched his mother's old dusty book of hours to find what potions called for that bark, but the only reference he had found to it was for making an acid used to scour diseased flesh and burn wax.

Zermatt pranced into Dornach, lighted now in the darkness, and he searched for Gavin's familiar face. The boy was nowhere in sight. The excitement of sleds on a first snow had probably worn him out. He smiled and greeted Thaddus, instead, handing over Zermatt's reins as he dismounted.

A huge, warm fire crackled in the great hearth where supper was being served to the men. Jonpaul took his place, and for a while he forgot Nichole as he satisfied his hunger. The men talked of the work, the likelihood of the weather putting them back a few days, and so forth. It wasn't until after the fruit and cheese plates replaced the supper plates that Jonpaul abruptly realized how subdued both Kurtus and Ari acted. The others, too, he noticed. Ari had hardly said a word.

"So how did Gavin do today? Is he still managing the Greek well?"

A sudden silence came over the table. "Fine . . ." Father Ari said in a strangely somber tone. "His Greek . . . coming just fine . . . fine," he repeated, and found himself suddenly fascinated with the rim of his brass goblet.

Sadly, anything but fine . . .

Nichole had begun two days ago. She started by puncturing his right ear, causing an eruption of bloody bile, all of which was cleaned—this alone took two hours of tedious, painstaking effort—before she proceeded with the salve that burned any hidden wax in the ear, leaving that for a day and night. It hadn't worked. Gavin awoke from the sleeping potion yesterday afternoon. At the very least he should have experienced a crackling, a tremendous crackling, but he reported no sensation. The part that tore Nichole's heart from her breast was that the boy was in pain. Today began the other ear but, as Nichole said, 'twas a bad sign, a very bad sign.

So lost in the anxiety of his thoughts, Father Ari did not notice how Jonpaul stared until his voice brought his gaze across the table.

"So something is amiss," Jonpaul said. "Something, I now see, that has to do with my son as well as Nichole. And you, my friend, will tell me what this is."

Not much later, Jonpaul quietly opened the door to Nichole's chambers. A candle lit the bedside where his son slept on his side, hands curled under the side of his face. Mary slept on her cot nearby. Nichole sat on a stool with her back to the door. She was soothing a cloth over Gavin's head. Jonpaul stood there staring, seeing her love for his boy like a visible light cascading over his form . . .

"Bettrina, I told you I wasn't hungry."

He still made no move. Sensing her mistake through the silence, she turned to see him there. Their gazes locked, emotions passed between them before he stepped quietly across to the bedside. The focus of his gaze fell on Gavin. "Nichole . . ." His voice was a whisper of pain. "Why did you not tell me?"

Her long pause filled with the same pain, rising from the wealth of the initiate's unnatural compassion. "I would not give you such hope, when . . . when I shall surely have to snatch it away again."

He said nothing for a long time as he took the cloth, smoothing it over his boy's forehead as she had done. His other hand reached to brush the wet blond curls back, and the gesture, so simple, natural, loving, brought a surge of emotion in her. Suddenly no matter what he had done in his past, no matter what sat between them or would come between them, all that existed in the moment was their love for a young boy.

"In the best of circumstances the treatment works rarely," she said quietly. "I watched Nanna do it on a child, a little girl of two, and even then, Nanna thought the reason it didn't work was because she caught it too late. 'Tis just that . . . I thought . . ."

She thought the Goddess had sent her blessing.

At last Jonpaul straightened, and he nodded, understanding. She had had to try. He had had to try. He closed his eyes as a montage of the blurred faces of doctors and surgeons rushed through his mind, the dozens of wise men he had courted in the beginning, each with their own worthless cure, and often a terrible cure at that. He had put the boy through leeches and bleeding and head braces, filling him with vile potions and poisons, and all for naught. Naught but his own desperate inability to accept what could not be changed. And still he probably would have kept putting the boy through cures if it were not for that dream . . .

In this dream he had been hunting. A white-gray sky melted into the horizon, empty save the light of the sun behind the smooth layer of clouds. The air had that curious stillness that arouses wonder and contemplation. In that strange sky he suddenly saw a magnificent bird circling high in flight. He took aim, but as he did the bird went through transformations: first it was a fly catcher, then, as he stared, a great tit, then suddenly a heron, a warbler, a woodpigeon, a sparrow hawk, a magpie, and thrilled at these tranformations, not cautioned by the magic or its beauty, he took aim. As the arrow flew, the bird changed once more, becoming two. Two magnificent white doves, the birds that Lisollette had cared for and loved, and with mounting horror, he watched the arrow strike one. The creature was felled at his feet. The arrow pierced his wing, crippling the creature with pain, and, as he withdrew his knife, knowing what he had to do, the other bird circled overhead, and he heard her voice cry without words, "Leave him be. Please to God, you've hurt him enough, Jcnpaul. Leave him be!"

As hard as it was, he let Gavin be from that time on, and it was hard, hardest to give up the hope, however small, offered by each new cure. Nichole did not have to tell him the danger of it, for if anyone understood the danger of hope, it was he.

She had so wanted to spare him the sadness and pain filling his dark eyes as he left the room. Startled, she looked down at her hands, hands that trembled with the effort not to go to him . . .

A dream appeared to the boy, a ripple through his consciousness. A familiar dream but one he had not heard in ever so long. A dream taken from long, long ago when he used to wake to hear his mother's voice softly rising with a song and, as before, he felt that familiar jolt of joy for it, his beautiful mother and her songs, but this was different, the voice had changed with the song. This song had no words he knew, and as he struggled to make sense of it, stirring with discomfort, the song faded with a sudden awareness of dull pain, then a crackling and a pop. The landscape shifted, fading into darkness where voices came to him as they used to come to his dreams, long, long ago before the world had turned silent . . .

"He is not back yet?"

"Nay. I doubt that he shall be back for some time."

"I've hurt him very much . . ."

A familiar silence fell, yet not familiar, for in this silence came the sound of footsteps, a distant sound he did not know. "He will get over it, milady. He always does."

The crackling sounded loudly, drowning out the voices so close, becoming even louder and interrupted by jabs of that terrible dull pain in his head. If he held still it settled. Yet when it settled he heard . . . why, how odd, he heard his heart beat . . . faster and faster . . .

Chapter Fifteen

How the mating of Lord Charles of old and the lady Lucretia had caused such disparate results as Charles the Bold and the beautiful Lady Nichole Lucretia was the question Gallman pondered as he left the dreary walls of St. Gallen. He had just endured a most unpleasant encounter with Charles and his queer friend or compatriot, the bishop. When he finally found Charles so he could sign the wedding papers he would now carry back to Dornach, he saw—

Gallman shook his head, unmindful of the soft, falling snow as his good horse started out, reliving memories of the unpleasant scene. After traveling to Lucerne, then sent to St. Gallen, he was told he might find Charles in the church and that he might interrupt since it was urgent business. Well, he *had* looked. The church was still lit from a recent mass, and with the devil's own blasphemy, beneath the gold-gilt cross of Christ, Charles the Bold of Lucerne was mounted on a young black cloth sister of Christ. The sacrilege seemed so much worse for the woman's struggle, and though 'twas hard to say for sure, it had the appearance of a rape. Then to endure that man's litigious insults—

'Twas a fool's journey to head back to Dornach in an

afternoon snowfall, but he could not stomach even a night within the corrupt walls of St. Gallen. Far better to brave the weather. He tried to rid his mind of the scene, staring at the tall, snow-covered mountains rising on both sides as his mount gently picked his way down into the valley. A foot of snow already. He could hopefully reach the next village by nightfall or shortly after—

The woman appeared from behind a tree. Her black cloth against the white snow startled his horse, causing a brief dance and a high toss of his red head. Gallman tightened the reins and stopped, staring incredulously at the misplaced sister on the snowbound road. "Greetings."

The woman approached. She wore no cloak or even shawl against the snow, and Lord knows how long she had stood there, for a thin layer of snow lay on her shoulders and head. One hand remained in the habit while the other withdrew a piece of cloth, tied with a woven string of straw.

This was extended to him.

"What goes here, good sister?" He looked at the cloth a moment before his mind produced the idea. "Is it a message?"

She nodded.

"For Dornach or—"

She nodded vigorously, then with a finger to her mouth she signaled her mute tongue.

"Oh . . . I see. A message for someone at Dornach?"

She nodded more vigorously but then seemed at a loss as to how to name the person. She looked helplessly around the snow-covered ground.

"Milord, perhaps?"

She shook her head as Gallman tried to figure who at Dornach might have business with a sister at St. Gallen, the very idea of anyone dealing with a mute sister of St. Martin unlikely. "Ari?" he asked doubtfully.

She shook her head and, spotting a fallen branch

beneath a tree, she struggled over there. She broke a limb off and then drew the picture of a crown and the sign of a woman in the fresh powder of snow. A crown and a woman . . . "Oh, why, you must mean the lady Nichole?"

The woman nodded vigorously, and then with a worried look, held out her empty hand and shook her head to indicate she had no way to pay. Gallman stared at the calloused red hand, trembling with cold or excitement. His smile bespoke his kindness. "Not to worry. God knows it won't be the first time. Prayers for a safe journey will be reward enough."

For the first time in many long years a weak smile of gratitude lifted on the woman's face.

Wild with apprehension, Nichole burst from the entrance hall into the snow flurry of the storm. Was he home? A dark morning sky against a world of white, at least another whole foot of snow had fallen in the night and she struggled to make her way to the solar garden's edge to see over the fence. No time for snow boots. The cold jolt of snow slid inside her day slippers, trickling down her socks as she sank with each step, not caring about anything but the question. She finally made it to the fence. Where were they? She looked toward the gate, then her gaze swept across the courtyard, past the smithy, the chapel across the way, and the piggery, until finally she spotted the fresh boot- and hoofprints near the stables.

Breathless all of a sudden, she tried to run, but the strong wind made progress slow, slower still with at least a foot of sinking with each step. Coatless, even scarfless, the blue muslin winter dress would be soaked by the time she reached the door, but she didn't care, didn't even think to care. Shivering against the cold, she finally reached the barely packed area of snow in front of the stables. The doors were closed against the wind. The sound of the men arguing inside barely rose above the fierce howl of the wind and, with effort, she pulled one door back and flew inside. The wind slammed it shut with a loud slap, as leaning against the wall, trying to catch her breath, her gaze flew around the large space. "Jonpaul? Is he back?"

She found the small gathering of men around Zermatt, but not Jonpaul. She looked around more. He was not here. Where then? The piggery? "Kurtus?"

All gazes settled on her: the girl who stood there coatless, wearing only a pretty winter dress, the long plait of her dark hair sprinkled with snowflakes, her cheeks flushed crimson with the cold and her eyes wild. "Where is he?"

"Not here," Kurtus said as he bent back down to continue rubbing the cold from Zermatt's legs. Wet and bedraggled, good Lord if the girl wasn't beautiful still, this on top of everything else she brought to Dornach. "Only Zermatt returned . . . but we best get ready. He should be here soon."

What? That made no sense, and she approached the news cautiously just as she slowly stepped to the group of men. Her eyes went from Zermatt to Kurtus back again. "I don't understand? What happened? How could Zermatt be here when he is not?"

"Well . . ." He brushed back his hair. "He's upset, Nichole. And when Jon gets upset he usually goes for a long swim. Like other men drink, Jon swims, and I suppose what happened is the storm naturally prohibited the idea of swimming and so he took to running instead. Seeing how Zermatt is just about spent, I'd wager he set him free and decided to do the last miles on foot."

Startled blue eyes looked to the familiar faces of the men watching her, then to Kurtus as she instinctively reached up to stroke Zermatt's head. "What? I'm not sure I understand?" She looked at Zermatt. "Are you telling me Zermatt has returned alone and you . . . you think that my husband is witless enough to walk or swim or run in this storm?"

"I know it sounds . . . ah, improbable—"

"Improbable!" She gasped the word, not thinking, only acting instinctively. "How could you, Kurtus? How could you just kneel there worried over his horse when he might be lying in the snow, injured or worse?"

Kurtus came quickly to his feet. "Now look here, young lady. Listen to me—"

"Oh, but Kurtus! You don't know, you just can't know for sure! What if you are wrong? Don't you see?"

"First of all, if he were injured or wounded, Zermatt would never leave him and—"

"What if he sent Zermatt home to tell us? What if Zermatt came home because he knew he needed help? Oh, Kurtus . . ." She grabbed his arm. "You, all of you, must go find him! This instant, or so help me God . . . so help me, I'll mount Maseen myself and go out there!"

No amount of arguing changed the fear in those blue eyes, though the thought of heading out into this storm made Kurtus try. All Nichole knew was that never in seventeen years had she ever heard anything so stupid as the idea that Jonpaul had purposely gotten off his horse in this storm—she knew that hadn't happened—and she panicked, spinning in her wet boots to the tackroom, meaning to get a saddle and go herself, which finally seemed to convince Kurtus. With a curse, he saw that he would have to do this.

Nichole waited shivering in the stables beside Zermatt. Bundled up and mounted, Kurtus stopped behind the others to say a short speech. "I have never met a woman who caused as much trouble as you, milady. Luckily you are also the only woman I've ever met who is worth it. So here I go, milady," he said with more irritation than anger as his hand swept forward, "out in this freezing wind and for no good reason at all, past the excessive worries of a young girl's heart. Aye, worries," he repeated for her confounded confusion that he was tired of humoring, "'tis very queer, my dear Nichole," a certain bemusement hid his mischievous intent, "one would swear that any decent person would relish the idea that this monster of atrocities, this maniac, this murderer of women and children you imagine, was now lying wounded and maybe dying in a cold winter snow. No decent person I know would send three good men out into the cold, dead winter to rescue the brute. Ah, you look shocked now, I see. Well, you should!"

Quietly, with urgency, "Go, Kurtus . . . please, just go."

He kicked heels to his mount, passing through the stable's doors and into the winter storm, and for no good reason past the excessive worries of a young girl's heart.

The horses picked their way carefully down into the valley, and some good long mile later Kurtus spotted the lone dark figure moving swiftly across the snow-covered landscape. They had waited a week for him, everything had been arranged. "There he is," he pointed. "And thank God, too, we can get back and dry off in plenty of time."

Snow covered and gathered in man-size drifts around the towering gray stone walls of Dornach Castle. The haunting quiet of the snowfall buried the castle as the next centuries of wear and weather never would.

Darkness approached rapidly and yet the hour was still early. Still, few lights appeared in the windows, and this silence rang eerily, interrupted only by the crunch of his boots on the snow and his labored breathing.

He had known, though; he had spent the last long week preparing for this very moment. A long week indeed, where the pursuit of that band of thieves served to ease the emotional strain of this crushing burden he no longer seemed able to carry. Accompanied by three men-in-arms, he spent the week following the tracks of these trade thieves, a small band of less than a dozen men who had been periodically raiding the trade houses along the Dornach's routes to Basel. Like his wedding night, and if only he hadn't left then—

'Twas useless; he banished the "what if."

In the dark dead of night these men ambushed the posted guards, slaughtering them mercilessly before stealing everything they could carry away. A couple of leads brought them to a country house on the farthest western outskirts of the Lucerne Canon—Lucerne, Charles's domain and not a coincidence, as he had guessed. The men had escaped, and there was no proof. With little food and less sleep, twenty exhausting hours each day, this search had done little to exorcise his demons, only he had been too tired to realize it. Until—

He made his way inside the snow-covered courtyard, and a sudden gust of the chilled wind came against his strength, hitting him like a thrust into a great impenetrable wall he could never scale. Gasping for breath, the icy air felt like a blade in his lungs and he stumbled, dropping to one knee as he tried to stop the sudden swell of emotion in his chest. It was the silence, the silence of the snowfall, the deserted battlements, the empty courtyard. What had he been expecting? A miracle? As if his pitiful emotionally tattered senses deserved, nay demanded such a gift, and so simply got it?

Less likely than Nichole ever coming to the truth . . .

With a curse to her, he struggled to his feet and made his way past the snowbound fence through the garden and into the entrance hall. He quickly discarded the binding of his snow clothes before climbing the stairs to enter his chambers. He called for young Williams as he tore off his damp clothes, replacing them with clean, dry ones. He called again, wanting a fire and some food before he collapsed into what he prayed was a dreamless sleep.

He pulled on a moccasin boot, stopped midway, and looked around as if to spot the trouble. Too quiet, even if everyone was trying to avoid him. And where the hell was Williams for that matter? He went to the door and shouted at the top of his great, loud voice.

No one and nothing.

With a curse he descended the stairs, two at a time, passing quickly through the entrance hall into the great hall. The door was shut. "What the hell?" He pushed it open but then stopped, staring at the unexpected sea of smiling but silent faces. As he stood in the doorframe for a long moment, he could make no sense of it, this, the crowded hall. "What the devil goes here—"

The silence sang again in his mind. All of Dornach's people, his people, over fifty people stood in a strange silence, smiling with a secret he could not guess. He looked at Mickeil and Williams, the farmers, the maids and serving and kitchen wenches, the stable grooms, and a dozen of his guards, Stefano, Peter, the smithy and his son, many of the villagers and all of the children, it seemed. Quiet children? Even little Mary held her mouth to stop a sound. There was Ari and Kurtus, looking most foolish of all—

The crowd parted and still kept this silence as Jonpaul watched his son emerge from the very center of the people. Gavin wore the same grin as the others, the same grin, only wider on his flushed cheeks, accented by a mischievous light in his bright blue eyes. Jonpaul felt his heart stop, afraid without reason, before, in this miracle of silence, he heard this one word, haltingly, with much effort: "Father . . ."

The cheer went up and did not stop. For many long minutes, the people's joy sounded like trumpets through the room. Jonpaul did not know what he was doing, that he was kneeling as Gavin ran to his arms, then lifting to hold his son tight against his chest where the emotions burst upon that one word he had never heard before . . . Father, Father, Father. His joy swung Gavin round and round, and Gavin was laughing, still laughing silently, as it would take many months to grasp the happy fact that his laughter had a voice and many more to begin exercising it regularly . . . But still he was laughing.

Through blurred eyes Nichole watched from behind as the people gathered around the father and son, their collective love visible in smiles and tears and eruptions of laughter as Jonpaul swung his son round and round. He finally stopped and set the boy down to stare, as if the change would manifest in his physical appearance, but he could not speak yet, as dumb as Gavin once was.

Kurtus saw this and explained, "So far as we can tell he has normal hearing in one ear, partial in the other, but even that seems to keep getting better as he still feels crackles and pops, he says. Yes, he says!—though this is very hard for the boy . . ."

Which had surprised all of them, Nichole especially, imagining, she said, "that once a deaf person heard, they would speak like all others." Every single word and sound had to be practiced over and over as, with effort, Gavin tried to mimic it. A voice so strange to him. Yet Father Ari and Nichole had taught him one sentence to say to his father. With a smile Kurtus said to Gavin: "Say the words to your father, Gavin."

The people fell silent again, and Nichole held her breath as Gavin's voice came haltingly again and obviously practiced. "I love you, Father."

The voice he had never heard before was such a surprise, high like all young boys' but musical like Lisollette's. "I love you, Father." Gavin said it again, and with the very emotion in his eyes as he watched the curious effect of his words change his father's eyes. Nichole saw this, too, and it triggered the pounding of her heart, a stream of tears sliding down her cheek, and with a sudden vulnerability, a weakness she could not fight, she turned away and disappeared quickly down the hall.

Later that night, long after the celebration, footsteps sounded outside her door. Hearing the boots stop outside her door, she tensed, lifting her head from the wet pillow. He had come at last. A soft knock sounded. "Nichole?"

The pause sounded loud and lasted longer, and into this pause the desperate prayer flew that he would leave her be tonight. *Oh, please, Jonpaul . . . please.* One look in his eyes and 'twould be over. The world lost or gained by a look of his eyes. Lost or gained . . . Lost or gained, she didn't know. If she conjured her brother's picture she knew the world would be lost, yet if she conjured the vision of Jonpaul staring at his son as he said those carefully practiced but heartfelt words she knew the world would be won. A gamble of consequence, but not one she could take until she knew, no matter how much she wanted to.

The knock sounded a bit louder, and like the whisper of her name, it echoed with the tenderness of his own feelings, of his love, the gratitude of the gift the Goddess sent him through her. She could almost feel his love reaching her, her mind, mind and soul, desperate to answer, so desperate . . .

She clutched the pillow tightly, and buried her face, terrified she would rise at any minute, and she wanted to, she wanted to. Oh, God, how she wanted to fall into his open arms, for she knew now how desperately she loved him. Hopelessly, desperately, she loved him. A terrible, doomed love for sure . . .

Finally the footsteps turned and left. She could almost guess how hard the measure was, almost but not quite, if she saw the clenched fist at his sides, a futile effort to stop their shaking.

Father Ari and Kurtus sat with an uneasy silence in the relative darkness of Jonpaul's study chambers. Abandoned by both Nichole and Jonpaul on the auspicious evening, young Gavin had at last fallen asleep in Kurtus's arms before the man set him on the cushioned sleeping cot in the corner near the blazing hearth.

"How could she!" The frustration finally pushed Kurtus from the chair. "A blind man would know by now, a blind, stinking . . . Dear God, Ari, there must be some way to show her where she is wrong."

"A signed confession writ by a black glove might do it. Might, I say. The whole thing shows how strong and deep her loyalty and love runs once got—"

"There must be a way . . . Let's say we go to her now?"

"Useless. She would only spit the litany of deceptions in our face—"

He stopped of a sudden as the door opened. To their surprise Nichole stood in the doorway. She was the last person either expected to see after the grief she had brought Jonpaul. Grief, they both saw, that she obviously felt, too. She wore a long blue robe over a nightdress, bare feet on the cold stone floor. She was hugging herself tightly. Even in the darkness, her eyes appeared red, swollen from many hours of tears, but when she spoke, her voice held an incongruent lucidity, as if she had banished by force of will the emotions plaguing her.

"I need to talk to you. Both of you."

Kurtus exchanged confused glances with Ari before

sinking back to his chair. "At your service, milady. Forever at your service."

"I am confused," she began, and then stopped, changing tracks, wanting to get to the point. "You know the dilemma tearing me in two. Jonpaul says he did not slaughter the village of Stan, that he is not this pretender I think he is. You, too, add voices of protest to his. Everyone at Dornach does. I woud never believe him, *never*, if his appearance did not consistently contradict this picture. Yet there are just so many other things . . . so many that say he is a pretender. Things he has even admitted, as you both know full well."

"I hope you don't mean the day 'terrible' came to his name?"

"I try to understand," she cried, distressed, her voice trembling with emotion. "I do. I know what happens to men when they're filled with bloodletting. 'Tis a kind of madness. They say they can't stop the killing, crazed—"

Father Ari gasped his surprise and looked at Kurtus before, "Dear God, you still think that was Jonpaul?"

"Do not lie to me now! He admitted it, he said—"

"That he was responsible, that is all. I was there, Nichole. I was there!" Kurtus slammed his fist on the table, rising to speak with heated emotion. "He stopped me from telling you once, and do you know why? Because he does still feel the responsibility, that 'twas his fault it happened, and, aye, he was responsible to the degree of this . . ."

Kurtus paused, desperate to get a grip on his emotions. Nichole's eyes shimmered with her own as she waited, expecting the common masculine explanations of the madness of killing, of blood lust and war and how once a man starts, he loses his mind and, really, could she blame him after her brother . . . and so on.

"Battle-worn, weary beyond belief, no one had fought as courageously as Jonpaul had in that war. He had not slept more than an hour or two in those terrible two weeks of fighting, and by the end of these two weeks of his valor, he was suffering a deep chest wound, as well as a number of leg wounds and a head wound that wracked him with pain, left him trembling with fever and weakness. In this state the news was brought to him: a portion of the army had broken away and was spreading terror across the land, heading, aye, to revenge the cowards in Lucerne while raping, killing, and burning along the way." He waved his hand in dismissal, quietly adding, "Such has happened after almost every war throughout history, a consequence of being drowned in the blood of our fellows, the devil's curse, they say.

"'Twas after Bruno and Wesmuller and their armies had already left. I, like all the others, was too weary to care. I had been to hell, fighting as man after man after man, friend after friend fell dead. I had not known a single moment for two weeks when I wasn't absolutely certain mine would be the very next body slain, and I was still absorbing the miracle of being alive. So many dead"—he shook his head, looking away for a long moment before returning his eyes to her, "So many. What could a few more matter?

"I say this to you, milady, that if it were not for your husband, we would have been glad to have those wretches bury your precious forest people. Not one man would have risen against them, not until Jonpaul's voice rallied what remained of his men. Oh yes, 'twas Jonpaul's heart and mind, so firmly fixed on the just, that made us struggle to our feet, made us ignore the aches and wounds long enough to get into saddle. 'Twas Jonpaul who made us ride and ride and ride, through the three days and three nights it took us to catch up to these wretches, 'twas Jonpaul who led the battle again until every last one of the outlaws were banished from the living earth."

Without anyone knowing, Gavin had awakened to

hear this story, one Kurtus loved to tell him. He rubbed his eyes as his mind caught up to the scene in the room. Was Nichole finally going to lose her blindness? For a long moment she said nothing. Her eyes swept to and fro around the floor, then she suddenly fell into a chair. "But they said 'twas him, Jonpaul—"

"'Twas his army, a portion that stepped from the circle of his control. That is all, though, that is all."

Silence sang in the room, a silence still so strange to him, the way it was silence but not, filled with the feather-soft sounds: the crackle of the fire, her small, quick breaths, the clink of a goblet.

Nichole suddenly jumped up and cried, "But, Kurtus, I saw it, with my own eyes! Oh, the hellish scene that haunts so many of my moments. So terrible," she cried, seeing it now. "We had argued all that night and argued until finally Charles ended it by saying he would take me to a place that would change my mind. We left that morning before dawn. We rode for seven hours at least, and all the while I could not reason where he would take me . . . this place that would change my mind until . . . I saw it. The village . . . smoke still rising in the midday air behind a terrible pile of bodies, the blood still red . . . a mother lying slain with her babe . . ." She stopped, shook her head as she turned to Kurtus, and cried, "And he said Jonpaul himself was said to ride here! There were witnesses! Jonpaul, the name of our enemy, the name, dear God, of my husband—"

Kurtus grabbed her shoulders, stopping just short of shaking her senseless. "Milady! Wasn't him, couldn't have been him! Upon my life, his sword has never been raised to the just, yet alone to a child. To this I swear. I swear!"

"But if you don't know? What if . . . what if he does want Lucerne? All his reforms, all his ambition! What if . . . what if he thought a village was not much sacrifice to his plans to unite Switzerland, and sometimes I try to think like that, I try to see it as he did—"

Gavin had never heard Kurtus or Father Ari shout as they did now—so much noise!—everyone shouting it couldn't have been his father, how they would have known, how he couldn't have planned it, let alone done it, pointing out other lies her brother had fostered against his father, how they knew every move his father made, and all the while Gavin sat there figuring seven twice was ten and four, minus two again and smoke and red blood and it was obvious. A woman, even smart like Nichole, might not figure it, especially as his father said her emotions were scrambled like eggs in a pan, but surely Kurtus and Ari—

So Gavin waited for Ari's explanation that always came. He waited. He waited more until he began to wonder if they somehow missed it. It, the obvious.

Confusion made his young face look cross. Say it, Kurtus! Tell her! Yet now Kurtus was going on about the people of Dornach and how they loved his father and Holy Mother, the way his heart hammered hearing these things now.

"Think, girl! Is it possible to deceive not just all of Dornach's people and Basel and beyond, but Ari and Bruno and Hans, those who know him best? His love of life, his children, the little girl you found him—does a man who slays innocents have such easy love for such things?"

"So I ask myself over and over." She was crying now, "but, then . . ."

Ari grimaced when he saw Gavin was not only hearing this but that the boy rose to come to the table where he scrambled for a piece of his figuring scroll and quill, then started searching wildly in the dark for the jar of ink, finally found on the shelf above the bookcase. Only Ari watched Gavin's hands shake with the urgency of what he had to communicate. "What is it, Gavin? What are you doing?"

The boy made no reply. He wrote shakily for his speed. Nichole looked up and finally Kurtus, too. Kurtus was just about to try to get the boy out of the room and to his own bed when Gavin rushed to take Nichole over to the scroll of paper. Wordless she came, expecting some picture he drew for her amusement, and she tried valiantly to overcome her struggle long enough to get him off to bed, too.

Yet, 'twas numbers there. Gavin tipped the candlelight so that she could better read the words written in his child's careful, large numbers.

7 & 7 is 14! 14 & 7 is 21

"What?" she asked, then shook her head as if to clear it long enough to produce a reply. "I know you're good with figures, Gavin, but—"

"Now is not the time," Kurtus said, irritated. "Time for bed, young man—"

He shook his head wildly, then wrote very carefully as he tried to spell the words next to the numbers.

No smoke. No red blood. He knew! He knew!

"What?" Nichole asked in a whisper. Kurtus read it too. "Who? Knew what?"

A desperate finger pointed to the paper, then to Nichole. So desperate he tried to make the words . . . but only garbled sounds emerged in his anxiety. Then he wrote more:

Brother knew Stan! Too fast!

Then in his excitement, he grabbed his ears as the ache

washed over him again. "Oh, darling." Nichole rushed to his side, but he pulled away, pointing to the words.

"Oh, my God." Father Ari was the first to grasp what Gavin was trying to say. "Oh, my God . . ." At first he couldn't say it. The proof. It would crush her, she would—

"What?" Kurtus asked.

"Nichole . . . Nichole. What he means, what he is trying to ask is how could your brother have known about Stan the night it happened if it takes seven full hours to get there and then seven back. How would there still be smoke and red blood?"

Nichole did not understand, not for long minutes, yet her body reverberated with the hard pounding of her heart as she heard Jonpaul's voice in her mind, "Why would a man take a girl to see such a sight? A young girl? To show her why she must marry a man she holds in contempt and loathing? To show her why he says he keeps a standing army of one thousand, an army he means to join with another? If it wasn't the men of the Alliance, then who did kill those innocent people? Who, Nichole, who? He did it, and the reason he did it, the reason he had those poor people slaughtered, was to show a young girl . . ."

The devastating truth dropped her suddenly to her knees with the single word "no." Charles was the bane, the enemy, the horror of the people, Lucerne's and the Alliance's, and she had been little more than a pawn for his malevolence. Charles whom she had loved and worshipped as a father, a man she had elevated in her heart and mind . . .

Kurtus, Ari, and Gavin watched in mute shock, too shocked to move to comfort her until she suddenly jumped to her feet and raced from the room. She ran through the door, turning down the dark hall before flying up the steps. Kurtus raced after her. "He's not there, Nichole! He left again!"

At the top of the stairs she turned and stared down at him. Her eyes were wide and frightened, refusing, absolutely refusing to believe this last. She fled down the last hall to his great, wide doors and burst through. The dark, empty chamber greeted her. The bed was empty. No fire played in the hearth. Outside, snow piled quietly on the windowsill, and she didn't know she was staring at it until the sight blurred, then blurred some more.

Kurtus stepped quietly behind her.

"Where, Kurtus? Where did he go?"

"Elkhorn. He told me to send Gavin as soon as the weather let up some. He said he would not be returning for some time, perhaps as late as spring."

"My brother is going to kill him."

"He knows this. And, milady, trying to kill Jon and doing so are two different things, separated by the possible."

She prayed this was so. "He does not have the Bible, does he?"

"No."

She turned to him. "You will take me to Elkhorn . . . now. I want to—"

"In this storm? No! Absolutely! Not for all the gold in Spain."

"Tomorrow then! We will leave tomorrow—"

"Get the idea out of your head, milady. You're not going anywhere in this weather. Jon would kill me if I even tried to take you through a snowstorm. Nay, he'd torture me slowly—"

"I must see him, Kurtus! I must—"

"Aye. And I suppose that means tomorrow I will head out in the cursed weather, twelve hours behind him. There is a chance, small, but a chance I can catch up to him, but in all likelihood 'twill take at least four days there and four days back."

"I cannot wait eight days . . . I, oh, Kurtus—"

"Hush," he whispered as she fell into his arms. "Just think of the reunion when you can finally meet him in trust."

Only a man would not understand this was the exact reason eight days was a purgatory of eternity . . .

Chapter Sixteen

A fire crackled in the hearth where Mary played with Jonpaul's Michaelmas gift on the bearskin rug. She moved the small, wood-carved figure of the Mother carefully through the tall three-story house, past the lovely little furniture, in and out of each separate room as she called out for the father over and over again. The mother ignored the children because something was wrong. A big people's story the children wouldn't understand, but something bad and troubling that made the mother call for the father over and over.

The mother stopped suddenly to look out the window, then wail over the beautiful snowfall that would not stop.

"May I get a bucket of snow for my house?"

Nichole made no response. She kept writing.

"May I get a bucket of snow?"

"What, Mary? Oh. No, darling. 'Twould melt fast near the fire and get everything wet. Pretending is always more fun anyway, don't you think . . ."

The advice made Mary nod. She would pretend the snow melted and the father came home and the mother was happy again . . .

Everyone at Dornach contributed to the purse, and with her own monies, Nichole had collected a pretty sum.

This would be sent to the bishop in Basel, payment for a mass to be said for Jonpaul on the morrow. She didn't know if she believed in these things. Nanna always mocked not the idea of collective prayer, but the idea of paying for it. "A French whore might listen for a price, but, God, even the Christian God, does not."

Nichole signed the letter. Picking up her wax, she held it over the candle until the green stick began dripping onto the seal, this made of the horns of two elk, the ancient symbol of the strength of life, and she thought, as she watched it fill, that Nanna would have approved of the old symbol, of Dornach's colors, of Jonpaul's mother, and especially of him— Approved of almost everything about him, it seemed so strangely clear now.

Oh, Jonpaul! Can you forgive me my blindness, a blindness owing to my woeful feeling for my brother, this man who returned my favor with mendacious maliciousness and malevolence. I see that now. 'Tis so clear, all of it—his greed and unholy hunger for power that made him head down this wicked path to spread and fan the vicious rumors about you and the Alliance, the premeditated horror of Stan, even the forced marriage to you—a marriage I pray to be worthy of someday, one, that despite its false origin, is surely blessed by all that's holy . . .

I love you, with all my heart, I love you . . .

If only the paper truly existed! Never had she wanted the paper more than now. She'd ride to Lucerne today, this very day, if she had the slightest chance of finding it. She had searched the Bible again and again, and it was not there. No one at Lucerne would ever believe Charles had ordered the destruction of Stan, no one. To lay the claim would put her word against her brother's. All the men who had committed the atrocity were either silenced or their loyalty assured. To even propose the idea that he had done it without proof, absolutely, would cast the name of traitor on her name. The people would assume she was no more than a puppet of Jonpaul—

A knock came to her door just as she sealed the letter. Bettrina swept inside. "Milady. 'Tis Gallman. He carries a message for you."

She stood up. "By all means see him in."

Gallman stepped into the warmth of the room. "Milady, I've a message from St. Gallen."

"Yes?" Nichole asked, watching as Bettrina knelt to see Mary's house arrangements.

"Here." He handed her the bound cloth. "From a sister of the Order of St. Martin, I believe. She did not say her name as she was mute. She seemed most anxious, and after I finally grasped who she meant it for, I said I would take it to you."

Mute? Katrina, it must be Katrina, she realized as she took the wrapped cloth. Gallman left then, and quickly, fearing there might be a return message, and nothing but nothing could make him willing to leave the warmth of Dornach again.

Nichole tore the straw that wrapped the cloth. Potato cloth. Moving to the light of the window, she spread out the cloth. There was no red ink at St. Gallen, and, dear God, this must be writ in blood, dried red blood made into crude figures. First a . . . a six-fingered hand, the cursed hand of six fingers. Then a . . . a, why that looks like a glove, carefully, completely shaded with blood, then an eye pointing to a cross on top of wings or, why, yes, a habit.

She stared for some time, her mind turning over this. The curse of six fingers and a glove, a dark glove, or, yes, a black glove, Charles's own. Charles and his black glove, the deformity that had so distressed her mother! The curse of the sixth finger, like Katrina's? Oh, my God . . .

What could it mean? Katrina and Charles, both sharing the curse of the sixth finger. Well, she could believe it now, but did Katrina send this just to tell her? Written in blood . . .

A shiver raced up her spine. There was an eye pointing to a cross and a habit. Eye and seeing, see a habit . . .

Nichole abruptly grasped the meaning.

Katrina knew the damning secret.

"Milady . . . milady, what's wrong. You look, why you look quite shocked?"

Nichole made no response. She knew how to get there. 'Twould take a day and a night, perhaps a day more. She could reach Zurich by nightfall, St. Gallen the night after. She could be back with the secret before Kurtus returned with Jonpaul, a secret that would ruin Charles. Yet she could not just walk into St. Gallen to visit a mute sister. She could not just walk into St. Gallen period. There must be a way, though . . .

"Milady—"

"I know . . . Yes!" Nichole jumped up and clasped her hands together, her eyes flying wildly around the room. Yes, it could work! "Bettrina, stay here with Mary. I'll be right back."

Nichole rushed down the hall, down the stairs. Father Ari's room sat in the northwest corner of the solar, yet which one was it?

Chatting, laughing, Gregory and Bebe turned down the hall.

"Bebe, wait," Nichole's voice stopped the woman. "Bebe, which is Father Ari's room?"

Bebe turned. "Oh he's not there, milady. He be in the study now—"

"Yes, but which is his door?"

She looked a moment, confused, before, "The second on the right, milady, but—"

"Oh I . . . I just want to drop off a potion I made for him. 'Tis a surprise. Shh . . ."

Bebe smiled conspiratorially, thinking, like most

others, everything the lady did was a miracle and a happy one at that. She hurried on to catch up with Gregory. Nichole hurried to Father Ari's room.

The door was unlocked. She stepped inside the small, dark room. No fireplace or window here, really little more than a servant's bed. The austerity of the room did not really surprise her, for, with the exception of drink, Father Ari lived more in his mind than most all others.

She fell before his plain wood trunk and unscrupulously, opened it. Nothing on earth or in hell would stop her from saving Jonpaul and, aye, Gavin, too, certainly not the borrowing of Father Ari's cloth. He had two extra robes.

Now he had one.

She shut the lid and rushed out. There was no time to waste, much to do, many miles to travel if she was to reach Zurich before the nightfall next.

Bettrina held Mary's hand, heading to the hall to get the midmorning meal. Nichole practically ran into them as they descended the stairs. "Bettrina, I need you. I must go—"

"Go?" Mary's green eyes widened with alarm. "To heaven?"

"Oh my, love," Nichole dropped to face her girl. "No, Mary, I'm not ever going to leave you." She kissed her. "I love you too much! 'Tis just that I've just been called to Dornach. A woman there is having a baby. She needs me to help her."

"Can I go, too?"

"Not this time. 'Tis too cold outside and, besides, Gavin needs you to help feed Mr. Glutton."

"Who is it, milady? Not Teresa, 'tis too soon—"

"No, 'tis a woman named . . . named Katrina. A breech birth—"

"Oh, no!" Bettrina grabbed her protruding midsection.

"Aye. Oh, please, I must hurry. Have someone saddle Maseen and pack me a meal. A big one. I am starved. I'll get my things."

Not much later Stefano and Nichole headed through the gates. She wore an ermine fur cape and hat, her blue cloak over that. Mink gloves kept her hands warm. Father Ari's robe hung loosely beneath these heavy clothes. A small cloth bag carried enough coins to pay for lodging, a plain anlace she stole from the tackroom, and the meal Bettrina packed for her, that was all. She would travel light to give Maseen all speed . . .

Which the fine horse wanted badly. Maseen threw her head back, prancing prettily and wanting to run. "Soon, my pretty, soon," she whispered. Just as soon as we lose Stefano.

Snow fell in soft flurries over the white, snow-covered land, swirling into a dreamlike mist. Visibility stretched no more than ten paces in any direction. Dornach lay ahead, but remained completely hidden in the distance. Nichole abruptly gasped and pulled tight on the reins.

"Milady!" Stefano quickly rallied to her side.

"Stefano, I forgot an instrument. A . . . a mixer. Aye, the mixer. Bettrina knows where it is in my trunk. Could you race back?"

"Then meet you?"

"Aye, at the third house from the north well. You can't miss it, they say. Two stories, thatched roof—"

He turned his mount around. "Aye, aye, milady."

"Oh, do hurry!" she called as he kicked heels to his mount.

He waved acknowledgment. Nichole waited until he disappeared into the white. Then she, too, kicked heels to Maseen. That fine animal leaped into the air and stretched her wings. Nichole rode first into Dornach so her tracks would disappear among the many others, but then she headed east . . . east, where a distant sun would set behind an impenetrable layer of clouds.

With each crunch of Zermatt's hooves to the snow, Jonpaul felt a heightened physical tension. A madness had come over him, 'twas the only explanation for the sudden pace of his heart and breath, the tension seizing him as if . . . he were about to face battle, that was it. All the pieces were in place, and what was he thinking? That Charles would wait a respectful amount of time before killing him, and once he was dead, who, in God's name, would protect his son? Who could protect Nichole? And Charles did threaten Nichole, as well. He did not know how or why, but somehow she, too, was threatened by this dark shape in human form wearing the name of her brother. This threat went to her life—

Nichole's life was threatened!

A man was no more than what he could protect. Foremost, above all else, he was a warrior. He was no longer willing to wait for a mistake that would put him in battle or that which would bring the land to war. He was no longer willing to endure these threats to everything that meant everything to him.

No more . . . no more . . . no more. In his mind's eye he exploded the dark image with a great burst of light, over and over, the meaningful exercise granting him knowledge that the time had come. The means would soon follow. It always did, it always would.

He stopped Zermatt as his gaze lifted to the snow-white heavens above, and he vowed in a prayer: When his sword sliced neatly into that black heart, dear God, grant her the knowledge. Grant her the knowledge that his death had saved all the people she loved—the people of Dornach, the Alliance, and, aye, the forest people of Lucerne; that her brother's death had saved Gavin and little Mary, the nearby souls of the unborn. Their children, especially their children, Nichole, I did it for them!

The snow-filled wind seemed to answer the prayer with a high, pure whistle of a female voice murmuring "aye" through the snow-covered trees. The sudden presence alerted him. A warning, but not. Zermatt pricked his ears, too, standing with perfect stillness. The keen green gaze searched the surrounding snow-covered forest even as he reached behind him to withdraw his crossbow and arrow.

With bow and arrow firmly in hand, ready to aim, he waited. The wind's song reverberated with the sudden race of his heart. Nothing. Swirls of white flakes fell in silence to the smooth white blanket of snow. The fifty-foot pine trees disappeared into the misty white sky. A branch dropped its weight of snow. His gaze flew to the spot. A badger hissed from its place there, and then he saw them . . .

Two red wolves peered cautiously from behind the tree with bright, curious eyes. Mates they were, brought together and inseparable for life, loyal beyond death. Their sad fate revealed itself in thick red winter coats that could not hide a thin frailty beneath. The way the creatures stared and made no move to turn from him said death would be soon, too. They would lose this timeless battle, and why, dear God, did the idea fill him with grief?

The creatures' battleground spread around them, this deserted snow-covered forest that had nothing to hunt. Now they were desperate enough to wait for what their instincts must know would never happen—that badger would never descend. The female would die first, he knew, the male shortly after, and from grief long before his hunger.

With mercy, Jonpaul took aim.

The arrow dropped the badger at their feet. A clean kill. Death for life. The female pounced quickly, and while the male hesitated, staring at him still, Jonpaul, not normally given to fancies, smiled when he imagined gratitude in those bright eyes. A sudden gust of wind, the high whistle of a song seemed to approve his choice.

Jonpaul kicked Zermatt forward, and as he traveled on he found himself wishing the haunting song of the wind would play for Nichole—

The arrow flew from behind. There was no pain at first. The thick fur coat and tunic offered no protection, as the arrow pierced neatly between two ribs. The second arrow cut into his arm, stopped there by his biceps, and with a searing pain that filled the silence with his anguished cry. Then he hardly noticed the pain as he stared at the horror of an arrow stuck in the dead center of his chest.

Zermatt reared high in the sky with an angry snort.

The leap saved his life. Jonpaul fell backside to the cushion of snow, and the thrust pushed the arrow straight through. Almost. With inhuman will, Jonpaul reached to the point and, using the last of his consciousness, he pulled it the rest of the way out.

The last memory came as he suddenly heard Nichole calling to him, "Jonpaul, I love you . . . I love you . . ." but his eyes closed. Dear God, the words came too late after all.

The horse seemed to go wild, rearing, turning in circles around the still and unmoving body of the lord Jonpaul.

"A clean hit."

"Jeezus, look at the blood. He's got to be dead."

"Aye, and by the night's end he will be buried as well."

Kurtus always spoke French to women he was about to lay, a habit initiated the first time he visited one of the more famous Parisian brothels as a boy. Young Arabell could hardly breathe. She had never been more than five miles from Kotkin, which made her a provincial victim of the wide-spread rumor that everything French was superior, especially the language, and though she didn't understand a word of the handsome man's whispers, they were producing a mostly curious effect on her senses. She laughed gaily, feeling dizzy and flushed, and while she might not know the words, his greedy hands and lips were making the meaning perfectly clear.

The day dress dropped to her feet and Kurtus eagerly worked the ties of her camisole, anxious to lay her backside to the bed. A knock sounded at the door. Terror instantly replaced the excitement in the girl's eyes and Kurtus, too, panicked.

'Twould be her father, the innkeeper! Christ Almighty, he had waited till midnight to reach his room, where she promised to wait. She swore her father would be asleep by then! He had purposely spent three hours getting the old man drunk for insurance, and as far as he knew Mickeil and the guards were still passing cups with her brother. He'd have to disarm the man and leave the warmth of an inn for a winter snow at midnight—

A hand covered her mouth. "Quick, under the bed!"

Too late. The door opened. With alarm on his face, Holbien, the captain of the guards, entered.

"What the devil—"

"A problem," Holbien said, looking alarmed, even frightened. "Come. You have to hear this for yourself."

"What is it? Can't you see—"

"Aye, I can see plain, but I tell you Jon's life is more important than a prick of a pretty lass!"

Minutes later, Kurtus descended the stairs to the common hall—the room with a great, hooded hearth and four tables arranged neatly over the hardwood floor—where supper and drinks had been served. Holbien pointed to Arabell's brother. "We were still sharing cups when the boy tells us, well, say it, Andrew."

Mickeil stood next to Arabell's twin brother, a tall, lanky youth, handsome, with straight blond hair and bright brown eyes, eyes that nervously lifted to Kurtus only to lower again.

"Tell him!"

"I was saying to—" Andrew pointed to Mickeil and Holbien—"that two men stayed here last week. Knights they were. Frenchmen, aye, but . . . but they let me ride their mounts . . . and, well, they said they had a matter to discuss with the lord, and they paid me two guldens to bring them word of his passage. No matter how long it took, the one said, the whole winter even, if I would just get word to them when he was coming through Kotkin's southeast pass."

Kurtus's eyes focused hard as his mind absorbed the threat. "When?"

"A week ago today. Jonpaul passed yesterday. He graced my father's house and that . . . that night—oh, God forgive me!—I left for the small hunting lodge—"

"Where, boy?" Kurtus grabbed the boy's shoulders. "Where!"

"Four miles south of here on the Kotkin Pass—"

The door opened with a great burst of frigid wind. The fire leaped in the hearth as two men walked inside, scraping their snowshoes on the snow-grating by the door. Spurs, expensive sheepskin and fox fur coats, and the steel sheaths of swords at each side put them in the class of knights. Travelers at midnight cast suspicion over the two warriors, increasing as their laughter stopped a moment as the taller one shouted, "Ah, you're about, boy! See to our horses. Nothing but the best—"

Kurtus shot his gaze to the boy's face to confirm the idea in the exact moment the two men absorbed the shock of Kurtus and Mickeil's colors, tunics blazing with the bright green of Dornach.

Kurtus froze; for one split second he froze. His sword

sat upstairs. Mickeil and Holbien were also unarmed. Not a good situation, one worsening as the sound of swords pulled from their sheaths rang in the suddenly silent room. The two blocked the stairs—

In a stream of motion that began as a blur, Kurtus saw Mickeil grab a chair, ready to charge, while Holbien suddenly flew through the air, landing with a slide on the table and his hand on a carving knife and, dear God—

Arabell was quick, she had always been quick. After hearing this and seeing the two, she rushed back from the room to the upstairs banister. "Kurtus! Here!"

Arabell—God bless her!—tossed down his sword. Kurtus was quick, catching it with his good arm in a backswing. The practiced movement dropped it from its sheath, and the upswing neatly countered the man's forward thrust.

The odds were better than even now.

A furious clamor of steel against steel rang through the rooms as the swordfight was on. Kurtus knew within a minute the man had precious little time left in the world as he led the French dog away from the stairs to let Holbien up, leading with his strong right to the man's weaker, slower left.

The other man advanced on Mickeil, but too late—the butcher knife flew through the air. The tall, heavyset man cried out as the blade pinned his abdomen a long minute before his sword dropped with a clamor to the ground.

Andrew pounced on him as he fell, but there was little need. With an agonized cry as he clutched the reddening spot, he passed out. Holbien raced up the stairs as Arabell raced down with his sword. Mickeil was quicker—grabbing, raising, throwing a chair against the man fighting Kurtus. He stumbled back, then fell over a bench on to his back. Before he even hit the ground, a deadly thrust of Kurtus's sword knocked him across the room.

The man's very next breath made him feel the sharp point of Kurtus's blade on his throat, and he looked up into Kurtus's darkly malevolent eyes.

A simple question. "Did you fell him?"

Fear, anger, twisted the man's face. "No . . . No—"

Kurtus pushed the point harder until a fast trickle of blood appeared.

The man gasped, "Aye! Aye! We killed him. He's dead now! Fallen many hours past."

Upon hearing those words, emotion filled Kurtus's eyes; he could not now speak. Shocked, too, Mickeil fell on the man. "Where? Where will we find him?"

"Oh, no." The man shook his head, seizing this unexpected lever. "Not until you let me up."

Kurtus fast rose to his feet, his sword dropping harmlessly to his side. "Where?"

"I want a horse—"

It was as far as he got. With a quickness that shocked, Kurtus thrust the blade into the man's stomach; the next thrust would kill him. The question was repeated: "Where?"

The man made no answer.

Kurtus lost any semblance of objective calm. One look at his eyes said he was a madman as he ran the blade hard across his waist. "The next goes deep. Where?"

Blood quickly manifest over the cloth of the man's tunic, seen through the parting of his fox fur coat. He grabbed his side and groaned. Kurtus pricked him again.

"In the forest. About four miles south of here—"

"On the road?"

The man wiped his mouth with the back of his hand, feeling more than faint as his tunic continued to absord his blood. "Aye," he said slowly, his fate sealed, and now he wanted it only to be quick. "That bloody horse of his would not let us close enough to drag him off. Shot the horse three times before giving up, but . . . but he's dead,

I say; the man is dead."

The price of those terrible words, symbols of the deed itself, was death, and Kurtus's only regret was that it was quick and merciful. The man left the world without so much as a whimper. The entire house awoke by this point and a number of shocked faces stared at the carnage below, stared until Kurtus snapped, "Call to arms! Get the horses and gather the men. Now!" He stopped once before rushing out with all the urgency and fear of the thought that Jon was dead. "Arabell. Tend to the other. Try to keep him alive. I would have the name of the personage behind this."

As Kurtus, Mickeil, and Holbien rode at a gallop out of Kotkin onto the snow-covered pass, the great trumpet sounded into the quiet, snow-filled night, a sound that called every able-bodied man to duty.

The searing pain came from Jonpaul's arm, rousing him from the depth of an unconsciousness he had never before trespassed. Something jerked there at his arm and, weakly, he tried to move it, to ease the licks of fire as something tugged and jerked there. Unable to move, he tried desperately to open his eyes. A great opening in the clouds showed the pinpoints of stars, stars shining onto the snow-covered ground where he lay. The stars were too bright . . . too bright—

He closed his eyes. Strange sensations enveloped him. Something furry licked at his chest and arm. A great, comforting warmth came from his back. His booted feet were numb, then not, burning with the snow fever that kills faster than any arrow could, but . . . but, oh God, he realized, he lay against a huge great warmth. Zermatt. Zermatt was felled as well. No . . . no . . . Zermatt. His mind produced the name and a cry, too weak for sound.

Not Zermatt, too—

Jonpaul tried to listen for the strong beat of Zermatt's heart when he realized a sudden 'twas Zermatt's great, huge warmth that was keeping him from a snow burial.

How did he get here? Someone dragged him to Zermatt. He struggled to open his eyes. The bright stars hurt to see. With all his strength he managed to cast his eyes down his length . . .

Only to see the nightmare shape of a wolf at his wound and another at his arm. Just as his mind produced the idea that he was being devoured alive by the creatures, his feverish gaze locked to the male. The creature's eyes caught and reflected the bright light of the stars, revealing a sentiment there. As if he had spoken. He realized he must be hallucinating to imagine such things, and as he thought this, the wind suddenly picked up. The soothing whisper of that song made him close his eyes again. For one wild moment he wondered if Nichole's Goddess was real, if the strange haunting lilt of a woman's song was not her calling to him.

And in this dream he imagined the male wolf curling at his head, while the female wolf took first one gloved hand in her mouth and brought it to his chest, then the other before she, too, curled into a tight, warm ball there on his chest . . .

Kurtus pulled sharp on his reins. Five miles and nothing. Dawn changed the landscape from the blinding darkness to a strange blur of a melting gray. A dark gray permeated the snow-covered land and sky and, God, it was cold. The frigid air seemed to penetrate his very bones, producing the fear as he said, "We lost him. We've gone too far."

Never had Kurtus felt the desperation he felt now. A despair of inexpressible agony as he tapped all the courage he knew to face these next few minutes where the new light of this day would finally let them find him—find him long dead. Even if by some miracle Jonpaul was not dead by an arrow put in his back, if he lay wounded and bleeding in a snowbank, he would most certainly be dead by now. No one, not even Jonpaul, could survive a night in this cold, lying in a bed of snow.

They came back down a hillside, rounding the bend below. The gray dawn gave the riders their sight. Mickeil saw it first, reining his mount behind the others. Kurtus and Holbien came to a quick halt, seeing the huge dark shape beneath the tall pine on the edge of a snow-covered forest.

Zermatt woke to their noise and let out an angry neigh, the first miracle. The great beast struggled to his hooves, making two attempts before he managed the trick. Almost simultaneously, Holbien and Mickeil reached for their crossbows as they made out the red shapes of two wolves lying on Jonpaul, the sight naturally producing the idea of winter scavengers on prey, but Kurtus, staring with a wide-eyed look of disbelief, reached across to grab Mickeil's hand tight. "Nay, look! The creatures move not! They rest for his warmth!"

Mickeil slowly lowered his bow, watching the wolves watch them as in a whisper of awe he said, "'Tis not possible! Wild creatures would die before taking a man's warmth, but . . . but—"

There they were.

The miracle kept the three men still and unmoving. One wolf rose, watching warily as if a guard to the fallen man. The other wolf came to his side. A low growl sounded above the wind. Zermatt neighed, a strange urgency to the sound. The wolves looked up at the beast, their gazes locked, a message exchanged. And then, then, the wolves disappeared like apparitions beneath the sun.

So now they were staring at no wolves, and that seemed more real. Kurtus fell at Jonpaul's side. The cloth of his tunic was ripped, torn, and the wound lay bare to his sight. A clean hole. Straight through. No blood. The idea repeated in his mind: no blood. Like his arm wound. "My God—" The exclamation was never finished as he saw the second miracle. Jonpaul's chest rose and fell with strong, deep breaths. He laid his hand over Jonpaul's heart and felt the swift steady beat of it.

"He's alive. Oh, God, he's still alive . . ."

The next miracle lay in five fallen arrows in the snow, three they discovered belonging to Zermatt, two to Jonpaul, but all pulled from flesh by a predator's sharp teeth, and as they got Jonpaul on to the stretcher, Kurtus would have sworn it was Zermatt long before he believed the other possibility that was not possible. If only the teeth marks on the arrows weren't so small, the exact size of say a . . . a wolf.

The snow had stopped and the sky darkened as Maseen brought Nichole to the narrow wood bridge crossing a hundred or so feet over the Fionnay River a mile or so outside the small valley of St. Gallen. Here the river cut deeply into the mountainsides, carving a deep ravine of maybe a hundred-foot drop over which the bridge spanned. Nichole discovered Maseen did not like heights over water. The horse stopped at the edge of the bridge, unmindful of impatient heels kicked to her side.

"Oh, please!" Night was falling fast, the gates would be closing soon . . .

Not known for a firm hand with the animals, Nichole's philosophy was to beg cooperation through bribing, pleading, and reasoning before ever attempting force. "Come, Maseen! I promise there will be a warm stall and hay just ahead. Oh, please. We shan't fall!" She looked again at this bridge, seeing how old and ill kept it was. Neither observation would she share, however. "Hundreds pass over this very bridge every week. Forward, I say!"

The horse reared up and turned around the other way. The philosophy did not always work with the more stubborn creatures, she knew from experience, and, really, any person with half a simpleton's wit would tell her one must master a horse firmly with force to win its absolute obedience. Thinking of this, cursing the creature, she dismounted and drew the reins over her proud, stubborn head to lead her across.

This did not work, either. Maseen would not cross, and the horse was far stronger. Tired, hungry, and more than anything, frightened of the night ahead, Nichole lost her patience. She mounted again and let her friend find its own way across. Rain and snow flooded the river, and it was deep, and no matter what, she was not going to get her feet wet in the raging icy water, she kept saying over and over as Maseen picked her way along the cliff two hundred or so paces until she found a narrow incline leading down. "Oh, no you don't—"

Too late. Maseen plunged into the frigid waters to her chest, and Nichole cried with the shock as her feet disappeared in the swift-moving stream. She closed her eyes, one foot more and she would be sunk. For several tense moments she clung desperately to the saddle horn with her eyes closed, braced to feel the raging cold waters to her waist. Maseen neighed as if to reassure her or perhaps comment as she leaped to the bank across.

Nichole drew her first easy breath. Then she started shivering. Her boots were soaked, Maseen too, and knowing the best answer to cold, she set out at a gallop up the steep incline and raced into the small valley of St. Gallen on the other side.

The chill chased her weariness. By law all abbeys had to offer one night of free lodging to traveling fathers, just as all castles had to offer one night to traveling nobility. So she had spent the last night in an abbey at Winterthur, the small township several miles outside of Zurich. No one had seen through her heavy disguise, this thick green robe that covered her head to foot. With her eyes downcast and her face hidden in the overlarge hood, she gave the gatekeepers the universal sign for the mute tongue or, in a prelate's case, a vow of silence. They led her to a small, cold room, brought her a simple meal of bread and broth, and closed the door, and that was that. No one had even spoken to her.

She was counting on the same treatment at St. Gallen.

The rest of her plan seemed improbable, even when set against her natural optimism. She would sneak to the woman's quarters in the dark middle of the night. Somehow in the darkness she would find Katrina without waking anyone else. Then somehow they would find a way to sneak out to some secret place where Katrina could somehow—through gestures yet!—tell her the secret of the black glove, a secret that would ruin Charles. A good plan if she had a week, but difficult in a single night.

If there was a will there was a way, and now more than ever, her will felt strong. She closed her eyes, remembering the strange dream last night, a dream taken from a memory. She must have been so young, and when she thought of it, the forest elk, she thought her mind must have conjured it, but, no, she remembered it. It happened. She had been passing her father's room when she heard his falconer describe Charles carving a felled forest Elk . . .

The memory set Nichole's heart apace.

"The difference between bad and evil is not just the matter of degree," Nanna once tried to explain. "'Tis hard to tell, but bad is usually an obvious cycle—for instance, the angry and cross mother makes an angry and cross child, creating a bad life altogether. Evil is something else entirely, for its source is darker, not of the earth, yet in it . . . a phenomenon that transcends human comprehension."

"Like Satan?" she had asked.

"If I've told ye once, I've told ye a thousand times—do not listen to the tales spun by these dark-clothed priests of the Church. Their Satan is no more than a symbol of evil, such a creature, be he a God or fallen angel, does not actually exist in the form of a horned, tailed devil. The image is man's creation, a . . . a, well, like a personification in the attempt to understand the force that is evil—a Christian creation at that. The image is made by the mix of the old god Pan and from the time long, long ago when the forest people worshipped the Goddess through the elk—'tis why the image of Satan is given horns. True evil is not a single shape, though, a single person, a single God. True evil is the absence of God, the opposite of light, a darkness that takes many shapes."

"Human shape?"

"I don't know," Nanna had said slowly. "Sometimes I think aye, evil will actually form into a person or an animal, while other times I think nay, that evil might enter a human heart and make a person its agent . . ."

The vision of innocent folks laying slain in a pile rose in her mind, and Nichole knew her brother was not bad but evil. Evil had entered her brother's heart and claimed his soul. Her father had never cared for her and she, in her desperation for a father's love, had found a willing substitute in her brother. Oh, Lord, how it blinded her! All the while he had used her love for the most malevolent purposes . . .

Jonpaul, I'm sorry . . . I'm sorry. Forgive me . . .

Charles had to be stopped. Now. Before he killed Jonpaul and Gavin, before he brought Switzerland to war. She had to do it. There was only one way and that was to unveil the secret Nanna had promised to her. The images drawn in blood raced through her mind as Maseen trotted quickly through the walled city of St. Gallen. The abbey rose in the far distance. All city shops and houses were closed, shutters drawn tight against the winter snow and cold, the darkness of the night. The dark cobblestone streets were deserted, too, and there they were—

The fortress walls of St. Gallen.

The abbey bell rang five times as Maseen quickly approached the guarded gate. The movement of a guard on the wall-walk caught her attention. She pulled back on the reins. Maseen slowed to a fast-paced walk, then stopped at the gates.

Moen approached. "A good evening to you, Father."

With a lowered head, the air of solemnity, Nichole nodded.

"Shelter for the night?"

Inside the courtyard a long line of the sisters of St. Martin trudged slowly through muddied snow on their way to the rectory for the supper meal, and just as Nichole nodded, she caught sight of this. Frantically she searched for Katrina, but . . . but they all looked alike—

"Will you be wantin' an audience with the bishop's advisory?"

Nearby, as Kuno dwelt on the question, he watched the guards question the traveling friar from the church steps where he awaited the retinue before officiating the evening mass. He was counting the projected revenues from the most recent success of their trade bandits in Dornach, debating the question to have the men killed or no. On the one hand, if these men were killed 'twould save them a healthy split of the pie, but on the other hand if they let them live—

Nichole shook her head. The sisters were disappearing. How could she attract attention without revealing her sex? If she pretended to lose control! Trust lady luck. Oh, hurry—

She looked quickly down at the guard, whose gloved hand petted Maseen's neck with admiration. "A fine piece of horse flesh—"

With an angry neigh, the great horse felt the prick of a hairpin and reared high in the sky, crashing to the ground with hooves charging. Using all her strength, Nichole pulled back on the reins. Maseen leaped into the air again, and quickly grabbing her hood over her head, Nichole went flying. She landed backside onto the packed snow, the breath knocked hard from her lungs. Stars floated dizzily around her head. The few minutes it took to recover surrounded her with the anxious, concerned faces of the sisters.

She dared a glance up only once, a fast sweep to find the familiar face. Hands came to her arms, lifting her up. The guards were trying to calm Maseen.

"Oh, heavens!"

"Are you not hurt, Father?" another sister asked.

Nichole nodded, then gave the sign for silence. The sisters nodded, understanding. "Please come warm yourself in the rectory."

Nichole nodded again, brushing the snow from her robes, careful to keep her eyes down and her face averted. The guards led Maseen toward the stables. She froze, for one second, she froze.

Somebody pinched her from behind.

"Are you quite all right?"

She nodded. As they moved on, she dared a glance back. Katrina walked behind her. Katrina nodded ever so slightly, then quickly pointed to herself, then toward the strange father. Nichole looked quickly away. The message was clear: Katrina would come to her.

Kuno witnessed the interaction, not seeing at first, but like a sudden frost, he went rigid with alarm. He knew well the tall, black-clothed woman behind the hooded figure who appeared short for a man, and thin. He caught a brief glimpse of pale skin—otherwise covered completely. His gaze shot to the horse. Not a common piece. He looked back, and saw, why, yes, a straight, proud back that he suddenly recognized.

What was taking so long?

In dim light Nichole paced back and forth in the small cubbyhole of a room, a stone-and-wood room no bigger than Dornach's smallest linen closet. One pallet sat in the corner and a plain wood cross hung on the wall over a small stand that held only a basin of water and a tallow candle, that was all.

'Twas well after midnight. Surely if she could have gotten away by now, she would have. What if she couldn't? Would she see her in the morn? What, dear God, if she didn't?

A knock sounded on the door.

At last! Nichole rushed to it, pressed the lever, and swung back the door, only to find herself staring up at two huge men, guards, and not common ones, either . . .

"I tell you he can't kill me! How could he?" Nichole asked Katrina for the hundredth time as she paced back and forth in the cold, damp dungeon. "There would be questions to answer, hard questions, none the least of which put by my husband. Milord Jonpaul is not just anybody, you know. Why . . . why the whole world knows of him."

Wringing her hands, pacing, Nichole faltered of a sudden. Dear God, who was she trying to convince? Nobody knew where she was, and this was obvious. Women were not allowed to travel a mile without an escort, let alone a highborn lady. The poor disguise said as much, too. Yet surely—

He couldn't kill her, he just couldn't—

Nichole threw herself against the heavy wood door, pounding as if will alone would make it open as she shouted, "I demand to see the bishop! I demand it! You can't keep me here like this, you can't! In my father's name, you will be punished—"

No one answered because no one was there. She sank to the floor, her heart racing, her mind spinning, her fear rising. The reason Katrina refused to even try to communicate was because it was hopeless. Why waste these few last breaths? He would kill them both now. Oh, God, the guards were not even common. They were something else entirely, these two hard and worn giants who had simply lifted her to the air and into the dark dead of night, carrying her kicking and screaming down into the cellar, then swiftly through darkened halls into this cold, dank dungeon, where they locked the door without so much as a glance of acknowledgment to her screams of protest, let alone her fallen disguise. They had seen her face clearly and they had not cared.

Nobody knew she was here but Kuno. Yet if he killed her, if he—

Would he not have done so by now? What was he waiting for? She just couldn't die, she just couldn't. She was too young and she had too much to live for yet. There was Gavin and Mary and Dornach and Lucerne and, more than anything, the untried love of the blue flame . . .

She closed her eyes and conjured that night, the one night she lost her doubt and opened her heart to his love. She saw the darkly green eyes as he held the rose beneath the flame and said her name. Oh, those eyes as he took her disbelief and changed it beneath the compelling warmth of his kisses, the gentle touch of his hands and—

Oh, Jonpaul, I love you . . . I love you . . .

Bright blue eyes shot to the woman sitting so still and unmoving across from her. There had to be a way. There had to! She had to get out of this. Somehow she would survive.

"Why won't you talk to me now? I have risked everything to talk to you, only to find myself now imprisoned with you. Why can you not tell me, at least try to tell me the mystery of the black glove and the mark of the sixth finger? What in heaven's name do you have to do with it?"

Nothing in heaven, Katrina knew well.

Two days and nights passed. For two days and nights Nichole tried everything she could think of to get the woman to talk. Begging, pleading, cajoling, she even reminisced out loud about the time Katrina resided at the Castle of the Lower Lake. This only seemed to irritate or bring the woman discomfort. Then she tried threatening, to no avail. Yet Katrina only stared in her terrible, mute silence, her face almost expressionless. Almost. Every once in a while Nichole caught a flash of anger, but this disappeared quickly, as if it, too, like all other emotions, was pointless.

All the while, the passage of time fed Nichole's apprehension and fears, none of which were helped by the cold dankness of the terrible place. There were no blankets given for their comfort. No midden passes, either, only a slop bucket in the corner of the airless stone dungeon, which so far had not been emptied. A cup of fresh water each day, and no food past a broth and bread, and the first time she ate it was the last. A mouse tail in the bottom of her wood bowl made her heave and vomit. The despicable treatment did not bode well for their eventual release.

The men of Dornach would be searching for her. They would first look in Dornach. How long would it take before they realized she wasn't there? Not long. They would no doubt have turned to Lucerne, thinking she left for her lost home. Jonpaul, would he know yet? What would he do? What would he think?

Holy Goddess, 'twould be bad . . .

*   *   *

Kurtus, Ari, and Gavin waited and watched Jonpaul as he slept, the quiet interrupted by the activities of Kurtus and Mickeil as they orchestrated the activities of every available man in the search for Nichole. Bruno and Hans had been sent the urgent message. Jonpaul slept soundly; one might not know he was injured. His breathing was deep, even regular. His arm and rib cage were bandaged tight. An enormous fire in the hooded hearth kept the chambers warm. Now his skin felt cool to the touch. He kept kicking off the covers in his sleep, as if impatient with the lethargy of his body.

Jonpaul . . . Jonpaul, he heard her calling him over and over. He was looking and looking but only darkness surrounded his vision. A desperateness set his heart racing. Something was frightening her. Suddenly a form took shape in the darkness, and as if viewing her from a kaleidoscope far far above, he saw her sitting in a cold, dark space, and she was afraid . . .

Kurtus had the bad luck to be leaning over the bed when Jonpaul first opened his eyes. The familiar room was not a surprise, Ari and his son were not a surprise, but Kurtus was. He caught his arm, the strength of his iron grip speaking well for his power of recovery and Kurtus knew to be alarmed. "Where is she?"

Less than a minute of stumbling about the terrible question put Jonpaul's feet to the floor.

"Oh, no. Oh, no!" Kurtus tried to explain. "You don't know. You were shot clean through and look . . . look, your arm, your arm will take weeks to heal and you can't—"

Jonpaul tried to swing his bad arm up and around but got only halfway before his face twisted with the pain. Blood slowly soaked the fresh bandage, but this was ignored. "I have half circle motion . . . Zermatt? I remember Zermatt—"

"He was hit three times. But . . . well, somehow, like

you . . . the wounds, they are superficial. Jonpaul, I tell you she is not in Dornach—"

"So she is in Lucerne. She is in trouble, Kurtus, I know she is sitting somewhere now . . . somewhere dark, and she is frightened . . ."

Alarm reached Gavin's face and, like his father, Ari and Kurtus's protests met with a quick temper. Jonpaul stopped suddenly braced on the brass hood of the hearth, fighting the dizziness washing over him. Only Gavin fully understood as his father turned to Kurtus and said in a flat, emotionless voice of deadly certainty, "I mean to find her, Kurtus, and then I mean to kill him. And I mean to do it on this cursed day."

Within the hour, Jonpaul and Kurtus sat on their mounts, outfitted for speed and snow, but dressed for battle. Another horse waited on a lead, in the unlikely event Zermatt failed him. Snapping orders to a worried Ari, he was drawing gloves over his hands when Gavin raced outside, pulling an excited Mary and Bettrina after him and not to wave his father off.

"Father!"

The still-strange voice caught his full attention. With effort, Gavin lifted little Mary up, as if to put her closer to his father to say goodbye, but Jonpaul knew his son. Gavin was all boy, he had not those sentiments. Bettrina hastened anxiously to explain, "He thinks . . . Gavin thinks 'tis important—"

"Nichole went to fix Katrina," Mary told him when Gavin could not.

Gavin dropped the girl to the ground, watching the effect of the name on his father's face.

"What?"

"Just before she left," Bettrina said, scared, nervous, out of her mind with worries. "A message came from St. Gallen. Then, then, you see, Nichole said she was going to aid the birth of a baby of a woman named Katrina. But she said the woman was in Dornach and I should have known. That's it, milord, I should have known. I know no one in Dornach by the name and—"

Gavin now rushed to Father Ari. He pulled hard on his robes. "Gavin . . . Gavin—"

Jonpaul's gaze focused hard.

"Oh, dear God, the boy means that I tell you someone has stolen my robe. Just before Nichole left, I discovered a robe missing from my trunk but, holy heavens, boy, now is not the time for—" He stopped suddenly. Robe, the robes of a friar or parish priest, and St. Gallen, an abbey and mayhaps—

"Oh, no, I just can't believe she would . . ."

The memory played quickly through Jonpaul's mind. A lovely young lady in blue velvet running from his insolence toward a line of the Holy Sisters of St. Martin. "Katrina! Katrina!" A message from St. Gallen and the stolen robes of a parish priest—

Keen admiration changed Jonpaul's gaze as he turned back to his son. "Gavin, you have most surely saved her life. To St. Gallen we go and to you, Gavin, I vow, upon my life, to bring her back!"

Strange dreams visited Nichole as she slept. The woman on the distant hillside waving her hand marked by the sixth finger, her brother bending over the forest elk, and with his knife, he slowly etched the devil's turned cross and then Nanna at Michaelmas, laughing as she searched and searched for her present. "Oh, please, Nanna! Where is it? Where is it?"

"I'll never tell ye, girl. If ye can't find the clue in the Bible, our Bible, then ye don't deserve the gift."

"I've looked! I've looked—"

"Not good enough. Gracious wind, but only eight years and ye are already a disappointment . . ."

"See the land from far above through small black eyes! Feel the shape of his body and the stretch of those wings! Do ye feel it, girl? Do ye?"

She felt the rush of wind off feathers as he soared. "Yes . . . yes, I do . . ."

The last memory woke Nichole. A dim, gloomy light filtered into the small, dank room where she sat curled against the cold stone wall. Father Ari's robes were made of the thickest wool, a small mercy. There were no windows and she had long since lost track of the time, minutes and hours blurring into days. Still, some dusky light from somewhere let her know 'twas daytime, that somewhere the sun shone and people went about their chores as the world still turned.

Katrina slept across from her. She, too, sat on the ground, leaning against the cold stone wall. The white habit of bird's wings spread in flight seemed to have gathered the rank dust of the cellar, changing into a dingy gray. The lines of her face cut so deep, so terribly deep. Life itself was a sculptor's knife, carving into the very flesh to make a picture of . . . of what?

"See through their eyes, feel through their bodies, know what they know . . ."

The trick was used exclusively for animals, to gain another kind of knowledge, an understanding of another form of existence. Nichole was so adept at it, far better than Nanna herself. "Training for empathy, the Goddess's greatest gift . . ." 'Twas how she knew the creatures better than most others. She had spent a good deal of time upset at people who could not grasp that the creatures were living, breathing, feeling beings and in this way not so different from people. Not so different at all. Still, Nanna had never mentioned it could be done with people . . .

She had nothing to lose.

Nichole closed her eyes and focused, concentrating on

the leap of consciousness that would put her soul inside another's mind, in Katrina's mind.

At first there was nothing, an emptiness or darkness that might have been the very cell she sat within. Yet, gradually, sensations piled. Not the physical sensations of an animal's experience. No, not that at all, but rather the sensation of feelings, but they were so . . . so—

A whirlwind appeared in the corner of her mind's eye, moving toward her. She knew to be afraid, but she didn't understand, not at all. The whirlwind was white, made of white light, and as it moved toward her, the light brightened. A blinding white light! Closer and closer and—

The white whirlwind touched her person and burst into red. An unnatural sea of simmering red anger. The fury washed over her in a violence that shook her to the soul and oh, God in heaven, such anger and hatred and rage, rage shimmering and waiting and waiting, undulating with a pressing urgency of the very beat of her heart. Yet it was imprisoned, trapped in a terrible prison. Like this dungeon, only . . . only, the prison was her heart where this rage devoured her life, herself, the heart it lived within, and then, then—

Nichole cried out in a soft, pained moan as she felt the helplessness and its despair. The terrible despair, a living hell on earth where she walked day after day, night after night. Tears filled Nichole's eyes as she opened them. Katrina stared back, and in a voice much changed by this vision, she said, she knew, "He did this to you? My brother did this to you?"

Katrina nodded.

"He has kept you a prisoner here, all these many years? You are not a sister of God . . . You never did take the vows, did you?"

She shook her head.

"Your tongue . . . Oh, God, he did that to silence

you . . . He—" Katrina blurred before her and scared, frantic, she wiped at her eyes to see. "He silenced you . . . He tore you from the world and silenced you because . . . because you know the secret. The secret, the secret, the black glove worn over the hand marked by the sixth finger. Like you—"

Nichole stared, she just stared as her lips formed the words, "Because, because, dear God, you are his mother."

An anguished cry uttered from deep in Katrina's throat as she threw her head back, staring up at the place where she saw, had always seen, only ceilings or empty sky. She was his mother! He had done this to her! Her flesh, her child, her boy had done this to her!

The agony and despair began the day, the hour he was born to her. The last natural feeling she had was banished as Nanna ignored her desperate cries and pleas, her screams and tears, and using her hellish strength and force, she wrenched the boy child from his mother's arms, her arms.

"You have done well, Katrina. He is a healthy boy—"

"No, Nanna! Please to God, I've changed my mind. I want him back—"

"That will pass. Drink the potion—"

Yet suddenly the old woman dropped the child. The babe fell from her arms as if suddenly hot. The tiny scream brought her flying out of the bed, but she fell with her weakness. The old woman swept the babe up again before turning her unnaturally bright eyes to where she lay crying on the floor. "The babe is marked by your sixth finger!"

"I don't care . . . Oh, God, Nanna, I don't care. Give him back. He's mine . . ." She choked on her tears, screaming now, "He's mine—"

"He is not yours. You gave him to his father—"

"You mean *you* gave him to his father! A trade for the

lady Lucretia's stillborn child—"

"Nay. 'Tis a trade for the girl child she will bear later—"

"May God see that there is never this precious girl child! Oh, God—"

"Oh, God, nothing. 'Twill be a child of the Goddess and, aye, she will be born, of that I know. I know this, too, Katrina. The sixth finger is a curse. Ye would do well to never see the boy again. He will bring ye despair or worse if ye do."

"He's mine . . . he's mine . . ."

Nichole finally overcame her shock to jump up and, grabbing Katrina's shoulders, she cried, "You were my father's mistress! Weren't you? I remember now. Charles is my father's bastard! But, oh God, my mother, my mother knew, but didn't. She thought, she thought—" Nichole's eyes widened with the horror. "What did he do to her true son? Did he kill—"

A sudden clamor and the heavy door opened. "Nothing so dramatic, sister mine."

Nichole swung around to see her brother. Her half brother. He stood fully dressed in his finery, staring at her, and with unconcealed antipathy. No not for her, for Katrina. "Charles . . ."

The iron door swung back. One of his men stepped inside. The room shrank and Nichole retreated as if the pale gaze was a cold wind that pushed her back. Unnatural sentiment shimmered in a bright light in his eyes as he studied the terrified woman he always hated. "Take her away. I have endured her presence on earth long enough."

Nichole gasped as Katrina's guttural moan rang in the small space. Those eyes deplored her son. To no avail, as always to no avail, and she tried to fight as the man's hands came at her with cruel force. Nichole leaped to intercede, but Charles stepped in the way, grabbing her by her shoulders. "Of course the great wealth of your sympathies would extend to the most pitiful. Save it, sister mine."

Nichole cried, "She is your mother!"

"My mother and my curse. I have endured much from that woman, threats and demands and more threats my whole life long. Almost as much as your own Nanna. I should have killed them both long ago."

A wide, shocked gaze looked up. Her lip trembled and she shook her head in denial, "No, Charles, oh, no—"

"You never did know, did you, sister mine?"

Katrina's very next cry sounded from somewhere down the hall, muted and distant, and Nichole felt it physically as a blade to her heart. As if part of her consciousness had remained with the woman, and she collapsed; helplessly, she collapsed. "She didn't deserve to be killed like that. After all you made her suffer, she didn't deserve to die—"

"She died some long time ago."

"Oh, God, I cannot believe this is happening. Did you kill my real brother, too? Or did our father kill him for you?"

"Our father, our father." Anger reached his eyes, or perhaps a more simple irritation. "You were too young to know him as I did. What a fool he was. He should have killed your mother and married mine. 'Twould have saved me a good deal of grief. Yet, no, he loved Lucretia till the day she died. The child I replaced was born still. All of her children were born still but for you. You, my lovely little sister, the jewel of my court."

Nichole greeted his very real affection with a dawning horror, more as he said, "Nichole, Nichole, you should not have come here."

The way he stared at her, she didn't understand and she couldn't think, couldn't think of anything past all those years and she never did know her own mother. "My mother never knew—"

"Of that I am doubtful. 'Tis a hard thing to convince a woman a child is hers when it's not. The way she would watch me, the confusion in her eyes. If it weren't for the old witch—"

"Nanna?"

"Oh, aye, your precious Nanna. She orchestrated the entire scenario. Oh, yes, and do you know for what? For you, Nichole, for you. Before I was born, long before you were born, she struck a bargain with our father. I'll give you the son you want if you give me the girl child that will be born later. He agreed, and why not? You know better than any his sentiment for a girl child. 'Twas a perfect solution to a barren wife—"

"No," Nichole shook her head, doubt like a song in her voice, "Nanna would not do that."

"But she did. She brought the young widow of his best friend to his bed, and within the year two children were born within weeks of each other. The second one dead, but the other not. The old woman set me in your mother's arms and then spent the next years trying to convince her of what she always knew was a lie, that I was her son, the rightful heir to the realm."

Nichole's eyes searched the familiar face, familiar but not, and she saw it was true, the incredible story was his history but there was no proof, nothing to show the world but, "The paper . . ."

"Ah, the cursed paper. Like you, sister mine, I have never seen it, though she took pains to remind me of its existence whenever she wanted something from me, which was often. Like my mother. She said that my father wrote a paper in his blood that disclaims my birth, a thing only to be presented upon the birth of a son by your mother. Or when that old witch decided to ruin me. And because that never happened, I have reasoned at last it must not exist."

They stared at each other. She slowly shook her head as she saw his regret, regret that he would have to kill her, too. The idea dropped her to her knees. Tears came to her eyes in another rush. She wiped the running tears from her cheeks with the back of her hand, desperate to think how to save herself—

"You should never have come here, Nichole. I curse you for that. Now more than any time past I curse your recklessness, this wild heart that made you, despite everything, bring such constant amusement in my life. And yet," his gaze filled with the familiar fondness, "if you were as the others of your sex and not my half-wild beautiful young sister, 'twould not be so hard to lose you now."

"No, Charles, don't do this . . . please—"

"Curse that old woman you loved, Nichole. 'Twas always a battle between us to see who could claim more of you, and if she did not own so much of you, then . . . it might have been different."

"You cannot get away with it! I am not an unknown peasant woman from a country village—"

"Nor am I a fool. I've arranged it to appear as if he did the deed before he died."

"Before he died! Jonpaul—"

She stopped, unable to speak as she froze on the idea, froze save for the abject denial of the shake of her head, this as Charles bent down to kiss her mouth. For the last time he kissed her. Startled eyes shot to him as he rose, moving to the door. And that one startled moment she stared at the empty space where he once stood cost her life. The door shut, and with it her only chance and she screamed, "You coward! You coward!" She threw herself on it, pounding her fists against the hard, cold iron. "You coward! If you must kill me now, do it yourself! Charles . . . no . . ."

She dropped to the floor, collapsing in so many tears.

Dear God, Charles could not plunge the knife in her heart, but the men who raped and murdered and burned at Stan would have no such trouble! Like Katrina, she would be killed in the dank dark cellar of St. Gallen and no one would know. Jonpaul and Mary and Gavin—

The very names made her jump up again, pounding on the heavy wood door with all her strength, screaming until—

Until she heard the footsteps. With a weak, terrified cry she backed to the farthest corner of the room. The creak of the door opening brought a scream. Another sounded as she looked up to the face of her killer and said his name. "Kairtand!"

Not far from St. Gallen, the maroon-and-black colors rode quickly from St. Gallen south to Lucerne. Purple and green rode faster north to St. Gallen, and as Charles and his party raced up Rudolph Pass, topping the crest, the snow-covered valley vista swung into view. They saw the colors. Far below the tree line, Zermatt's purple-and-green colors shone bright in the snow-laden valley. "The lord Jonpaul! He is alive!"

The fateful crossing gave the black-and-maroon colors a supreme advantage, not just in numbers but in the deadly momentum of a downhill advance. Charles chuckled as his four men drew swords and halberts and lowered their bonnets before kicking spurs to their mounts, all split seconds before Charles's exclamation rang through the valley: "To the death!"

Jonpaul dropped his fur coat. His right arm felt like a throbbing mass of pain, the wound open and bleeding, the limb he fought with rendered useless. No halberts could be tossed. He raised his sword in his left arm.

"You cannot fight!"

"Nay." Jonpaul slowly shook his head. He could fight. He could fight because he knew what Charles beating him to St. Gallen first meant. The idea reverberated through his body, and while leaving him trembling of a sudden and weak, he also felt more desperate than he ever felt.

To Kurtus he said, "Take a wound—"

"Never! To death!"

The darkly green eyes met his friend's and he said his last words, "You have been the best friend a man could have."

Kurtus's bonnet dropped and his spurs hit his mount when Jonpaul's last terrible words crashed through his mind and now, now, he felt the full force of the great fear of death work upon his racing heart.

Chapter Seventeen

"Kairtand!"

The huge red-haired giant held a knife in one hand, while the other held a huge sack. Like a potato sack, and when Nichole grasped the purpose of the bag, she screamed again, pressing hard against the wall. One step and he was upon her. A calloused hand came to her mouth as he held her still, careful not to let the knife touch her during the frantic seconds it took to stifle her struggle.

"Easy, milady, easy." With urgency, "As you put your trust in our lord Jonpaul, it belongs, too, to me, for I am his servant."

For I am his servant, for I am his servant. The merciful words took several seconds to penetrate her terror, several more to believe. Then she collapsed all at once like a puppet minus strings, collapsing breathlessly in his arms. She turned to see his face.

"I am his servant."

The memory of the man sitting on his horse, watching as Jonpaul stole her away, spun dizzily through her mind. Cowardice made him do it, she had always assumed, but no—'twas Kairtand who was Jonpaul's spy. She had completely forgotten in the rush of terrible days, the matter of a single man's cowardice seeming inconsequential. "Don't you know, milady?" Kurtus had asked. Kairtand was the reason Jonpaul would never let her speak to Charles.

I am his servant. The words echoed in her mind and she was suddenly crying and he was holding her now, and as he held the young girl in his strong arms he thought, Jonpaul was right, he was always right. Thank God for that. The last communication was specific. "Nichole is threatened, I know not how or why or how I even know this, but my fear keeps running to her. She who means most to me. Act for her now, only her. The time will come."

So he had, and it was not easy. It was not easy accumulating favors from the beasts that were the lord Charles's men. There was more than one terrible thing he had done, things he would carry to the grave, things done so that when Charles motioned for one of them to step forward to this cell, he could hold the others back and grab the bag and take out his knife and say simply, "The girl is mine." More than one terrible thing done to convince them he was like them, he was a man who could, would, relish the raping of a helpless girl twice or thrice before sending her to her death, an act so unconscionable to his mind the knife trembled with the effort not to plunge it into the man who said, "And for God's sake do not linger with that lucious little tart. I need you to catch us before we reach Lucerne."

"Is . . . is he dead, Kairtand?"

The pain in Nichole's voice brought Kairtand up sharp, then made him lie. "I do not know . . . I think, I think . . . first we must get out of here. Milady . . . milady," he pulled her back to say, "I have seen you ride, and thank God for that. For I can get us to the stables and on our horses, but then—"

The urgency in his voice gave her hope. She looked in

his eyes and found her courage and strength. She nodded, a nod that meant she was ready to face the race for their lives, and he smiled, a sad smile she tried not to understand. Not now, not when their lives depended on her courage.

Kairtand hurriedly put the bag over her head and, wrapped in this way, he lifted her to his shoulder and made his way out the door. No one stopped him, not until the stables. He dropped Nichole to the ground. Two unsuspecting grooms were little match for his strength, and skill, knocked unconscious long enough to saddle and mount their horses. Maseen tossed her head back excitedly, rested and anxious to run. Nichole bent forward, petted her head, and whispered words of encouragement as they stopped at the stable gates, waiting for the passing of guards on the wall-walk. Each extra minute gave them a better chance.

With a booted foot, Kairtand kicked the doors open. Two horses leaped into the courtyard at a gallop, then through the gates. Nichole pressed against Maseen's neck. The icy wind whipped her face; she could not even see as the world became a great blur of Maseen's speed.

Kairtand could not hear Nichole's call above the rush of water below and the thunder of his horse's hooves as his stallion raced across the narrow wood bridge. Maseen reared high in the sky. Nichole dug her knees tight to her sides as Maseen crashed back to the ground and threw her head down with an angry neigh to fight for the bit.

Kairtand stopped and turned on the other side of the bridge. Maseen turned into tight circles, refusing to cross, not caring at all that the refusal could cost them the advantage of a precious five-minute lead.

Nichole cried over the rage of water below. "There is an incline upstream!"

She never waited. She turned Maseen and kicked heels to her side, certain the move had just cost their lives, and with a curse, seizing a halbert and his sword, Kairtand turned his mount and chased after her. Their mounts were climbing down the hill when, from down river, they heard the thunder of the chase crossing that bridge. They reached the bottom stopping to listen.

Nichole's heart thudded as she held her breath.

The ploy seemed so obvious then, that Kairtand wondered if she had not planned it and he laughed. "A lovely spot for a rest. Shall we, milady?"

"Aye, by the grace of the Goddess," and she petted Maseen's neck, "I believe I will."

Five men lay dead or dying in a bloody pool in the snow-covered valley. Charles lay on his back, and at this moment of his death he had only the thought of revenge. One thought that made him say, "You are too late by hours, milord. My dear sister is now dead."

The words changed the warrior's face. "Nooo!" The cry echoed in the snow-covered valley as Jonpaul raised his sword for the last time and plunged it deep into Charles's chest, pulling savagely down. Then he stumbled back from the dead body, his head pounding with the swift beat of his heart that said simply "no." Over and over again the word "no" as he half walked, half crawled to where Kurtus lay still and unmoving in a pool of blood.

A head wound felled Kurtus, but not before two had fallen to him. Still gasping, Jonpaul pulled his knife from his sheath, quickly cutting his tunic into strips. After tying two strips together, he wrapped it carefully, tightly around his friend's head. Once tied, he fell backside into the snow and there he lay. A wild frantic gaze stared up at the dark sky where the clouds opened to begin dropping a light snow to the ground.

* * *

Nichole and Kairtand had waited a spell at the bank of the river. Two more parties crossed the bridge before Kairtand felt it was safe to go on and then, cautiously, at a trot. Still, it was a precarious journey to say the least, and only luck would keep them safely behind the search parties. Only luck would let them know when the search parties were to turn back, for there was only one road out of St. Gallen to the first township of the Alliance and the whole warring world was on it.

Maseen raced up the pass, cresting the top. Nichole reined her horse to a halt as the valley scene came into view. Circled around a bloody massacre gathered the men of St. Gallen. Zermatt's colors appeared against the white, and with a gasp of recognition, she knew, she knew . . . Kairtand came up behind her, took one look, and reached for her reins. Too late by a fraction of a second.

Maseen leaped into a breakneck speed down the hill.

Jonpaul stood in the middle of a large circle made of over forty armed men. Cruel red blood covered one arm like paint. He stood on his feet, bare-chested in the snowfall, breathing deeply, his eyes wild as he shouted viciously at the perimeter of the circle.

No one noticed the fast-approaching rider until she broke through the center of men. The horse rose in the air, but Nichole swung off before the hooves crashed to the ground. She flew with the song of his name, not seeing anything but that he was alive, he was alive.

The thin arms came around his neck and he did not move, frozen for a long minute with the miracle of her presence. "Nichole . . . Nichole." He softly gasped the name with each hard breath as gratitude to God, and Kairtand swelled in an emotional avalanche in his chest that put his lips to her face, covering the tears with kisses.

Nichole clung to his neck without the support of his

arms. She slipped to the ground, suddenly seeing. He was half naked in the snow. Amidst the angry scars covering his chest was a torn and ripped bandage, an angry red hole the size of a gulden, and she looked at this with first confusion, then horror. Blood covered the hooded robe that draped her form, this streaming from his arms. Yet the thing that made her spin on her heels were the chains binding both his arms and feet.

"He is chained!"

As if her horror was an invisible magnet, it riveted her gaze to Kuno, who watched this scene impassively, sitting atop a horse. If he showed any surprise that the lady Nichole Lucretia was alive, breathing, standing before him in outrage, he had long since thought to hide it. There was, however, the barest hint of that as Kairtand rode into the circle, but this was quickly concealed as he announced, "Indeed, the Lord Jonpaul is chained. He will remain that way until an eccleciastic court is convened for his trial—"

With outrage still, coupled with stark disbelief, she cried, "On what charge?"

"The murder of the lord Charles of Lucerne, your brother."

Shock lifted in the wide blue eyes as they flew around the space, stopping at last on the fallen body of her brother. She stepped to him cautiously, afraid, not of his death but that he might still be alive. He wasn't. Then she swung back to Kuno. Fury changed her eyes as she shook her head and clenched her fists. "You will never get away with this. Never. The murder was just, as you know full well. My brother tried to murder me and you know it—"

"I know no such thing, milady—"

"That man will testify," she cried, pointing to Kairtand.

"That man? Your husband's servant?"

A sudden desperation entered her eyes for the first time, and her face reddened more as she tried one last time. "My brother was evil, a bastard, too, he just confessed. Not a lord, unfit by rights and character for his title! He coveted Dornach and plotted to kill me, my husband, and our son. He has had an entire village, his own people laid to the ground by plunder—"

"My dear girl," Kuno interrupted, anger entering his voice, "I do hope you have wits enough to realize there is no person alive who will believe the good lord Charles of Lucerne is bastard to the title, much less that he had murdered his own people or that he plotted to win Dornach or kill his dearly loved sister who obviously has betrayed him for her own gain."

"My own gain!?"

"Aye, this as your husband ambushed the good lord Charles in this deserted valley where we all stand as witnesses, slaying him like an animal!" His eyes shimmered with hatred, as if he had rehearsed this whole perfect end to a less than perfect plot, ordained by God for sure. No paper and no proof, the lord Jonpaul might as well be dead after all. "Your husband plotted all these many years for Lucerne, while he has slayed village people to bring terror to the borders."

A grumble of anger rippled through the men upon hearing this long list of crimes. They believed him! With mounting terror and disbelief, Nichole backed into Jonpaul, shaking her head, her mind racing, trying to think—

Kuno's gaze narrowed as he said the last. "Unless you can create more believable lies, your dear husband will hang by the final papal authority of the Holy Roman Church. God's will be done!" He turned his mount away, as if sickened by the sight of him. "Get him to the dungeon. Be sure that he walks."

As if to amend for the long, terrible winter, spring came to Switzerland not just early, but with a flourish.

Rain alternated with bright sunshine, and within the space of the month of April, the valley's snow melted and the world turned green. Cumulus white clouds appeared whiter against the rich blue sky. Gentle breezes ruffled the new growth of green leaves and grass, the tiny pearldrops of edelweiss and poppies growing wild in the fields, all just waiting for a predestined moment to bloom. Seeds were gathered and prepared, farmers worked from dawn until night tilling and plowing the soil in preparation for planting. Winter coats were laid neatly into trunks. Horses and cows were set to pasture again as the sheep were herded, shorn and set loose again, too. Another winter had at last passed.

In the morning mists Dornach Castle looked like a silver crown upon a green-jeweled mount. Towering pines, glistening with morning dews, appeared so perfectly erect and tall around the castle wall, as if the very best knights. Nature blessed the place, the forest filled with its newborn life: deer and elk fawns, wolf cubs that would be forever protected now, too, and of course birds of all kinds. The fields filled with plenty of mice and rabbits to feed them. Three new cat litters were hidden in Nichole's abandoned room, one new set of hounds were lovingly whelped, a number of calves, pigs, and lambs folded, and two new colts were born in the stables. Yet none of the few people left at Dornach appreciated the fancies of this early spring now, not its new life or fresh green foliage. No one had even discovered how, nearby, the new warmth coaxed tiny leaves and new buds of a wild patch of roses. Like the rest of Switzerland, the people of Dornach and Basel waited only for word from St. Gallen as tension mounted, culminating on the eve of the last day of the lord Jonpaul's trial.

For war threatened. Lord Bruno held the amassed army of the Alliance on the border to wait the word of the verdict. These men, numbering in the thousands, faced the combined army of Lucerne and Uri, a considerable force if joined by the army of St. Gallen, as surely they would be. If Jonpaul was sentenced to death, and this seemed certain, blood would spread across Switzerland, spilt from the mountaintop to valley. The fateful sentence rested on the judgment of five far from impartial men: the Bishop Kuno of St. Gallen, the Bishop Pol de Swquin of Basel, the two red-robed cardinals of the Vatican, Gioacchino Rossini and Metternich de Milan, and the monsignor, Jean Luke Bysshe. Facts had little to do with the outcome. The church had seized this chance to rid itself of the threat of our lord Jonpaul, his steady break from the orthodoxy of the Church, and the dangers of his reforms, the power of the Alliance, and the threat of a united Switzerland, and the Church would have war to get it.

Hans and Kurtus tried everything they knew to convince Nichole: reasoning, threatening, begging, pleading, but the girl was more stubborn than a rusty dungeon hinge and cursing her, Hans finally slammed his goblet down. "I forbid it! I will not let you!"

Nichole closed her eyes. His image appeared in her mind, so vivid, so real, she felt her hand raising to touch him. Dear God, if she could have one thing, one thing only, it would be to touch him, to feel the smooth hard lines of his face beneath her fingertips or place the palm of her hand over the beat of his heart . . .

Jonpaul, I love you. I love you forever . . .

She opened her eyes. "Your words are empty, my dear friend," she replied quietly. "You can not stop me. I can not make it easy for them. If they take Jonpaul—" the mere pronouncement of his name filled her eyes and made her lip tremble. She caught the emotions quickly. "If they take my husband, they will have to take me, too. I will not lie to save myself. I will not lie under oath."

Kurtus and Hans exchanged unkind glances as she put

her back to them, her resignation to the unthinkable fate hanging in the silence. Seeing it frightened Kurtus more than anything else.

She had changed. With the exception of her testimony, she rarely spoke. The weight of her sadness could not find expression in words. The impending tragedy had changed her beauty, too: Her dark hair seemed an inky midnight halo against the unnatural paleness of her skin. A mist appeared permanently in her eyes, one never shed in tears, though, but making the lovely blue eyes larger, so hauntingly drawn.

The martyr's otherwordly beauty, Kurtus thought. Over a dozen witnesses had been called to tell their story. Nichole's testimony had been the longest, and to have seen her kneel before the judges, more beautiful, more courageous than any other, was to love her. She began her story at the beginning, the night her woman told her of the paper and the day Charles took her to Stan. One of the worst moments came as Charles's widow, the lady Anne Marie, stood up to announce she knew that much was true. Like everyone else, she was obviously desperate to save Nichole. Trembling and nearly hysterical, Anne Marie told what she knew of Charles's wickedness, about the serving girl Mayra, and that very night, how she overheard something—she did not know exactly what, but something—about a paper that would ruin Charles. The court stopped the distraught lady when she fell into incoherent ramblings about Nichole and her goodness, but then Kuno followed the dubious testimony with three other ladies of the Lucerne court who reluctantly confessed under oath that the lady Anne Marie had a great deal of trouble with her husband and was generally not liked for any number of reasons, reasons that cast considerable doubt on her wits.

None of the people of Lucerne wanted to see Nichole hurt, especially the women, which was not to say they believed her damning story. Like the rest of the world, they felt certain it was the strain, that any girl would face collapse after all she had been put through. They all seemed to believe Kuno's proposition: 'Tis obvious the lady Nichole Lucretia is drawn into this wild plot of obvious lies by the weakness of a woman's heart for the man she lays with, that she was bewitched by the lord Jonpaul's terrible, dark powers!"

Only one thing could save them, and that did not exist. Only the paper could prove her claim, and do it twice over, for not only would it prove her story was the truth, but if it proved that Charles was not rightful heir to Lucerne, then his murder was not a high crime and Jonpaul could not be hung for it. The Bible now sat in her chambers above. No sinner ever looked longer or harder for salvation in these pages. At last, each one of them had read the Bible thrice through, each until the pages wore thin with the oil of anxious fingertips, until even Nichole finally saw that it was an empty threat Nanna'd used to bend Charles to her will, nothing and never more.

Kurtus's anger made him try one last time. He stepped to her and turned her around to face him. "Nichole, milady, if you say one damning word against Kuno, you will be tried for heresy." Solemnly, with fear, "And you will be hung! He stands well above your accusations. If you won't do it for yourself—do it for him. For Jonpaul, milady, you must save yourself!"

She only lowered her lashes but not before Kurtus saw the unyielding rebellion in the misty blue eyes, and he cursed her. Stopping just short of shaking her senseless, and he cursed her.

Hans knew what he had to do. "Enough, Kurtus," he said quietly. "There is one person still alive who can make her see the reason."

Nichole had not know what Hans meant, not until in the dark dark hours of the night when Kurtus, accompanied by a handful of guards, interrupted her candle vigil to escort her out. She hesitated, confused, half afraid he would force her into hiding in hopes of saving her. "But where shall you take me?"

To heaven before hell, he knew more than any other what it would mean to her, but he said only, "You shall see."

Nichole searched his eyes, seeing only a strange light there. While she didn't understand, she saw to trust him. She was wearing a plain white cotton dressing gown, remarkably simple with short sleeves and a high bodice that dropped folds of unadorned white material to the floor. She turned to her trunk to dress.

"No, milady. There is not time. Here . . ." Kurtus picked up her cloak to set it about her shoulders. He then raised the hood to cover her face and hair, a precautionary move. Followed by the guards, he led her through poorly lit halls outside. Confusion lifted on her face as they quickly passed along the curtain wall, but as they approached the bastion tower behind, she stopped with alarm.

"Kurtus . . ." She pronounced his name with a pain-filled desperateness. "Dear Kurtus, is it . . . are you—"

"Aye, milady," he said in a whisper of his voice. "For one night. For one night only."

He did not say the last night.

Not a word was said as the lady Nichole emerged at the end of the long dimly lit stone hall that led to the dungeon where the lord Jonpaul was held. A stunning, rich purple cloak covered her head to foot. Only her pale face showed, her lashes lowered to the cold stone floor beneath her slippers. The few minutes she waited behind Kurtus were the longest in her life, as her whole being echoed with fear that the iron wood door would not open for her.

It had been arranged in secret, a small fortune had exchanged hands for the illicit favor. Kurtus carefully kept the Dornach guards back so as not to threaten the others as still no one spoke. Blue eyes flew up as the door suddenly swung open. Hans stepped out from the dungeon, nodding to Kurtus. Kurtus took Nichole's arm and led her to the door.

The cell was mercilessly small, five paces wide and ten deep, smaller than a stall. Yet gifts from the people had transformed the small, cold space. An enormous velvet down comforter spread across the cold stone floor like a rug. Green-and-purple cushions, with gold fringe, filled the space, too. The Dornach Castle tapestry hung on one wall. The stone seat against the wall was transformed into a table, lined by a green silk cloth. Books were piled there, alongside a dozen lit candles and two wood bowls of fruit, imported oranges and apples, dressing water and another plate of roasted fowl, bread, cheese, and a large wine cask and goblet.

Nichole noticed none of it . . .

For, after two long months, she at last beheld her husband alone. He stood to his full height, an inch or two from touching the ceiling. Despite the chilly spring air, he wore only leggings rolled just beneath his waist . . . that was all. Angry red scars remained from his wounds. Tension gripped the thick, corded muscles on his bare arms, shoulders, and chest. His thick blond hair was tied behind, pronouncing the harsh lines of his unshaven face and accenting the anger alive and fierce in his remarkable green eyes.

Nichole did not care.

She flew in his arms as the door closed behind her. Emotions, an avalanche of emotions, exploded with the contact. He closed his eyes as his strong arms came around her, lifting her from the ground to hold her small body tightly against his.

"Jonpaul! Jonpaul, do not let me go. Hold me, hold me forever . . ."

Never, he would never let her go, and he shut his eyes tighter, fighting the weakness rocking through him. The promise of a single night. His passion and desire for her had been a ferocious thing from the first, but now, facing the near certainty of death, it became an avalanche of terrible need, desires that could not be appeased in a lifetime.

The force of it rocked him back and stole his breath. He could not hold her close enough as his senses filled with the sweet scent of her, the press of her small body against the hard outline of his. Yet even through her thick cloak and gown, he felt the pounding of her heart in her breast. Her heartbeat, at last, was infinitely more precious than life. Death was nothing compared to losing her, nothing, and using all the force of his will, he lowered her to the ground.

With one arm wrapped around her to keep her close, he pushed back the hood to stare down at the lovely upturned face. Tears sparkled like gems in her eyes and, with agony, he studied the changes grief had already made on the lovely face.

"Deny it."

"Nay," she cried in a whisper. "I cannot—"

"Deny it!"

"I will not make it easy for them to take you from me! I cannot! If you must die, then so must I."

"Curse you, girl!" Emotion blazed in his eyes. "The only thing harder than leaving you in death is leaving you to face death. I will not have it! You will lie for me on the morrow. You will swear to me now."

Wide, tear-filled eyes pleaded with his, but his will was stronger, so much stronger, she knew he would not touch her until she promised him. Yet she could not, would not do it.

"Jonpaul, Jonpaul . . . do not do this to me!" Small hands came over his large ones. Tears slipped down her cheeks as her trembling hand brought his under her cloak and held the warmth of his palm tightly against her breast, where her heart pounded beneath the thin cotton gown. "My heart, Jonpaul . . . My heart and soul are filled with your love. I feel it everywhere, in each breath and sigh, in every movement, in every thought and feeling. When you are gone, when they take you from me, I will be empty, a hollow shell with but one memory to hold me. This night, Jonpaul. Give me this night. Love me, Jonpaul," she cried in a whisper. "Love me now—"

A desperate light came to the green eyes as his breath caught again, released with the sound of her name, once, twice, and then again. The sound was a prayer, an invocation as his fingers ran through her hair, stopping to hold her tear-streaked face back. His lips brushed the soft pliancy of hers, stopping where he felt them tremble. He closed his eyes, tasting the hot sweetness of her tears before his mouth came over hers.

Warm, firm lips molded to soft tear-moistened ones. The touch was devastating, changing, becoming almost savage with the warring desperation of but a single night. The desperateness of her emotions swelled, then trembled through her, lit by the hot flames of his mouth, tongue, the feel of his arms, and the alignment of their flesh. A kiss without end.

She reached her arms around his neck, clinging to him tightly as his impatient hands at last unclasped her cape. The cape dropped unnoticed to the floor. His own leggings came next, so that when he pulled her small, trembling frame back, the only thing between them was the maddening tease of the thin cloth of her gown. His hands ran through the long silky hair, over the curves of her thin shoulders, then reached under the trail of her hair along her back, rocking over the gentle curve of her hips, and all the while he was pulling her closer and closer.

The kiss ended, but only to let his lips graze her forehead, her closed eyes and flushed cheeks, as he drank the perfume of her tears and skin. His hands slipped under her arms, his fingers moved with sure, deft strokes over her breasts. The heat and strength of his hand made her shudder and gasp ever so slightly, gasps that he leaned over to catch in his mouth, kissing her as he did.

"Your love, Nichole . . ." His lips moved to her ears before he pulled back to drink the sight, all of her, the long dark hair falling in waves down her back, the pale, petal-soft skin, the blue eyes filled with emotion, emotion he had so longed for! "How I longed for the gift! Endlessly, day and night, night and day, I longed to feel this, your passion unbridled by love. And now, now I would give anything to lose my treasure . . . To save you—"

"No! No." She shook her head. "Don't think of it. Not now. We have but one night."

"But one night . . ."

Aided by his arms, she pulled herself up and pressed her lips to his mouth. All restraint broke in the instant as they dropped to their knees. His hands reached behind her to pull the neat row of tiny pearl buttons apart. Strong, warm hands caressed her shoulders as he pulled the material over her thin arms, breaking the kiss to watch this unveiling. The gown slipped over her waist. The magnificent green eyes darkened, filling with the beauty before him as his hand brushed over a breast, cupping the rounded peak, smoothing the pink crest with his thumbs over and over until her breath came hard and fast. Then he caught her mouth for another long, hard kiss.

Hot flames leaped where he touched her. His hands reached her buttocks to hold her flesh urgently against the hard press of him. The fullness of him matched the swelling of her own sex. Emotionally and physically she needed to feel him everywhere, inside and out, and with wild urgency, she broke the kiss with a soft moan, arching her back to offer her breasts to his mouth. She clung to him with quivering abandon, her nails raking the muscles along his back as his lips played over the hard, tight buds as he lowered her backside to the quilt.

She felt the scratch of his unshaven chin as he drew the tip of her breast into his mouth, rolling his tongue around a bud, then biting it softly. Quivers of fire shot through her loins. The burning heat of his mouth and body made her dig her nails deep into his skin. She said his name, writhing beneath him until, "Jonpaul . . . Jonpaul, please . . ."

"Sweet Mercy," he whispered before his mouth claimed hers again as he joined her to him. The pleasure that was theirs bordered on pain, the hot joining of their flesh melted together as their souls seized the miracle of flesh, clinging desperately to the heavenly abyss as if these moments could make up for all time stolen. When it couldn't, when their love was spent and after he had pulled her small form over his, his hands caressing the smooth skin of her slender back, and she held still to listen to the swift steady beat of his heart against her ear, she started crying.

"Time is not enough, Jonpaul. It's not enough."

Jonpaul slipped his hands under her arms, lifting her partially up to see her. The long dark hair fell in chaotic disarray around her flushed face and slender shoulders, cascading about the round curves of her breasts. Her tear-filled eyes were wide, speaking volumes of poetry to his. She was more beautiful than ever, the press of time making her so. The palms of his hands were warm against her breasts, and his slight movement there caused her small hands to brace against his chest. She gasped as she felt how hard and full he was against her, again when his hands slid to her hips and he slipped into her still-moist, feverish flesh.

He rocked her slowly over himself. One hand brushed the long hair from her breasts, sending shuddering licks of heat through her as he did. "Yet it's all we have, my love. This one night. Ride me, Nichole. Ride into the night . . ."

The blue eyes opened to sweep the ground where she knelt, and in the space of her long silence, she knew to tell the truth. Only the truth. She had never looked more beautiful. The strain of these last long months only added to her air of dignity, the very nobility that was her birthright, the conviction that she spoke the truth. A pale-green gown draped her kneeling form, with long, flowing sleeves that dropped to the floor as she clasped her hands in prayer. A pale-green-and-violet woven band held the long dark hair back, and as she had closed her eyes to this last, silent tears slipped down her cheeks.

Tension changed Jonpaul's face as he watched her. He shook his head with an unvoiced warning, a plea, the imperative that he would have her lie. She could not be sacrificed in a futile attempt to save him. She must not!

Over two dozen dignitaries from the church stood in somber black back to the right of the dais, while all of Swiss nobility watched from the left.

This now was worse, the present silence brought by the tension as Nichole shocked the hall by finishing the story of Katrina's revelations of the truth, all acknowledged, she swore, by Charles before he had killed his mother and sent Kairtand to kill her. Like all other, this last testimony was directly contradicted by Kuno, who stood to shout in furious indignation, "I assure the court no such woman as Katrina or Sister Mary Teresa ever existed in the holy cloister of the sisters of St. Martin, much less was ever found murdered here, as I further contradict that the lady Nichole was ever, ever held in the dungeon of St. Gallen!"

Ripples of shock raced through the crowd, falling to tense silence as startled eyes glanced around the room. As before, no witnesses willingly stepped forward to support the outrageous claim of Nichole and the man Kairtand.

Then Nichole cried out, "The sanctity of his robes hides a wicked heart from our view! I submit to the good men of this court that 'tis not the first time in a long history of the Holy Church that a bishop's cloth has covered such a profane affront to the holiness that is God! If it were true, would not he say exactly thus to save himself? If it were true—"

"Silence!"

The forceful voice made all gazes rivet to Jonpaul, whose gaze angrily held his wife. The light there was startling; only one person could meet it and she did. "Enough, Nichole, enough. I will not have you lie more to save me!"

Gasps of more shock and surprise raced through the crowd as all eyes turned back to Nichole, shaking her head, crying, "I am not lying! My husband's love makes him try to save me! I will not have it. May God strike me dead now if I have uttered one lie before my judges!"

The entire court held their collective breath, as if waiting for God to indeed decide the matter with a bolt from the heavens. Just as Kuno was about to blast them both to everlasting damnation in hell, the cardinal moved to end the trial at last. End it with the last question.

"As God is merciful, so is His court," the red-robed Cardinal Gioacchino Rossino stood now to address the lady. "The good bishop of St. Gallen is not on trial here. And," his voice rang with solemnity, "I would remind you too that the eternal love of God must rise above your love for the accused. If you admit now you are lying, the court will excuse both your sins as well as the last, most venial of these vilifications against Bishop Kuno of Stoffeln. Save not yourself, Lady Nichole Lucretia, not your honor but your very soul. Admit finally you are lying."

The terrible words rocked her back. Tear-filled blue eyes lifted to the green ones across from her. Jonpaul was shaking his head as he said her name in a warning, "Nichole . . ." but she didn't see, she didn't hear as all she thought of was last night, their last night—

"No," she cried in a whisper, "as God is my judge, I verily march to my death with my words, the truth, and the refusal, absolute, to renounce."

Except for Jonpaul's hard gasp, silence landed into the room. At first no one moved; the lady's denial hung with its own heavy indictment in the still air. The idea that the lady Nichole would be tried next, hung alongside her husband, brought two women to their knees and many others to tears. Lady Fiona fainted, and as if to balance the sides, Lady Adline, normally so strong and sure, fell back into Kurtus's suddenly weak arms. There was a sudden rush to aid the women as the cardinal's gavel landed angrily against the table and he said, "Sentence will be passed tomorrow. May God's wisdom guide us, one and all."

The court was adjourned and still no one moved as they watched Nichole rush to Jonpaul's open arms, where they clung to each other as if they could never be parted, as if it were the last time they ever would.

That night rumors flew about St. Gallen. The army of the Alliance advanced on St. Gallen, these eager warriors already marching past Olten and certain to reach St. Gallen by dawn. Some rumors reported this as the result of Lord Bruno losing control, others said the lord led the march himself, that it was his call that sent a thousand and more men to marching. With Zurich remaining neutral, the army of Schwyz, Lucerne, and Uri countered the advance to reinforce the army of St. Gallen. In ever-heightening agitation, Nichole waited alone in the guest chambers as Hans and Kurtus petitioned the cardinals to let her spend this night with her husband.

The women gathered outside Nichole's doors, over thirty of them, and their collective voices raised in the alternating harmony of song and prayer, and it was strange, this situation, how as their men prepared to wage war, the women joined their voices in prayers and songs. It started as both the women of the Alliance and the women of Lucerne found themselves outside Nichole's door to offer support and what comfort they might. Lady Adline bridged whatever gulf might have developed, and she did this by reaching for Lady Fiona's hand, then Anne Marie's, and raising her fine, melodic voice with an old Swiss folk song, a song each woman had been taught by her mother. And when the voice of the lady's young daughter joined her mother, the sight and song seemed to swell in their hearts, becoming at once a chorus. Prayers followed, then more songs—

Mary sat on the edge of her seat alongside Bettrina, her green eyes focused hard on Nichole's door. She did not know these songs, nor did she care at all for all these endless prayers. Prayers, Nichole had told her, were like tying your boots. Once was enough. She wanted only to see Nichole. The urgency of this need made her feverish. If only Bettrina did not have such a hard hold of her hand—

The door, Mary, 'tis open. Pretend to sleep.

Ohh, the green eyes shot shyly to Bettrina. Crying again? Everybody kept crying. It made her want to cry too . . .

Mercy in heavens, do not cry, child! 'Twill do Nichole no

good. Ye must tell her. Pretend to sleep until Bettrina lets go of yer hand. The door is open . . .

Mary sniffled, wiped at her nose with her free hand, then slyly curled up at Bettrina's side. Then Bettrina let go of her hand to bury her face for her tears. Like a mouse, Mary slipped quickly from the bench and raced to the door. She grabbed the latch and pressed down. The door swung open. Inside, Nichole knelt in prayer before the light of ninety-nine candles. For a brief moment the little girl forgot her message as she stared at the wonder of so many candles. The open door brought a warm draft into the room; the light leaped and flickered like tiny little dancers—

"Mary!"

Bettrina's call made her step quickly forward. "Nichole . . . Nichole, I have a secret."

Nichole opened her red, tear-filled eyes to see her little girl. She opened her arms. Mary needed no other invitation, and Nichole held the little body to her breast, tightly, with the fear that she might soon have to let her go. Bettrina rushed into the room to retrieve the little girl. "Oh, Mary, ye cannot be botherin' the lady Nichole now." A number of other women followed, crowding into the doorway.

"I have to tell Nichole a secret."

Nichole pulled back a bit to look into Mary's wide green eyes. With effort she tried to concentrate. "What is it, darling?"

She held up a finger. "I cut myself."

No, no child—

"But I did," Mary said crossly.

"Well, yes I see." Nichole took the finger and, with trembling lips, she kissed the tiny cut.

Bettrina came to take Mary's hand. "We must leave Nichole, be—"

Tell her Mary! Tell her!

"I will," Mary answered the persistent voice, and sighed. "The lady says to tell you there is one, two . . ." She held up two fingers and smiled at Nichole.

"Two cuts?"

"Noo," Mary laughed. "Two books—"

Not books! Bibles!

"Two Bibles," she corrected herself.

A strange light came to Nichole's eyes. Bettrina went to take Mary's hand and usher the child from the room, but Nichole's look stopped her cold.

"Mary, what lady told you this?"

"The beautiful lady."

"Where have you seen her, Mary? Where?"

"When I close my eyes and I go to sleep. After Bettrina gives me my cup of milk and sings a song."

Nichole's brows crossed as she searched the child's face. *Two Bibles, two Bibles. The hint is in the Bible, our Bible. If ye can't find it, ye don't deserve the gift. Put ye hands on the Bible, the Bible, our Bible, Bible, two Bibles . . .*

"Nanna, oh, Nanna," Nichole jumped up and rushed to her trunk, her heart suddenly hammering as she lifted the lid.

"What is it, milady?"

"Nichole," Lady Adline and Fiona said almost simultaneously, confused, like all the women watching, not knowing what to make of the emotion on Nichole's face.

Nichole lifted the old woman's thick blue book of hours. She had never opened it. The cumulative book of recipes and prayers passed down from more than five generations, hundreds of years, had never been opened by her hands and simply because she had assumed everything in it of any value had long since been copied into her own green book.

The women watched in silence.

Nichole quickly untied the plain dark string. The thick blue velvet cover fell back. It wasn't even hiding. It didn't have to be. After all, only she would ever own this book, only she knew how to read Nanna's Romanesque. Pasted on the cover were the words:

> My last legacy to you lies in the family Bible on the cover such as you see here. Write a single letter in the space of the family tree reserved for the secondborn son of Lord Charles the first and the Lady Lucretia Marie, the place for a son never born.

The Christian Bible, worn from the tireless search of each page by so many, sat innocently atop her altar now. She grabbed a quill from her trunk and moved to it. She turned the cover to the carefully marked page of family names and titles. The quill marked the blank spot reserved for the secondborn son of her parents.

The top layer of paper ripped. Beneath this, concealed inside as if by a glove, was a paper, the paper, the tool of salvation. She quickly unfolded it to read her father's words signed in blood and marked by the seal of Lucerne.

A different kind of tears filled her blue eyes and Nanna would have approved them, these tears of the uplifted heart as she said, "I need Lord Wesmullar to take me to an audience before the cardinals."

Epilogue

Ribbons of blue flame died in the night; the last fire the hearth would hold until late fall. The open windows let in a stream of diffuse morning light with waking sounds of a spring day: the incessant alarm of roosters, a sleepy-eyed kitchen maid drawing water at the well, the hogs rooting about the mud near the haystacks, a faint hum of bees leaving the hive beneath the window in the garden, and the quiet coos of the doves that had returned to the cots, creatures like the wolves that would forever find sanctuary in Dornach. These peaceful sounds of the waking castle made Jonpaul smile as he lay at his wife's side, the small, lithe body pressed against his length making him release his breath in a husky sigh, a sound of pleasurable discomfort and a familiar, heightening tension.

Nichole, Nichole, Nichole . . . she was a warm, bright light in his heart and life; she brought him so many things, laughter, gaiety, song, purpose, and more, so much more, things never to be put to words—the love and passion of the blue flame.

The girl also brought him a more than indecent share of lust, plain and potent lust. Like now. His hand lifted her dark, silky plait and he drew this to his face, drinking the rich scents, lilacs and roses—that sweet flowery scent that was just her, a faint trace of his lovemaking last night, and the lingering taste of . . . grapes.

Grapes and erotica, he never would have believed it. Last night he had returned from Basel with his men to find Nichole and little Mary dancing knee-deep in the grape vat, their laughter and smiles smeared a comical trollop red. He kissed Mary's mouth to taste it and needed more, so he had picked his wife up, unmindful of her protests, and carried her off to—not his solar, the maids would hang him for that—but rather the stables. Still unmindful of her protests, but very aware of her laughter, he backed her into the nearest haystack—

The memory of what had followed did little to ease his growing discomfort. He shifted to better align her warm, pliant form with his as his calloused hand slipped, light as a feather, beneath the full mound of her breast, and his lips found the nape of her neck . . .

May Day was only the second happiest day in Dornach. The most fun was the day before, a day spent on grassy slopes with picnics and laughter as everyone, even the men, did nothing but gather all the thousands of flowers necessary for any fair May Day celebration. As warm morning sun streamed through the open windows and Nichole awoke, the excitement for this day came with her first breath. Her second breath brought a gush of hot, voluptuous sensations as she felt Jonpaul's warmth against her. His warm, large hand rested just beneath her breast, her back nestled against his chest, and her buttocks pressed maddeningly against his shaft. A very hot warmth, her body seemed to suddenly be reliving last night, and the memory of his passion made serums throughout her body heat and simmer. Careful not to wake him, she arched ever so slightly, the movement bringing his hand—

His chuckle was warm and light against her ear. "Love,

are you purposely teasing me?"

She bit her lip as if to contain her excitement as his hand began kneading, stroking, her arched breast until it burned beneath his touch. Any idea of rising, of being the first to the new day vanished with the next soft moan.

"I love the sounds of your pleasure," he whispered, igniting a furious rush of shivers. "I love the sounds of you wanting me. Oh, yes, love, yes . . ."

He threw back the covers to reveal her beauty to the sunlight and his gaze. His free hand lifted the braids of black silk hair from her ear so his open mouth could plant kisses there. Shivers erupted from the spot, a reminder of the quivering heights he brought her to . . . he always brought her to. The blood began to pound in her throat, throughout her body, an echo of the joy of feeling his huge body come over hers. She felt his breath come quicker, too, and her lips formed his name just before he turned her to kiss her mouth, but—

He stopped as the long rope of her plait slid across her face. He picked it up again, but stared into the darkening blue eyes, the soft light that always seemed to surround her beauty in the morning. "Did I leave this last night . . ."

She ran her hands over his broad shoulders, beckoning innocently as she felt a stirring, warm moisture in her loins, a swelling of anticipation that cared not a whit for conversation and this made her smile. "In our haste last night, milord . . ." She laughed. "To save time . . ."

Her warm, sleepy laughter was the very meaning of seduction. A wicked smile answered as he slowly began unweaving the braid, first one, then the other. "I am not interested in saving time." His hands combed the silky hair over her form. Delicious shivers made her laugh again, for she knew this torment. "I am rather interested in spending it . . . slowly . . . bit by bit—"

"Oh please, Jonpaul." She knew this game, he had

taught her, and she knew how to give as good as she got. "Not too slowly—"

"Nichole!"

The call of her name replaced the morning memory with a crimson blush. "What?"

All the women sitting with her on the bright blue quilt burst into laughter. "Oh, to have the thoughts that made that blush!" Madeline fell back on the blanket, laughing, thinking at once of Kairtand, whom she had met but once, but . . .

"Not a thought, but a memory, I'd wager," Marguerite added as she watched their three young girls, Adline's Carolyn, her own Sherrine, and Nichole's Mary rolling down the hill over each other, giggling all the way. "I was newlywed, too, at one time."

Adline nodded knowingly as she deftly strung daisies into a crown, then threw a wink to her oldest daughter, who seemed of late to always perk up with these conversations.

Laughing at herself, Nichole had to ask, "Oh, Marguerite, do tell me it goes away then?"

"The gift of love? No . . . never. It might shift and change like this goodly spring breeze today." She stopped her sorting of blossoms to tilt her handsome face toward the breeze. "But no, it never goes away."

Bettrina nodded; it seemed the common experience.

With exasperation, Nichole fell back on the blanket to stare up at the bright blue sky with Madeline and, laughing, "Well, then, I am alarmed. I can hardly hold a coherent thought before, suddenly, without even knowing, it turns to him . . . like—"

"Like honey bees to a flower?"

The ladies grimaced but laughed at Adline's overworked metaphor, but then, like everything else this day, it quickly became a game. "Like a moth to flame?" Madeline said.

"How about an ant to sugar?"
"Oh, that's the worst so far—"
"How about this—like a stream into a lake, or rain onto the earth . . ."
And so the morning passed. The blossoms had been gathered, falling from dozens and dozens of baskets, and the women sat among scattered blankets spread over the wide green meadow beneath the castle. The blankets appeared like a patchwork of bright colors: dark and light blues, green and yellow, oranges and purples from afar, all of this laced with the tiny dots of the even brighter colored flowers and the pretty prints of their skirts and ribbons. Children laughed and played in the forest and the swings nearby. Dragonflies and butterflies danced in the breeze. Songs started and ended or erupted into laughter, and into this idyllic scene the men began to arrive, first in ones and twos, as the day's work had been hastily finished, and then a large party of over twenty from the morning's hunt, including the lords Bruno and Hans, all in time for the afternoon picnic . . .
Nichole pretended not to notice Jonpaul had yet to grace the picnic as she pushed a giggling Mary on the swing high in the sky. He had been called down to Dornach unexpectedly. Not a day passed without meeting with bishops or merchants, representatives from this court or that, talk of expanding trade routes and new alliances. Her husband was ever ambitious—and all for joining the cantons of Switzerland and increasing the welfare of the people, and she loved him so for it. Today was special, though, and, well, normally he included her . . .
"Kick up . . . and down, kick up—" Nichole stopped to watch as Bruno and Hans, Holbien and Stefano lifted—rather threw—Marguerite onto a blanket despite her protests. The men took the corners in hands and, with a great heave, Marguerite flew into the air and,

smiling at the sight, Nichole turned to steal another anxious glance to the road behind her—

She gasped, not at Zermatt or Jonpaul riding up to the picnic at last, but at who was with him. Mary forgotten, she was suddenly running. "Kurtus! Kurtus!" and, "Kairtand!"

Marguerite was high in the air as the men's attention turned to the sound of Nichole's voice, and she screamed, catching the gazes back to her precarious fate, just in time to stop her certain hard fall to the ground. "Kurtus and Mickeil are back," Hans cried just as they managed to set the terrified lady gently to the ground again before they, too, set off to greet the party . . .

As one by one the people turned to see the party of four approaching, they rose with excited greetings to join the widening circle. Nichole was first. She fell happily into Kairtand's arms for a warm embrace, Kairtand who would forever more own a special place in her heart. Like Kurtus. Kurtus swung off his horse and, with laughter, managed to open his arms just in time to catch her next. A wide grin spread over Jonpaul's face as he watched, knowing perhaps that no one was as anxious for Kurtus's return as Nichole.

Kurtus set Nichole on her feet, staring down at her pretty, upturned face. "Milady, you are as fetching as the day is bonny—and daisies everywhere." He pulled a blossom from a stream of her loosely bound hair, but the blue eyes filled with anxiety, urgency. "Ah, but I see your question." He looked back to the crowd to announce, "'Tis over, all but the hanging. We did not stay for that—"

The news hit her physically. Like a blow to her head it was. The news then seemed to lift a tension, a tension she had not even realized she carried, as if it had been a burden all this time, and she supposed it had. She felt a lightheadedness, not all pleasant. She took another uncertain step back, only to be drawn into the security of his arms. Jonpaul held her in an embrace, and she closed her eyes, savoring his comfort that was now always there.

Bruno, too, came to her side and put his strong hand on her arm, "'Tis over now, milady . . . 'tis finally over."

She nodded. The people fell silent again as Mickeil addressed the crowd. "This will not blight our May Day. Let me say this once, then put the subject, like the very history itself, to rest. First I read Milord's testimony, then Bruno's and Hans's," Mickeil explained. "Kairtand and Kurtus testified and then the blackguard that shot you, milord. 'Kuno paid me from 'is own fat purse,' he said. At sunrise the next day that man hung. Same with the thieves we caught, all five testifying that Kuno ordered and paid for their raids on the Basel trade routes. Three sisters of St. Gallen testified, but the judges were most moved"—his voice lowered with solemnity—"by your testimony that I read to them, milady. The cardinals themselves planned to sing a mass for you the morning Kuno of Stoffeln was defrocked and . . . hung."

The blue eyes anxiously searched his face. "Excommunicated? Dear Lord, was he?"

Mickeil shook his head with a sad smile, and as Nichole seemed to swoon with relief, he thought again how true it was that men might make religion but the women kept and honored it. Hanging was one thing, but eternal damnation was another, far worse fate, not that the man didn't deserve it.

Nichole could not help but be glad for this. Just in case there truly was a hell . . . though Nanna never was wrong. She sighed. If she lived to a hundred she would never be able to reconcile completely the dual inheritance of her religions. Somehow, though, she did think the Goddess minded—

"'Tis over, love," he whispered. "'Tis all over now."

She nodded, and the men seemed suddenly to be

talking at once—not of the trial, for the news was enough and, as Mickeil said, they would not blight the picnic by returning to the subject again; but rather they talked of the sights of Rome, the high comedy the Swiss found in everything and anything Italian. Just then Mary raced to her father to show him the crown of daisies Nichole had made her and the ladybug that came with it, while Kurtus helped Gavin up to his horse and made the boy guess what gift he brought back from Rome. Little Mary was giggling as Jonpaul teased her, and somehow the moment changed, shifting, becoming a kaleidoscope to the future, filling Nichole with the bright promise of this beautiful day. A day like that depicted in the tapestry hanging in the solar. A castle of dreams. Her heart seemed to suddenly lift and soar as the words sang in her mind. 'Twas over, 'twas truly over . . .

A perfect moment in time. After the feasting and laughter, as the people paired into couples to lie against the blankets and watch the sun set, when finally no one, not even Father Ari, could eat a single bite more, Nichole's sigh, as she leaned against Jonpaul where they sat on the blue blanket, was one of perfect contentment. Kurtus softly strummed a mandolin, his fine, deep voice lifting with a pretty lullaby, joining the gentle rustle of the warm breeze through the leaves. Mary lay sound asleep on her lap. Nearby, Adline and Bruno, Marguerite and Hans, all seemed to sleep, surrounded by their children, too. Bettrina leaned in Holbien's arms as well, and Nichole smiled as Holbien's hands lovingly caressed her rounded belly. Gavin and Father Ari were playing a game of cards, and from the sound of Ari's complaints, young Gavin was winning again. As it should be. A day even more beautiful than the one depicted in the tapestry, for she was in it.

Jonpaul had no mind for the sunset, not when Nichole looked—dare he think it?—more beautiful than ever.

She wore a pretty yellow skirt and white blouse, covered in a pale-blue apron, decorously embroidered with birds and flowers and the blue set her eyes off like—

No, don't think of those eyes . . .

He searched for a distraction. A discarded red rose lay at his side. Nichole smiled when she felt the velvet-soft petals tickling her neck. She grabbed his hand, bringing it to her nose with another deep sigh of contentment.

He said, "'Tis early for roses . . ."

"Gavin found them for me. There's a wild patch growing yonder . . ."

Father Ari was desperate for a distraction, too. Just long enough to get young Gavin's sharp gaze from his sleeves. He seized this topic and, with a chuckle, he asked, "Ah, roses. Well, I've long held a question in my mind. What happened on your wedding night with the roses? I've imagined the scene a hundred times: Jonpaul, so . . . ah, desperate for the success of his seduction, holding the blossoms over the flame only to find his normally smooth-honeyed tongue twisted as he tried to explain the ashes made of your blossom, milady—" True to his words, the very idea of Jonpaul blundering through some wildly implausible explanation made him laugh again.

Having been told the story, too, Kurtus stopped the strumming and laughed as well. "I, too, have wondered how you explained the bad omen to your . . . ah, most reluctant bride, Jon?"

"Why are you looking like that?" Ari asked Jonpaul, and Nichole, noticing, "Is it a sore subject still? Or are you, dear God, remembering to be angry at me. 'Twasn't all my fault. Oh, no." He shook his head. "I sent Bettrina to dip the blossoms in wax, but then—"

"Well, I didn't do it," Bettrina said petulantly. "I was still mad that Holbien did it to me on our wedding night, too, and that 'twas a trick and a rake's trick at that. I was probably the only maid in Dornach who hadn't heard of it—"

"My dear girl," Holbien laughed. "I don't remember you regretting it then!"

Jonpaul was not listening. He held the rose to Nichole's face as the lovely blue eyes searched his with confusion and, yes, a certain desperation to know. Slowly, with his own caution, he asked, "Are you saying you never doused the wedding roses in the wax?"

"I did mean to fix it when Bettrina told me she hadn't," Ari explained, "but somehow I forgot and then when I finally remembered, you were not willing to wait, as I recall—"

Those blue eyes held him in a trance as the miracle of it began manifesting in a transparent mist of tears. She started to speak, but he stopped her, and with his own urgency, "No, love, don't question it." He added softly, "In your heart you've always known it was true. I've always known it was true. Our love, the love of the blue flame . . ."

And with these tender words, he kissed her, a kiss that sang a song of eternity, a love that would last forever and a lifetime, the love of the blue flame . . .